THE DARKLING CHRONICLES

Shadows 1

TRICIA ZOELLER

Blue Portal Press, LLC

Marietta, GA

Published by Blue Portal Press, LLC
Marietta, GA
www.triciazoeller.com

ISBN-13: 978-0-9893963-3-2
Library of Congress Control Number: 2015902495

Cover Art by Robin Harper, Wicked By Design
Cartography by Jared Blando
Book Formatting by Angela McLaurin, Fictional Formats
Editing by Nancy S. Thompson

TABLE OF CONTENTS

MAP OF MONTENAI

DEDICATION

For my sisters, with love!

SHADOW
BLUES

The Darkling Chronicles #1

TRICIA ZOELLER

PROLOGUE

Anka Rehmling, Age Four

"Did you hear me, Anka?" Pops asked.

"Yep." I looked at Pops's fuzzy eyebrows. They made me laugh.

A big darkling came into the room. "Anka Rehmling and Bianca Rehmling?" he asked. One yellow eye. Funny skin. *Scales?*

I looked down at the floor. My finger followed the squiggles.

"Stop, child," Pops said. "Get up and pay attention."

"I'm Lord Akton, and these are my brothers, Lord Leasith and Lord Bulosk."

One lord smiled and talked to Bianca. She was quiet. The tree was scary inside. I closed my eyes. Squeezed Pops's finger.

"Say hello to the Lords," Pops said. He sounded mad.

I waved. My sister bowed. I bowed, too. Lord Bulosk laughed.

"They are four and six, right?" asked Yellow Eye.

"Yes, Sir."

"Very well."

Yellow Eye kneeled in front of me. He smelled like smoke and apple juice. "Anka Rehmling, you are assigned Patrick Benjamin Solomon."

"Eye?"

Pops pinched my arm. "Don't point. It's rude."

"Pay attention," Lord Akton said. His one eye moved round and round. My tummy hurt. I saw a boy in my head. He had yellow hair and green eyes.

3

Next, Yellow Eye walked to Bianca and told her the boy's name, too.

"We're done, sweetie," Pops said. He held Bianca's hand. I walked behind them. They went out.

Someone sang. He had a rumbly voice like Pops. The room was empty, but I liked the song so I stayed. My shoes clapped loud on the floor. I put my ear on the wall. It was so hot. Singing. Talking, too.

Yellow Eye ran at me. "Get away from there!"

He picked me up. I couldn't breathe. I touched his face.

"Don't do that," he growled.

Pops came back with Bianca. Yellow eye put me down, and I ran to Pops. Bianca started to cry.

"She cast a dark shadow at me. Who taught her how to do that?" he asked.

"I'm sorry, Lord Akton." Pops's eyebrows went up. "She's just a fledgling. She doesn't understand."

Yellow Eye frowned.

"Anka, we don't cast dark shadows," Pops said.

Bianca hugged me, and I cried. "I want a lollipop."

"Quiet." Pops's face was red.

I pointed to the wall. "Somebody talkin'."

"I'm sorry, Lord Akton. She's usually such a good fledgling." Pops grabbed my hand, and I fell. "Stand up, child."

"I wanna go home."

"We are going home. Hush now."

Yellow Eye stared at me. I hid my face in Pops's legs and squeezed his hand so hard it hurt.

CHAPTER ONE

MY HAND SHOOK as I reached out and pushed the hair off Ben's sweaty forehead. When he sat up suddenly, I took a step back. Could he see me? He looked around the room with cloudy eyes that passed right over me.

When he turned on the lamp, I flicked my fingers, casting a shadow on the wall of a bird flying. He gasped before looking around once more. Now, he knew something was here. After peeking in the corner, the closet, and under the armchair for where the shapes came from, he shrugged his shoulders. He used his hands to create a barking dog. I used my magic to create a meowing and hissing cat with fur standing on end. I barely stopped myself from snorting out loud from his goofy face as he scanned the room. He looked scared but excited.

Anka Rehmling, you are in big trouble. I'd just broken three shadowcaster rules. I tried not to think about it. Instead, I focused on my superhero, ninja, and dinosaur forms, complete with sound effects. Ben looked so happy, I told myself it would be okay just this once. He had been sick all day.

Each pull of my magic started in the pit of my stomach. The energy swirled out to my arms before releasing from my fingertips like thread. That's how Dad explained it. Then, it snapped as it broke free and became the shadow on the wall or floor. It wasn't a bad feeling, but felt normal, right.

When Ben grew tired, I watched him lie back in bed and drift off to sleep, a smile on his face. He had light hair with white skin that burned and freckled in the sun. My skin and hair were darker, like the shadows I cast.

In human years, we were both eight. However, shadowcasters, by nature, acted more mature than humans. Our world expected us to be responsible from a young age. The Shadowland Council had assigned Patrick Benjamin Solomon under my charge at the age of four. I cast shadows in his world and would for my lifetime, as long as my strength held. *"That's a lot of responsibility riding on your shoulders"*—direct quote from Dad. I removed my hand from Ben's arm as I thought about what I'd done.

Dad.

Shadowcaster rules flooded my head.

Cast true to form. Don't talk. Don't touch the human.

My heart pounded in my ears. I hadn't cast true. My palms grew sticky. I'd created my own make-believe shadows. Technically, I hadn't talked, just made sound effects. However, I'd touched him. This realization caused fear to spark in me like fire; then it burned out, and I was so tired. I couldn't wait to go home.

My family shadowcasted for the Solomons. The Council assigned my dad to shadow Ben's dad. My mom followed his mom. Bianca and I took shifts with Ben. I covered him by day; she watched him at night. Other shadowcasters rotated in if we needed a break.

As a shadowcaster, I didn't go to school but trained with my dad. My grandparents, Nana and Pops, ran the household since Mom and Dad worked so much.

Ben's sigh brought my attention back to him. He looked peaceful. Maybe his fever had broken. When Mrs. Solomon slipped into the room to check on him, my mother followed, casting her shadows. My mother was really tall—five-foot-ten. She wore a flowing dress of purple, the family color. Jeweled combs sparkled in a ring on her head, which was the darkling custom.

As I watched Mrs. Solomon worrying over Ben, I felt jealous. He had a normal life. Not every darkling had the ability to cast shadows, and so it was a privilege and honor to serve the Council. However, the other young darklings went to school and played during the day. Most of them would never journey to the human world, but they benefited from the power shadowcasters brought back to Shadowland.

My mother's brown eyes found mine. I met them briefly before looking away. Had she heard my sound effects? I forced myself to glance back up. She gave me a smile before leaving the room with Mrs. Solomon. I sighed with relief.

"You need to rest."

I jumped. "Geez, Bianca. When did you get here?"

Bianca crossed her arms and squinted the evil-all-knowing-older-sister glare. "Anka, why are you so jumpy?"

"Long day," I said with a shrug.

Bianca's brows lifted. Her eyes were so much like Mom's, sometimes, it was plain spooky.

As I stood up, an awful taste filled my mouth. Guilt tasted like brussels sprouts. I stumbled to Ben's bedside and touched the center of his palm, which acted as my portal back to Montenai.

Immediately, I fell through to a tunnel of air. It felt like I was riding a speedboat with winds coming at me from every direction. Then, I dropped so fast I didn't see anything but crazy colors. My stomach tickled as the ride came to a sudden stop and I stood in the middle of a hollowed-out sequoia tree. Looking forward, I saw the small fir tree that marked the portal entrance. When I tilted my head back, I looked up inside the tree into a blackness that went on and on. I couldn't believe I had just dropped through that place. The lords set up the portal so only one darkling could go at a time. This way we didn't crash into each other.

It always took me a second to catch my breath before leaving the tree. Tonight, I came out to a fresh pine scent and colored stars in the sky. Once I walked around the small fir tree, I raced down the path of pine needles, headed to the river. I didn't feel excited like I usually did in the forest. Instead, that taste filled my mouth again—guilt. Would Ben give me away? I should have thought about how he would react to the strange shadows I had cast.

The yellow moon beamed down, and I ran faster until my ribs

hurt. Reflections bounced across the ripples on the Montenai River. They came from the glass domes that made up the west side of the river, Kirka Village. The nymphs cast reflections in the human world. A kirka named Korena made reflections for Ben. Most darklings had dark hair and skin, but the kirka had light hair and skin. Their beauty mesmerized everyone. Sometimes, you forgot what you were saying when you talked to one of them. We had our own history with their kind, but now we lived together without fighting.

I had slowed to a walk, but started to jog again when I heard the soft hum of a cart driving my way. I knew from the jazz music playing and the purplish light it was Pops coming to meet me. Darklings drove in carts almost like human golf carts. While I was slightly more mature than Ben, I was still a fledgling, a darkling child, so Pops watched out for me.

"There's my pretty, green-eyed genius," he said as he braked to a stop next to me. His bushy, black eyebrows framed bright, brown eyes. Pops usually wore crazy colorful shirts with baggy jeans. Tonight was no exception. This one looked like purple asteroids had collided with neon green space creatures and left their guts splashed across his shirt. When I climbed in, I smelled Pops—cinnamon, sugar, and chocolate.

In his retirement from shadowcasting, Pops had become a candymaker—a decision that made my sister and I really happy. Shadowcasters' powers get weaker as we age. Young darklings have a strong essence, which is why shadowcasters start training and working at such a young age.

I felt older tonight as we whizzed down the path by the river, glimpsing the kirkas' homes. I knew it had to do with how tired I was from pulling a double shift to watch over Ben. I had wanted to stay, so Bianca had held my hand the night before when his fever was at its highest.

The nymph light across the river caught my attention. Light bounced off their homes bringing to life their wide field of enchanted yellow grasses and wildflowers. Because they loved sunlight, the nymphs built their houses out of a material like glass but much sturdier. No one could see inside their two-story domes because the nymphs cast reflections of their surroundings on the surface. Most kirka stuck to the guidelines of reflecting nature.

I giggled, and Pops shook his head as we took a curve and one nymph's house came into view. She had cast her own reflection upon the glass surface so it looked like a billboard of a curvy supermodel.

"Could she be anymore full of herself?" Pops asked. "Her neighbors can't be pleased."

I just shook my head. The kirka had a matriarchal society. That was the big word Pops had taught me. It only took me about ten tries to pronounce it. I gathered the females ruled the village—the whole idea that girls rule, boys drool. No males lived within their boundaries anymore. However, the kirka did hang out with the satyrs who lived down the river in a fishing town called Port by the Sea. My mom and dad sometimes whispered about the nymphs and satyrs, which caused Bianca and me to listen even harder.

While the kirka basked in the sunshine, most darklings loved the shade of the thick forest on our side of the river. Shadowcasters absorbed excess solar energy to protect humans. Although the sun strengthened us, by the end of a shadowcasting shift, we liked to feel the cool breeze off the river. It helped us relax. The smells of fresh moss, pine needles, and hickory nuts helped calm me. Home was a comfy cottage built at the base of a grove of enormous sequoia trees in North Village. We used the goosepen or large hollow in the trunk's base as a storage shed or garage.

Tonight, even though I wanted my bed, I craved chocolate even more. Pops must have read my mind. He headed for the main square located along the riverbank. We traveled to the boardwalk, which had the community center and many stores such as the shoemaker, the baker, and the candymaker. Darklings loved sweets. Pops stopped at his all-night chocolate shop, Chocolate Syncope, to grab some chocolate-covered strawberries. My Uncle Vincent usually worked the counter at night.

Pops let me eat the treat in the cart. I was careful to hold my hand under my chin to catch the juices so Nana wouldn't bust us later.

After a short ride through the woods, we pulled up to our two-story cottage built in front of an enormous tree. The hole at the trunk's bottom provided Pops room to park two carts. He kept his fishing boat docked by the bridge in South Village, though.

I rushed to join Nana in the kitchen. The smell of her cheesy-bacon potato soup caused me to drool. After I stuffed myself, I stumbled upstairs to the room I shared with Bianca.

In the top loft, I burrowed under my light purple blanket. On the wall, my mother had painted the darkling Wishing Tree with a tremendous shadow. Human artists didn't do much with shadow. My mother painted it with as much detail as the tree itself. The tree represented the essence of every darkling's existence. It was the center of Shadowland, but it could be frightening. It grew in South Village where the expensive shops and five-star restaurants were. It was also the home of the Shadowland Council.

Paper leaves decorated the tree branches. Each week, we wrote a wish on the back of a leaf cut from construction paper and placed it on the tree. We changed the leaf colors with the seasons. In the winter, we added snowflakes. Each month, we took down the wishes so we could start over. Looking at it under my nymph lights, I considered adding a wish, but knew Mom counted them.

I finally fell off to sleep after reading half a book of our folk tales—a very different storyline from human stories.

THE NEXT DAY, as Ben stretched in his room and removed his pajamas, I cast the appropriate shadows for his movements. When he turned around in his underwear, he shrieked. Quite frankly, like a girl.

"What, who, what's going on?"

I froze. I knew the rules, but I just couldn't think. He could see me.

"Hi," I said. "I'm Anka."

Just then, Dad walked in the room with Mr. Solomon. I backed up until my legs hit the chair behind me, and I fell into it. Ben followed my movements. "Are you okay?" His blond hair stuck straight up in back.

"Ben?" His father looked at him. "Who are you talking to?"

"The girl," he said, pointing at me. My father's eyes grew wide. I gave him a nervous smile. I'd just been upgraded to Imaginary Friend. "Anka," Ben said.

Uh oh. My father glared at me. The only way Ben would know my name was if I'd talked to him. I shook my head and mouthed to him that it was an accident. I'd broken two rules. I'd talked and I'd given him my name!

"What the devil…" Mr. Solomon grabbed Ben and put the back of a big hand to his forehead. "You don't feel like you still have a fever."

"Whataya mean, Dad?"

"Benjamin, there is no one in here."

Ben stood, hands on his hips, looking from his dad to the chair where I sat, wide-eyed, shaking my head. He took the clue and brushed it off as a joke. "I'm just kidding. I don't even know a girl by that name."

His father clapped him on the back and steered him out the door toward the bathroom. He turned his head around like an owl so he could watch me as he left the room.

My father paused briefly and mouthed, "We need to talk."

I nodded and followed him. There was no such thing as modesty in our world. I provided shadows wherever my assignment, Ben, went. Female shadowcasters didn't only cast for female humans and male shadowcasters for male humans, because we worked in family units. Also, there were more female than male shadowcasters.

I always shadowcasted from a distance when a human used the bathroom. It was just common decency. But now, I'd need to make sure to shadowcast from outside the door when he dressed, because humans were particular about their privacy, and he could see me.

I stopped abruptly at the bathroom door. My father indicated with a nod that I should shadow Mr. Solomon. I guess he didn't want to upset Ben any more.

My breath caught. I'd always shadowed Ben. What if I didn't do things right? Before I had time to think, Mr. Solomon darted down the stairs, and my dad shooed me. I shot after him, excitement rippling through me as I matched his pace. I cast a bunch of complicated shadows at Mr. Solomon's incredible speed. Then he sat down. All day, he worked at the computer doing accounting. I did my best to cast shadows from his pen, his calculator, and his tapping foot while not falling asleep on my feet.

I thought Dad would come to exchange with me, but he didn't. When Ben came into Mr. Solomon's office at lunchtime, my Dad flew in ahead of him, motioning for me to hide. I slunk behind the floor-length silk drapes and perched on the sill to keep my feet off the floor.

Before my shift was up, Pops tapped me on the shoulder.

"What are *you* doing here?" I asked him.

Pops's cheek twitched. "You need to go see *them*."

My stomach dropped to my feet. *Them?*

"I'll shadowcast just for today, but you and Bianca must go to the Wishing Tree."

My feet felt glued to the front hall floor. As I looked at the neon green swirls on Pops's shirt, I felt like they were spinning.

"Go on, little fledgling. Nana and Bianca are waiting for you."

When I got to the stairs, I took the steps two at a time just as I'd seen my Dad do. My legs had just gotten long enough to do it. In the hallway, I almost bumped into my father.

"Dad?"

He hugged me. I smelled the cherry tobacco from his pipe. "It was an honest mistake." His green eyes were so serious. With his long fingers, he brushed my bangs out of my eyes. "Just listen and apologize. Okay?"

My feet began to move, but they felt cold and numb. I entered Ben's room where he sat on the floor playing a video game. Since he was my portal, I had no choice but to approach him once more.

When he noticed me, his character died in the video game. He didn't seem to mind. "Ben, I am not supposed to give my name." *Or talk!* I clamped my hands over my mouth.

He waited. I found him to be more patient than other boys.

Well, the damage was already done. "You should give me a name if I'm to be your Imaginary Friend. Don't use my real name again or I'll be in big trouble." I was already in trouble.

He tilted his head as he considered this. I sat down in the overstuffed chair I had fallen into earlier.

"You made the shadows for me."

I placed my finger to my lips.

His eyes grew big. "Okay. I get it. Top secret stuff," he said, giggling.

I nodded.

"Are you from outer space?"

"Really? Do I look like an alien?"

"No. You look like a…a princess." His cheeks turned red, and I assumed mine did too.

"I can be your friend for a while, but you can't act like you know about the shadowcasting or make a big deal about me in front of your parents. Dad says it will just lead to a lot of unnecessary doctor appointments."

He chewed his lip. "Well, a princess name has to be pretty different like Eugenie or Hosanna or Eureka—"

I put my hand up and wrinkled my nose. I guess he'd accepted my terms. "Ben, Eureka is a vacuum."

This didn't discourage him. "Fiona, Per*smell*ope, Atawatha…" He stopped when he saw my face. "Maybe, I'll think on this a bit. Although, I'm thinking Per*smell*ope."

"I have to go now," I huffed.

"Why?" he cried.

"I just do. When I return, I can't talk to you." As I walked toward him, his eyes grew wider, like he considered I might steal his body and take over his mind. "Relax." I touched his hand and returned to my village.

CHAPTER TWO·

NANA MET ME in the full sunlight right where I came out. Her cheeks looked red. A chill ran up my spine, and I dove into her arms. Her yellow hair was like the nymphs. It flowed halfway down her back. She had a darkling father and a nymph mother. She'd spent her childhood in Shadowland because the darklings had accepted her just as she was. The nymphs, not so much.

As she hugged me, I smelled her—lavender.

"Deep breaths, Anka, dear." Her purple dress felt soft and cool on my warm face. I tried not to get tears on it.

When I found my sister in the back of the cart, her brown eyes looked at me. Yeah, the older sister thing, like, *what did you do*? Once in the cart, Nana drove it like she stole it. Pops always teased her about her driving. I couldn't reach the top bar, so I grabbed the side of my seat as she took each turn back to the house. Our cart had seatbelts, but today, they didn't seem like enough. I didn't often see Shadowland during the day. I couldn't enjoy it because Nana's driving was making me cartsick, and I kept thinking about dragon lord claws.

Once inside the garage, Nana jumped out and pushed us into the house. "Go downstairs and wait for me," she instructed.

Bianca and I went to Pops's basement den. He kept all kinds of old stuff down there. Nana said he tinkered with it when he needed to think or *not* think. I touched the horn of an antique gramophone before sitting on the flowered couch. With my hands, I tried to smooth the wrinkles on my shiny, purple dress. I kicked my black boots up on the stool like I always did then decided I better not.

"Anka, they're rumbling," Bianca said from next to me.

My mouth went dry as the room moved. Definitely might throw up, even though I'd never done that before. I squeezed my eyes shut, which only made me dizzy, and I saw the Council in my head. Opening my eyes didn't make it better. They weren't like other darklings. Three old dragon lords were on the Council. But they didn't look old. They looked a bit like darklings but had dragon parts. Pops said, without them, there would be no Shadowland.

"Are we in trouble?" I squeaked.

"They're gonna talk to us."

I didn't want to go to the Wishing Tree. "Will they hurt us?"

"No, silly. We're just fledglings." She sat back farther on the couch and played with the pretty flower buttons on her dress. She stared at the floor.

Nana rushed into the room carrying our dressy shoes, gemstone combs, and a brush. She had smoothed her hair, applied lip gloss, and pulled her hair back like Mom's.

She sat on the footstool in front of me first. "Anka, the human world cannot know about us. It would jeopardize our existence and theirs. Your charge has seen you. This is very serious. You must not encourage him." Her earrings quivered as she shook her head at me.

I nodded as I took a deep breath. My chest hurt when I thought about being a shadowcaster.

"Always follow the rules. They're there for a reason," she said in the sternest voice she'd ever used.

I nodded again as my bottom lip trembled. She brushed my hair none too gently. I felt her hands shaking as she drove the combs into place.

She looked at me and wiped my tears away with her thumbs. After she kissed my forehead, she tried to wipe her mark off with some spit. She switched out Bianca's shoes and brushed her curly hair, placing the combs around the crown in the darkling way.

With shaky hands, I grabbed the railing and leaned on it

as I walked to the top of the stairs. I knew our history. The dragon lords helped restore darklings' vitality. We owed them our lives. It didn't mean we liked them, but we respected them... and feared them. Pops said vitality meant our life energy. I kind of understood.

The ride to South Village went by in a blur. My palms felt sweaty, and I struggled not to cry. I barely noticed the fledglings playing on the playground at the school or on the slide at Lady Pia's Park. My brain felt cloudy.

Nana stopped the cart by the side of the Wishing Tree. A nonshadowcaster stood as a door attendant in front of the double doors. He wore a uniform of dark pants, boots, and a red jacket with the dragon lords' symbol on the pocket.

The same symbol hung above the two doors. The gold shield showed a dragon looking down at his shadow. Pops said it reminded us that we were a team, dragon lords and shadowcasters. We'd been a team for a hundred years.

The attendant opened the doors to the Wishing Tree, and Bianca gasped as a black cloud of bats launched into the air from the upper branches, making a chorus of chirpy squeaks. She leaned against the darkling, as if she wanted him to save her. He held Bianca's shoulder to steady her.

His face changed then. "This one is strong."

Nana nodded to him before shooing us through the doorway.

Bianca slipped her sweaty hand into mine and squeezed. Nana walked behind us, a hand at each of our backs.

My shoes pinched my toes. A smell I remembered from when I was four hit me suddenly. The dragon lords smelled like...cedar, pine, cinnamon, burnt apple cider, and smoke.

It was hard to see, at first. Fancy lights hung on the walls, but still it was so much darker than the bright, sunny day outside.

We heard deep voices coming closer. From the dark tunnel below, eyes glowed gold, blue, and green. Nana clutched the back of our dresses. I didn't dare tell her she'd pinched some of my skin.

Lord Akton appeared before us. "I told you. Not in the Rotunda.

We'll talk to them in the Council Room."

Bianca and I stood with our heads tilted back and our mouths wide open. I felt like screaming.

"Coooool," Bianca said. Then, "Yipe." I was pretty sure Nana had pinched her.

One golden eye stared at us. Where there should have been another eye, Lord Akton instead had several wrinkled lines through darkling skin mixed with red scales.

My heart beat so fast, I thought I might just die.

"Hello, Rehmlings. Thank you for bringing them here, Violet."

"Of course, Lord Akton."

Inside the Council Room, they told us to sit at a large marble table. I remembered tracing the squiggles in the marble of the Rotunda floor when I was four. Now, I did not want to touch the marble. I wanted to disappear from the room, play invisible fledgling.

Nana sat next to the youngest dragon lord across from Bianca and me. We faced the doorway where Lord Akton stood on one side and Leasith on the other. Were they guarding the door?

Bianca kept staring at the red-scaled lord across the room. Nana kept whispering for her to stop. I couldn't take my eyes off Lord Bulosk. His blue scales were the prettiest color I'd ever seen. I'd never seen that kind of blue in my life.

"Hello, little shadowcasters. I'm Bulosk. I'll be your tour guide for today."

Bianca giggled. Nana hushed her.

"What? He's funny," Bianca said.

Lord Akton growled. It vibrated my chair and tickled my whole body. Lord Bulosk rolled his green eyes up into his head, like, "*don't mind my grumpy brother.*"

My breathing got faster, and, suddenly, I hiccupped loudly. Nana's lips mashed together, and she gave me her mean look.

"Sorry," I whispered.

The lord opened a leather case and pulled out some paper. He set a piece in front of Nana, Bianca, and me. "You are all aware of shadowcaster rules. I'm placing them in front of you in a contractual form. This is standard procedure when a human discovers you as an Imaginary Friend. Please review."

I followed along as he read aloud. I understood most of the words:

Shadowcasting Rules

1. Always cast true to form.
2. Never talk to the human.
3. Never give the human your name.
4. Never touch the human other than to use him/her as a portal.

Exceptions and Addendums as it pertains to Imaginary Friendships

1. If a human child shall see you as an imaginary friend, you may play with him/her, but never converse. Please do not encourage the child. Touching is allowed as it pertains to playing games, but keep affection to a minimum.

2. Imaginary friendship shall be terminated by the age of thirteen. This is the maximum age and is extended as a courtesy to shadowcasters who may have charges who have special needs or are terminally ill. There are no exceptions to this age limit.

When he finished, he tapped a claw on the paper. He hadn't had a claw out before. "Now, we just need your blood bond there on the "X" then my handsome brother will give you a short history lesson, and you can be on your way."

I watched Nana's mouth fall into a frown, and her eyebrows drew together. She pushed back from the table and turned on the biggest lord. "Standard procedure, you say? I've never heard of this."

Lord Akton left the wall. "I assure you it's required of certain shadowcasters, if they've broken rules."

"She is just a baby."

"Well, if you don't have them sign the decree, we can think of other ways for them to make amends for little Anka's mistakes."

Nana gasped. "Don't work your hocus-pocus on me." She spun around and sat back down at the table. She sat with her body so rigid, I thought she'd get a spasm. Her blond hair flowed in the air a bit. It only did that when she was angry.

"It will be okay." Lord Bulosk smiled at Nana then us. He stood up and went to Bianca's side. Suddenly, I saw a flash of all the claws on his right hand.

I screamed. He glared at me and rubbed his forehead. "Ow, that really stings, little one. No dark shadows."

I froze. I'd done it again. "I'm sorry," I squeaked. Tears filled my eyes and made my cheeks sting. I hiccupped again. "Don't hurt Bianca because I was bad."

"It will only be a finger prick." He pointed to the paper. "For the contract."

If Bianca's eyes got any bigger, they'd pop out of her head.

"No worries. Just a tiny spot," he said to her with a wink.

Bianca bit her bottom lip then sat up straighter and gave him her hand. He pricked the finger and smeared the dot of blood on the paper. When done, he blew on her finger, and the bleeding stopped.

She giggled. "That tickles."

Not to be outdone, I offered my finger and let him poke it then heal it.

Once the blood dried, he put everything back in the pouch and stepped back from the table. Lord Akton came over. He didn't sit but leaned forward on the table, his big hands spread wide.

"We are why you live. It is our power that sustains you."

I gulped.

"Before the Blessed Incursion, darklings lived with the kirka and satyrs on the west side of the river under the House of Hanleith.

"Hanleith was an evil nymph queen. She punished darklings and treated them like dogs. Your kind only had the ability to bend light. Compared to the powers of the nymphs, who can control plants, light, and heal, your measly abilities to cast a shadow just did not compare."

He stood up and held his arms behind his back. "Under her reign, darklings got sick. Shadow Fever killed many. Hanleith soon banished the rebellious and the weak. Darklings banded together on the east side of the river, and Shadowland became a place for the forsaken and the dying.

"Then, my father came into this world. Drakos slayed Hanleith and caused the change needed in Montenai for the rise of my brothers and me. It's why you live the happy lives you do in Shadowland."

Nana had told me it was also why some nymphs avoided darklings. They still thought we weren't good enough, and they resented the death of their queen.

"So. Anka Rehmling. What happened today at the Solomon

house?" The lord came and squatted next to me. It felt like he took away all the air.

Nana nodded to me. Something in her look told me to be careful. "Ben saw me."

"And?" The golden eye glowed in front of me.

I looked away. "Well, Dad came over. And then, I shadowed Mr. Solomon. I think Dad wanted the boy to calm down."

"Do you know why you are here?"

"To go over the rules about being an Imaginary Friend?"

"Yes. But how do we know about Ben seeing you?"

I wiggled in my chair. "Because you have magic?"

"Look at me."

I flinched, but I looked.

"We hear you in the human world. When you talk to a shadowcaster, it flows right over us. But when you talk to humans and they talk to you, it tingles inside our heads. We hear you and we know."

So many things went through my mind. Had they heard everything I said? Everything Ben said?

"This part is very important. Don't break the rules again." He stood up and walked to stand next to my sister. "Bianca, will you tell me what the penalty is for breaking the rules."

In a clear voice she said, "Harsh punishment, banishment, or death."

"Do you have any questions, Anka?"

"No." I shook my head so much, I made myself dizzy.

"Good, because I wouldn't want anything to happen to your family. And I wouldn't want you to lose your privileges as a shadowcaster."

Nana looked like she might explode. Her hair was definitely moving on its own the way nymphs' hair did when they were pissed.

"You may go now," he said.

She stood up and rushed to pull our chairs out for us. All color had drained from her face. Lord Akton and Bulosk left first. That left the quiet one.

Lord Leasith didn't dress fancy like his brothers. He wore jeans and boots with a short-sleeve shirt. He had a lot of muscles. His face had the most scales.

"Ma'am." He nodded to Nana and took us to the double doors. Once we stepped outside, Bianca and I blinked in the bright light.

"Get in the cart," Nana said. Bianca waited by her side. "Go, loves."

I let Bianca get up front. I sat in the back with my stomach feeling like it was doing flips.

Nana actually touched Lord Leasith's arm. Even though she spoke quietly, we heard her.

"They are just fledglings. Threatening them with death is completely inappropriate."

"Their actions endanger us all."

"I understand that. But I don't like grown darklings, part dragon or not, threatening my grandchildren."

Lord Leasith nodded once. "Noted." Then he turned and went back inside, and the door attendant closed the doors.

Nana took her hands off her hips and turned to us, her cheeks red.

She blew out a long breath and scooted into the cart. "Breathe in and out several times, fledglings. Their magic gets inside you." She began muttering as she drove crazy again. "Calling me ma'am. He's older than me."

Bianca and I puffed in and out for the whole ride back to our house.

Nana's mood didn't change when she made us lunch. I tried to eat a turkey sandwich but had trouble swallowing. After lunch, I walked into the forest. Feeling confused and scared, I looked up into the tree branches. I promised to follow the rules because I didn't want anything to happen to my family and I didn't want to be taken from Ben.

Pops woke me up the next morning. He brought me outside to the picnic table. I smiled when I looked down. He had made my favorite chocolate chip smiley-face pancakes.

"Nana said the lords were pretty scary."

I stopped chewing and nodded.

"Here's what I know. This is the only time I'll talk about it."

I put my fork down.

"They hear it when a human says your real name. That's why your dad told you to never give them your name."

Oops.

"They know when you talk out loud to a human. They don't know when the human talks back, unless your name is used."

Pops came to my side of the table and sat on the bench. Today, he wore his fishing shirt, which had neon orange goldfish on a black background. His eyebrows went up. "They don't know if you hug your buddy. They don't know if you give him a high-five when he makes a basket." He winked. "So zip your lip."

CHAPTER THREE

WHEN I TRAVELED through the portal to Ben's room, he was already dressed. I thought maybe he had slept in his clothes so I wouldn't see his underwear. He rushed up to me and blurted, "I'll call you Jade because your eyes are like my mom's necklace." I smiled. I put my finger to my lips to remind him about the no-talking rule.

"Let's go play by the creek," he said. I nodded and ran down the stairs after him. I felt pretty excited to get to play with him and not just watch him do things. When we got to the stream, we found sticks and floated them in the water, having races with them. I laughed quietly, trying not to make a peep.

Ben slipped in the mud and got it all over his shorts, legs, and hands. He started chasing after me, saying he was a swamp thing. I wound up covered in mud, too. I didn't usually feel things on earth, but now, I could.

Ben lived in Georgia. It was a hot place. It had never bothered me until now. Thankfully, the water was cold when we splashed our feet in it. My nose itched suddenly, and I knew that Korena, the nymph, was nearby. She didn't always show herself to me, but today she did. I flashed her a quick smile before Ben noticed.

I think she was my age. Her dark blue eyes were the color of Lake Hanleith at its deepest part. Her long, blond hair seemed to do its own thing. The frilly pink dress she wore reminded me of something Nana would pick out. She wore a flower bracelet. I knew it was how she

24

moved about.

"Well, look who has a new friend." She walked through the water without disturbing it. She got right in Ben's face. "I wonder why he can't see me." Puckering her lips, she managed a fish face.

I kept quiet even though I wanted to tell her the phantoms might freeze her face that way.

"Yeah, so, Dad says I can't have a dog because Mom's allergic," Ben continued.

I made a sad face to him.

"I wish you could talk."

I shrugged.

Ben leaned forward and looked into the water. I did the same. He crossed his eyes and stuck his tongue out in a funny face. I made a silly face in the water, too. Korena cast reflections for us.

I wondered why she wouldn't leave. The nymphs didn't have to stay with their charges. They had a powerful magic and could cast long-acting spells once a day that would follow the human. After setting things up, they could return to Kirka Village then just come back to check their spell the next morning.

Today, she watched as we played. Ben spit into the water, which brought the fish to the surface.

Out of the blue, he sat back on his butt and said, "You're the prettiest girl I ever met. I'm pretty sure I'm gonna marry you when I'm big."

Even if I could talk, I wouldn't have been able to. I felt my cheeks get hot.

He looked at our reflection again in the water. I scrunched my nose up then put my finger to it, pretending to pick it.

Ben looked at the reflection and laughed. "You're funny, too." He stopped suddenly. Confused, he looked at the reflection, then me.

When I looked down at the water, I saw a girl with frizzy hair, buck teeth, and a huge nose with a black wart on it.

Ewwwwww. When I looked to Korena, she was laughing so hard, she had to sit down on a rock.

I didn't want Ben to hear me, so I didn't yell at her, but I gave her my "die" look. I could have cast a dark shadow, but I didn't.

She disappeared, and I breathed easier. Ben looked at me a few times, and I let him feel my nose and face to see for himself I didn't look like a little witch.

From that day on, we spent all of our time playing together. My sister called me a tomboy. I had no problem with that. Ben and I raced each other. I was faster but sometimes let him win. I rode on the back of his skateboard and bike. Certain games remained off limits, such as catch. A ball stopping in midair would attract attention. I kept Ben company during homework, ballgames, even punishments. When you're friends, you take the good and the bad.

As BEN GREW older, he gained more friends and had less time to spend alone with me. I accepted the fact that some days, I would only be able to "shadow" him and not "hang" with him.

It didn't bother me that much because I got to experience new places and things alongside him. The first chance he'd get alone with me, we'd talk about everything that happened that day. See, I had a secret. I could communicate in Ben's head. I didn't know of any other darklings who could do that. If they had discovered this, none of them had told anyone. The lords could communicate in this manner. I tried not to think of them, though.

When Ben was eleven, his class took a trip to Six Flags Over Georgia. I spent the noisy bus ride squished in the space at Ben's feet. Others couldn't feel me, but that didn't mean I wanted his larger friend, Will, sitting on top of me the entire trip. For one, he farted all the time.

The bus came to a rocking halt. Kids bumped and jostled each other to get off the bus, everyone except a girl named Sarah. She looked like she'd rather be at the dentist than at an amusement park.

When I followed Ben off the bus, I looked over my shoulder to see her two friends swarming her, planning which rides they wanted to go on first.

"I want to do Goliath, the SkyScreamer, and Acrophobia," said one friend.

Sarah stayed quiet.

Her friend noticed and hooked her arm through Sarah's. "Don't worry, we'll teach ya how to do all the rides. You'll love it."

"Not everyone likes rides. She got carsick on the bus."

Ben did a mini nod—one he did to acknowledge a comment of mine in public. His eyes scanned the crowd and watched the three girls make their way to the SkyScreamer. I looked up and watched the spinning swings that were twenty-four stories off the ground. In Montenai, we didn't have skyscrapers. Most of our buildings nestled low to the ground, blending in and respecting the environment around it. I wondered how Sarah would handle being that high off the ground.

Ben headed toward the SkyScreamer, and Will followed. He made his way up to the girls. He looked genuinely concerned for his classmate. Her face had turned white.

"I might wait for you guys here," she said.

Her friends teased her and told her she'd be fine. She bit her bottom lip until it bled.

When Ben drew closer to the girls, the tallest girl with a dark pony tail, Amber, turned to Ben. "You want to ride next to me?"

I noticed Will poke Ben's side. Amber was the prettiest girl in the class.

"I think I'm going to ride with Will."

Will shook his head like, *you dummy. I don't need you next to me.*

As they got closer to the ride's entrance, I watched Sarah's face. I guessed she didn't like heights or spinning.

Somehow, Ben managed to work his way to stand next to her. "Hey, Sarah. You ever been on a ride like this?"

"No," she gasped. Her brown eyes were huge.

Unlike everyone else, he didn't try to convince her it would all be okay. "Do you like to swing?"

"No."

"How are you with spinning?"

"I get dizzy if I spin around when dancing."

"And heights?" Ben asked.

"I can't look over the side of escalators."

Ben furrowed his brow. "You don't have to ride this. You may want to start with something like the log ride first."

"Geez, Ben. You're a lot of fun," Amber said. "She'll get used to it. After her first ride, she'll be fine."

But she wasn't. In fact, she screamed in terror the whole ride and was so dizzy when she got off, she couldn't walk steady. She also threw up in the garbage can. Her friends laughed and teased her before leaving her behind to get in the next line for the Goliath rollercoaster.

Ben and Will helped her to a picnic table. Will ran to get her a cup of water while Ben waited.

"You don't have to stay here with me, Ben."

"It's no big deal."

"You're going to miss all the rides."

Ben shrugged. "So? It's not like I can't come back here with my family or friends."

She rested her chin on the table. "I'm so embarrassed."

Will returned at that moment with some waters. "Don't be," Will said. "My mother hates rides. So, my dad always brings us. We don't force her to do something that makes her miserable."

Sarah gave him a weak smile.

Ben chimed in. "Yeah, my dad doesn't do spinning. He's very picky about what rides he'll go on. He'd never go on the SkyScreamer. See, you did and you lived to tell about it."

The boys took turns going on rides alone or finding a random classmate while the other waited with Sarah or took her inside the fun shops. She went on the Log Jamboree with them and did okay on the one big hill because she clutched Ben's back and tucked her head into his shoulder blade.

By the end of the day, she was glad to be going home. Her friends stopped teasing her because they saw it bothered Ben. As one of the popular kids at school, what he thought actually mattered to people.

In the dark, as the bus rolled along and my sister came to take my shift, I wanted to hug Ben for being the sweetest boy I knew. I'd never seen him be cruel or mean. Tired from the trip, I returned to Montenai. I felt a bit jealous of Sarah. She got to cling to Ben on the log ride and talk to him openly all day.

Overall, I couldn't complain. I was just happy to be around him.

CHAPTER FOUR

ON A BEAUTIFUL summer day, I dressed as fast as I could. Ben had gotten a new mountain bike for his birthday, and we planned to test it in the woods by his house. We decided to do it first thing so no one else would be around, and I could take turns riding it. I wore purple shorts and a white tank top. The Georgia heat always felt stifling in the summer time, especially in comparison to Montenai's fresh, cool breezes.

When I emerged in his room, he met me with a huge grin. He was in the middle of a major growth spurt, and I now came to his chin. I nodded once to my sister as she stepped toward him to go back to Montenai. Ben's eyes traveled from my light brown legs to my hair. Something had changed in the way he looked at me lately. It caused Bianca to roll her eyes whenever I stepped through the portal for my shift. It caused goosebumps to pop out all over my body, accompanied by a rather pleasant tingling sensation.

I laughed without making a noise. He took my hand and led me down the stairs to the garage. His family had spared no expense. The red bike had a light aluminum frame with heavy-duty shocks and suspension system.

"Get on."

"This is awesome!" I said in his head

"I know. I'm so excited." His blond hair had grown longer over the summer and curled at the nape of his neck. Indoors, his green eyes looked darker. Outside, I could see little golden flecks in the outer edges.

He got on first to steady the bike, and then I climbed onto the seat. He pedaled standing up while I held on to the tail of his t-shirt. At the end of his neighborhood, we entered a small stretch of woods with pine trees and large oaks. No one was here this early in the morning. In July, the sun struggled to break through the thick morning haze. He waited until we were out of the public eye to talk to me. We both got off the bike to look down the path. Situated between two thick trees, the first jump hit thirty yards down. A thin layer of mulch coated the path and was uneven from use and run-off from rains.

"So, don't aim for the trees," he laughed.

"Ha, ha."

A light dusting of freckles covered the bridge of his nose. "You want to go first?"

"No. You're the birthday boy."

"You go first," he offered.

I smiled up at him in challenge. *"You need someone to show you how it's done, don't you?"*

He folded his arms across his chest, and his mouth dropped open. "You really do talk a lot of smack."

I smiled.

He poked my side as I stepped in front of him and raised my leg to straddle the bike.

"Wait. You are absolutely not riding this unless you wear the helmet."

I scrunched my nose up at him. His freckled hands undid the straps. With one hand, he brushed my long hair off my shoulders then tucked it behind my ears. I reminded myself to breathe. Once the helmet was on, I pushed his chest to make him back up. *"All right already!"*

Exhilarated, I took off into the haze, reveling in the speed as I took the first jump.

When I went to land, I noticed some downed branches and tried to twist the handlebars to avoid them. The bike turned sideways, and I crashed on my side with my leg stuck under the bike. I hit my head on a larger branch. Darklings don't get hurt easily. However, sprawled out with my limbs contorted, I felt stunned.

"Jade!" Ben stared down at me. "You okay?" He grabbed the bike off me and held my leg before I had time to prop myself up on my elbows. Struggling so fast to regain my composure and cool, I bumped his forehead with mine.

"Ow," he said.

I was still wearing the helmet. Flustered, I pushed his hand aside. My skin had already started to knit closed on my knee and the side of my leg. The wound would heal in the next few hours and leave behind just a purplish mark. In a few days, it would fade to nothing.

My cheeks flamed hot with embarrassment. I got to my feet and brushed mud and pine needles off my butt.

He reached over and helped me get the helmet off. "How's your head?"

"*Fine.*"

Ben hugged me tight. "Are you okay?" He pulled away and looked at me.

I flashed him a dazed smile.

He just kept looking me over, not paying any attention to the bike. "That was a terrible crash!"

"*Yeah, but how'd I take the jump?*"

"Like a boss."

We both laughed hysterically. I leaned in to put my head on his shoulder, but he caught my chin in his hand and pulled it up. He kissed me square on the lips.

Something pulled at my stomach where my shadow magic rested, and I felt weightless. The world hushed. All color faded from my surroundings. When I caught my breath, I stood at a distance at least ten feet from him.

"Jade?" He looked right *through* me. "Where'd you go? Jade?" His voice sounded strangled as he blinked repeatedly, like things were too bright.

Without realizing it, my legs took me backward, away from the bike…from him. As he scanned the path, my stomach seemed to jump into my throat. I wanted to run to him. Instead, I continued my slow progress backward, driven by the droning that filled my ears. It was a dreaded sound for a shadowcaster. It meant the dragon lords' magic hung in the air. Lord Bulosk's voice rang in my head from when I was eight: *Imaginary friendship shall be terminated by the age of thirteen. This is the maximum age and is extended as a courtesy to shadowcasters who may have charges with special needs or terminal illnesses. There are no exceptions to this age limit.*

My body ran cold, and my eyes blurred from my tears. Why hadn't I remembered this? I could have warned him. I could have…why didn't someone in my family remind me? Of course, none of them knew I communicated with him.

"I can't see you. I know you're here," he called. "I'm so sorry. I won't do that again. Come back. Please."

My sister appeared next to him, her eyes huge. She waved her hand, indicating I should go away. She must have heard the discord of the lords, as well. Fear held her body rigid and hardened the warning look she shot me.

Her brown eyes conveyed sympathy but also a severity that brought back visions of the Council. I cupped my hands over my ears like when I was a little. I couldn't stand it, not another second. If I heard him pleading, I would give in.

My father met me in the open doorway of the Solomon's white colonial home. He held part of the newspaper. His wavy hair seemed more unruly than usual.

I'd interrupted his morning ritual, which entailed sitting with Mr. Solomon and reading the newspaper with classic rock playing from the stereo. They always looked like two friends studying together. I wondered what my father would do with his life if he didn't have Mr. Solomon to look after.

One look at my face and my father stepped off the stoop and gathered me into his chest. I muffled my cries in his shirt as he stroked my back. My mother peeked through the doorway, her lips pressed together.

She kissed my cheek and whispered to me. "You know it's for the best, Anka. It's time he ventured more into this world without you, and you paid more attention to your own kind."

I knew she meant well, but it felt like she'd slugged me in the stomach. While my father held my arms tightly, I turned to watch as Ben walked his new bike toward the house. He didn't look like he ever wanted to ride it again. Bianca walked by his side. He whispered my name as he approached the house. His eyes continued to search behind the blooming hibiscus plants then to our favorite tree where he swung as a kid.

Ben put his bike back in the garage and climbed the stairs to his bedroom. From the doorway, I watched him stare out the window as if he were searching for something, someone. Bianca's eyes were red from crying. As much as my sister could be bossy, she really did care. She hugged me tightly.

The droning continued in my ears.

"They want to talk to you," Bianca said.

My mouth went dry.

"I'm sorry, Anka. They sent a messenger to the house."

I stepped away from her and toward Ben. I heard Bianca scream my name as I touched Ben's palm.

Pops met me on the path. "What happened?" he asked. His shirt today was banana yellow.

"He's thirteen!" I shrieked. "He turned thirteen!"

Instead of hugging me and comforting me, Pops grabbed me by the shoulders. "You need to stop and listen to me."

I tried but choked on my sobs. My best friend had just been torn from me, and I couldn't get a hold of myself.

"Anka."

"What, Pops?"

"They didn't just work a spell; they are summoning you. Do you hear a noise?"

"Like bees," I gasped.

"That's not good."

With my heart doing a crazy dance in my chest, I climbed into the cart. No matter how many times I took gulps of air, I still felt lightheaded. Darklings didn't usually throw up or get sick like humans. But at this moment, I felt like I might.

I don't remember the ride to the Wishing Tree in the South Village. Pops kept talking, but his words just ricocheted off me. He patted my thigh several times.

Finally, he pinched me.

"Ow," I said.

We were almost past Drakos, the restaurant named for the first dragon lord. The smell of gourmet food caused my head to swim.

"I'm going in with you," Pops insisted. He grabbed my hand so hard, I winced.

"Pops."

"I got you."

"Pops?"

I could feel him shaking. I didn't know if it was from fear or anger. Goosebumps broke out all over my body. The Wishing Tree loomed overhead. Darklings had cleared from the grassy area by the water in Lady Pia's Park.

Just as we stepped up to the doors, they crashed open. Hundreds of bats erupted from the treetop. A force yanked me forward. Pops yelled and tried to hold on. As I sailed away from him, his nails scratched my arm. The doors slammed shut at my back, and I crashed to the cobblestone path inside the tree. On my hands and knees, I gasped for breath. I stayed in that position until I saw a shiny dress shoe.

"Get up."

I did what Lord Bulosk told me. Today, he had no winks, no reassurances.

"Follow me." His footsteps echoed as he took me into the Council Room.

It looked the same, except for the mess. Flowers were scattered across the table and spilled onto the white marble floor. Water ran in a tiny river and dripped off the table's edge. Broken shards of glass sparkled under the blown glass fixtures floating in the space above. Something had destroyed what once had been an extravagant flower arrangement.

The heavy wooden door slammed closed behind me. I startled, hunching my shoulders up to my ears.

He dried a corner of the table with the cuff of his shirt sleeve. "Sit."

I balanced on the edge of the seat and tried not to inhale the smell of the dragon lords. I remembered Nana telling us to puff out air the last time we'd escaped this place.

"Patrick Benjamin Solomon is thirteen today. He is neither sick, nor has special needs of any kind. And yet, somehow, he has continued to see you."

Beads of water quivered on the table as his low bellow shook it. The air seemed to press on me. I caught myself blinking and breathing through my mouth.

"You're lucky I convinced Lord Akton to let me handle things." His green eyes met mine. "In my hand is a decree of suspension," he rasped. "Take it, read it, study it. Follow the instructions and don't ever get summoned here again."

When I grasped the rolled parchment, it quivered in my hand, as if there were magic trapped inside it.

As Lord Bulosk escorted me out, my knees and hands stung from when I'd fallen in the Wishing Tree's hallway, but I was too upset to care. I wanted to burn the decree or toss it in the Montenai River; just get it away from me.

When the doors swung open, and I saw Pops standing just past Lord Leasith, I swallowed my anger. Pops supported his right hand like it hurt. *They hurt him?*

"Just let me see it a minute," Lord Leasith commanded.

"No. Don't touch me," Pops said.

"What's the matter?" Lord Bulosk asked.

"He won't let me heal him."

"Ernest, just hold it out a moment," Lord Bulosk said.

"I mean it. Don't you touch me." Pops looked like he might explode. I'd never seen him like this. "Get in the cart, honey."

Without looking at the lords, I rushed to the cart. Pops got in, cradling his injured hand in his lap. He drove along the river, and I didn't dare talk. Every hair on my body stood on end. When we were halfway home, I remembered to take deep breaths and breathe out the magic of the Council.

I held on to the top bar. No tears came.

Pops parked the cart inside the sequoia. Neither of us made a move for the house but just stared at the bark in front of us. Finally, I found my voice.

"Are you okay?"

"Are you?" he asked.

"They didn't hurt me." My bottom lip trembled, and I tried to hold back the tears. "What happened to your hand?"

"I'm not proud of myself, but I thought they were going to harm you." Pops grimaced.

"Pops?"

"I punched Lord Leasith in the face. Mother of Montenai, I saw stars. It was like hitting granite." Pops's eyebrows shot up. "I don't think his head even moved an inch."

With my mouth hanging open, I thought about what my grandfather had just done. I didn't know what to say.

CHAPTER FIVE

I READ THE decree that night in the glow of the nymph lamps in my room. After a weeklong suspension, I would return to the Solomon house. I would cast shadows for one Patrick Benjamin Solomon. And I would watch my conduct. This was their second warning.

When Pops worried, a muscle in his cheek twitched from clenching his jaw. For several days, I watched that muscle jump. It became more pronounced with my endless crying. When the tears finally dried up, I wandered to the river's edge and considered the nymphs across the way.

Before the Blessed Incursion, we had lived as subjects to the nymph queen, Hanleith. It must have been miserable over there if darklings accepted the ruling of the dragon lords. Something dark reared in me, but I pushed it down. I needed to abide by the rules of Shadowland or my family would suffer. Pops's hand had healed within a few days, but his eyes had lost some of their sparkle.

After I cried my heart out, I started to think of my family. I couldn't look at Pops without feeling guilty for causing trouble. I hadn't meant to...it just...Ben was my best friend. I treasured every day I had with him, and I hadn't ever wanted it to end.

My family moved around me, talking to me as if nothing had happened, except for Bianca. She took time to talk to me when our parents weren't in the room. She listened to me whine, complain, and feel sorry for myself.

For weeks, my stomach felt tied in a huge knot. Seeing Ben, yet him not seeing me, hurt physically.

Even though I accepted the terms of my position, the knot stayed. Ben never gave up, though. He'd whisper when no one was around. I never flinched or made a move to show I was there. Fear caused me to swallow my sorrow. It nestled in the pit of my stomach with my shadow magic. It leaked out of me with each pull from my energy as I cast shadows for him.

Ben's loyalty persisted even until he was fourteen and he named a star after me. At fifteen, he grew at least a foot. He loved baseball and he excelled at it. Girls started to call. At sixteen, the calls increased. I knew I shouldn't interfere. However, every once in a while, a phone cord magically disconnected from the wall or a call terminated on his cell phone.

At first, I would stew in the corner during these calls while he flirted. I understood we lived in different worlds, but I still yearned to talk with him like the other girls did. I realized he would date humans, eventually. It was only natural, but it didn't stop the pangs of jealousy when he did interact with sweet girls like Sarah. Luckily, my sister covered Ben in the evenings so I didn't witness the few dates he had.

Some of my fellow shadowcasters tried to encourage me. Others distanced themselves. They had no idea what I had done. They just knew the dragon lords had reprimanded me twice. Shrouded in mystery, I attracted some of the rebel shadowcasters in the crowd. I went on a some dates, even kissed a few darklings, but I didn't fool myself or anyone else. My mind was never in Montenai. Instead, it stayed on Ben and our kiss in the woods on his thirteenth birthday.

During this time, I became more aware of Korena's presence. As was the way of the nymphs, Korena never showed herself to Ben. She emerged every morning to re-spin the web of her reflections spell. She'd grown tall and breathtaking. At sixteen, her body reminded me of a human supermodel's. Sometimes, we talked. I got the feeling quite often that she thought she was better than me.

"Don't you wish you weren't stuck to humans like leeches?" she asked one morning.

Ben was in the shower, getting ready for school, so I sat in the hallway waiting for him to finish.

"I like my job," I said.

She wrinkled her nose. "I can't imagine following a human around like a kicked puppy."

I knew she was baiting me. "Well, Korena, we can't all be perfect, can we?"

"Darklings have always been so weak."

Before I could respond, she disappeared. I shrugged it off.

Since Korena usually appeared early in the day, I took advantage of the evening time, just before Bianca came, as mine and Ben's quality time. Ben must have sensed it, as well. He talked to me in the dark, whispering so his parents wouldn't hear. He covered everything from sports to the injustices in the world. At times, I wanted to whisper back about darklings, nymphs, and our struggles with dragon lords. What must he think about my life as a mute? How did he remain faithful to the idea of me when he received nothing in return?

I considered this one night as I looked at his seventeen-year-old frame stretched long atop a new bed that fit his legs. The room had changed, as well. Sports team paraphernalia covered much of the walls, along with anything to do with astronomy and the stars. I wondered if he still thought of me as an alien.

Tonight, he wore a white t-shirt and boxers. With his arms behind his head, he sighed. "I know when you're here."

Breath held, I drew closer. *I will always be here.*

No matter what happened in Montenai, things didn't seem so scary when I was with Ben. He didn't have a pretty face, but a handsome masculine one with a slightly crooked nose—compliments of a wrestling match. He'd won despite the broken nose. One look at his face and I felt trust and loyalty, two things I hadn't found much of in my life.

"I know when it's someone else."

I watched his muscular chest rise and fall. It took every bit of willpower not to attempt talking in his head. Fear lodged in my throat, and I had to remind myself to breathe.

"You smell sweet, like sugar. See, Per*smell*ope was fitting."

I smiled. I smelled like Pops's chocolate shop.

"I wish I could still see you."

Trembling, I bent over him. The rules swirled in my head. For some reason, I couldn't get past how he looked, how much I missed him. I knew I shouldn't, but it hurt not to. My body moved on its own. When I kissed his lips, he wrapped his arms around my lower back, pulling me on top of him. My breath whooshed out of me as we made full contact.

He deepened the kiss. As I rested my palms on his chest for balance, he ran his fingers through my hair. He smelled of musk and tasted minty like toothpaste. I felt the muscles of his chest through his thin shirt. He rolled me onto my side with extreme care.

The movement broke our kiss. With his hand, he felt his way up my arm, leaving a path of goosebumps. His fingertips caressed my neck, swept across my collarbone, found my jawline, and then my lips. Once he'd located my mouth again, he leaned in. I met him halfway. Both of his strong hands cupped my face as his kisses became more urgent. Warmth traveled from my chest down to my stomach, creating a fluttering sensation in the core that housed my shadow magic.

His one hand held my chin, the other found my hip and squeezed. Everything inside me melted. I kissed back, exploring his mouth with my tongue. My heart hammered in my chest.

"Jade," Ben whispered in my ear in a husky voice. The emotion in his voice brought tears to my eyes.

I touched the center of his palm.

Back in Montenai, I stood at the edge of the portal by the small fir tree. My eyes scanned the forest as I listened. After a minute, I took a few cleansing breaths. My lips tingled. I smelled him, still. Felt dizzy from his touch. A giggle burst forth before I could stop it.

"Holy hotness!"

He shouldn't have been able to feel my touch, but he had.

Within seconds, the epic dose of euphoria I'd swallowed felt like a stubborn pill of worry lodged in my throat. Ben wouldn't give me away to Bianca. And no one had witnessed the encounter.

But the lords…

I walked down the path. My pace increased the more anxious I became. He'd touched me. At some point, would he be able to see me, too? Soon, I was running to see Pops who had to work at the shop tonight.

Sultry blue jazz notes hit me at the entryway. Pops had opened the rolling windows to the summer air, and the luscious smell of desserts lured me into the space. Pops had an immense glass counter he'd purchased from the nymphs.

Nymph lights floated like tiny orbs throughout the space, changing colors with the mood of the music. The light, ethereal touch of the nymphs contrasted perfectly with the dark space within the tremendous sequoia that was Pops's shop.

I perched on a leather stool at the counter, attempting not to appear as breathless as I felt. I checked my reflection in a metal napkin dispenser and hastily fixed my lip gloss with my finger.

Pops placed a decaf coffee and two chocolate-covered strawberries in front of me. "Hello, my green-eyed genius."

"Hi." My fingers traced the purple musical notes painted on the plate.

"You look *thoughtful*," he said.

Not the word I would have used to describe my current condition.

"What's going on in that dark darkling head?" he asked with a chuckle.

"Nothing, Pops. I just want to relax and listen to the music." My voice sounded strange to me.

He nodded, but I caught the muscles twitch in his cheek. "Well, you've come to the right place."

I rested my chin in my hands and darkling-watched as I pretended to enjoy the treat. It felt bittersweet watching the other couples who laughed and held hands as they swayed to the music.

I'd crossed a line tonight. What was I thinking? I sat up straighter. Nana's stern reprimand from when I was eight played in my head. If I couldn't control my impulses, I would endanger my family. *I just won't talk to him or touch him again.* I recalled the taste of him, his smell, the feel of his body pressed against mine. *Life is so unfair.* It couldn't be helped. I needed to maintain my distance.

It seemed like a good plan, but when I returned to Ben's room the next morning, Korena stared back at me from the bureau mirror. Ben stood transfixed by the nymph's reflection. With my hands balled into fists, I watched him touch the mirror.

"Who are you?" he asked.

Korena gave him her name. My jaw dropped. What did she think she was doing? I lurched across the room to stand behind Ben. When I scowled at Korena, she winked at me from the glass. Ben whipped around. "Jade?"

I stepped back out of his grasp. He still couldn't see me. This would not bode well. Korena *knew*. She didn't answer to the Council. She was toying with us. It dawned on me that she had always known.

Ben searched his room, but I stayed out of reach. Frustrated, he headed to the shower. I flicked my fingers, sending shadows into the bathroom after him. My power didn't match the nymph's, though. Korena appeared in the mirror before me, waving her hand haphazardly in Ben's direction so he'd see his reflection when he got to the bathroom.

"Well, haven't you been naughty," Korena challenged.

"I don't know what you mean," I hissed.

"You know exactly what I mean." Korena fluffed her golden curls. "He's a handsome devil, isn't he? I just thought I'd give him options."

"This is a dangerous game, Korena."

"Maybe for you, but not for me. I don't have any overgrown lizards to hide from." Her enormous blue eyes stayed on me. Darklings had a sturdy build. The nymphs were waif-like and graceful. I felt the sudden urge to cast a dark shadow at her scrawny figure. It would sting, give her a migraine, and make her queasy.

I gave her a scathing look. "Don't hurt him." With my hands still curled in fists, I turned and walked away from her.

The day lasted forever. I tried to ignore Korena and not make eye contact. My brain whirred like Pops's old computer. If I mentioned

Korena's appearance to any of the darklings, Korena would tell the others I'd kissed Ben. Somehow, she knew. I'd been so wrapped up in things, I hadn't felt her presence.

That night, as Ben lay in his bed, he tried to communicate with me again. "Who is the woman in the mirror?"

I bit my lip.

"Jade? Why did she appear to me? Is she a bad person?"

Yes. I never trusted nymphs. Not after the history we had. Not after how they treated Nana. Although we now traded with them for goods and worked together on the human plane, we always kept up a protective wall when it came to them. I didn't know what to do. After stroking his arm, I touched his hand and fell through the portal.

I spent the night brooding in my room. I'd redecorated the space in soothing tones from nature after Bianca had moved out two months ago. She lived in an apartment in North Village, just off the boardwalk. Pops had contributed to the space by tossing in some nymph lights. They changed with my mood. Tonight, they shone a dull gray. I fought the urge to hurl them out the window since they reminded me of Korena.

Restless, I scanned my room for some distraction. My eyes landed on my CSP, Compact Satyr Player. It looked much like a human's digital music player, but its inner workings were some satyr creation I couldn't begin to explain. The satyrs created the external brass shell to be the size of a cell phone. They often engraved tiny symbols from nature on them. Mine had a tremendous wave on the front, reminding me of the Aglatian Sea. The cradle for the player was the shape of a satyr hoof. My device rested in the space or cleft in the middle of the hoof.

After selecting a darkling jazz band called the Shadow Blues from my playlist, I paced the floor. The darkling Wishing Tree loomed in front of me. Mom had painted a more realistic image with pine needles when we outgrew the wishing game. Now, it more closely resembled the sequoia that housed the Council. I knew it was my mother's subtle way of reminding me to behave. I felt a burning need to get away from the tree, as if it were monitoring my movements.

"Wow, Anka. You are really losing it." I considered my music selection might be contributing to my somber thoughts. Eventually, I climbed into bed and drifted to sleep, not feeling any better about life.

CHAPTER SIX

THE NEXT AFTERNOON, Ben dressed in his baseball uniform. His blond hair curled out from the edges of his cap. He looked stoked for the upcoming championship game. The Solomon house was astir because college scouts planned to attend to see Ben play. He played right field, but his strength was the bat. He had a batting average of .330. When he grabbed his glove and pounded down the stairs, I followed. I smiled at my parents in the living room as he discussed plans with his parents. Ben would leave early to warm up with the team. The Solomons would come later.

Ben drove an old, red Dodge Demon his father had helped him restore. I slid through the crack of the door and into the passenger seat—a wicked cool trick Dad had taught me on my sixteenth birthday. Not many shadowcasters could do it. Korena sat in the back, wearing a cheerleading outfit. *Not cool.*

I scowled at her. She winked at me then waved at Ben as he adjusted the rearview mirror.

"What the—" He swung his head around between the seats. "I'm sorry, but you need to get out." He licked his lips and fidgeted with his cap. As he turned back toward the front windshield, he gasped, "Can anyone see you besides me?"

"Sometimes," Korena chirped.

"Why are you here?"

"I've always been here, Ben. I know you have a birthmark on your left hip."

"Creepy," he whispered. He smoothed his hands on his thighs. "What do you want?"

"Just a ride to the game, silly."

We drove in utter silence as I glared back at Korena. I didn't like her attitude. Nymphs could be such slinky creatures.

At the ball field, Ben fielded grounders and long balls and talked with his teammates as fans filled the stands. Korena took her place among the other team's cheerleaders. I scanned the crowd to assess if they could all see her. I found Dad sitting calmly behind Mr. Solomon in the stands. I pointed to Korena. His jaw dropped.

The game started, and I did my best to cast the most accurate shadows, but none so dark Ben couldn't see the ball. As the game progressed, I noted many of the humans appeared mesmerized by the new cheerleader. Darn nymphs and their wily ways. Ben kept his head in the game.

His team, the Cardinals, led the game, but the Seminoles were last at bat. Ben's team needed one more out. As the sun moved across the sky, I watched as strange glares bounced off the metal chain-link fence behind home plate. What was she up to? I positioned myself as far away from Ben as possible while still able to cast shadows. As the opposing team got a hit, the nymph sent a glare up in the fielder's eyes, causing an error. Now, they had a man on first base.

I couldn't scream at her. Instead, I moved even closer as the nimble nymph kicked her boot up to her shoulder and shook her pom poms. The next batter hit a pop fly, which should have been caught, but again, Korena interfered.

"*Stop it!*" I mouthed at her.

My parents sat in the stands doing nothing. They never interfered in the human world, even with a wayward nymph causing mayhem. Korena continued to jeopardize the next play. Now the bases were loaded. Sweat drenched Ben's jersey, and he glared at Korena. Did he know she was responsible?

The Seminoles' batter looked like he should be in the big leagues.

A full-grown man, he swung for the fences. The ball sailed toward right field. I watched as Korena cast an unusual reflection in Ben's eyes. He struggled to get under the ball.

Fuming, I ran past Ben and screamed, "Another foot to the left," before diving and tackling the cheerleader. The crowd roared. I couldn't discern the game's outcome since I was busy rolling Korena and pinning her beneath me.

"Why?" I screamed at her.

My parents' disapproving stares didn't hinder my interrogation. Instead, a sound like the swarming of bees filled my ears. It prompted me to stand. I fixed my skirt in the process. The Shadowland Council had summoned me. When I looked to Mom and Dad, I saw fear had frozen their mouths and eyes wide open.

I sprinted toward Ben who was sprawled at the bottom of a crazy heap of celebrating teammates. With a touch of his hand, I slipped through the portal to the Sequoia Forest.

On my plane, they no longer sounded like bees, but rather what they truly were—enraged dragon lords. Darklings ran from the boardwalk. Shop owners closed their doors and drew their shutters. I kept running, because I feared, if I didn't, they'd summon my family. I headed for South Village.

Darklings scrambled out of my way as I raced toward the end of the boardwalk where the tallest tree stood. When I was almost there, an incredible force whooshed past me. With a sonic boom, the bridge to Kirka Village exploded, sending splinters of wood into the air. I dove to the ground and covered my head with my arms. I couldn't be sure the bridge had been their target.

After the storm of debris settled, I raised my head. Their strike had taken out half the boats at the dock. On trembling legs, I completed my journey to the tree. No door attendant met me at the entrance. In fact, all employees had evacuated the area. Since they were predisposed toward Shadow Fever, many nonshadowcasters believed close proximity to the lords' power would keep them healthy. Perhaps, after this incident, they'd rethink their employment and living arrangements.

I didn't want to be close to the lords. In fact, I was sure overexposure to the Council would be hazardous to my health. *Breathe Anka.* My heart felt like it would launch from my chest.

The gnarled wooden double doors stood before me like the mouth of some menacing monster ready to ingest me. Each creature of Montenai stood in relief upon the doors' surface. Just above the door, hung the golden shield of the dragon and his shadow. It represented the communion between the dragon lords and the shadowcasters. It all started when a red dragon dropped through the sky from another world and changed our lives forever—the Blessed Incursion. Right now, I felt more doomed than blessed by it.

Behind me, the sun set over the glass domes of the nymphs. It struck the shield above the door, causing it to shimmer. The early evening breeze stirred, surrounding me in the thick, undeniable scent of dragon lords and their magic. I smoothed my hair and straightened my black skirt before reaching with trembling fingers to ring the bell. It felt like such a human thing to do. The bell echoed throughout the old tree, sending bats scattering from the tree's crown. I'm not a fan of bats. I prefer winged creatures to have feathers.

The doors creaked inward, revealing the cobblestone tunnel leading down to the Rotunda where the dragon lords wielded their power. Empty. Each room I peeked into looked abandoned. A messy countertop with spilled milk indicated the hasty departure of the darkling kitchen staff.

Enchanted mosaic sconces lit my descent. My thigh muscles spasmed as I walked like I'd just run across all of Montenai. I didn't have time to think. Lord Akton waited just outside the vestibule. His seven-foot frame dwarfed my five-foot-seven. His red facial scaling could be mesmerizing under certain light. He turned abruptly, and I followed him into the inner chamber before I could fully study the mottled flesh and scarring on the right side of his face.

When he turned, his one golden eye focused on me, driving me to my knees. I gritted my teeth as my kneecaps cracked on the marble floor. The pain brought with it a reality check. *Don't think about what they did to the bridge.*

I noted the other dragon lords had halted their activity of cigar smoking and brandy drinking. Today, they all wore fine silk shirts and tailored pants. Leasith stood, rolling up the sleeves of his shirt to reveal the bronze scales of his arm and the claws of his hand. Bulosk stepped up next to him with his enchanting blue scales. He didn't unsheathe his claws.

To distract myself from my impending doom, I scanned the surroundings. If you're going to go, go out in style. Apparently, one can amass quite a bit of wealth living for over a century. Exquisite paintings covered the walls, but I didn't dare peek at them too long. The last time I had been in this room, I was four years old. The room itself felt alive. That hadn't changed.

My labored breathing was a pitiful sound. Bowing my head, I focused on steadying it. Being so close to all three of them at once caused my head to throb. I didn't understand their magic, but I knew it was strong. It bound every fiber of my body and caused the shadow magic in the core of my belly to flip-flop like a dying fish.

When I saw a pair of enormous loafers in front of me, my head flew back and fixed in position. Akton locked his eye on me. He used no words to communicate. Instead, he raged, igniting a fire that simmered over the surface of my body. His images attacked me in a relentless storm.

A red dragon burst from Montenai's layered sky; an astrei rode upon his back. The dragon's fierce bellow shook the world as scarlet blood poured from the astrei's wings. She clutched a dragon's egg, which glowed and shimmered with power.

My body quaked as I fought Akton's hold, but his golden eye sucked me back into his world.

The egg came into the care of a brave darkling named Toren who was heavy with child. Childbirth was long and harrowing for her, but she produced the first dragon lord—a stunning creature with golden scales. Drakos was magnificent but menacing—a mutation caused by proximity to the glowing egg. He had three sons. Akton was the oldest. They named him for the grand dragon who fell from Montenai's sky.

Tears streamed down my face as I felt Akton's fear under his father's dominion.

In a dark room, young Akton reached for the glowing egg, which soothed with a lulling tone. Out of nowhere, golden claws lashed at his face.

My eye! My eye!

The images jittered, stuttered, and skipped as agony suffused my every fiber, and I screamed. On the marble floor, I struggled to separate myself from the red-scaled dragon lord and the trauma of his father's brutal punishment. *That's how Lord Akton had lost his eye.*

My fingers fluttered in front of my eye. *Not your memories, Anka.* Nonetheless, I wailed until I lost my voice, curling in on myself as if to disappear.

I knew then there would be no jury, no side to my story.

Akton pulled me to sit as he rumbled from above. "In the name of Toren, our grandmother, we revoke your powers, shadowcaster."

White noise filled my ears. I would never see Ben again. I would never use my talent again. I saw all of their fancy shoes before three searing lashes filleted my back. I tried to escape into the floor's cool marble as my back sparked with intense fire. Looking up, I saw Bulosk's green eyes as he looked down on me, and if I didn't know better, I'd say with concern.

CHAPTER SEVEN

I LAY ON my stomach in my bedroom while Bianca sang a childhood darkling song. She wrung cool water over my wounds and tried to use her energy to heal me. The sensation offered some reprieve from the pain for a minute, but then the searing feeling started anew. Dad squeezed my hand, attempting to soothe, joining Bianca's song in his baritone voice. Mom wept in the corner chair. Even in my daze, I understood they couldn't take me to the hospital. The lords managed almost everything in Shadowland. They had named Toren Hospital for their grandmother, the first keeper of the egg, the Torensphere.

I don't know how much time passed. At some point, I realized my wounds didn't heal but continued to fester. How long was the Council's sentence?

Through the bedroom window, I watched night come. My eyes remained bleary, my brain in a fog. In the middle of the night, Pops stood over me.

"Princess. Hang tight. I got you."

I tried to nod but couldn't. At some point, I'd rolled onto my side, which was a miserable position. I was aware I may be naked, which would be embarrassing, but I didn't linger too long on the possibility. Pops pulled the sheet from the bed and wrapped it around me.

"Shh," he warned.

He pulled me up to cradle one arm under my knees and the other at my raw back. I choked back a sob.

"Anka, my child, you're on fire. But not for long."

Despite being in his sixties, Pops was still strong as a bear. I smelled Nana in the hallway. The entire house remained quiet as he walked down the stairs and through the kitchen. Nana opened the back door for him and followed us to the cart. He propped me up in the passenger seat with an apology. The red star, the Father of Montenai, shined brightly down on me, as if mocking. It was said to be the red dragon's soul. He'd fled to the sky in grief over the dead astrei.

After Pops and Nana worked together to strap me in with the seatbelt, I leaned forward in my toga, bracing my arms on the dashboard. Nana kissed my forehead.

"Hang on, honey. Pops will take care of you."

Pops didn't turn on lights or music as he took a back route away from the main boardwalk and the half-destroyed pier in South Village. Pops's boat had been a casualty to their anger. He almost drove the cart right into the river. My head whipped forward before the seatbelt yanked it back. I mewled like a cat when someone has stepped on its tail.

Pops jumped out and freed me from the seatbelt. I moaned despite my best intentions to stay strong. He plunged into the Montenai River with me and fought the current to the middle. The shock of the cold river water on my burning skin sucked the breath from me. Did Pops plan to drown me? Put me out of my misery?

When I caught my breath and gazed up, I saw a dark figure standing on a rock.

A satyr greeted Pops. "No worries, my friend. I'll take extra care." He tilted his hat to me. "I'm so sorry to find you in this condition, Dark Beauty. Cornelius Jeremiah of the Fardoragh herd at your service."

I managed a weak smile for Cornelius, the head buck of the satyrs. His lot was an interesting bunch with their ability to beguile females, despite their lower limbs being that of a goat. They tended to have ripped torsos and incredibly muscular posteriors. Musicians and artisans at heart, they could make anything with their hands and created instruments, home goods, even tremendous sea vessels. In addition to their handiwork, they possessed an uncanny ability of shifting the winds to their favor when fishing.

I'd met Cornelius before, but only briefly. Everyone knew who he was. He helped Pops position me astride him. I leaned against his massive back, my arms and legs wrapped around him as he stretched his own arms backward to hold me secure. The satyrs dwarfed darklings. Most were at least seven feet tall.

"I hope they aren't coming after us," Pops said, his voice tight.

"Something powerful is shielding her. I can feel it," Cornelius said.

"What is it?" Pops asked.

"Why question. Just accept it for now," he answered.

I didn't hear Pops's response. My eyelids drooped as I struggled to stay alert. With my cheek against the satyr's back, we launched onto the rock.

"I'll meet you there," Cornelius said to Pops. He rock-hopped across the river while Pops struggled through the current behind us. At the moment, I knew Pops wished he still had his boat.

Cornelius increased his speed. He was so graceful, he barely jostled me. Before I knew it, nymphs surrounded me inside one of their domed dwellings.

"No," I gasped. I attempted to push them away.

"It's okay, love." Korena's mother looked down at me with her exquisite blue eyes.

Pops burst into the room, still huffing. "Magda. Thank you," he said.

"Don't thank me yet," she replied.

An awful keening came from the corner of the room. When I searched the area, I found Korena hunched over on herself with swollen eyes from crying. "I'm sorry, Anka," she said.

"Take her out of here," Magda commanded.

Pops held my hand as the nymphs cut the sticking sheet from my back. They sang to me as they applied a cool, gelatinous treatment to the wounds. I didn't drift off to sleep, rather it rose up and pulled me down. When I awoke, my back still hurt, but the fire had gone.

Pops stood over me, a steaming mug in hand. "You need to drink this."

On my side, I attempted to push up with my right arm. So many hands rushed in to support me. Slowly, I drank all of the tea.

Birds sang sweetly nearby, and the room glowed. How did they sleep in this glass bubble of light? I looked down at the white nightgown I guessed was Korena's.

"There's our girl," Dad said.

Mom, Dad, Nana, and Bianca stood behind Pops. The nymphs scurried out of the room.

"I'm sorry," I said meekly. It wouldn't suffice. Had I ruined everything for the entire family?

Dad knelt by the bed, brushing my hair off my forehead. "We're just glad you're okay."

"But what will happen to all of us?"

Mom looked down at her hands. "It's done, Anka."

"Those slimy lizards will leave us be as long as we accept their terms," Pops said.

Confused, I looked at my sister.

"I'll watch over him," Bianca said. My sister's hair looked tousled, her eyes red.

I nodded as my eyes brimmed with tears. Everything I'd done my whole life had been so I could stay with Ben, and here, I'd thrown it all away over the outcome of a baseball game. Inside, I knew it stemmed from something more. Love will make you lose your mind.

My family stood silent as Pops explained my banishment from Shadowland. My eyes locked on a tiny prism of color cast upon the wall from the sun coming through the nymph's special glass.

They would go on with their lives. Relief and resentment swirled as a nasty potion in my stomach. How could they go back to work under the Shadowland Council after what they'd done to me?

CHAPTER EIGHT

MY SENTENCE WAS the ultimate rejection. Before the Blessed Incursion, nymphs had treated darklings as a lesser caste under the House of Hanleith. They'd mistreated and banished my kind. Shadowland had been our new home, a place of peace, health, and prosperity under the dragon lords. But now the lords had removed me from my safe haven to live with the creatures who had first rejected my kind.

Thankfully, when Magda accepted me into her home, I learned that beliefs and attitudes had changed on this side of the river.

The darkling law disallowed me from crossing the water to Shadowland. However, my family visited often. Pops made the trek every day, bringing an array of chocolates with him. The satyrs acted as his ferry. Pops planned to wait for the lords to simmer down before ordering a new fishing boat from the satyrs.

Korena had run off with a satyr and now lived in Port by the Sea. I swallowed a dose of bitterness each time I thought about her antics. She still cast reflections in the human world for the Solomon family. It didn't seem fair. I missed Ben every single minute of every single day. I did my best to stay busy and keep my brain occupied. When I wasn't helping Magda around the house, I spent time painting. I'd inherited my mother's artistic talent.

My sorrow hijacked my mind when I was left alone. I snapped out of my latest haze to find my paintbrush paused mid-air. Magda's voice sounded in my ear.

"Well, that's an interesting interpretation of our sunset," she said.

Behind her glass home, several terraces spilled down the hill to Lake Hanleith. It was the perfect setting for an outdoor studio.

"So dark," she said, as she surveyed my latest creation. Her puzzled eyes left my canvas and traveled to the scene in front of us. "Look at all the colors exploding across the lake with the changing leaves and the sun setting."

I didn't take her criticism too much to heart. As a nymph, she wanted everything to be bright.

"Magda, just accept that I'm going through my Blue Period."

She chuckled as her strong hand squeezed my shoulder and a bouquet of frankincense, peppermint, and lavender filled my nose. It was Magda's scent—a collection of her favorite herbs used in healing.

"Come in when you're ready. I've made your favorite lamb stew."

"Thank you," I said, despite not having any appetite.

After she left, I took a moment to analyze my work. I'd painted the lake, but it didn't dazzle. Instead, it held layers of shadows from an encroaching dark forest.

"It's the happiest painting I've created in a while," I said aloud to no one.

I had to admit it was dark. But it wasn't as haunting as Bianca's favorite series of mine, which showed the human world as it would be if we didn't cast shadows. When we absorbed the sun's radiation, it disturbed the molecules around us. If we didn't cast for them, all humans would have eerie shadows that warped and melted into their surroundings like a Salvador Dali painting.

Several of my paintings featured Ben, but I could never finish them. It was just too painful. Almost daily, I wondered what he thought. Did he think I'd abandoned him? Would I be more at peace if I could just say goodbye?

At first, my sister had shared tidbits of his life. Over time, Bianca became more tight-lipped. I guessed Dad had instructed everyone not to speak of Ben, so I would forget him and move on. It didn't work. Time felt different now that I was trapped on earth's plane. The days stretched long and unforgiving.

I cleaned up my painting supplies and went inside so I could help Magda. I know I wasn't much company at dinner because I was too anxious and distracted in anticipation of my sister's visit.

When Bianca finally came, I found myself full of nervous energy. During the past two visits, I had sensed she was burning to tell me something.

"What?" I finally asked her.

We stood outside in the tall grasses under the moonlight. The enchanted nymph grass bent to the side to allow a path for us. Two years older than me, Bianca was shorter but so lovely. Her hair grew in ringlets down her back, and her dark eyes held the same kind of shine as Pops's.

Bianca squeezed my hand. "He's in the army."

"The army?"

She nodded. "He didn't want to go straight to college."

Closer to her now, I saw worry had creased her forehead and fatigue had turned the skin under her eyes ashen.

"Are you shadowcasting in a war zone?"

"Yes," she said, bringing her hand to her mouth. A flowered nymph bracelet sparkled around her wrist. "I gotta go." She disappeared using the nymph bracelet to travel through their portal.

Numb, I let her leave. *Ben was in a war zone?* I felt sick to my stomach. Bianca must be miserable witnessing so much pain and violence. I couldn't imagine Ben in that environment. And yet, I could. He stood proud and protective. He would no doubt consider it his duty to serve, feel obligated to be a catalyst in ridding the world of so many injustices.

I didn't sleep at all that night. The next day, I helped Magda with her charms. She showed me how to combine frankincense, myrrh, and some unknown element to develop love doodads. I doubted the nymphs needed them because the satyrs were enthralled with the golden haired maidens. Magda lassoed a purple doodad around my neck.

"Thanks. Just what I need. If a goat creature comes to steal me away, I'm blaming you."

She laughed huskily, her eyes shining. It was hard to imagine her kind had wronged mine a century before. I felt her desperation to make up for it and the ill will her daughter had rained upon me with her meddling ways.

After I completed my tasks, I strolled to the river's edge and plunked down on a log. I did this too often—stared across the river at my former home.

A flurry of leaves flew into my face. Bianca appeared, her hair everywhere and her eyes wild.

I bolted to my feet to go help her. "Are you hurt?"

She smacked my hands away. "No. No. He's hurt," she said.

A slithery energy uncoiled in my stomach. "Go help him," I insisted as I nudged her.

"I can't. He can't see me. He can't feel me. I'm useless."

"Do something!" I shrieked. "I can't go to him. They took my magic." I pushed her this time. I had no patience. I wouldn't accept her declaration of defeat.

Bianca grabbed my arm to still me. I suppose I was a bit hysterical. "I have an idea." In a storm of leaves, she vanished.

I looked across the river and up and down the bank. "What idea?" I asked the wind.

Desperate, I paced. I looked to the residual footing that was left of the bridge. The lords had never approved reconstruction—I guess to discourage any nymph/darkling coalition. My thoughts only grew more frantic as I looked at the broken structure.

A gentle breeze came up from the river. The unnatural current brought with it Korena. I took a step back when she approached. She wore a golden gown. I would have called it exquisite except it hung in tatters, covered in blood and grime. Had she managed to take corporeal form on earth's plane? How? Her face held my attention. It looked haggard and ravaged, which is almost impossible for a nymph.

"Come now," Korena said, hooking her arm in mine. I wanted to pull back, but she didn't allow any resistance as she touched a flowered bracelet on her wrist. She gathered me into a nauseating flight to a place of screams, smoke, and sand. It clung to my clothes and formed grit in my eyes.

Noxious fumes choked me as Korena led me down an abandoned but not tranquil road. Burned-out vehicles littered the street. I flinched when I glimpsed charred remains inside.

Mortar shells exploded nearby, shaking the ground and causing me to lose my balance. Korena hauled me up and kept moving as if accustomed to this. She appeared immune to the surroundings. I attempted to block out the scene that contained mountains of garbage, piles of rubble, and streets riddled with potholes from artillery shells.

My head swam as we traversed one particularly morose alley. A battle had just been fought here. It didn't look like any side had won. We clambered around huge slabs of concrete to approach a building that stood in ruins. Shattered glass, twisted metal, and gouged concrete with gaping holes comprised what used to be apartments. I doubted the structure was safe.

Just as I thought this, Korena pulled me inside. The gloom blinded and disoriented me. After stumbling, I put my hand out to feel along the gritty wall next to me. We stopped for a moment; I assumed to let our eyes adjust. Light filtered through a window up ahead. Looking down, I could start to make out the paper-littered ground. Part of a child's drawing rested at my right foot.

"Over here," Korena insisted. It was the first time she'd spoken to me since traveling through the portal.

I saw something on the floor in the corner. As we drew closer, I discerned a soldier sprawled on the rubble. Where was the rest of his squad?

So much blood. He lay on his side, wheezing and mumbling prayers to himself. When I knelt beside him, he turned his green eyes to me. *Ben.*

"Where's my sister?" I asked the nymph.

"I told her to leave," Korena said.

It was all too much for my brain to process. Ben's eyes grew wide. "Jade."

He could see me? My attention snapped to Korena. I wanted her help, but I knew she couldn't administer to him. I didn't have the power to touch him, either.

"You need to make a decision," Korena said.

I wanted to cradle his head and soothe him or find something to staunch the bleeding. *So much blood.*

"Help him!" I pleaded.

She frowned. "I can't transport you both."

"Then take him," I demanded.

She gave a curt nod, which set my body to trembling. What was I asking her to do?

My nerves all but consumed me as I reached for his hand. A jolt hit me—it was the familiar pull of the portal, my portal.

"My magic," I exclaimed.

Her eyebrows shot up as we both realized, some power still resided inside me.

"If he goes home, he'll die," Korena warned.

I didn't know how it worked or where this portal would take us. If it yanked us back to Ben's home, then at least his loved ones could be around him.

I thought of Magda and the love charm she teasingly had placed around my neck earlier. I leaned over Ben and locked my one arm around him in a hug. Then, I reached down and touched his palm with my free hand. In a flash, we disappeared.

So many arms rushed in to support us. Magda looked at me, her face white.

"A human made it through the portal!"

Three other nymphs helped her maneuver him inside their glass dome.

"Anka, this may not work."

I couldn't find my voice.

"But I'll try." She rolled up the sleeves of her pink dress, now stained red with blood. While chanting, the nymphs administered their salves and teas. Magda's hair stood straight out from her head, and her eyes became brighter as she attended to Ben.

On a stool in the corner, I rocked back and forth, unable to think, to wipe my tears or runny nose. Mute, I remained in the background, allowing the nymphs to work on him.

I thought back to when we were eight, and I had cast funny shadows on his wall to cheer him during his illness. When I looked up, Magda was beckoning me to the bed.

"Come now. Hold his hand. Sing to him. Let him know you are here."

Grasping his hand, I pulled it to my cheek. It felt so familiar, like home.

Hours went by, and I swayed on my feet, but I didn't leave his bedside. At some point, Magda drew a chair up and I sat in it, resting my head next to his.

The next morning, bird song woke me. The empty room felt ominous—no nymphs, just us. He looked so still. I slid my head across his chest to listen.

When I turned, his eyes stared into mine. "Persmellope."

I smiled.

He winked. Then his face grew serious. "You came for me, Anka."

"Always," I promised.

SHADOW FIRE

FIRE

The Darkling Chronicles #2

TRICIA ZOELLER

PROLOGUE

WHAT IS HE? I held my breath as I met Anka's green eyes. They conveyed both wonder and fear.

"Thanks for coming, Bianca," she said to me as she yanked her hood back, sending snowflakes cascading to the floor. Ben stood next to my sister, eyes focused on the fire, but I caught a glimpse of his profile under the hood.

I took in the bleak surroundings. The cabin stood bare of any furnishings except for a broken stool in the corner. A barred owl sounded in the night with its characteristic call, *Who cooks for you. Who cooks for you, too.* A cold shiver slid down my spine, and I listened more intently for any approaching sounds of hooves or large prey.

I heard the crunch of snow underfoot before the door creaked open. Mom's tall frame looked almost gaunt today as she entered the room. Her brown eyes reflected a worry she couldn't control. Ice crystals shimmered on the hood of her purple cloak as she drew close to the fire and revealed her raven hair pinned back with gemstone combs. Dad followed behind her, bringing with him the smell of cherry tobacco. His wavy dark hair brushed the collar of his wool jacket. He took his place by Mom's side, his determination apparent in the tight muscles of his face and neck.

All eyes traveled to Ben. I hadn't seen him for weeks, since he and Anka went on the run after the nymphs had healed him. My gut twisted as his hood fell, revealing a different face than the one I'd grown up with. *What had the nymphs done?*

CHAPTER ONE

BELOW ME, THE fierce dragon lord stalked, filling the cavernous space with his magic. I couldn't hold my breath forever. I had to gulp the heady magic rather than forego breathing at all.

Suspended from the ceiling by my wrists, I couldn't quite catch my breath. At first, the stretch to my vertebrae hadn't seemed so bad, but soon, my arms felt like they might come loose from their moorings, while my gut launched spasms of protest from the pressure.

"My sister…is with…the nymphs," I gasped. "Where you…sent her."

Lord Akton halted his pacing. He found me with his one golden eye and bound me in place.

Like I'm going anywhere.

Helpless, I looked up from the Rotunda into a cathedral ceiling that reached up for hundreds of feet. Light streamed down from tiny, round windows carved out of the sides of the sequoia's trunk. I hung inside the dragon lords' lair. It wasn't a dank, musty dungeon but a well-appointed room dripping with the finery of original art pieces, ornate rugs, marble floors, and gold-leaf accents. It smelled of expensive cigars, brandy, and aftershave.

I wanted to study my surroundings more, but funny thing pain; it can be so distracting. All of my sister's experiences with the three dragon lords, starting from the age of four, had been negative. By the time she turned eighteen, the lords had banished her from the east side of the river, the town known as Shadowland, where darklings made their homes in the shade of a lush sequoia forest. Over the summer, the three lords, Akton, Leasith, and Bulosk, had delivered a punishment to Anka for breaking shadowcasting laws. They had sent her away with horrendous wounds. The nymphs had saved her life.

Lord Akton strode across the white marble floor to stand at my right foot. His skin resembled any other darkling's, except for the bloom of red scales on the one side of his face. Despite his scarring, he was still a handsome creature. At seven feet tall, he towered over most darklings. Some described the lords as hideous, but I'd never thought that, not even Akton with his missing right eye.

I had hung out with my friends in the South Village where the lords lived. I'd even had a conversation or two with the youngest brother, Bulosk, and middle brother, Leasith. Despite being close to a century old, they had come across as reasonable creatures. That is until they almost killed Anka and now had me hanging like meat to be aged.

"Why didn't the termination spell activate, Bianca?" Lord Akton asked. He referred to the recall of a shadowcaster when his or her human charge died. Normally, once the human breathed his or her last breath, the dragon lords' magic pulled the darkling shadowcaster back to the Wishing Tree.

If I attempted to explain the circumstances, I'd only endanger my family. I hated getting in trouble. I believed in rules and followed them, but now I needed to lie. My mind raced as I cursed my sister in my head. If Anka hadn't fallen in love with her human charge, I wouldn't be in this predicament. I'd been dealing with the repercussions of her actions my whole life.

"I...don't know."

The force of his power pressed against me. I attempted to swallow as the heat from his fire seared me. I couldn't even scream. The suspension stole my breath, and if he didn't let me loose soon, I knew I'd pass out.

A piece of parchment suddenly appeared in his hand. The burning sensation subsided, and I gasped for air. Looking down at my white blouse, I noticed nothing had burned; it just felt like it had.

"You must recall the blood contract you signed at the age of ten."

My fingers tingled as they turned numb from the lack of circulation. A dark curl fell across my face, but I didn't have the energy to blow it away. I leaned my head into my armpit and closed my eyes. It's hard not to panic when someone takes all your air.

"Look at this," he insisted with a growl.

Bleary-eyed, I peeked at the scorched piece of paper.

"I've never seen a contract do this," he said.

The stabbing pain through my shoulder blades helped strengthen my resolve. "I…know…nothing…a—"

"You see, when a shadowcaster's charge dies, the contract turns to ash. My sources tell me that human Patrick Benjamin Solomon died in Afghanistan from wounds suffered in battle. His human family just held a funeral, complete with military honors.

"This happened days ago, and yet, you didn't come to get reassigned. Why is that?"

His one golden eye began to whorl so I looked away because I remembered what he'd done to Anka. He'd gotten in her head and shown her horrific scenes of violence from his childhood. I felt a force slide into place; an invisible shelf supported my feet. My arm sockets throbbed, but with this new footing, I started to draw more air. I knew he hadn't put the shelf there out of compassion but because he wanted answers.

"Speak!"

"I…want—" My eyes closed, and I panted.

"What?"

"To go to…Dis…ney…land!" I dared to look at him then.

He grinned, causing the scar tissue on his face to distort his nose and pull the outer corner of his eye down.

Maybe not so handsome. I braced myself, expecting him to snatch the invisible support from under my feet.

"Why don't you shake?" Lord Akton asked, tilting his head. His eye shone with curiosity, and he wore a puzzled look.

At the moment, I was more pissed-off than scared. If I wasn't, I'd be peeing down my own leg. Anka's mess-ups had made my life hell.

"Leasith has the old guy in the other room," he said.

A surge of anger helped me focus on his face. "You're ly…ing," I said through clenched teeth.

I jerked suddenly from the force of the French doors exploding inward. With my eyes squeezed shut, I stiffened as shattered glass rained onto the marble floor.

Through slitted eyes, I spied a flash of copper before dropping through space.

"Akton!" a male voice bellowed.

My body collided with someone, and I squalled like a wounded rabbit. My agony filled the air as all my pain registered at once. Stabbing pain in my arm sockets and joints accompanied a burning in my oxygen-starved lungs. Tears pricked my eyes and white dots danced in my vision. A thrum of energy enveloped me, and the misery dampened to a dull ache. I closed my eyes in relief.

"Get her out of here," commanded Lord Leasith.

When I tilted my head back, I saw blue scaling and a strong jawline. Lord Bulosk carried me over the shattered glass and up the cobblestone path of the Wishing Tree. He moved at such a rapid rate, the enchanted sconces blurred into one continuous streak of colored light.

"Pops," I rasped. If they did anything to Pops, I would personally hunt them, skin them, and make them into kickass boots and handbags.

Deep laughter rumbled from the youngest dragon lord's chest. "Thank goodness you prefer red."

We stopped in the grand entranceway. Lord Bulosk's green eyes gleamed in the subdued lighting. "Dragon-scale boots, huh?"

My mouth dropped open. "What?" *Did he just read my mind?*

His face changed into one more serious. It happened so quickly, I wasn't sure if I had hallucinated the boots comment.

"We don't have your grandfather. Lord Akton was just trying to get information from you."

Without realizing it, I relaxed my head against his black silk shirt. The scent of lotus, bergamot, and musk filled my nose.

"I need you to stand," he said.

My body felt boneless. I couldn't imagine standing, but I didn't want a dragon lord touching me any longer. Again, I felt the thrum of energy, warm and soothing. He set me on my feet, and I stared up at him. He was several inches shorter than Lord Akton but heavily muscled and just as imposing.

Green eyes and black hair contrasted with the design of blue scales on the right side of his face. Of the three brothers, his features appeared the most like a normal darkling. Against his tanned skin, subtle blue scales traveled along his hairline in an arc. They swept across the top of one brow, edged his right eye and cheek, then trailed off at his chin. Many darkling females thought Lord Bulosk was all kinds of fine.

He flashed a blinding white smile.

"Nice shirt," I said, touching the fabric. *What was wrong with me?*

He looked handsome and mysterious in all black. His eyes widened, and, if I wasn't mistaken, he straightened his shoulders a bit.

Shadowcaster log November 10th, year gazillion of the dragon lord: have interfaced with the dragon nobles. Youngest one likes ego stroked. Oldest one is a maniacal bastard. Middle one I have yet to assess.

Just then, Lord Leasith appeared and snatched me from Bulosk. He held me by my shoulders with my feet dangling in the air. "Is this one full-grown?" He cocked one eyebrow.

"Put her down, brother. Her respiration just regulated."

Lord Leasith set me on my feet and folded his arms across his muscular chest.

"Remember, she's the older sister. She follows the rules and volunteers when she can in the Shadow Fever ward at the hospital. Has some strong healing essence, too."

How did he know that?

Lord Leasith's light blue eyes scanned me from head to toe. I looked at Lord Bulosk. He winked. My mouth dropped open. I shook my head to regain my bearings.

I crossed my arms because they didn't seem capable of doing much else. "What is the purpose of this kidnapping?"

Lord Leasith's expression hardened. "Something strange happened to your charge. Care to discuss?"

"He died." My head swam from the close proximity to both of the powerful creatures. I wanted to cover my mouth, but my hands and arms wouldn't move right. Although, something had definitely relieved much of the pain. "I think I might be sick."

Both dragon lords froze. Darklings didn't vomit like humans. Well, there was a first time for everything.

CHAPTER TWO·

OUTSIDE, NO BATS launched from the crown of the Wishing Tree, as I'd grown accustomed to seeing during the warm months. I was relieved they were hibernating because I couldn't handle any more adrenaline tonight. Most darklings valued bats because they kept the nasty sprites away. My family, the Rehmlings, had never been fans. My sister and I had been terrified of them since we were young fledglings.

Under the full, yellow moon, I breathed out the dragon lords' toxic magic, clearing the fog that had muddled my mind. On shaky legs, I walked through South Village, which glowed with enchanted blown-glass lanterns, compliments of the lords. They blew the glass with the heat of their breath. I didn't want to acknowledge my tormentors had created anything so exquisite. Each piece stretched into a unique shape with a swirl of colors too dizzying to be natural.

Despite having thrown up on the lords' shoes, I felt so much better. No one would suspect what I'd just endured. It was hard for me to process it all—the violence of the eldest lord, the teasing of the middle one, and the flirting of the youngest, Lord Bulosk, who had escorted me out after feeding me chocolate. I'd cast shadows in the human world since I was six. I knew chocolate was not a common remedy for nausea. However, I couldn't argue with his methods. I truly felt much better.

As I moved to fasten my gray cloak, I felt something just inside the neckline, something soft but textured. My hand came away with a blue diamond-shaped scale. Lord Bulosk must have shed it when he helped me put on my cloak. No matter how angry I felt, I couldn't toss it aside. It was too extraordinary. Opening my mother's large cage locket, I placed it inside and snapped it shut. I was too freaked out to consider how creepy the action was.

As I continued through South Village, fall leaves skittered across my path before the wind hijacked them into the dark night. My stomach growled as I passed Drakos. The five-star restaurant, named for the first dragon lord, glowed with a scarlet light. Classical music drifted to me as patrons exited the establishment. It used to be one of my favorite places. Once a month, my friends and I would splurge and have dinner together before I worked the night shift casting shadows on the earth's plane for Ben Solomon.

Thinking of Ben raised such strong emotions, I had to stop and remind myself how to breathe. My strategy was to focus on the good smells coming from Drakos, but inevitably, my thoughts then strayed to Lord Bulosk. He ate in the restaurant often, a glass of Chianti accompanying his fourteen-ounce filet mignon, prepared bloody. I knew this because the only times I'd spoken to him directly had been inside this restaurant. I vowed never to eat there again and chastised myself for thinking about the dragon lord.

Rowdy voices from III Brothers' Pub distracted me and clashed with the classical music of the restaurant next door. Beside Drakos on the wooden promenade, which skirted the wide Montenai River, the pub was the lords' true baby. It housed a microbrewery featuring Akton's Red Ale and Bulosk's Blue Beer—and yes, it really was blue. Leasith didn't brew beer but had created a line of fancy liqueurs called Copper Spirits. The place had a tendency to get a bit rowdy, especially after soccer matches and hockey games, two darkling favorites.

Fledglings enjoyed their time just as much as adults did in the pub. It served Pia's Pop, which came in strawberry, blueberry, raspberry, peach, and pomegranate. Or, a darkling could brave Drakos Dregs, which came in black licorice, butterscotch, or the notorious cinnamon, a rite of passage for every darkling male. Known as The Fire Bomb, it was a bit much for me. The bottles were fantastic, though.

Each vessel held a unique shape of its own, created by a lord. They were definitely collector's items. Pia's Pop bottles exhibited intricate designs much like the inside of a kaleidoscope. Drakos Dregs came in gold bottles, except for The Fire Bomb. It came in a clear glass bottle with a rubber base. When a fledgling slammed the bottle down on the table, the rubber plunger broke a capsule inside the base, dispersing a colored fizzy liquid that warmed the drink and turned it into dragon fire. Because it ignited the sinus passages, only the toughest darkling could finish the whole drink without shedding a tear.

I'd had a lot of fun in there with Nana and Pops when I was younger. Nana liked the butterscotch flavor. Pops loved The Fire Bomb.

Had loved it. I doubted he had a taste for the dragon fire drink anymore. In fact, my family hadn't been in South Village much since Anka's banishment. Pops would be pissed if he knew Akton had burned me or at least simulated burning me. It had lasted only a second but had been intense enough I would never forget the agony.

My eyes traveled to the opposite riverbank where the kirkas' homes glowed. Their glass domes reflected the scenery around them. I knew the nymphs could and would help me.

When I fished a special bracelet out of my cloak's pocket, the inner fabric felt like sandpaper across my sore wrist. I gritted my teeth as I put on the jewelry. Magda, the head nymph of Kirka Village, made the bracelet for me so I could cross the Montenai River to visit my sister during her banishment from Shadowland. The dragon lords had blown up the one bridge in their fury over my sister's *betrayal*. The nymph jewelry allowed me to travel via the kirka portal.

Outside South Village, I stepped off the path to travel down an embankment. Leaves rustled underfoot as I walked to the water's edge. It had to be close to 9 p.m. I knew my roommates would worry about me, but I needed to talk about what had just happened with someone who would understand and not judge.

Clouds shifted in the sky, creating a milky, rippling veil. Despite the cover, the red star beamed down, steadfast. The celestial presence was believed to be the spirit of Akton, the majestic red dragon known as the Father of Montenai. I couldn't bear to look at it tonight because then I thought of his legacy, Lord Akton.

As the river roared in my ears, I checked behind me for any unwanted company before accessing the nymphs' portal by pinching a flower on my bracelet. A wave of power pushed me through a bubbling water slide in space. Once through the portal, I huffed up the embankment to a field of tall grass resistant to any Montenai frost. The kirka reeds parted for me as I traveled—a phenomenon that can be disconcerting until you grow accustomed to it.

Light from Reflections Celebration Hall spilled in all directions, outlining ten smaller domes in the middle of a field. The hall stood as the hub of Kirka Circle. Ten domes surrounded it—some were homes, others were specialty stores. While Shadowland was meticulously planned and orchestrated utilizing nature in its architecture, features of the Kirka Village flowed and moved together like parts of a living organism. Members of kirka households tended their plots of land and many kept livestock: cows, pigs, horses, but no goats. They wouldn't want to offend their male counterparts, the satyrs, who lived down the river.

The deeper into Kirka Village I walked, the better I felt. My home, situated in the lovely shade of the sequoias in Shadowland, had become a hostile territory. I actually felt safer here.

My indignation over this fact caused the nymph lights that swarmed me to burn red. The lights twinkled at varying heights across the field. They flitted about like a swarm of moths, adjusting color with the ever-changing moods of the creatures around them.

As my anger turned to despair, they darkened to a crimson-black. I just wanted to escape, set off through the Ballatian Woods, and leave all responsibility behind. Perhaps I could outrun my lies, which had taken on a life of their own.

It was a crazy thought. Darklings didn't stray from the dragon lords. Nonshadowcasters, in particular, feared becoming ill if they strayed too far from Shadowland. Plus, adults warned us as fledglings about the dangerous, haunted Ballatian Woods, which culminated in the imposing Faunlier Mountains. The woods provided a home to energy-draining phantoms; at least that was the rumor. They meant to scare us, and they succeeded. However, we also heard the surreptitious whispers of older darklings who indicated that some had made it through these woods and lived out simple lives in the mysterious mountains beyond.

As I approached Magda's door, I shut off the flow of wayward thoughts. Magda's dog, Pan, barked just before I knocked. Pan was Montenai's equivalent of the humans' beagle. He had appeared on Magda's doorstep a month ago. Magda has a soft heart for lost souls. She took in my sister, so of course she took in the dog. Many kirka whispered he was a gift from one of the satyrs down the river. I couldn't determine whether the rumor started because she'd named him Pan or if she'd named him Pan—Greek god of the wild hunt and music—because of the rumor.

When the door swung open, Pan shoved his snout into my legs. He made a hound waffling sound as he tasted and scented the heady essence of dragon lord on me. As he gazed up at me with golden eyes, my chest felt tight. This is where our beagle differed from the earth's version. Our hounds' eyes signaled impending danger, joy, or loss. Gold meant danger, red—joy, gray—loss. If things were status quo, they remained a soulful brown.

"Aw, buddy, you're not happy to see me?"

He whined softly and backed away.

Smart beast.

"What's the matter?" Magda's impossibly blue eyes searched my face and entire body. Her hair flowed in waves to her mid-back. Although I knew her to be close to sixty years old, she looked twenty years younger. She wore an elaborate rose silk nightgown and robe that clasped together with corded buttons shaped like peonies.

"I'm okay. Just a slight misunderstanding with The Brothers Grimm." I showed her my wrists, and she swore. It wasn't a special nymph word, but a well-used human curse.

Magda instructed me to come inside and sit by the fire situated in the middle of the open floor plan. A klenin-burning stove vented through a long, glass tube out the roof of the dome. I didn't know what the nymphs did to their special glass, but it didn't discolor, change shape, or break. Klenin is moss they grow in their meadows. It's a cleaner solution to wood. With the nymph's magic, one clump can burn for an entire day.

I sank into a soft daybed decorated with furry pillows as Magda knelt before me to examine my wrists.

"It looks like someone partially healed these wounds." She stared up at me and waited for an explanation.

As I shrugged, I realized my arm sockets didn't hurt, just felt a bit stiff. Lord Bulosk had attempted to ease some of my pain. I didn't want to spend time considering his motives.

"They know something is up with Ben," I said. "I didn't tell Lord Akton anything."

Her brow creased as she stood up. "Let me fetch you some tea."

"Thanks."

As utensils clattered in the kitchen behind me, I looked across to the water feature occupying the wall closest to the door. Tiny white nymph lights twinkled against a silver rock wall, highlighting climbing lotus flowers in a miniature waterfall. I didn't know lotus blossoms could grow on a vine, but I guess, for this nymph, they did whatever she told them.

Down the hallway, a room awaited Anka, decorated in greens and oranges to suit her taste. It remained as a cover should anyone investigate whether or not she still lived with Magda.

She didn't, and now the lords suspected. However, instead of summoning me to discuss Ben's death with them further, Lords Bulosk and Leasith had told me to stay away from the tree.

I leaned back against the pillows and shut my eyes. Despite my best intentions, I often had violent flashbacks to the time I shadowcasted for Ben in a war zone. Tonight, one golden dragon eye appeared in my head. My eyes popped open, and I looked into a different set of golden eyes.

Pan nudged my hand with his wet nose, and I scratched his velvety ears. "Things are scary, aren't they, buddy?" I wished his eyes would go back to their brown color.

Magda returned with the tea. She handed me the steaming cup

before positioning herself on the ottoman upholstered in a rustic swatch of colors. It looked like the handiwork of a satyr. They wove and knit clothes, as well as fabric and linens for home goods.

Across the room, the lotus blossoms rustled as they swiveled on their stems to face Magda. I'd always considered her to be a benevolent force of nature, but this close, her presence raised all the hair on my body. I took a sip of tea and tried not to wince from the bitter brew.

She looked down at her hands. "I didn't even think when Ben landed on this plane."

My stomach dropped. None of us had anticipated that Anka would bring Ben *here*.

"Humans don't usually make it through a portal to Montenai. If they do, they age before your eyes and perish within twenty-four hours."

The room felt off kilter, and I found myself clutching the linens on the daybed as my body wrestled with which way was up and which down. No one had ever spoken of this to me.

"Ah. A subject no doubt taboo to you darklings. Well, many a nymph and darkling have grown attached to their human charge." Her eyes darted to the side as she squirmed.

It made sense. The nymphs cast reflections in the human world. They were the light to our dark shadows. While we protected humans from excess radiation and, in turn, received added energy from our shadowcasting, the nymphs also benefited from close proximity to humans. They reaped increased longevity and beauty.

A tear formed in the corner of her eye and clung to her lashes. "The darklings only tried it a few times out of desperation when their human was terminally ill. But…"

"Hanleith," I said.

She nodded. "As you can imagine, Hanleith wanted to harness that part of humans that added to her own vitality. She made many disastrous attempts to keep humans alive on this plane."

I shuddered. The glass dome had felt warm and inviting, but now the chill of the tale seeped into my bones.

Before the Blessed Incursion, the satyrs, nymphs, and darklings all lived on the west side of the river under the notoriously cruel nymph queen, Hanleith. That all changed when a red dragon named Akton broke through a portal from a world called Fallon, bringing with him a mystical egg and a dying winged fairy-creature called an astrei. Both the red dragon and astrei perished, but their presence lives on, reigning in Montenai's sky as red and blue stars.

The essence in the egg survived and fell into the care of a pregnant darkling named Toren. It caused mutations in her offspring, resulting in the first dragon lord, Drakos. He was the first to call the mystical egg the Torensphere. He slayed the evil queen, freeing many Montenaians from a desperate existence, although Drakos was known to be quite cruel himself.

Magda and I looked at each other until my eyes watered. I found myself fixated on the softness of Pan's ears. He didn't complain as I stroked them. My fingers traced over the soft, braided material that comprised his collar. Somehow, these little things were a comfort.

"I don't know how long Ben has." She straightened her back as if bolstering herself for the impact of her own statement.

I needed two hands to steady my teacup. Despite wearing the gray, wool cloak and drinking the warm tea, I couldn't stop the shivers that persisted throughout my body.

"Who knows? He could outlast us all," she added, I think only to appease me.

Just as I drummed up the nerve to push her further, she turned her head. "Someone followed you."

My heart jumped to my throat, and the teacup rattled against the saucer as I failed to control the tremor in my hands. I glanced down at the coral-colored tea. Usually, I drank the nymph tea like a shot of liquor. It was potent stuff, which could never be described as palatable. I tossed it back. If someone meant me harm, I wanted the medicine to have taken effect.

Terror rooted me to the spot as Magda glided to the door. If it was the lords, I didn't know what I'd do. They hadn't forbidden me from seeking the nymph's aid. They were upset they hadn't sensed Anka's movements over the summer, despite having set some kind of tracking spell on her. I figured they didn't know what to do with the charred but intact shadowcasting contract.

I leaned forward for a better view of the door. A hooded figure stood just past Magda. Thinking of the Wishing Tree, I burped up Magda's nasty tea. *Not palatable the first time. Disgusting the second time.* The visitor removed his hood.

Zack. My whole body relaxed back into the furry nymph cloud behind me. "Mother of Montenai. You gave me a heart attack."

My roommate looked ashen. "Are you okay?"

He came across the room and knelt in front of me, oblivious to the river water dripping from his pants to the pristine, white marble floor. "What did they do to you? I overheard some shadowcasters talking about Lord Akton. I ran to the tree, but one of the darkling workers intercepted me before I could confront the old lizard and get myself fried. She told me they released you. I saw you go down by the river, but then you disappeared."

I patted his shoulder. Zack wasn't a shadowcaster, although he hung out with a few of us. He and my cousin, Liza, had been such loyal friends, even when crap hit the fan with Anka.

"I'm okay. They were just trying to harass my family some more." I hadn't confided in my friends about my family's secret.

The sleeve of Zack's hoody felt damp as he gently touched my left wrist. His brow furrowed.

"How'd you get here?" I asked him.

"One of the satyrs actually helped me cross the river," he said.

That was a big deal. The satyrs didn't pay much attention to darkling males. Occasionally, they attempted to woo a darkling female, but usually, the lords nixed that courtship.

I smiled. "Cornelius?"

"Yeah. He's a bit intimidating." The marks on my wrists captivated Zack. He seemed to struggle when answering me, too intent on gently stroking the tender areas on my skin.

"Cornelius Jeremiah of the Fardoragh herd," I said, mimicking the satyr. He had helped rescue Anka and brought her to the nymphs. As I gazed up, I caught Magda's sudden interest at the mention of his name.

Hmmm. I wonder if he had anything to do with Pan?

"I'm so sorry, Ma'am. I'm dripping all over your floor."

Magda scowled. "Don't worry about the water, but don't ever call a nymph ma'am."

Zack's dark eyes widened. "I'm so sorry, Ma—"

"Magda," I volunteered.

He flashed his goofy smile that could charm the pants off many a female, and had—mine. It had been a moment of weakness when the whole Anka ordeal blew up. Now, we were just good friends.

Magda nodded her head to the lotus flowers, which stirred the air around Zack. Beads of water shimmered through the air, flying off his clothes at a rapid rate before landing on the leaves and blossoms of the plant.

Once dry, Zack whispered a thank you to her before situating himself on the fluffy furniture next to me.

"I'll bring you some hot chocolate," Magda said, then retreated to the kitchen.

Just as I was wondering how we would both return across the river, a jazz ringtone sounded from my pocket. I retrieved my cell phone to see Pops's phone number. I guessed the lords' magic had bound my phone as it had me and it was just coming out of its stupor.

We had one cell tower in Shadowland and one wireless company called Three Brothers Wireless. Yeah, they held a monopoly on our lives. Some darklings even gossiped they listened in on our cell phone conversations. Pops had said that if they were doing that they had too much time on their hands and needed to get a life.

"Bianca? I've been trying to reach you for hours!" Pops said.

I let him know where I was and that I'd been entertained, not detained, by the lovely lordly lizards. He didn't buy my toned-down version of things, but I wasn't divulging any more. I needed time to process things myself.

"Don't worry, Pops. My friends are here. They've got my back."

Zack smiled.

Magda whispered in my ear that two could use the portal. I nodded before assuring Pops he didn't need to come get me. He insisted I come by the house that evening. I explained I just wanted to go back to my apartment and crash. After a few stubborn minutes, he finally relented as long as I promised to see him in the morning.

After placing my empty teacup in the kitchen sink, I kissed Magda's cheek. I valued her like a second mother. Zack thanked her, as well, before we both stepped outside. He remained uncharacteristically silent.

"You haven't been to Kirka Village lately, have you?"

"No," he replied. "Not since the bridge has been out. The satyrs have been bringing much of the fresh produce and food across." Zack worked part-time at Drakos Restaurant, in addition to studying culinary arts at Montenai College. He looked down at his feet.

Things had changed in our world. As fledglings, we'd taken field trips to see the kirka farms.

"Something tells me there won't be any more field trips like when we were young," I said.

Zack waggled his eyebrows. "Maybe we could convince a herd of satyrs to ferry students across the river."

I just chuckled as he flung his arm around me. I leaned my head against his side as we walked toward the river's edge. Zack smelled like cypress and sandalwood and felt...innocent and young. I'd turned twenty last month. Even though I was only six months older than he was, I felt eons older. I knew it was because of my shadowcasting. It had stripped me of a normal childhood.

He stopped a moment and looked down at me. I'm five-foot-two; everyone looks down at me. "I don't think you understand how scared I was, Bianca." Zack swallowed as he studied my face. "You know I really care about you."

"I care about you, too."

He blinked several times, looking first at the river before returning to my face. "I don't know what I'd do if I lost you."

After the stress of the day, I didn't have the strength to handle such a serious conversation. His body language and tone of voice indicated strong feelings I wasn't ready to acknowledge or accept.

"Thanks, Zack." Eager to change the subject, I fumbled with the nymph bracelet. "So, here's how we get back without getting wet."

He followed my instructions, and we both stumbled a bit when we came out on the darkling side.

"That so beats a stupid golf cart for travel." He rubbed his lower back. "Or having a goat-creature give you a piggyback." Zack looked up and down the river. "Don't tell anyone a dude carried me across the water."

"As long as you don't tell anyone I used a nymph portal."

"Deal."

We trudged up the embankment and entered North Village. We lived in a duplex apartment just two blocks north of Pops's all-night chocolate shop, Chocolate Syncope. The shop called to us like a beacon in a storm. My Uncle Vincent worked the counter tonight so we would avoid an inquisition by Pops.

Sultry blue jazz notes hit us as we entered the shop housed in the base of a sequoia tree. Nymph lights floated throughout the space. I batted them away as they attempted to swarm me, alerting everyone of my crimson-black mood.

Uncle Vincent stepped up to our tall table to take our order. He was a shorter, more serious version of my grandfather. While Pops had a predilection for crazy, loud shirts and wore a carefree air, Uncle Vincent donned bankers' vests and had a habit of rubbing his balding head. He always darted around full of nervous energy. The nymph lights often flickered magenta and orange around him. I giggled. At least, he got them off me tonight.

My decaf cappuccino and Pia's fizzies arrived. Pops had come up with the idea for the frozen treat and obtained rights from the lords. I popped one in my mouth. Once I broke the hard chocolate shell, the half-frozen raspberry soda burst in my mouth. *Delicious.*

Just as I considered downing the whole plate of them, Liza accosted me on the stool, squeezing me so hard I choked.

"Holy crap, Bianca. Are you okay?"

"I'm good, just having some trouble breathing."

"Oh. Sorry." She stepped back and examined my face before acquiring a stool at the tall table. The nymph lights swirled the new patron, emitting a peachy light to reflect her essence. Her hair held a reddish cast unlike any other darkling's. Her eyes were the same green as my sister's. At the moment, they were locked open in a doll's stare.

As she studied me, fear and intrigue warred on her face. Liza was a nonshadowcaster like her dad, Uncle Vincent. She attended Montenai College to obtain a degree in education.

With our crazy schedules, we were lucky Zack cooked and baked for us all the time. I glanced to my side to see him stirring his Café Amore. It was a blend of cognac, amaretto, and coffee topped with whip cream and toasted almond slivers. The drinking age in Shadowland was eighteen.

Liza ordered a Café Caribbean. I could smell the rum when Uncle Vincent placed it in front of her. She stirred the warm drink then licked the cream from the stirrer.

"Thanks, Dad," she said. He kissed her temple before darting back to the coffee bar.

Liza tilted her head back and rolled it from side to side, cracking her neck. "I so need this tonight. I spent the entire day with fifth-graders." She nabbed a fizzy from the plate and popped it in her mouth. Her mini-internship would be for three months. Her next one would be with the high-schoolers.

Zack laughed. "If you can't handle fifth-graders, what are you going to do next semester?"

"Eat a gallon of fizzies every day," she joked. Her smile fell as she seemed to remember the type of day I had. "You're not going to tell me, are you?" She thrust her bottom lip out in a pout.

"I think I'll let Zack fill you in later." I managed a tight-lipped smile as I caught his eye.

"Okay." Liza's shoulders slumped. She put her head down on the table. "I'm just so tired."

Zack eyed her. Liza glanced his way then forced her head back up. Something was going on there. I was too tired to pursue it.

We finished our drinks and made our way back to the apartment. Too tired from the day to stay up late watching a movie, we all crashed. What a wild bunch we were on a Friday night.

CHAPTER THREE

THE FIRST TIME I threw up that morning, I became concerned. It startled me so much I hadn't made it to the bathroom. By the third time, I stood on shaky legs in front of the sink and splashed cool water on my face. Deep circles had settled under my eyes. I heard a soft knock at the door.

"Bianca?" Liza called.

Crap. I'd woken my roommates. Darklings rarely were ill, particularly shadowcasters. I cracked the door. "It's okay," I said.

"No. It's not," Zack said from behind Liza. I opened the door farther to see him. He stood shirtless in black drawstring pajama bottoms. A gray-purple rash stretched from the corner of his right eye to mid-cheek. It resembled human spider veins in appearance, but it wasn't a benign mark.

"We need to talk," Liza said.

I scanned her face—puffy eyes, blotchy skin, but no rash. "Give me just a minute." I closed the door and exhaled a long breath. I could feel my heartbeat pounding at my temples, giving strength to the epic headache brewing. As I brushed my teeth, I tried not to cry.

When I entered the small living room, they were sitting next to each other on the couch. Liza didn't have the markings of Shadow Fever, the Silton rash named for the first darkling to have died from the illness. However, her eyes looked a bit feverish like Zack's.

"You guys should get dressed. I'll take you to the hospital."

"No," Zack said.

"We need to ask you something, Bianca," Liza managed. "And we want the truth."

I eased into the beanbag chair on the floor.

"Have you been at work?" Zack asked.

"Yes," I answered, as I studied the dusty wooden floor.

"It doesn't *feel* like you have," Liza offered. I could tell she was uncomfortable confronting me because, when I looked up, I caught her biting her nails.

I clasped my hands in front of me. Again, I felt pulled in two directions. I lied to protect my sister and family. I lied to protect my roommates from an interrogation by the Brothers Grimm. But now, my friends were sick. With all the stress over the last several months, I'd never stopped to consider how much radiation I was absorbing or not absorbing and what the effect would have on my friends and me. With the dragon lords' magic, it shouldn't have mattered.

"Crap." I leaned my head back and stared at the ceiling. It felt like it was spinning.

"Something happened with your human charge," Zack stated.

Busted. When I sat up, the nausea hit me again. I waited a moment. "The only reason I haven't told you guys anything is because I'm afraid." My squeaky excuse sounded phony to my own ears. "I've been so distracted and stressed by my sister's situation, it never occurred to me this could happen." When I mustered the nerve to look at Zack, I immediately began to cry. Darklings could die from Shadow Fever. "I don't shadowcast for Ben because he was a casualty of war."

Zack's hand flew to his mouth. "Are you serious?"

"Yes." My eyes found the floor again. I wouldn't be able to continue the charade if I looked at him.

"Why didn't you tell us? Are you okay?" he asked.

"Not really," I rasped.

I peeked at Liza. Her hands clutched the edge of the couch, her lips pressed flat, and her eyes glistened with tears. She knew that Anka and I had shadowcast for Patrick Benjamin Solomon since Anka was four and I six. We'd talked about him often. As a shadowcaster, your human charge becomes much of your life, particularly if you cover him during the day as Anka had Ben. Liza leaned forward as if she considered coming over to console me.

"They held the funeral just a few days ago," I said, pulling my knees to my chest and hugging my legs.

Ben had been missing in action for a month before the army looked through the evidence and deducted that he had perished from an explosion.

Zack sat up on the couch, eyes intense. "I can't believe it. He was so young." He blinked repeatedly. Zack had heard so many Ben stories, he probably thought he knew him. His Adam's apple bobbed in his throat, and he licked his lips. "Why didn't you tell us?"

I bristled.

Zack's tight jaw warned me he planned to pursue this subject until I squirmed. He'd always felt betrayed when I didn't tell him something first or when I failed to trust him.

My shoulders shook as I cried. I could tell him *how* I felt but not *why*. My cheeks burned from tears, my gut churned from the betrayal. I hated myself at that instant. I had played hooky from shadowcasting for over a month, not just a few days. What would they do if I told them the truth about Ben?

Liza chewed her nails as she looked from me to Zack. "Bianca, please let us know if there's anything we can do. You must be heartbroken," she said.

Grimacing, I wiped my tears away and took a breath. "I can't really talk about the details right now. It's just too painful."

They both nodded, but Zack could always read me. His eyes watched me, analyzing. He knew something was up.

"Tomorrow, I'll be checking in with the temp pool and starting work again. I'll be able to recharge and bring back more energy." I couldn't meet Zack's eyes. "Sorry I've made us all sick," I whispered.

"Don't blame yourself," Liza said. "It's like we've become a couple of leeches."

"I don't think the dragon lords have been doing their jobs," Zack added. "It's making us sick and zapping all the shadowcasters' energy."

"I've been at the school every day. Other students are showing fatigue," Liza said.

Shaking my head, I pulled myself out of the beanbag. "Their collective power should more than compensate for one shadowcaster's lower energy." I paced the small space in front of the coffee table. There were millions of shadowcasters all over the world. My playing hooky shouldn't have upset the balance of things so much. My stomach rumbled, reminding me I still didn't feel so great.

"What do you think's happening?" I asked.

Zack raked his fingers through his short hair. "Payback. They're sending us a message."

I nodded. "If you don't follow our rules, look what will happen to all of you."

"It's an effective way of turning darklings against our family," Liza said.

I appreciated that she still associated herself with my immediate family, the trouble-making Rehmlings. I understood the danger if every darkling fell in love with his or her human charge as Anka had with Ben. Sometimes, human children saw their shadowcasters for a time. They became the human's Imaginary Friend. Anka had taken this one step further with Ben. She'd let him see her until the age of thirteen, and she had interfered in his human life.

"You two take it easy today," I said. "I'll see what I can do. If things don't improve by tonight, I'm taking you to the hospital."

They both nodded.

Back in my room, I put on my favorite long-flowing black skirt with a purple sweater that fell off my shoulders. A thousand thoughts pecked at my mind. Although I couldn't help but feel hurt by my roommates talking about me behind my back, their scrutiny was warranted; my behavior had been erratic. In the bathroom, I applied extra makeup, perhaps thinking, if I looked better, I'd feel better.

With my black leather boots on, I stepped out to a gray-blue morning. Feeling desperate and depressed, I raced to see Pops at Chocolate Syncope.

Pops wore an orange shirt with white musical notes on it, which caused me to smile. I sat on a tall stool at the coffee bar and ordered a tea, while my short legs dangled in the air.

He gave me a puzzled look as he placed orange blossom tea in front of me.

"Just need something a bit lighter today," I said. Darklings rarely drank tea unless they required some energy from the herbs.

Pops began to buff the nymph glass counter in the same spot. A muscle twitched in his cheek. We were all under some major strain.

"I'm reporting to the temp pool today."

He stopped his work. "Are you sure you're ready for that?" Bushy eyebrows raised, he didn't blink.

"You know I should have reported *days* ago."

"I don't want you going anywhere near that Wishing Tree." Pops leaned in and whispered, "Do you understand?"

"If I don't report, Lord Akton will hang me from the ceiling again."

Pops flinched like I had hit him. His face blanched from a light brown to yellow.

"See? No choice."

His lower jaw jutted forward, and I thought he might explode. He placed the rag down on the bar top and leaned on the glass, undoing the results of his previous hard work. After a long breath, his expression shifted to one less murderous. "Make sure to call first and set up an appointment with Lord Bulosk. He seems the sanest of the lot, which isn't saying much."

I nodded and covered his hand, hoping to be reassuring. I don't think my hand shook, but my insides quivered like human Jell-O. I never understood the allure of that food.

After I thanked Pops for the tea, I stepped outside to a wintery Montenai day. A layer of frost covered the wooden boardwalk and crunched underfoot as I walked toward South Village. I retrieved my phone from the pocket of my gray cape and touched my thumb on the icon of a tremendous sequoia tree. It immediately dialed the Wishing Tree's main number. I'd never called the Wishing Tree before. My throat tightened, and I struggled to swallow.

When a darkling receptionist answered, I asked to speak to Lord Bulosk as Pops had suggested.

"And what is this regarding?"

"This is Bianca Rehmling. I need to be added to the temp pool."

"One moment please." Violins wailed over the line. Not the kind of hold music I would have picked.

"This is Lord Bulosk."

My breath caught in my throat. "This is Bianca Rehmling. I need to schedule a meeting to discuss temp work until you assign me my new charge."

An uncomfortable pause followed. "Meet me at Drakos in half an hour."

I continued to hold the phone to my ear long after the call terminated. *What?*

Darklings scurried about as I walked through the tiny tunnel of mountain laurel trees that led me into the prestigious South Village. To stall a bit, I stepped into the cordwainer's riverside shop, Good for the Sole. Darklings not only loved chocolates, they loved boots. My mother called this boot therapy. Entering the shop immediately calmed me for several reasons, number one being that Zack's mother was the cordwainer. She had the same warm caramel brown eyes and luxurious eyelashes as Zack.

"Little B! I'm so glad you dropped in."

Ever polite, I endured the nickname she'd bestowed on me when I was six. "Hi, Mrs. Salva. I have a shadowcaster meeting but was early, so I thought I'd pop in to see your latest creations." I'm not sure what she said because a killer pair of boots stood up in the window, and I could have sworn I heard Adah, the Mother of Montenai, singing.

She giggled.

I looked up and felt my cheeks flush warm. "Sorry. Those are spectacular."

"Size six, right?"

"Yes, but I really only have five minutes, and I don't think that I could possibly wear above the knee boots since I'm short, and those are probably so expensive, and I just shouldn't be—"

A black suede boot appeared before me. Many shoes and clothes in Shadowland are adorned with snaps, buckles, and buttons shaped or engraved with dragons. These, however, laced all the way up and cinched closed at the top with two silver flower-shaped bells that jingled.

Must have the jingle boots. I am a darkling through and through. You can lure me to my death with good chocolate or a seductive boot. Before I realized it, the boots were on me and laced up perfectly for comfort and still practical for movement.

"I need to go," I said, still in my boot hangover.

Mrs. Salva winked. "I'll put these on your tab. And don't worry; I gave you a super discount." She placed my old boots in a box and stowed them behind the counter. "I'll send these home with Zack."

"Thank you." I didn't have the heart to tell her he was sick. She looked content and happy, which told me he hadn't spoken to her about it yet.

Five minutes later, with my boots jingling, I darted into the doorway of Drakos Restaurant, the place I vowed to never step foot into again. While the Wishing Tree dripped with finery and embellishments, the restaurant stood simple and minimalistic. Contemporary paintings hung on the walls. The furniture felt unassuming, comprised of a light beech wood. The familiar dragon blown-glass lights filled the space, but they were of only one or two colors. The smell always sedated me, like I'd already eaten an amazing meal and needed a nap.

The restaurant stood empty.

Someone cleared their throat next to me, and I looked up to find Lord Leasith standing guard at the door. He wore utilitarian navy blue pants with a matching long-sleeve, crew neck shirt and black combat boots. He always looked ready to serve and protect, and I wondered if he sensed something brewing. I knew I did.

I tried to smile, but I think it was more of a grimace. "My bad, restaurant's closed. I spun around, but his arm blocked my way, and I felt like I'd just taken a sequoia tree branch in the chest.

"Better for the meeting."

Darkling of few words.

"Right," I said.

The walk to the table where Lord Bulosk sat seemed like a mile. My boots jingled, and I felt more self-conscious than I ever had in my entire life. *Should have worn my other boots.*

"You look well."

"I puked this morning."

His eyebrows rose and his blue scales did the wave along his forehead.

"Sorry. Too much information," I said.

Quiet, he gestured for me to take the seat across from him. In the background, I heard the wail of violins. What was with them and the depressing violin music?

My eyes flitted to the window blinds, the kitchen staff, anywhere but at the dragon lord in front of me. I crossed my legs and my boots jingled.

Lord Bulosk leaned in and tapped the tabletop with his index finger. I found myself mesmerized. If I hadn't seen his claws, I wouldn't have known he could produce them. It looked like just an average darkling's finger. Then I remembered my baby sister's raw back, and I felt a seething rage. I wanted to declaw him.

He stopped in the middle of his sentence.

"I'm sorry, what were you saying?" I asked.

"How did Ben Solomon die?"

"Multiple wounds. IED. You know, improvised explosive device."

"I know all about human weaponry."

I nodded.

A nonshadowcaster appeared at his side. "My Lord. Would you like some wine with lunch?"

The lord tilted his head toward me like *did I want some wine.*

"Some sparkling nymph water for me, thank you." Nymphs made the best water. They infused it with mint or peach or some unique organic flavoring. It really quenched the thirst.

"You don't like our soda?" Lord Bulosk asked.

"Sure." I looked to the darkling server who pulled his chin back as if I had affronted *him* with my selection. "But I would really like Magda's Mint Julep, please."

The server's eyes darted to Lord Bulosk.

He smiled. "I'll have one, also. Thank you, Jacob."

Jacob remained by his side and looked to his Lord like he had just ordered algae water, which was a nasty drink the satyrs loved but no darkling in his right mind drank.

Eventually, the waiter retreated.

"Do you know the story of Adam?" Lord Bulosk's tone changed drastically.

I sucked in air and pinched my thigh to keep myself grounded. "No."

Jacob darted in and placed our water in front of us. Magda stared at me from the label. She looked fantastic with her golden hair shimmering. She moved on the label much like a human's hologram.

"Adam, termed for the first man according to their Bible, was Hanleith's first subject."

My sour stomach returned instantly. "Don't."

"He didn't fare so well on this plane or in her *care*."

I fiddled with my necklace and attempted to swallow.

"Tell her, brother," growled Lord Leasith from across the room.

"He went mad. Tore at his own skin while he withered away, slowly."

My nostrils flared, and I swigged the rest of my drink. Magda said the humans had died quickly. I didn't dare disclose my conversation with the nymph. "That's a lovely story. Now, could you let me know who I should report to for work?"

Jacob returned with my favorite appetizer at Drakos—lobster and crab stuffed mushrooms dripping in a melted herbal butter sauce. I didn't move.

"It's fresh, caught in the Aglatian Sea this morning. Try one."

Some alarm rang in my head. I sniffed the air. It smelled and felt like the thick soup I'd come to recognize as dragon lord magic.

I stood up suddenly, my napkin slipped away, and my chair crashed to the floor. "In the words of my Nana, 'don't work your hocus-pocus on me.'"

When I turned to leave, Lord Leasith stepped in to block me.

"Who will give me my next assignment?" I asked him, hands on my hips.

He looked to his brother to confer first. My heart raced like a rabbit's. I needed to get out of this place.

"Report to Marcus. He'll set you up on the temp circuit," Lord Leasith said in his gruff voice.

"Thank you."

He stepped aside, and I ran out to the cold air and threw up in some shrubs. I scared the crap out of several darkling nonshadowcasters who had never seen vomit.

CHAPTER FOUR

MARCUS PUT ME on the shadowcasting list, but nothing happened. When I found out someone had a scheduled vacation, I stalked him or her, but all the shadowcasters made some excuse or told me another had already filled the slot. It frustrated me to no end that my family's views and rebellious actions were holding me back from helping my friends.

My family had trained traditionally, which meant under the tutelage of our parents. The new method, spearheaded by Marcus, utilized a shadowcasting pool. It called for better hours and shifts for shadowcasters and their families, so the shadowcaster fledglings could go to school like nonshadowcasters. The dragon lords were open to the new model and were aiding Marcus with his efforts for the program termed Out of Shadow.

Pops hated it. According to him, it took the tradition out of the art of shadowcasting. In the new model, darklings shared human charges. I never told Pops that I understood the theory behind it. There was less chance of a disaster like what had happened with Ben and Anka. If a darkling had more to life than shadowcasting, he or she would be less likely to form an unhealthy bond to the human world and be more in tune with Shadowland and its culture.

Two days had passed since my confession to Liza and Zack. Liza looked pale but still didn't have a rash, while the rash on Zack's handsome face had bloomed close to the size of a fist. Desperate for some of the earth's rays, I cursed the current politics in Shadowland. Finally, my mother put in for several vacation days and *told* Marcus I was to fill in for her.

Relieved to have work, but unsure of myself, I stood in front of the bathroom mirror and rubbed sparkly blush on my cheeks. My hand tremored as I applied lipgloss. *Will anything I do even make a difference?*

Before leaving the duplex, I peeked in on Zack. I watched his chest rise and fall, and tried not to stare too long at the mark on his face. It only brought tears to my eyes and paralyzed me with fear.

Outside, I met a daytime moon as I trudged through fresh snow on the path leading to the portal in the northeastern part of the Sequoia Forest. Because of the different time zones on earth, one often found shadowcasters of varying ages and sizes in the woods as they came and went from the earth's plane.

Today, I encountered only two shadowcasters returning from a night shift. Once I passed them, I walked in silence while the sunrise bathed the woods in a golden glow. I was early for the usual shift of casters who left for work in this particular time zone. When I turned the corner leading to the final stretch before the portal, I startled a herd of mule deer. Their golden eyes glowed like those of a dragon lord. Only herds in our darkling forest had reptilian eyes. They stotted in retreat, springing in the air with all four legs off the ground at once. Their big ears and black-tipped tails contrasted with the white snow, but still, they disappeared into the camouflage of the forest as if they had never been there at all.

Uneasy, I followed the path worn in the snow from other shadowcasters, passed the familiar fir tree, and entered the hollowed-out sequoia, which acted as our portal to earth's plane.

Once inside, I felt the usual pull into a tunnel of air. At first, I soared straight up, before jerking in a horizontal path. Strong winds buffeted me and roared in my ears as colors swirled in my vision. In five seconds, silence took hold, accompanied by bright white light and a "pop." I stood in the Solomon home. For the first time in my life, Mrs. Solomon, rather than Ben, had acted as my portal.

One look at her sad eyes and I wanted to go back. She sat at the round kitchen table, looking out the bay window, a cup of coffee grown cold. In her late forties, she had a series of fine wrinkles around her eyes. I thought they gave her character. From the time I was a little fledgling, I had always thought she was so elegant and pretty. Today, she had her chestnut hair pulled back into a ponytail. Her gaze never faltered.

She thought her son had died. I felt responsible, deceitful, and miserable. Unlike my sister, I had never been tempted to break my silence. Today, I wanted to talk to her, hold her hand, and tell her everything would be okay. Her son was alive and adjusting to a new world and new abilities. But I couldn't. I wiped tears away, swallowed a knot as I maintained my silence, and remained invisible.

When her cell phone buzzed on the table, she moved.

"Of course, Judy. I'll be right there."

I cast shadows for her as she grabbed her fleece jacket off the hook by the back door. The neighbor waited for her at the end of the driveway. Tarah, a plump darkling my mother's age, shadowcast for Judy, the neighbor. She nodded once to acknowledge me before we walked down the street.

Mrs. Solomon stared straight ahead as the neighbor jabbered on, obviously uneasy about her friend's grief. In Montenai, snowfall was inevitable this time of year, but in Georgia, the weather remained mild. The sun shone brightly in a clear blue sky. My solar-deprived body approved of the activity.

By the afternoon, my father came to my side and gestured for me to cover Mr. Solomon as Mrs. Solomon climbed the stairs to her room in order to nap, something she would never have done before.

Mr. Solomon carried a bucket of soapy water to the driveway and began to wash the cars. I found this endearing. He'd always washed his own cars despite being able to pay for an expensive detail job. Today, he buffed the cars beyond the point of "shiny." Nerves sparked like live wires, twitching in the muscles of his neck. Grief sucked. Shadowcasting for Mr. Solomon just plain hurt.

By early evening, I felt better physically, but drained emotionally. My mother returned to cover the night shift.

"Thank you," I whispered.

My father and mother usually stayed at the Solomons' around the clock. They took turns keeping watch once the Solomons went to bed. One slept while the other read or monitored in case Mr. or Mrs. Solomon rose to use the bathroom or get a midnight snack. Every third or fourth day, they would take the day off and have temps fill-in so they could get a break. They enjoyed their role as shadowcasters. They never resented the freedom nonshadowcasters experienced.

Freedom had its price. Nonshadowcasters were more vulnerable. This fact hit me in the gut as I stepped into the apartment at 9 p.m. and found Zack lying on the couch. "Where's Liza?" I asked.

"She went to hang with the shadowcaster crew by the river. Hopefully, she'll absorb some of their energy. I didn't go because of this," he said in a hoarse voice. His forehead glistened with sweat as he pointed to his face. Darklings tended to panic at the distinctive webbed mark. It started with quarantine, not that there had been any indication over the years that the fever was contagious.

I sat next to him and pulled off my jingle boots. Within a minute, he relaxed and breathed deeply. With a guilty look, he reached for my hand and placed it on the mark. I used my other hand to stroke the damp hairs that stuck to his forehead. "It's okay, Zack. Lie down."

He lay on his back with his head on the throw pillow. I lay on my side so I could fit next to him on the couch. After nestling my head under his chin, I reached up and cupped the spider web pattern on his cheek. Without looking at him, I spoke. "Better?"

"You have no idea." He swallowed. "How come you can do this?"

"Don't know," I whispered. Since I was young, I'd always harnessed some strong energy. It was why nonshadowcasters often doted on me when I entered their boutiques and restaurants. I knew they weren't aware of their actions. As a teenager, I'd put two and two together, particularly once I began volunteering at the hospital.

He wrapped his arms around me, and we accepted each other's silence. My breathing naturally synced with his, and we napped like that for several hours.

The creak of the front door woke me. A glance at the ornate

glowing clock on the wall, told me it was midnight. Liza tiptoed in, carrying her computer bag. I waited a few minutes after she'd crept down the hall to her room before extricating myself from Zack. He squirmed a bit but stayed asleep.

I made my way down the hall and tapped lightly on her bedroom door. Liza opened the door wearing her t-shirt and sleep shorts.

"You doing okay?" I asked.

Shrugging, she turned from me. "Suppose so," she called over her shoulder. She weaved her way through discarded items of clothing she'd abandoned on the floor and entered the bathroom.

As I followed her in, I tried not to focus on the mess. I had a bit of a compulsive streak when it came to orderliness. If I really focused on Liza's room, the disorder would give me heart palpitations.

"What does that mean?" I asked, as I stumbled after her. I placed a pair of shoes neatly together under her bench and returned a brush to the top of her bureau. I hesitated just at the threshold of the bathroom.

"It just means I'm good," she said. She flipped her hair up into a clip and turned on the water to wash her face.

I didn't move. "Are you mad at me? I mean, you have every right to be. I feel like a nasty sprite's butt for jeopardizing your health."

After a quick rinse of her face, she dried it on a black skull towel, a vestige of her rebel/Goth days, as was the piercing in her nose. Her cheeks looked rosy and I wondered if it was from anger.

She exhaled, obviously exasperated with me. "I'm good, okay?" She grabbed her toothbrush and toothpaste off the sink.

My stomach churned. I really *needed* my friends right now. I really needed them to be *okay*. I cleared my throat.

Through a mouth full of toothpaste, she spat at me, "You are such a bulldog. I slept with him, okay?"

My stomach lurched. *She slept with Zack?* If that was the case, then I needed to explain the nap on the couch. "Zack and I didn't do anything. I was letting him absorb some energy. We didn't kiss or hold hands or remove any clothes," I babbled in a high-pitched voice.

Her mouth hung open. I felt the urge to point out she had

toothpaste in the corner of her lips.

"Eric. I slept with Eric!" She dried her mouth before pushing past me and heading for her bed.

While she settled under the hot pink and black comforter, I sat down on the corner, making sure to avoid a little pile of discarded socks and underwear. I dangled the sock in the air. "Is this dirty? Like, how long has this been here? Have I disturbed some ancient relic?"

"Ha. Ha. I know where everything is. I have my own system."

Raising my eyebrows in question, I dropped the sock. I'd made her smile, mission accomplished.

"I'm sorry," I said.

Eric was the tall lead singer of the band, Shadow Blues. They had dated several months ago, but his schedule became too hectic. He shadowcasted during the day and had gigs at night, quite often at Pops's shop. Knowing Liza, she was beating herself up for sleeping with the guy. I knew she wouldn't sleep with anyone just to gain energy. However, Liza was incredibly insecure and hard on herself.

Brow furrowed, she chewed her nails. I suspected her insecurities had teamed up with her conscience and were creating an epic crap storm in her head.

We stared at each other for a while.

"You're a good darkling, Liza."

She bit her lip as her eyes filled with tears. I meant what I said. Uncle Vincent had raised her by himself. She'd been going to school, as well as working, since she was twelve to help support them. Her mother had been a lone shadowcaster who ran off with another shadowcaster. Infidelity did not happen often in Shadowland and carried a harsh social stigma. Growing up, Liza had endured many cruel comments.

"I feel like I haven't been here for you."

She shook her head violently. "It's the other way around, Bianca. I can't believe you lost Ben and didn't tell us." Leaning back against the headboard, she closed her eyes. "I can't believe we didn't notice something was horribly wrong."

I was glad her eyes were closed because if she looked at my face, she'd know how much I was hiding.

When she opened her eyes, I wore what I hoped was a neutral expression.

"So, how's Eric?"

Her neck and face flushed red. "He's good." A smile teased the corners of her mouth.

"How *good* is he?"

She giggled. "You are so nosy."

"Can't help it. It's my nature."

As we hugged, I felt better and worse at once. I worried she went back to Eric because she was sick. I felt she was sick because I hadn't been doing my job as shadowcaster.

CHAPTER FIVE

EARLY IN THE morning, I visited the Shadow Fever Ward of Toren Hospital, named for the lords' grandmother. It looked like a French chalet on the outside. The Fever wing had knotty pine walls, huge picture windows, and skylights. As I walked through the wing, I realized the number of patients had doubled in the last month. *What's happening here?* The only nonshadowcasters in the unit were the healthcare workers. Shadowcasting volunteers and nymph healers made the rounds, but nonshadowcasters still kept their distance from their loved ones, despite being told repeatedly that the illness was not contagious.

In one of the first rooms, I found five-year-old Sonya. The Silton rash stretched across the entire right half of her face. As I took her small hand in mine, anger simmered just at the surface of my skin. I'd had enough of the lords' reign of terror. Punish my family but don't hurt little fledglings.

Her body remained so still, I wondered if she had slipped into a coma. Would she ever gain consciousness? As I touched her face and concentrated, she slept, her breaths shallow and rapid. She never indicated she registered my touch or my voice.

After an hour, I stepped out of her room to find Pops standing at the end of the hallway, bathed in morning light. He waited with his hands in his pockets. A lump formed in the back of my throat. No matter what was going on in my life, Pops's appearance always caused me to become emotional.

I couldn't believe he was here. Not every family member inherits the ability to shadowcast. Pops had lost a son to Shadow Fever. Nana had blamed herself, saying it was because of her nymph blood.

I met him halfway, and he pulled me in for an epic hug. I would not cry.

"Zack told me you were here." His big brown eyes stayed on me, accusing. I knew he must have stopped by the duplex and knew the state of my roommates. "Bianca, don't do anything rash." His eyebrows hunkered low on his forehead.

"Maybe not the best word to use on this ward," I said.

He gave me a tight-lipped smile. I knew his sad eyes would stay with me the rest of the day. As I walked toward the exit, I looked back to see if he was coming.

"You go on. I think I'll stay here a while," he said.

"Okay."

Once in the hallway, I looked down the wooden staircase and felt dizzy. I grabbed the immense wooden railing and took the steps slowly. Outside the hospital, the cold Montenai air bored right through to the bone.

With my head down against the wind, I made my way through the snow-covered path toward North Village. Darklings brushed past me, but I never looked up at their faces. Something drew my attention to the locket around my neck. I touched the golden cage pendant that housed the blue scale. When I stopped to look behind me, I thought I saw Lord Bulosk's wavy black hair. *Is he following me?*

I quickened my pace and breathed a sigh of relief when I stepped into the forest. After checking to make sure I was alone, I used the portal to earth's plane.

With my mother and father's disapproval, I sunbathed in the Solomons' back yard all afternoon. My mother shadowcasted for Mrs. Solomon, even though she was supposed to be taking her days off. I realized all of us were bending the rules now.

Although the autumn sun wasn't as bright as the summer sun, it still charged my body. My mother wrung her hands and argued with me that the solar absorption came through the human in a siphoning fashion. The human acted as a conduit. Purposefully drawing in direct radiation for hours could be detrimental.

Ignoring her, I lounged in the chair with the sleeves of my sweater pushed up. The temperature hung in the mid-fifties. Sure, it was brisk, but I tried to expose as much skin as possible without freezing myself. I had foregone the tights and wore a pair of thick socks with my skirt. Mr. Solomon had left the solar panel for his car windshield on the deck chair when he washed the car the previous day. It acted as a blind, blocking the wind, so I could tolerate the temperature.

By 3 p.m., I felt a bit lightheaded from the sun's radiation. *Perhaps, this is the way humans feel when they have downed too many energy drinks.*

"Bianca!"

I shook my head to clear the spots from my vision. My mother's tall frame loomed over me on the lawn chair. Her thin eyebrows were drawn in a V.

"You should see yourself. Your skin's as brown as satyr fur, and your pupils are dilated."

I tried to get out of the chair but fumbled a bit. My mother snatched me up by my elbow.

"I hope you know what you're doing."

That makes two of us.

I found Mrs. Solomon in Ben's old bedroom, looking out the window. She made my heart hurt. I used her palm as my portal back to Montenai.

As I walked quickly through North Village, I hugged myself, trying to shake off the image of a distressed Mrs. Solomon. The cool air drifted up my skirt, causing my bare legs to turn numb. Zack was my first priority, so I headed straight home.

When I opened the apartment door, I saw he hadn't moved from his spot on the couch. His eyes widened when I approached him. He had the faintest trace of the rash at his hairline. "What did you do?" he asked. "Your eyes are funny."

"Well, your face is funny," I snarked back.

He smirked. "Seriously. Are you okay?"

"Of course. I just stored up some extra energy," I said as I pulled my red sweater over my head, leaving on just my tank top.

"Whoa." His eyes found my every curve.

"Cut it out," I warned.

"Sorry."

Without any more questions, I knelt next to him on the couch, perching my elbow on his shoulder and allowing my hand to rest on his hairline. I leaned against him, my entire body touching his side. He remained seated with his culinary notes in front of him. He was preparing for his cooking final.

"Are you okay?" he asked.

"Yeah, why?"

"I can feel your heart going a hundred miles an hour."

"I may have overcooked myself in the earth's sun."

He turned his head and looked into my eyes. "Bianca," he reprimanded softly.

Without warning, he touched my cheek, slid his hand to the nape of my neck, and pulled me in for a kiss. Before I knew it, I was underneath him on the couch with the armrest serving as a pillow.

After a few moments of reveling in everything Zack—soft hair, long muscular legs, ridiculous biceps—I nudged his shoulder to break the kiss. "What happened to being friends?"

He sat back to his original position on the couch, pulling my feet into his lap in the process. I continued to lie with my head on the armrest as my raging hormones cursed like a satyr in my head.

"Honestly, Bianca, I never wanted to be just friends. I've always wanted to be your steady." He didn't look at me but out the front window of the duplex.

My eyes scanned Zack's sharp jawline then took in the luxurious lashes that fringed his round, brown eyes.

What's wrong with me? Why can't I match the intensity of his feelings? I was attracted to him and had a wonderful time with him, but he didn't drive me to obsession the way Ben did my sister. Maybe true love shouldn't be about obsession. Did I really want to be like Anka, who had done what she liked for Ben without too much thought to anyone else?

Zack wasn't forbidden. I tried to reason with myself that Zack was just what I needed. I knew, at the moment, I was just what he needed. The rash had disappeared. Healthy color flushed his cheeks. I gave him a rush of euphoria. Did he mistake it for something more?

When I met his gaze, he shook his head and swallowed. I could see he was frustrated with me, but I had no way to fix the situation. My brain and body were already working overtime, processing too much of earth's sun.

His eyes lowered to my chest. At first, I thought my female parts mesmerized him, but then he scrunched up his face, and I realized he was studying my locket. The hollow, ornamental cage of the pendant gave a close observer a glimpse of its contents.

I shot to my feet and grabbed my sweater off the floor.

"When did you start wearing your locket again?"

This was a loaded question. For the brief period we had been romantic, I had worn the locket with a piece of dragon glass inside he'd found along the riverbank. After things had fizzled out, I had stopped wearing the locket.

If he saw the blue scale, I was screwed.

"I don't know. I just put it on the other day."

He was in my face so fast, the locket in his hand, I could only gasp. Apparently, he was feeling much better, at least physically.

"Is this what I think it is?" Every muscle in his face and neck stretched so tight, I thought something would snap.

"No." I put my hand on his, attempting to pry it loose. "Let go."

He dropped the locket. "Why, Bianca?"

The excitement of the day had given me a raging headache. It hurt to even blink my eyes. I couldn't answer. I didn't understand myself. Looking down at the floor, I searched for a reasonable response. "He saved my life."

"What?"

"Lord Akton had detained me and was tort..." My eyes brimmed with tears. I didn't have a handle on any of my emotions or actions lately.

His face shifted from anger to disgust. With his arms

across his chest, he waited.

"Lord Akton planned to sear me like a fine piece of steak. But Lord Leasith restrained him and Lord Bulosk carried me to safety."

Still shaking his head, he walked into the kitchen. He started pulling items from the cabinets, making a complete racket as he opened and closed them, retrieving baking items.

He had all the makings for double chocolate cake. Now I knew I'd really upset him. Zack always turned to sugar when troubled.

As he mumbled to himself, I disappeared into my purple bedroom. Purple was the Rehmling family color. For some reason, I had needed the color as comfort when I moved out of my family's house. I slipped on wool tights and donned my cape and jingle boots. I needed fresh, cool air to clear my head. It would take an arctic blast to rid me of my shame.

With a curt, "I'll be back," I left the duplex and found my way to the Montenai River. I watched the geese floating together like flotsam on the river's icy surface. They launched as one unit into the sky, honking to each other as something startled them. The ducks followed suit.

Despite searching the water, I couldn't find the source of their anxiety. I tucked my head as the wind whipped off the water and a wall of clouds hunkered close to the horizon, promising snow. I walked through the archway of twisted tree trunks to the South Village. My thoughts created a traffic jam in my head that would have a human swearing.

I had liked the way Lord Bulosk smelled. Since the day he carried me out of the Rotunda away from his brother, I had been thinking about all my encounters with him. He had always winked at me when I saw him in III Brothers' Pub. Once, he even bought a round of drinks for me and my friends. *Good grief, maybe his scale is affecting me.*

When I reached Toren Hospital, I headed to the second floor. The sun began to set, casting a peachy glow through the ward. I walked as quickly as I could to Sonya's room, hoping to bypass the medical staff. They used to greet me with warm smiles, but since the fiasco with Anka, they cast suspicious glances.

A family stood at the nurse's station, occupying the head nurse, so I slipped into the tiny room where Sonya sat up, looking out the window. When she turned to face me, I noticed the rash on her face had diminished. Her large, green eyes studied me as she drew her stuffed, pink dragon closer to her. "Are you gonna give me a shot?"

"No, sweetie. I'm a volunteer. I visited you this morning while you were still sleeping."

She continued to stare as if assessing whether I were friend or foe. Darklings didn't have the same "stranger danger" engrained in them as humans. When she smiled, I stepped over to her and perched on the edge of her bed. I held her hand and reached across to touch the rash on her face.

Sonya jerked her head back. "Don't. You'll get sick."

"I won't get sick. It's okay." With my hand on the rash, I distracted her with talk about the upcoming winter games, the impending snow, and whether nymphs or shadowcasters were cooler. Definitely shadowcasters. She had a brother who played on the college hockey team and would be in the winter games, a friendly tournament that pitted nonshadowcasters against shadowcasters. Sometimes, the satyrs made an appearance. They were surprisingly adept at skating, with better muscle definition than any human Olympic speed skater.

The longer I sat with her, the more animated she became. I knew it was the energy. Several times, I shushed her, politely reminding her of the other sick darklings. Eventually, she climbed into my lap. To entertain her, I cast shadows on the wall of horses, dogs, cats, and dragons—her request. I gave the largest dragon a low, gruff voice. "'Don't you love my pink polka-dotted underwear?'"

She giggled.

As I turned us toward the window, utilizing the largest wall for my shadow production, she leaned back on me. I continued with the dragon brothers because she thought they were hilarious.

"'I just got a mani/pedi,' said the copper dragon. 'Do you like my magenta claws?'"

"'I sleep with the light on because I'm so scaaaaared,' said the blue dragon."

Sonya howled with laughter.

"I do not sleep with the light on," said a deep tenor.

I froze. Sonya peered around me. Her eyes grew wide as a curious kitten's, and she extended her neck in a feline way to study our guest better.

"I have my blankie and my thumb, which make me safe even in the dark," he said.

My throat grew dry. I looked at the person behind me via the reflection in the dark window. I couldn't make out his facial expression.

Sonya opened her mouth and belly-laughed. "Hi, Bowlie!"

"Hello, my little hatchling," Lord Bulosk said in a gentle voice.

I still didn't move. My face grew warm. Sonya scrambled from my lap and off the bed before I could stop her.

"Whoa," he said. "Look at you. Strong as a dragon now."

When I finally found the courage to turn around, my breath caught. Lord Bulosk held her in his arms as she rubbed his forehead where his blue scaling was the most pronounced.

"When do I get my scales?" she asked.

I tried to shut my mind off about my locket's contents.

He pressed his lips together. "Hm. I don't think you need scales. You look perfect just as you are."

She poked her bottom lip out in a full pout, and his face grew distressed.

"But you said I would probably get 'em once I was all better."

His mouth dropped open. It must have seemed like a safe thing to promise a dying hatchling. The reality of her condition just twenty-four hours ago must have hit him, for he stared at me. I held his gaze in a challenge.

"Yeah, Bowlie," I said.

He continued to stare. I cocked an eyebrow at him.

His eyes flitted over every inch of Sonya. "Amazing work, Miss Rehmling."

I didn't know how to take his compliment.

He carried Sonya back to the bed. "Okay, Pumpkin. It's late. I think you should try to rest now."

"But you just got here, and you didn't sing yet."

With pursed lips and furrowed brow, he looked uncertain. I tilted my head and matched Sonya's imploring eyes.

"Miss Rehmling. Don't you have some other darklings to visit before you go home?"

I had planned to check on each patient to assess which ones were the worst and needed immediate attention. "Yes. I do." I kissed Sonya's forehead. "Good night, little hatchling." I ran my eyes over his face before exiting the room. What a charmer.

He's a killer, Bianca.

In the hallway, the head nurse nodded to me and even managed a half smile. Had he talked to her? No one bothered me as I poked my head in each room and spent time with four patients, dividing my time into fifteen-minute sessions. Like Sonya, the rash had spread to a size greater than a fist on their faces, which was the unofficial measurement for Shadow Fever. If the Silton rash reached a size larger than the average fist, then you were doomed.

By the time I was done, the cloud of gloom, which appeared to hang in the air above the patients, had descended and cloaked me in a suffocating malaise. My bones ached. I tolerated it because I knew what I was doing was important.

My thoughts drifted to the blue-scaled dragon lord. He had looked vulnerable in the hospital room. Even with all their magic and healing abilities, the lords were impotent at curing Shadow Fever.

Or were they?

CHAPTER SIX

I SPENT THE morning resting in my room because attending to the Shadow Fever patients the previous night had sucked all my energy. A pot of Pops's robust blend of mocha coffee at least got me up and dressed. Late in the afternoon, I ventured out in warm, black leggings, a turtleneck, and long cardigan sweater. Several inches of snow blanketed the trees, shrubs, and homes. At a sluggish pace, I walked away from the river toward the northernmost corner of the woods.

The methodical crunch of snow under my boots lulled me into a steady rhythm as the sun's rays set the snow to glistening with thousands of diamonds. A sense of wellbeing filled me as I moved through the soft, safe cocoon—until someone jerked me back and attempted to smother me.

I knew this smell. My eyes rested on the strong hand covering my mouth. The smallest blue scales appeared only on the thumb and index finger, and then swept onto the palm in a swirl. He thought to subdue me, but I bit down as hard as I could.

A growl vibrated against my back. I let go of Lord Bulosk's hand that now sported long claws. When I spun around, fierce green eyes met me. The pupils had changed to vertical slits. He folded me into his body before the ground dropped out from under us. I couldn't scream; I didn't have any air.

We landed in an explosion of snow. *Teleporting* felt very different from traveling through a portal—my head felt like it was still spinning. I wobbled around in a circle before falling on my butt. My surroundings caused my nerves to riot. These weren't sequoia trees but ancient oaks with arthritic limbs that twisted toward the sky. *The Ballatian Woods.* My heart raced as Bulosk plucked me out of the snow. He didn't use his claws, but his pace told me he meant business.

"Hurry," he insisted.

I didn't protest or scream or prattle at him in my snarky way. My gut told me to dive into one of the snow banks and burrow deep like a scared little mole. Snow thunder boomed from deeper in the Ballatian Woods, quaking the ground and sending an avalanche of snow from the branches above.

"You need to trust me," he said as he searched the area with a confused look on his face. His frenzied manner frightened me. He dwarfed me in size, and if he was nervous in these woods, then I was petrified.

Gray fog weaved through the trees, headlong in our direction, as if stalking us. He strode toward it while I wanted to run as far away as possible. It emitted muffled screeching sounds, which made me want to curl into the fetal position.

I dug in my heels and pulled back.

He ignored me and continued to plow through the snow toward the diabolical mass. I held on like a water skier.

What in the world of Montenai are we doing here? No one will hear me scream. The phantoms will eat me.

He whirled around and stared down at me. "Stop. Talking."

"I wasn't talking. I haven't even made a squeak."

He exhaled a long plume of smoke through his nostrils.

I pulled a hand free and waved it in front of my face as I coughed. "Do you know what the statistics are regarding secondhand smoke?" Smoking didn't actually have a negative health effect on darklings, but when I was nervous, I started to crack jokes.

Lord Bulosk stomped through the snow. "Stop talking. I can't think when you are in my head." He released my arm in the process of gesturing wildly.

I'm getting to him. Maybe he'll leave me alone if I annoy him to death.

He glared.

"Sorrreee."

When he unsheathed his claws, I screamed. My false bravado left me. *I know what those claws do to darkling skin.* Anka had almost died. The pain had consumed her to where every conscious moment, she had asked me to end it for her. I don't think Anka remembered that part, but I did.

"I didn't touch her," he said.

"What?"

Before he could answer me, an attractive female emerged from the woods, her dark brown hair unfurled in the smoggy wind. I'm sure she enchanted males when she was alive. Now, she haunted them. *Or, hunts them.* Her eyes and mouth were gaping black holes.

I clung to Bulosk like a tantruming fledgling.

"P-p-poof us back," I pleaded as I wrapped myself around his massive arm.

"Serena?" he asked.

Her mouth opened, and she shrieked at a pitch so high, I'm sure dogs several planes over leapt.

"Oh, not good. Did you just call her by another female's name? Nobody likes that—alive or dead."

"My mistake," he said. Lord Bulosk stood his ground as the phantom grew to three times his height.

"I don't think your charm is working on her."

The phantom's mouth stretched to the size of a car tire as dark, shapeless creatures swirled her skirts, screeching in a chorus.

A fierce suction pulled us toward her. My toes turned cold then numb. This was how they incapacitated creatures. They weakened and froze their victims until they curled up, became hypothermic, and died. Or, maybe they ate them, as the stories said. I didn't want to find out.

I reached in my pocket and touched my nymph bracelet. If this bull-headed dragon lord thought we were going to negotiate with a pissed phantom, I wasn't sticking around.

He yanked me forward and placed me in front of him.

You no good dirty rotten piece of reptilian afterbirth. Now I understood his strategy. Antagonize the creature so she eats me. I had other plans. I slid my wrist through the vines of my bracelet and pinched a blossom before she'd freeze us to the point where we couldn't move a muscle.

As I traveled through the portal, he clung to my ankle. I landed flat on my back in a field on fire. I rolled to my stomach and saw Lord Bulosk five feet to my right. Groaning, I pushed to my hands and knees then sat back on my heels. Smoke burned my eyes and found my nose and mouth, causing me to cough and sputter.

In front of me, scorched land and dead plant matter replaced what once was a field covered in drifts of pristine snow. Through the smoke, I caught glimpses of the destruction—Kirka Circle was broken. *This can't be happening.* Flames shot thirty feet into the air from the enormous dome that was Reflections Celebration Hall. Inky black smoke belched into the sky. Just as I got one foot out in order to stand, glass exploded, sending me to my stomach once more. I thought nymph glass was indestructible.

Dazed, I barely had time to duck as nymph lights darted by my head. Colorful wounded birds losing flight, they sputtered a high-pitched sound that accompanied their diminishing glow before they crashed into burning snow banks. *How does fire spread over snow?*

"It's enchanted," Lord Bulosk rasped. His mouth hung open like a cat's when it's sniffing and tasting the air. He jumped to his feet but immediately stopped. Vines as thick as my thighs writhed, twisted, and locked around his ankles, knees, and wrists. After pushing to my feet, I pulled my turtleneck over my nose and mouth before stepping in his direction. From behind me, I heard snow crunching underfoot. When I turned, at least thirty nymphs approached. Their hair sailed back off their shoulders and remained suspended in the air. Their blue and green eyes lightened to an otherworldly sheen. Their magic had Bulosk trapped.

Magda stood front and center. She nodded to the two on either side of her. They stepped forward, raised their hands to cast, and—

"No!" I lunged in front of him. "Magda. What are you doing?"

"They broke our treaty, Bianca. We can't put the fires out. It's taking all of our magic just to contain them."

I turned to look at Lord Bulosk. The vines had grown up around his neck, squeezed until his eyes bulged, and clamped his mouth shut. I couldn't reconcile the darkling who visited five-year-olds in the hospital with the one who tortured young females.

"He couldn't have done this. He was with me." *Kidnapping me. Trying to feed me to a phantom.* I really needed to champion better causes.

With a flick of her hand, Magda released the thorny bindings. He didn't make a sound when they ripped free, other than a loud exhalation. I knew he had magic, but he hadn't tried to use it from what I could gather, and he hadn't tried to barbecue the kirka.

"Magda, I can help, but I first need a word with you in private," he gasped.

When Magda removed the rest of the vines, his clothes hung in tatters and blood oozed from sores. He made no sign of distress or sound of complaint as he followed the nymph leader to her home, escorted by the ethereal squad of hit nymphs.

Despite protests from her posse, Magda walked into the home alone. I followed without asking permission.

Lord Bulosk looked toward me. "She needs to leave."

Magda flicked her eyes to me before studying his face. "She stays."

She sat down on the white daybed. He stood in front of her with his hands held behind his back, I guessed in a sign of good faith. I stood next to him because, frankly, Magda scared me almost as much as the phantom had. Power radiated off her, electrifying the air and making my joints hurt. The flowers on the water feature rustled and twisted violently.

"Talk fast, my village burns."

He shifted his feet and cut his eyes at me. I sensed how uncomfortable he was having an audience.

"Please respect that all darklings should not know the inner workings of the Council."

I just saved his dragon tail and he has the nerve to shut me out? That, of course, had me wondering...*does he have a tail?*

He scrunched up his face. "Nooo."

"No, what?" I asked.

"I'm losing patience," Magda said through gritted teeth.

"Akton isn't well." He pressed his lips flat as he shook his head. "Magda, please. This is not for all ears."

"You have fifteen seconds before I order you executed in front of the kirka."

His nostrils flared and he pulled himself taller. "Hear me just this once," he hissed. "I could have called to my brothers telepathically and had them finish all of you, but I am showing diplomacy. Don't threaten my life again."

Smoke came out of his nose and mouth. The space filled with his heady magic—the kind I'd felt when hanging in the dragon's lair and in the restaurant. I started to sway on my feet.

Maybe I should sit down. I stumbled to a white brocade chaise across from Magda. I didn't want to be sitting next to her, in case he turned her into a charcoal briquette. As the magic lulled me, my lids grew heavy. Dirty scoundrel. I would not be knocked unconscious. The air appeared to move around me, causing me to feel seasick. I leaned back on the lounge and fought with my eyelids.

Maybe I'll just rest my eyes.

"The darklings are unstable. Cases of Shadow Fever have increased. Some believe we are withholding our energy as punishment for darkling defectors and traitors."

"Why is my village on fire?" Magda demanded.

"Akton thinks you are colluding with the shadowcasters to gain them independence from the Council. This would be detrimental to humans, darklings, and the kirka. We know you healed Anka Rehmling. We suspect you interfered in human affairs. And Lord Akton believes you are teaching Bianca magic so she can eventually spearhead the rebellion against us."

My eyes popped open.

"He lost it with Anka Rehmling. He hasn't been himself over the last several months. Leasith and I have been working day and night to harness the power and re-establish the balance. It's not working. With Akton's mind in dark places, and his extreme paranoia, all of Shadowland suffers."

"And what of the Torensphere?"

Lord Bulosk's green eyes glowed. "Not. In. Her. Presence," he said. His voice had taken on a demonic edge.

My blood ran cold, and I shivered. I continued to feel the weight of his magic wash over me, causing me to sink farther into the chaise.

Magda stood up. Her peacock-blue skirt flared as she walked toward him. Her mood had changed within an instant. "Something's happened." Her anger still lingered but fear had caused her voice to waver.

"Yes."

"Akton?"

Bulosk looked down. Stress tightened the cords running down the sides of his neck. He nodded once.

"I see," she said.

"Leasith had nothing to do with these fires. I'll call him so he can help douse them. We can talk more, after."

With that decided, they hastened toward the door, suddenly on the same team or at least of the same mind. Lord Bulosk turned my way. "Stay close," he said with a strained look before disappearing through the door.

I couldn't lift my head due to the nymph/dragon lord cocktail. My thoughts lingered on the talk of the Torensphere. *What exactly did this entity do?*

"Uh. Little help here, please," I squeaked to Magda.

That earned a deep sigh from her. As she crossed the room to me, Pan padded in from the hallway. I guess he'd been waiting for the dragon-darkling to leave. *Nice watch dog.* He goobered my face, his eyes shining an intense gold. Magda instructed him to go lie on his dog bed. She lifted me to my feet and supported me around the waist as we walked out the door to fresh air. Actually, not fresh air but better than the heady magic-filled atmosphere inside the dome.

Night had fallen, and Lord Bulosk had already disappeared. I hoped he was rallying his one sane brother because despite the nymphs' chanting, the fire flourished. Twenty yards from the house, I finally found my stride. "Geez. You guys ever heard of toxic relationships?"

Magda smirked at me.

I lost my sarcasm as I viewed her village. "This is because you helped my family. I'm so sorry, Magda. What can I do?"

She tilted her head as if listening to the wind. "Stay close."

When our eyes met, I realized she was puzzling over something. I wanted to confide to her that Lord Bulosk had hijacked me to the Ballatian Woods, but I'd just stood up for him, and I didn't think it would help the temporary truce they'd established. I don't know why I cared if she took out the dragon lord.

She eyed my locket for an instant. I wished I'd left it in my jewelry box at home. I thought she might speak, but she turned and began giving orders. I followed alongside her, helping physically with debris cleanup, and assisting the displaced families as they moved to temporary housing. The fires had stayed in the main meadow and along Kirka Circle. The majority of farmland remained untouched. I had no idea if that had been an intentional show of mercy or just by chance.

I didn't have time to process Lord Bulosk's revelations. Adrenaline kept me mobile. When I noticed the satyrs had arrived to help, I finally stepped down a side path to clear my head and catch my breath. Pops's sad eyes from earlier filled my head, and I fumbled in my cloak for my cell phone. My family didn't answer, not even Pops. My roommates were fine, but Zack's voice sounded strained.

"Bianca. Where are you? I thought you were with your parents at the Solomon house."

"Uh, I got held up. I'm now with the nymphs."

"Are you okay? We can see the fires."

"Someone's having a meltdown and taking it out on the kirka."

The silence on the other end caused me to look for somewhere to sit. I settled on a bench formed from twisted nymph vines. "What's going on, Zack? Talk to me."

"Someone torched Pops's shop."

I felt like I'd been sucker-punched. "Is he okay? Did everyone get out?"

"I don't know, Bianca. No one was there or at the house when I went to check."

"Nana?" I asked, my voice trembling.

"Sweetie, I don't know."

I put my head in my hand as I kept the phone to my ear. A huge sob escaped.

"What do you want us to do?" he asked.

As much as I tried, I couldn't catch my breath. I rubbed my hand over the circle of vines, which comprised the bench's seat. "Stay in the apartment."

I terminated the call and stood up. When I returned to the chaos in the main circle, I couldn't find Magda. A flash of copper indicated Lord Leasith's arrival. Numb, I watched for a moment as the brothers strode through the rolling smoke, untouched by the flames. Leasith moved with the slightest limp.

Panicked about my family, I headed in the opposite direction, stumbling over charred debris to the river's edge. Snowflakes swirled in the air, mixing with the ash and causing a caustic, wintry mix. With shock setting in, my body rebelled. I shivered, and my teeth chattered. As my anxiety peaked, I pinched a blossom on the bracelet. My body anticipated the familiar push through the portal, but nothing happened. I tried another blossom. Nothing. Looking back up the slope, I searched for Magda. I couldn't be certain, but I guessed, with the nymphs' energies diverted, their portal system was malfunctioning.

Anger ignited in my belly and began to warm me. Tilting my head back, I looked up through the haze and gloom. Akton's red star gleamed through the murky night.

"Can't I catch a break?"

CHAPTER SEVEN

THE COLD, BLACK water flowed in a sinuous path in front of me as I paced the bank. *How do I get across?* I looked for a boat of some kind, but there weren't any on this side of the river. The nymphs didn't need a vessel to traverse water. The satyrs transported all their goods for them, either on their backs or in their boats.

Although Kirka Village remained matriarchal, the satyrs and nymphs continued to work together. If a mating couple gave birth to a female or nymph, the kirka took on the major responsibility of raising her with plenty of support from the male satyr father. If the nymph had a satyr or male, the father cared for him in the fishing town of Port by the Sea, teaching him all their trades and the secrets of manipulating the wind. It worked for them. The female and male counterparts remained strong, independent, happy, and fiercely protective of each other.

I could use a fierce, protective satyr right now to get me across the rapids in the dark. The head buck, Cornelius, had helped my sister across during dire circumstances, but there was little chance I could find him in the current chaos.

My phone buzzed in my sweater pocket. *Zack.*

"Hey. Any news?" I asked as my voice broke.

"Bianca. Where are you?" Based on his voice, I'd say his stress level had just ratcheted up ten notches.

"At the river's edge. I can't get across. The portal's closed."

He sighed. His frustration was palpable. "I know you're worried about your family, but it's probably better you stay there. They have the village on lockdown."

"What?"

"A militia of darklings representing the Council is running through the streets, brandishing swords."

"Are you okay?"

"We're safe in the apartment. Eric came over to warn us about the activity in South Village."

I thought I heard Liza's voice in the background. *She must have gnawed her nails into little nubs by now.*

"Bianca, I'm worried about you," he said.

"I'll stay close to Magda," I lied.

"There's nothing you can do over here until things blow over. There's rumbling coming from the Wishing Tree."

"I understand. You guys stay safe." My nerve endings felt electrified. I just wanted to get off the phone.

"Bian—"

I disconnected. I hoped he mistook if for Three Brothers Wireless cell tower issues. Desperation fueled my legs as I climbed up the bank and ran smack into Max, a young wild buck who caught me from falling by sweeping an arm around me.

"Oh," I grunted. It was like Adah, the Mother of Montenai, had answered my prayers. *Hero type? Check.*

"You okay? What are you doing over here?" Max's forest-green eyes widened in alarm and stood in stark contrast to his light brown skin.

"It's complicated."

Once he steadied me on my feet, he scrutinized my appearance. I realized I probably had cuts, bruises, ash, and grime coating me.

With a powerful, seven-foot buck towering over me, it was hard not to feel a bit self conscious, but I forced myself to push ahead. "Have you seen Cornelius? I need help crossing the river."

Max scratched his goatee. "We'd be hard-pressed to find him in that pandemonium. Why don't you let me ferry you across."

"Are you sure?"

He squatted low to the ground next to a rock. "Hop on," he said.

I used the rock as a stepping stool. From above him, I glimpsed the small horns on his head that usually stayed hidden under his hair, except for in the heat of battle. Once on board, I clung to ropes of muscle on his shoulders and arms as he rock-hopped in the dark without the slightest hesitation or misstep. While the satyrs' upper bodies resembled a heavily-muscled darkling, their goat lower half allowed them to accomplish such a daunting feat as scaling rough terrain and maneuvering across the treacherous river. Despite his obvious skill, I closed my eyes and held my breath.

On the other side, he crouched again, allowing me to slide gently to the ground. I gave him a peck on the cheek.

"I apologize for my curtness, but I really must find my family."

"Any time, Miss Rehmling." He winked before leaping to a sharp rock a quarter of the way across the river. Then he disappeared into the smog.

Still winded from the encounter, I huffed up the bank and through the tunnel to North Village. I didn't head toward Chocolate Syncope or my family's cottage but instead for the portal in the northernmost reaches of the Sequoia Forest. At the fir tree, I raked my fingers through the needles, releasing the familiar calming scent of pine. As I attempted to enter the sequoia, I cried out as a stinging sensation covered my face and hands.

"No! No! No!" Someone had locked down the portal with a ward or force field that felt like stinging nettles. I prayed my family was safe on earth's plane at the Solomon house.

When I turned from the tree, the woods stood empty—a sight I'd never seen in my lifetime. Not a single shadowcaster walked the worn path through the woods.

Are they all hiding in their homes or stuck on the other side?

Perhaps my shadowcasting family members had taken refuge at the Solomon home, but that didn't account for Nana. As a nonshadowcaster, she couldn't travel via the darkling portal. My stomach churned, and I grabbed my pounding head. In my mind, I saw

Nana's golden nymph hair and heard her laugh. For a second, stress and fear blinded me.

In the next moment, I laughed at my stupidity. Nana and Pops had probably taken refuge in the cabin deep in the Hinterlands where Ben and Anka now lived. Mom and Dad were no doubt with the Solomons. Relief began to soften the tension in my shoulders.

Exhaling a long breath, I started back toward North Village. I'd check on Zack and Liza then head back across the river, somehow. I could enter the Hinterlands by passing Magda's house and walking around Lake Hanleith.

A sound, like the droning of a million bees, halted me in my tracks. It sounded the same as it had over the summer when the lords had summoned Anka.

I ran. When I reached the boardwalk, I pumped my arms and legs harder, sprinting toward the Wishing Tree. When the lords summoned, you came. This time, I knew it was the one lord. With the smoke still billowing across the river, Lords Bulosk and Leasith had to be continuing their aid to the kirka.

I knew who had blocked the portal, just as I knew who had torched Pops's shop. I replayed Lord Bulosk's conversation with Magda about Lord Akton. The oldest dragon lord viewed me as some kind of traitor. I'd always thought of myself as just a silly little hatchling. Was he really threatened by me? What if he used my family to get to me?

Nana!

Once through the tunnel into South Village, I slowed a bit to take in the scene. Splotches of blood marred the snow. A small number of shadowcasting and nonshadowcasting darklings wandered the streets, aiding the wounded. I recognized the server, Jacob, from Drakos Restaurant. Frost coated his dark beard. His breath came in rasps. The manager, Ian, held Jacob's arm around his neck and supported him around the waist as they waited for a Toren Hospital cart to come to a stop. I noted cuts on his face but no blood on his shirt where he clutched his ribs with his hand.

It felt surreal to witness the bloody aftermath of darklings warring with each other. My only consolation was that whatever skirmish had played out now appeared to be winding down with shadowcasters and nonshadowcasters helping each other.

Lord Akton continued his summons from the grand tree, spurring me to run again. I slipped several times on icy patches, skinning my knees and abrading my palms until they burned. The snow whipped sideways, impairing my vision, but I knew the path well. I bumped into a few darklings because the wintry storm had intensified along with the summons of the dragon lord.

At my destination, a flash of silver greeted me. Ten darkling males stood sentry at the tree's entrance, swords raised. I could feel their adrenaline and see the whites of their fear-widened eyes.

"I'm being summoned," I shouted over the howl of the wind.

They didn't lower their swords but stepped back to create a path. I recognized some of the males but diverted my eyes. I didn't blame them. An incredible force had compelled them. I doubted they had much control.

The double doors to the Wishing Tree stood open. Before I lost my nerve, I entered. My racing heartbeat filled my head. No enchanted sconces lit my way. In the pitch black, I descended, feeling the rough bark of the wall as my wet boots made a squelch, squelch over the cobblestone. Lights shone from the kitchen on the left. Glancing inside, I found it empty.

The farther I traveled down the tunnel, the more I realized all darklings had fled. A familiar heady magic enveloped me like a wet cloak, weighing me down, hampering my breathing, and diminishing my will.

I recognized Lord Akton's magic. It felt heavier than the other lords' alchemy and left a metallic taste in my mouth. Lord Bulosk's and Leasith's magic smelled and tasted sweeter. While their magic blanketed, Lord Akton's *smothered*.

With legs heavy as lead, I continued my journey, anticipating I'd find the lord of the house in the Rotunda. A smart shadowcaster would have grabbed a sword on the way to her doom. Maybe the earth's sun had fried my darkling brain. With no hesitations, I reached the vestibule. The lights flickered like humans' fluorescent bulbs. The eerie light show continued into the inner sanctum. My eyes tracked to the infinite ceiling to see if any family members dangled there.

"They're gone," Lord Akton said in a gravelly voice. He sounded *different.* The room felt strange.

My chest tightened as I located his voice. He sat in a black leather club chair. It was the first time in my life I'd seen him sitting down. A rash bloomed on his face, but it wasn't the Silton rash. This looked dark as ink.

"Where are they?" I asked, trying not to stare.

"I believe they are on the earth's plane. I can't track Violet."

Seems my grandmother had dropped off his radar. I wondered if it had anything to do with her nymph blood or Ben.

"None of it matters now. Your selfish actions have already spurred apocalyptic repercussions."

My curiosity propelled me across the room, and I stopped in front of him. When seated, he was almost my height. I stretched my arm out to place my hand on his cheek.

He caught me by the wrist, but it wasn't a violent move. "You can't," he said.

I had instinctively reached for his rash as I had with the Shadow Fever patients. Even in danger, I couldn't contain my impulse to help.

"Why not?" I asked, studying the scorched pattern that traversed his whole face. Only the left side of his nose and good eye remained untouched.

"I have too much fire." His voice had lost its intensity. He released my wrist, and my arm dropped to my side.

"Is that why you did that to the kirka fields?"

His eyelid drooped, as did the corner of his mouth. It reminded me of when Ben's grandfather had a stroke. *Can dragon lords have strokes?* His blank stare indicated he may not remember his actions across the river.

"You can't fix me," he said.

I followed his gaze to the opposite wall. The space had not been exposed during my last visit. A fake wall had drawn to the side, exposing a black marble table veined with gold. Upon it rested a tabernacle; its golden-hinged door hung open, the space within empty.

When I looked back, I met Lord Akton's golden eye. "What happened?" I demanded, surprised by my own boldness.

"It's gone." A tear escaped the corner of his eye. "I don't know what will happen to you without the Torensphere." His speech sounded slightly slurred.

He blinked once. The rash began to spread like an inkblot stain. The air boiled. I leaned toward him, allowing him direct access to my face. Even with his power waning, Lord Akton locked his eye on me, which fixed my head in place. He used no words to communicate but blasted me with images.

A fire ignited and simmered over the surface of my body. Would I see his childhood abuse like he had shown Anka?

He stood in the Ballatian Woods. A beautiful phantom stepped out from the trees. Serena. "I couldn't find you," she said, anguish contorting her face. In her hand, she held a shattered mirror.

My whole body flooded with grief. I felt what he felt. The depth of his emotions overwhelmed me. He had loved her. *Why had Bulosk taken me to see her?* I didn't have time for further contemplation. A visual storm hit me and filled my head with chaos.

His grandmother, who was pregnant at the time, took the ancient dragon egg into her care. Her baby, Drakos, came into the world with golden scales. The egg passed down to the next generation. Akton's mother, Pia, bore three scaly fledglings—the three dragon lords. Akton protected his two brothers from their abusive father. His brothers fought with him about the shadowcasters. Akton delivered three lashes to my sister. Bulosk and Leasith created a binding to make him stop. Bulosk shielded Anka and Pops's journey across the river so Magda could treat her. I healed the darklings.

When he gasped for breath, the images stuttered. His red scales appeared to move under the black mottled rash as waves of heat radiated off his skin. One last time, he locked his eye on me. He showed me female eyes the color of the Aglatian Sea. I registered his confusion, fear, and...remorse.

My head snapped back, out of his hold. Lord Akton glowed yellow, as if lit from within. His eye closed, and the lines of the rash turned fiery red. A few heartbeats later, he ignited, shining as bright as a supernova.

I had no time to react. The explosion flung me back against the marble table that held the tabernacle. Woozy and stunned, I only processed the pain in my spine and the intensity of the jolt. As I struggled to make my lungs expand, I looked in horror toward the club chair, now ablaze and shrouded in a cloud of ash. *He's gone.* Incinerated.

Shock locked me in place. I needed to move, but I couldn't even breathe. Helpless, I watched the walls come alive with flame. It shot skyward through the 200-foot trunk of the Wishing Tree before coming down in an infernal rain. Charred pieces of the ancient tree began to crash to the marble floor and burst apart, shooting splintered shrapnel in all directions. Flinging my arms over my head, I curled in a ball on the floor, waiting for the worst of it to subside. Smoke swirled around me, and ash fell on my skin.

Shrieking reached my ears. *The bats.* When I removed my arms, the horror show continued as leathery corpses showered down on and around me. The floor writhed with the desperate, dying creatures.

Tears stung my eyes as I shook my head, trying to clear my senses and jumpstart my body to act. I grasped the hot surface of the table and pulled myself up. *Move, Bianca!* I raised my arm to steady myself, only to find the sleeve of my sweater engulfed in flame. Finally, I found my voice, but my screams were so hoarse from the smoke, I could barely hear myself. Thrashing about, I only knew panic and terror. Finally, I got a hold of myself. Desperate, I looked around me. I couldn't stop, drop, and roll. The floor was on fire. My legs weak, I lurched toward the door, amazed I couldn't feel any part of me burning.

It doesn't make sense. I should be in excruciating pain. Thank you, Mother of Montenai. I must be in shock.

Fire engulfed me, but I didn't burn. When I looked down, my clothes and boots turned to ash and sloughed off. By this time, I could only see a foot in front of me. I fumbled my way across the room, stepping on sharp items, soft things, but not knowing exactly what.

Disoriented, I could only guess how far I was to the doorway.

Finally, a blast of air hit my face, and I glimpsed the tunnel walls as flames licked up their sides. *I just need to make it to the surface.*

Voices came to me from up top. *Lords Bulosk and Leasith.*

"Bianca!"

"Akton!"

As I moved toward the sound of the two brothers, I opened my mouth but only produced a squeak.

A force like a truck hit me, knocking me back. I clutched onto someone's shirt as strong arms reached out for me.

"Bianca?" Green eyes glowed just above me.

Bulosk.

"Did you find them?" yelled Lord Leasith.

Blue eyes appeared next to green in front of me.

"He's gone," I gasped.

Lord Leasith darted past me. "Aaaaaakton!" he bellowed.

I felt a blanket or coat wrap around me. Lord Bulosk lifted me, and I rested my head against his chest before everything went black.

CHAPTER EIGHT

WHEN I AWOKE in Toren Hospital, I first registered the tremendous weight of a male hound head on my chest. Pan gazed at me with sentient eyes. One shone gold, the other gray.

"*Danger* and *sadness*? That is just depressing," I said to him. "What kind of therapy dog are you?"

Ears perked, he wagged his tail against my leg, which made me aware of how sore and stiff I felt.

"Caaan't brrreathe," I joked as I shifted him to my side.

"Drama queen," Magda teased. She stood across the room in front of a picture window framed by satin curtains. Over her shoulder, the white-capped Faunlier Mountains loomed.

This was not the Shadow Fever ward. I was in a suite decorated with fine linens and furnishings.

"Pan, come here," Magda called. The dog leapt down from the mahogany sleigh bed to pad across to his owner. With him gone, I could appreciate the handmade quilt that covered me. It also allowed me to stretch every limb and examine the tiny cuts and bruises on my skin.

"Not a single burn," she said.

Feeling self-conscious, I adjusted the flimsy gown I wore. It was quite pretty, although I wasn't really a pink kind-of-girl.

Magda approached and sat in an upholstered chair pulled up next to the bed. When she touched my hand, I felt her calm and reassuring energy. "Your friends just left. They were here most of the night. I told them to go home and rest."

Unsure, I grasped the locket in my hand and jangled it on the chain. I realized it was a new habit I'd developed. A lump formed in my throat. My family had always seen me through every major event in my life, but where were they now?

Tears stung my eyes, and I closed them, trying to block out the vision of Lord Akton, the fireball inside the Wishing Tree, the dying bats, the desperate shouts of the dragon lords, and the overall feeling that everything just sucked.

Magda stroked reassuring circles on the back of my hand with her thumb. "They're all safe, Bianca."

I shook my head. *Not Lord Akton.*

"Lord Bulosk fixed the portal, but I believe your parents must stay on earth's plane for a while until some shadowcasters volunteer to relieve them. Quite a few members of the Out of Shadow movement are refusing to go over there because they fear they will get trapped."

My throat felt scratchy and sore, making it difficult to talk. "Nana and Pops?"

"With Anka and Ben." She reached over to retrieve a glass of water for me.

Even the smallest sips hurt my throat. By the time I placed the glass on the nightstand, salty tears had found the corners of my mouth. I wiped them away. Magda was here for me, and I didn't want to be disrespectful by feeling sorry for myself. My family probably stayed away so as not to create any problems with the dragon lords. Mustering some calm, I looked into her blue eyes. "How are things with your village?"

"They could have been a lot worse. My crew fixed our portals and is transporting some of the shadowcasters, those who can leave their posts, back to Montenai."

Clearing my throat caused my eyes to water more. "I'm sorry about this mess."

Her eyes widened. "None of this is your fault." Her lips drew in a thin line, which I knew to be her stern look.

I didn't have much fight left to argue with her. Honestly, I just wanted to be alone and cry.

My eyes drifted to the window. I was surprised to see a relatively clear sky beyond the curtains. "The satyrs work their wonders?" I asked her. The talented bunch could finesse the winds.

"Yes. I'm grateful. They stirred the black air and smoke and drove it out to sea so the fallout wouldn't be so toxic for both the kirka and darklings."

I managed to smile, but tears still fell down my cheeks.

Magda rose. "I'm going to have the healers check on you in a few moments. You let me know if there is anything I can do."

"You've already done so much." I reached out to squeeze her hand. "Thank you."

When she left the room, my shoulders shook with sobs. I wanted to get out of here. My shame and grief were too much to handle, and I needed to walk by myself, not look anyone in the eye right now.

With a bit of work and discomfort, I freed myself from the linens and crossed to the mirror that hung on the closet door. A small cut at my eyebrow, another at the corner of my mouth. I didn't look like a darkling who had been in an explosion. Other than a sore back, slight ringing in my ears, and incredibly sore throat, I had fared well from the trauma—at least physically.

Inside the closet, I found my purple paisley tote bag. Liza and Zack must have brought me some clothes. I pulled it down from the shelf and put on loose-fitting jeans, an oversized sweater, and socks and boots. My old brown jacket hung from the rod.

They had included some toiletries in the bag, but I didn't bother. My curly hair looked like its own natural disaster.

Just outside the room, a plaque on the wall read "Toren Suite." That felt like a punch in the gut. I couldn't believe they'd put me in the dragon lords' special suite. A darkling healer attempted to stop me from leaving, but I ignored her. The ringing in my ears grew worse as I found my way to the stairs and out the building.

Before I realized it, I was at the river. My labored breaths hung in the cold air. *How did I get here?* My mind had been racing, and now I couldn't recall any details of the trip. The skeleton of the Wishing Tree lurked in my peripheral vision. I wasn't ready to look. By the time I reached my favorite bench, streaks of orange cut through the low striated clouds in the sky behind me, casting everything along the river in a fiery hue. How could the sunrise look so awe-inspiring during this moment of utter devastation?

I didn't want to face my friends, my family, and certainly not the dragon lord sitting on the bench in front of me. Did I come to this spot knowing he would be here? Or was he here knowing I would come?

"Sit down," Lord Bulosk said, patting the bench.

Without looking at him, I sat down.

"How are you feeling?" he asked.

His concerned voice only made me feel worse. I wiped more tears away, frustrated with myself for having sprung a leak. *He lost his brother. I watched him die. I should have died in the flames, too.*

"Stop," he said. His broad hand covered mine.

"Can you read my mind?"

"Sometimes I hear your thoughts," he confessed.

Great, like it's not weird enough to be sitting next to him, now I have to be careful what I think? My whole life, I'd revered him and his brothers. He didn't look so intimidating now in baggy jeans and a casual cable-knit sweater. I couldn't recall ever seeing him in anything other than a finely tailored shirt and pants. His hand still covered mine.

I tried to summon some courage by looking straight ahead. I found no comfort there. Instead, the sun lit the wreckage of Reflections Celebration Hall across the way. The once perfect sphere of glass was a series of jagged, tarnished shards poking into the sky at awkward angles.

"I'm sorry," I rasped.

A light touch on my chin drew my face toward him. "I want to make this perfectly clear, Bianca. This isn't your fault." Various emotions rippled across his face.

Unconvinced, my thoughts strayed to my rebellious family—my sister's actions, and my own. *Had we contributed to Lord Akton's decline?*

Guilt and anger warred inside me. I felt terrible about the dragon lord's death, but at the same time, I couldn't forget his brutality. The muscle in Lord Bulosk's jaw twitched. It reminded me of Pops.

"Akton has always been stronger than Leasith and I combined. That's not something I've ever told a darkling." Grief held his shoulders rigid. Regret darkened his face.

Was he making excuses for their allowance of my sister's brutal punishment, the attack on Pops's shop, and the damage to Kirka Village?

He grabbed my hand again. "We were supposed to scare Anka into complying with the rules. Akton thought fear was the ultimate motivator. Actually, Drakos raised all of us to believe this. Leasith and I weren't prepared for Akton to raise his claw to her. It happened so fast. Afterward, it took all our energy to contain him."

"You sent her home to die." My voice broke. I still couldn't forget the summer and my sister's suffering.

"No. I cloaked your grandfather and notified Magda that she was coming."

I fiddled with the locket, not sure what to feel. "You could have healed her like you did me."

"She broke the laws. I agreed with the banishment. She endangered lives, including the human's. And with Akton's mood, she was safer on that side of the river."

"I don't know. Those nymphs are fierce."

"You're just realizing this?" he asked. "What were you thinking, stepping in front of a nymph death squad?"

"I didn't know nymph death squads existed. I've never seen that side of Magda."

"They were only defending themselves." He sighed. "Leasith and I should have consulted with Magda sooner. But we kept thinking Akton would get better." Leaning forward with his elbows on his knees, he looked across the way at the wreckage. He shook his head. "Akton stormed away after lunch. Leasith went after him, and I came to find you."

"Why?" I asked.

He turned to face me on the bench. I squirmed from his intense attention.

"I didn't want anything to happen to you."

I scrunched my nose. "You tried to feed me to a phantom, and I had to save your scaly ass!"

Bulosk's eyebrows rose. The one was barely visible surrounded by the scales. "My ass isn't scaly, at least not all of it. If we'd found Serena, she wouldn't have eaten you."

I found that hard to believe after my brief introduction to phantoms.

"The phantoms have actually been known to help a wayward female navigate the haunted woods. I thought I could get you away from Akton until his latest rage episode abated."

Try as I might, I couldn't close my mouth. "You were trying to *save* me?"

His green eyes grew huge. Up close, they surprised me with all their layers of colors.

"What did you think I was doing?"

"Kidnapping me."

"Why would you think that?"

"Uh..."

"Because you always think the worst of me," he grumbled.

"You don't really make yourself clear. A simple 'run, my brother wants to kill you' would have worked. Or, 'here I come to save the day' would have let me know your intentions when you grabbed me."

He smirked.

I leaned back farther on the bench. He settled back, as well. Silence hung between us as we both processed the information.

My mind flitted over a thousand thoughts but came back to rest on the last images Lord Akton had shown me.

"Why did he show me Serena?"

"She was the love of his life. They were supposed to marry, but she became ill, confused. I suppose he knew he was dying, and his thoughts went to her."

"She looked so young," I said, puzzled.

He nodded. "Serena struggled with some mental health issues. She wandered off during one of the worst snowstorms in Montenai history. It snowed for three days. Akton never rested. A search party set out but couldn't find her. On that third day, Akton ran into her *spirit* in the Ballatian woods."

"Mother of Montenai." I couldn't imagine finding my loved one's lost spirit in the wilderness. How had he coped knowing she hadn't crossed over to Laith, our place after death?

The big dragon lord squirmed next to me. I heard him swallow. "It almost destroyed Akton, but he redirected his energies into making Shadowland what it is today."

I followed his gaze. The top of the Wishing Tree was gone. The Trunk stood mangled and charred. It hurt to see this powerful symbol of Shadowland completely devastated.

With sharp eyes, he studied me.

It hit me then. *How did I make it out of there alive?*

Lord Bulosk grabbed the locket.

I held my breath. *His scale.* I touched his hand as it grasped the locket. "It's your power that saved me?" I asked.

He stared at my eyes, my lips.

"No. It's your power," he said in his deep voice.

"I don't understand."

Our faces had drawn so close as he clutched the necklace. I studied his features without reservation. The blue scaling only made him look more exotic, particularly against his green eyes and dark skin. The iridescent scales decreased in size as they descended his face and reflected light when the sun hit them. The subtle design of scales hinted of the otherworldly dragon within, a trait both dangerous and alluring.

"Why'd you keep my scale?" he whispered.

My heart raced as I stared into his eyes. He stole a kiss before I registered what was happening. I kissed back as warmth crashed into my chest and spread in a wave to all my extremities. He cupped my face as he delivered soft, tender kisses, followed by a deeper one that curled my toes.

When he broke away, he reclaimed my hand. I looked into his eyes, surprised I wasn't nervous around him.

"Sorry about that," he said as he raked his left hand through his hair. *He* looked nervous.

"I'm not. You're a good kisser."

He chuckled. I snorted, which made him chuckle again. It was so inappropriate considering the depressing circumstances, but we both struggled for a few moments to regain our composure. I knew it was stress. We were both worn out and devastated.

My nerves returned, and I searched for something reassuring to say. "I think the Shadow Fever patients will be okay."

"Thanks to you," he said. "Not all shadowcasters can accept so much of the sun's direct radiation on earth's plane. They would wind up like Akton. Don't you think they have tried in the past?" His eyes watered. "You've always been special, Bianca. You have the power to process radiation, heal, and walk through fire unharmed."

That was a lot to digest.

"You possess some of the powers my brothers and I have." His smile dropped when he realized what he'd said. "*Brother* has."

I felt his desperation as he looked again at the destruction. The unmerciful rays exposed in detail the tortured wood of his destroyed home.

"Too many secrets. We thought it was the only way with the power the Torensphere created." He frowned. "Suddenly, Akton couldn't seem to control or balance that power. A fact none of us wanted to admit."

The Torensphere sounded like an entity that could be quite dangerous. "I suppose I understand why you had to keep so much secret," I said.

His head jerked away, and all the muscles in his body grew taut. "I understand why you hid Ben away from us."

My stomach dropped. A man stood at the water's edge. Not really a man, though. His blond hair had grown to his shoulders, and his eyes were a shade of green not of earth but Montenai. His hair moved on its own, just like a nymph's. The tips of his ears were slightly pointed. My breath caught. So many emotions swirled in my stomach:

regret, sorrow, relief, fear.

Lord Bulosk leapt to the river's edge and waited, hands clenched in fists at his side. I rose and stood next to him.

Ben crouched low before casting a reflection on the surface. The graphic image showed Lord Akton, his face contorted with rage, the kirka fields behind him ablaze while young nymphs fled, their eyes wide in terror.

Bulosk instinctively took a protective step back from his dead brother's reflection. Waves of heat emanated from him and warmed my chilled skin. Before he could turn from the hurtful image, a vine shot up through the snow, locked around his ankle, and anchored him in place. Without thinking, I reached a hand out to touch his shoulder, I suppose to steady him or offer comfort. The fierce dragon lord did nothing.

As quickly as the vine had grown, it withered and disintegrated. After the reflection dissipated, Ben rose to his full height and glared at us.

It had been several weeks since my family met in the cabin in the Hinterlands, and I'd first glimpsed the physical changes in Ben. No one had mentioned his new *skills* caused by Magda's nymph essence.

"I didn't know he could do that," I said. Mouth open, I continued to stare, dumbfounded. *Things just got more complicated.*

Ben gave us his back, a sure sign he didn't fear the dragon lord. We watched him bound up the icy bank and disappear into the enchanted tall reeds.

Lord Bulosk returned to the bench.

I remained in place, afraid to approach. *Would he unleash his rage on me as Lord Akton had?*

He shot me the saddest look I'd ever seen on someone's face. "I will never hurt you."

Wiping a tear away, I joined him on the bench. When my hand claimed his, he squeezed it hard.

"He's really not pleased with me," he said.

"He most likely thinks you're the root of all his and Anka's problems." Shaking my head, I tried to suppress my fury. Ben knew nothing about Montenai, Shadowland, or our struggles. I understood his frustration, but his outburst was immature and dangerous. Lord Bulosk could have killed him. I suppose he felt invincible after surviving the war and the trip through the portal.

"Once Leasith and I have re-stabilized Shadowland, I'll try to address your sister and Patrick Benjamin Solomon." His voice sounded weary. "Right now, we need to focus on harnessing enough power to keep all darklings healthy. We may need your help."

My shoulders relaxed as I realized he had no plans to harm them or punish them further for their behavior.

Jaw tight, he continued to stare at the glass structures across the way. The bright morning sun was as unforgiving as Ben had been in showcasing the wounded village.

"I'm sorry about your brother." My voice wavered. I couldn't imagine what I would do if I ever lost Anka. Ben's display made me worry about our relationship, but for the time, at least I knew she was safe.

Bulosk didn't meet my gaze. His nostrils flared as he tried to squelch the pain that arose. Bitter tears streamed down his face.

"He went crazy trying to wield all the power. He felt something coming and thought it was your family's rebellion. But it was the Torensphere's disappearance his visions had foretold."

All this time, I'd worried about darklings' wellbeing but never gave a thought to what these changes meant for the dragon lords.

"What happens to you without the Torensphere?" I whispered.

He shrugged. "Don't know. Never lived without it."

I didn't like the sound of that. "We'll find the thief," I said. A fire surged inside my chest as Bulosk placed his hand on my knee.

"Leasith is already in pursuit."

Reality hit. He had chosen to protect me yesterday instead of helping Leasith contain Akton. Now, he had stayed back to protect Shadowland while Leasith hunted the culprit. I prayed darklings would turn to him for leadership, not blame him for the tragedy.

"What do you want me to do?" I asked.

He leaned in and touched my cheek with the back of his hand.
"Stay close."

SHADOW
THIEF

The Darkling Chronicles #3

TRICIA ZOELLER

PROLOGUE

I AM A creature of fire, directing my own concert of shadow and light to cloak myself from the dangers in the world. My concealment has been effective—I don't even know who or what I am. The sea cliffs of Montenai have always been my home, the Aglatian Sea my private pool, and the phantoms my family.

Only one satyr and nymph have detected a whisper of my presence in the Faunlier Mountains. When I was a tiny hatchling, Cornelius Jeremiah of the Fardoragh herd, and Magda, the nymph mother of the kirka, heard my cries. Despite three protective phantoms hounding them, they braved the haunted woods each week to leave supplies for a baby they only believed existed but could not see. What if they had seen me—a fair-skinned Montenaian with wings, scales, and claws?

They tried to break through the phantom shield again when they heard the cries of another baby, my sister, Nalene. Apparently, my cloaking concealed her, too. My early years in Montenai were a blur until she appeared, bringing life into clear focus.

It was a starry night when the phantoms led me through fresh fallen snow to an abandoned baby at the river's edge. From my phantom Serena's stories, I guessed I was three years old when I wrapped my arms around the tiny, helpless creature. In an instant, I knew love. My fire surged to the surface, helping warm the baby, to restore color to her blue cheeks and steady breaths to her little body.

For my sister, Nalene, breathing had not been automatic but a rigorous fight.

From that night on, we have always been each other's balance. We have lived an isolated but safe existence in the sea cliffs. To her, I'm Natcha—sister and mother. To the satyr and nymph, I'm a mysterious secret. To the darklings, I've been *nothing* for over twenty-three years.

Until today.

Now, I'm the thief.

CHAPTER ONE

LORD AKTON WAS the tallest of the dragon lords—and the palest. His lighter skin caused the sprinkling of red scales to stand out more on his face. They lined his hairline, touched the scarring by his missing eye, and trailed off his cheek like a path of tears. Although I didn't think this dragon lord ever cried, I imagined he had made many weep.

His reputation of "seeing" with his one golden eye motivated me to take caution when spying in Shadowland. I usually avoided the Wishing Tree. Tonight, I braved the closeness due to my fascination with the Salvas. Nalene and I spied on their family shamelessly because the son, Zack, was my sister's age.

His father, Alexander Salva, had been the head chef for the dragon lords until recently when he lost his job in the Wishing Tree. Zack's mother, Marta, was the cordwainer for a new shop in the South Village called Good for the Sole. While she worked long hours making shoes, her husband drank...and drank. Most nights he found his way home to the apartment above their shop.

We often shadowed Zack. He never knew because my cloaking hid us from sight. We were drawn to him because he seemed so alone. It was difficult to watch him deal with his father, who once was responsible and loving, but now known as the town drunk.

Hidden from everyone, we saw things, heard things. Nalene didn't always comprehend, but I did. I had seen the fear in the dragon lords' eyes. All three dragon lords, Akton, Leasith, and Bulosk, had been watching Mr. Salva. I'm only twelve, but I recognize when a creature feels threatened. Tonight, I was so scared for Mr. Salva, fear roared inside my head. It made focusing on my cloaking difficult. Still, I drew from the shadows and shaped the light to cover my presence.

I'd left my little sister in the care of my phantom, Serena. Maybe not the best sitter for your fledgling but not the worst. If she needed me, Nalene could always communicate in my head.

I wasn't worried for my sister tonight but for the grown darkling who stood in the shadows of the Wishing Tree all alone with the leader of the darklings. Not even the usual door attendant was present at the entrance of the Wishing Tree, the grand sequoia where the lords lived.

Cicada played their music at full volume in the clear summer night while colonies of bats squeaked from the top of the tree. My excellent hearing allowed me to catch every word of the unfolding conversation.

"Alexander. Thanks for coming."

"Yesss, m' Lord." Mr. Salva slurred and swayed in place. A dress shirt hung from him, wrinkled and soiled, the collar half up/half down.

Akton's golden eye glowed softly in the dark. I studied the scarring on the right side of his face, marks made by his father's clawed hand. It caused me to shiver even in Montenai's summer heat.

"You don't look well, my friend. I think we should talk about what unsettles you."

"Lies. You spit filth n' lies."

The dragon leader relaxed against the trunk of the Wishing Tree and waited, one long leg bent at the knee. The lords wore fitted shirts underneath their finely tailored suits. His casual stance looked awkward with such fancy clothes.

I held my breath. *Please don't, Mr. Salva. Please don't.*

"You, you mean to shhhhame my family. Tellin' all-a-Shadahlan' l'us f-fired. Come unhinged."

Lord Akton folded his arms across his chest.

"I quit. Anyaknow sssomethin'...I'm not soooree. I know somethin's not right with you or this tree."

"Alexander. I'm going to ask you one last time. What is it you think you heard from the tree?"

He shook his head. "Doesn'matter. Doesn'matter." With a wave of his hand, he turned toward the boardwalk, dismissing the lord.

"Why don't you go home, Alexander. Skip the pub tonight."

Grumbling, the darkling wavered his way down the path. Lord Akton watched for a moment before entering the doorway beneath a golden shield that showed a dragon looking down at its shadow.

Everything felt off. For some sick reason, I followed the drunk darkling and waited patiently outside the pub for him. I knew Zack would come looking for his father, as he had done almost every night this week.

While I waited, I daydreamed about living in Shadowland as one of *them*. I would definitely live in the North Village, close to the portal to earth and in the shade of the Sequoia Forest. I'd drink coffee every morning at Mr. Rehmling's shop, Chocolate Syncope. The thought of chocolate-covered strawberries had me drooling. I don't know how long I sat on that bench along the boardwalk. Maybe an hour. When Mr. Salva stumbled out of III Brothers' Pub mumbling to himself about demons, I forgot about desserts and nice things.

Demons?

He carried a large satchel over his shoulder and turned his head from side to side as he walked. I tiptoed behind him, passed the Wishing Tree to the river's edge, just at the mouth of the *haunted* Ballatian Woods.

So not the right direction for making it home. I didn't like the wild look in his eye or the fact he'd chosen the river's edge as his place to sober up.

I kept looking through the trees, hoping someone would come collect him.

"Dad?"

The sound of Zack's voice off in the distance brought me both relief and dread. I retraced my steps along the path of South Village to find him walking along the wooden boardwalk beside the Montenai River. Wearing shirt, shorts, and soft leather moccasins, he didn't move like most nine-year-olds. His stance reminded me of an adult, his pace serious. He was the parent trying to find the wandering child.

Most nights, I let him figure things out on his own. Tonight, I broke twigs and rustled leaves up ahead to draw him on the correct course toward his confused father.

"Dad?" Zack yelled as he pushed aside the overgrown branches of mountain laurel. He never hesitated as he stepped onto the pitch-black path of the Ballatian Woods. He didn't draw the attention of the phantoms who guarded the woods like a dragon does its treasure. They usually nipped at a creature, freezing its will, until it turned from the borders of their home. But even my phantoms understood the troubled situation between the father and son.

My breath caught when we reached the river. Alexander Salva was not where I'd left him. The frogs croaked so loudly, I couldn't hear myself think. *Where did he go?* His satchel lay crumpled on the bank.

Panic twisted the features of Zack's face as he scanned the water. "Dad?" He paced the small opening between the trees. "Dad!" His voice cracked, and tears streamed down his cheeks. "What have you done?" he asked the river.

My vision is better than my hearing. I spotted movement twenty yards out and spread my wings. Mr. Salva's eyes widened at my approach, the whites showing under the starlight. He could *see* me. Soaking wet, he trembled on a wide boulder. Sand and grit clung to his black beard.

"Demon," he hissed.

"What?"

"You look like a fledgling. I guess that's the sick way of the *dark*. It tries to confuse me with a young face." He had been holding something down at his side but drew the object up in front of him. The heavy, steel longsword shook in Mr. Salva's hand.

My cloaking was still on. I knew by the soft whisper it made in my ears. Why could Mr. Salva suddenly *see* me? I stood still. Nalene had told me my shimmering wings were pretty, not symbols of evil. Why did he think I was a demon? My heart raced in my chest. I didn't know what to do with an *armed*, drunk darkling who was apparently scared of me.

"I'm just a hatchling. You look like you need help." My eyes darted back and forth from him to the immense sword with beautiful etchings of stars running up and down its blade. Where did he get it? I didn't remember him carrying anything when he spoke to Lord Akton. *He had the satchel when he left the pub.*

"I don't need your kind of help! The tree told me what I needed to do. I've lost everything because of this sword, and I will not let you or the demons within this vessel destroy my family or Shadowland."

The Wishing Tree talked to him? Why hadn't he confided in the lords? "What did the tree say?" My voice trembled.

Maneuvering the sword's tip much closer to my face, he tilted his head.

I put my hands up. "Mr. Salva, could you please lower that away from me. I like my face the way it is."

His jaw dropped. "A demon who knows my name? I'm more cursed than I ever imagined."

He lowered the sword for a moment, allowing me to see the wings that comprised the branched handguard. With his shoulders sagging, he looked down. His soaked shirt clung to him and was bunched up and twisted around his middle. Blood dripped from his wrist to the rock.

Face pale, he brought his attention back to me. "You're a beautiful demon-child, but your eyes give you away."

When I'm sad, nervous, or frightened, my fire surfaces, causing my pupils to change and eyes to glow in a nondarkling way. I tried to think of nothing but the cool Aglatian Sea. It usually brought my "dragon" down, and restored my eyes to their normal blue.

Apparently, this didn't change Mr. Salva's opinion of me. He drew the sword over his head with both hands.

"Dad?"

With the sharp sword glinting over me in the moonlight, I'd forgotten about Zack on the bank. There was no way Zack could see his father this far out in the river, but he could have heard snatches of the heated exchange, especially the loud shouts of "demon."

At the sound of his son's voice, Mr. Salva clenched his jaw tight and spun away from me, toward the opposite bank. He moved to throw the sword into the dark water beyond, but he went with it. Ten seconds went by before he surfaced. His blood-curdling screams startled birds from nearby trees. My sister's shrieks in my head accompanied his cries.

"Natcha! Natcha!"

"I'll be there in a minute, Leeni."

"I'm scared."

"You'll be fine with Serena," I said.

I blocked her out as I launched myself toward Mr. Salva. I found him clinging to another rock, his lower body submerged in the river. Coming to land above him on the rock's sharp tip, I looked down into his face. When I saw the blood coating the rock by him, my head felt fuzzy. My eyes snapped to his bleeding right wrist where his hand used to be.

CHAPTER TWO

HE'D GOTTEN RID of the sword, but at what cost?

"Adah, help us." I exhaled through my mouth. "Mr. Salva, what happened?"

"Demon!" he shouted.

"Dad!" Zack replied from the bank.

"Mr. Salva—"

"What have I done to die like this, claimed by the dark?" He trembled all over, his large, brown eyes filled with so many emotions.

"I'm going to help you up," I said, determined.

"Don't touch me. I won't go with you, Demon."

Why did he think I was some demon claiming him? My head swam, and I closed my eyes to keep my heat from taking over. "It's not your time to die." What did I know about anything; I was but a twelve-year-old hermit? My presence was making things worse. If he didn't get help soon, he'd bleed to death.

"Dad, I'm going to get help!" Zack shouted. He stood waist-deep in the river.

I could sense his conflict. He didn't want to lose the sound of his father's voice forever, but he knew he couldn't fight this current, especially in the night.

"Don't move. Hold on. Do you hear me?" he yelled.

"The demon is here, son. I need you to run to your mother."

"I'll be right back. Don't you dare move!" He sobbed out each word.

Zack was hysterical, and I couldn't blame him. He scrambled onto the bank and disappeared into the trees, leaving just his dad and me. His missing hand caused my head to swim. I looked away for a second and tried to get it together.

I was giving myself a pep talk in my head when the first glimmers of something pulsed from below.

Mr. Salva looked to me with first fear then acceptance.

"What is it?" I asked, my voice cracking.

"You don't know?"

The white-blue light shone from the depths of the river, almost blinding me. It was beautiful in a horrifying way. When I looked again at Mr. Salva, he was studying me.

"You really don't know," he stated.

"No, sir. My name is Natcha. I'm twelve years old. I live with my sister by the sea. I'm not a demon, but whatever is beneath us may well be."

His eyes grew wider.

"What is it?" I asked. "Did something touch you?"

"The astrei sword. It holds the demons." His chin quivered. "Do you hear them?"

I could barely swallow as my heartbeat filled my ears. I waited. Yes. I heard something—a strange language streaming up from the white-blue light below. As I stooped over Mr. Salva, the air around me chilled. I watched as his lips turned blue, and frost coated his beard.

He cried out and attempted to pull himself up but couldn't manage it with the weight of his soggy clothes and his missing hand.

Two steps took me to his level. I grabbed him under the armpits and pulled with all my might to get him out of the water where the glowing force had ballooned. The river bubbled around us as voices rose in a chant.

My mind tried to place the sound, but I couldn't. Sirens or naunies were known to live in the southeastern portion of Montenai, deep in the Aglatian Sea. Rarely did they show themselves, but when they did, a creepy singing accompanied them. The singing below us wasn't like any singing in Montenai. All the hair on my body stood on end.

Mr. Salva managed to kneel on the rock.

"I need you to trust me. I'm going to get us away from here," I insisted.

Before I knew it, he was standing, his face just above mine. His forehead wrinkled. "You're just a wee fledgling."

"Yes," I said as I slowly drew my sash from around my waist and wound it around the bleeding stump. I worked fast since I didn't know how long he would tolerate me touching him.

"I'm so cold." His teeth chattered.

This confused me. If anything, being close to me should have made him hot. "It will be okay." As I tightened the makeshift bandage, I felt a chill seep into the rock at our feet. I've felt cold before—I lived with three phantoms—but this was more than a change in temperature. This was some force or presence.

"You're not with them," he stated.

It's horrifying to see an adult so spooked.

"I told you. I don't know what that sword is. I live with my little sister by the sea."

He nodded. I'd finally convinced him I was not a demon from the sword. "You need to leave. They mean to claim me, child."

With my pearly claws protracted, I snagged the sleeve of his wet shirt. "Your son needs you. We'll get out of here."

Although my eyes had alarmed him, the show of my claws apparently did not.

"Dad?" Zack's voice called through the woods.

"Alexander?" Mrs. Salva's worried voice carried across the water.

The chanting below increased and vibrated through the rock. I clenched my teeth as the fierce power of the light gripped my ankles so I couldn't move.

"What is this?" I gasped.

He shook his head. "Whatever it is…it doesn't like that I tried to end it."

I thought about that and the fact *it* had already taken his hand.

One minute he was there, the next, the force sucked him off the rock and into the river. I tried to move, but the voices, the spirits, had my feet rooted in place. "Mr. Salva!"

Oh Adah! Completely helpless, I stared into the water, scanning from one area to the next.

"Mr. Salva!" I choked.

The water churned, spiraling around the rock. On the bank, I saw Zack and his mother staring into the river. *Can they see me?*

"What is that?" Zack asked.

Mrs. Salva screamed before gathering her son in her arms and dropping to the ground. I thought my heart would stop. *I can't move.* My legs prickled. Mr. Salva's icy demons held me hostage on the rock.

Water swirled into the air, blocking my view of the bank. Calling my fire released my fixed feet. I attempted to fly straight up, but a power slung me to the side. I bounced off the river's surface several times like a skipping rock, coming to land farther down the bank. Crumpled against an old oak's trunk, I attempted to draw breaths despite the pain radiating through my whole body. My mouth was open, but I couldn't scream, cry, or breathe.

The ground shook next to me, and I startled as something landed with a sickening, wet thud.

Tears burned my cheeks. "No. Oh no." I blinked several times, but the view didn't change. "Mr. Salva?" I squeaked. *This can't be happening. It isn't real.*

Eyes fixed open, Mr. Salva lay flat on his back.

I scrambled away, my claws digging into muck and grime, because the sword pierced through his chest still shone with a blinding light. It pulsed three times before it went out. The chanting voices quieted. Darkness returned to the woods.

I couldn't take my eyes off the dead darkling or the sword. No matter how hard I tried to shake myself free of my fear, I couldn't breathe or move or do anything. I simply trembled all over as the stupid frogs continued their croaking like nothing had happened.

"Alexander?" called a female voice.

"Dad?"

Oh, don't come this way. Sobbing, I tried to understand what had happened. What and why had something claimed him? My cloaking buzzed around me as I backed away, my feet stumbling over tree roots.

Get the sword, Natcha. Get...the...sword. My mind told me one thing, but my body just wouldn't listen. I didn't want his son or wife to touch it. Mr. Salva had died trying to get it away from them.

"Dad?" Zack called.

I kept looking at his face, waiting, still, for some sign of movement.

"Natcha?" My sister called to me in my head. The sound of her little voice woke me up.

"It's okay, Nalene," I answered.

With my hand over my mouth, I muffled my sobs and backed away farther to make sure I was out of view. Who would take care of Nalene if the sword claimed me as it had Mr. Salva?

My body shook as I tried to make sense of everything. As I thought of my little sister, I simply could not get myself to go back toward the weapon.

The Salvas' lantern light bobbed through the trees, creating haunting shadows in the canopy. Nymph lights swarmed past the Salvas. The pesky swarm of enchanted mini-lights surged forward and circled above Mr. Salva's head, revealing his condition to his family. The lights dimmed to an eerie purple-black.

The lantern crashed to the ground, and Mrs. Salva fell to her knees. "Alexander."

She flailed her arms to grab Zack, but he darted past her, stopping just in front of his father. His shoulders shook as he wept.

"No, Dad. Nooo."

"Zachary, don't go any closer," his mother hissed.

My chest tightened. It felt like my heart would break. *How did this happen?*

When Zack turned his head, I could see the devastation in his eyes.

"I need to get the dragon lords," she said, her voice trembling. "Stay away from the sword."

He turned fully to face his mother, fists clenched at his sides. "You will not get *them*."

What did he mean to do?

With one quick movement, he grasped the hilt of the sword in both hands and withdrew the long blade from his father's chest. I expected a gush of blood and gore, but instead, the wound closed to a long, dark line that looked like a bad scratch. No voices came from the sword.

Mrs. Salva rushed forward, but Zack stepped to the side. "Careful," he said, his eyes wide. The blade had to be heavy for a fledgling, but he held it off the ground.

Her bottom lip trembled. "Zachary, please. I don't want anything to happen to you."

"Get his belt and scabbard," he said, his voice stern and calm.

She glanced at her husband then at her son.

"Please," he added.

Grief strained the corners of her eyes and mouth. She turned back to squat next to her husband and do just as her nine-year-old asked. Her shoulders shaking, she sniffed and cried as she undid the belt buckle. Her face distorted with emotions, Mrs. Salva extended the belt with scabbard to her son.

"Maybe just lay it on the ground," he suggested.

She did, taking care to touch only the edges of the belt leather, not the long scabbard. Zack sheathed the sword. They both breathed huge sighs of relief once the sword was secure, but didn't have much time to relax before a dragon lord bellowed from the river's edge.

"That sounds like Lord Akton," she said, her face tight.

The lords were approaching. I stayed hidden in the brush, because, if I appeared now, I'd spook them even more. My cloaking buzzed, but I didn't trust it. I didn't trust anything just now.

Zack shook his head. "They can't find this. They can't find us." He wrapped the heavy belt around his waist and attempted to notch it tight, but it fell over his narrow hips and behind. With trembling hands, he looped the belt over one shoulder, barely keeping the sword from dragging on the ground.

"I think you're right." She bobbed her head. "They aren't meant to have it."

The first tendrils of fog began to curl through the trunks of the trees. *Serena and the phantoms.* The lords must have crossed the boundaries into the Ballatian Woods. Their presence tripped some wire in the phantoms' heads.

Three ribbons of gray fog curled around Mrs. Salva with black hissing trailers following behind.

"Father of Montenai," Mrs. Salva whispered.

They lingered briefly around the terrified darkling female before hurtling through the old oaks to find the dragon lords.

"Phantoms?" she whispered, dumbfounded.

Zack nodded. "Yeah. They've never bothered me. But they really give the lords a hard time."

Mrs. Salva looked at her husband. "I can't leave him here." Her trembling hands reached out to touch his cold cheek. Her brow creased as she found my blue sash around his stump. "What happened to you, Alexander?"

Zack's mouth dropped open. "His hand," he squeaked.

Mrs. Salva leaned in to examine the wrapping more closely. Then she did the most peculiar thing—she peeled the blue sash from around his wound. This area had not healed as his chest had. She shoved the bloody fabric into her skirt pocket. "I don't want them to find him like this," she pleaded with her son. "They think he's just a crazy drunk."

Zack bit his lip. I could see the disappointment on his face.

Mrs. Salva straightened. "Well, we know better. He was protecting us all from something."

Zack's face scrunched up as he cried and nodded in agreement.

With a big sigh, Mrs. Salva broke herself free of her dead husband. "Let's go." Hand in hand, they headed east to avoid the lords and phantoms.

Natcha?

"Stay there. I'm coming." I needed to get back to my little sister. She was alone since Serena was now battling dragon lords. Leeni's voice sounded weak and scared. Sometimes she heard my thoughts. Did she

know something horrible had happened?

Before I left the area, I reached down to touch Mr. Salva's wet hair streaked through with ice crystals. "I'm sorry," I sobbed. My head and chest hurt. I chewed the inside of my cheek as guilt tore me up inside. Why hadn't I taken the sword? *Because you're a coward, Natcha.*

I couldn't look at Mr. Salva any longer, but I swore an oath that I would look after his son, somehow.

Even as I cleared the trees, I felt his dead eyes boring into my back, my wings. He was the first darkling to have ever seen me, and now he was dead.

As I FLEW over the water, all the colors of the sea creatures and plants blinked to life as they did every night. I couldn't catch my breath because Mr. Salva's panicked eyes would not leave my mind.

Our cave sits in the middle of a sea cliff. When I landed on the narrow ledge that jutted over the water, I expected to find Leeni. Her absence snapped me out of my shock. A rocky tunnel leads into the main area of the cave where purple-blue stalactites hang like fancy light fixtures. On a table in our kitchen area, a compact satyr player blasted music—some light, silly song about nymphs with flowers in their hair. My eyes traveled to the corner where our cots were. She sat with her back to me, knees drawn up to her chest.

"Leeni? What are you doing?"

She rocked to and fro.

"I'm sorry I was gone so long. Something terrible happened to the sad darkling and his family." She had been with me several times when I'd followed Zack. She'd named him 'the sad darkling.'

As she continued to rock, my stomach dropped.

"What is it? Don't be mad. I came as soon as I could."

Then I heard the wheezing. From the time I found her as a baby, Nalene had trouble with her body temperature. It had always alarmed me how quickly it would drop, resulting in bluish lips and labored breathing. My heat had helped the blue baby recover from these episodes.

I sat on the bed and hugged her from behind. "I'm so sorry."

When she turned her face to me, I saw blue lips, a white cast to her skin, and a patch of blisters by her left eye.

"What happened?" I put my hand to the sore patch and tried to soothe.

"I-I w-was ssso c-cold."

CHAPTER THREE

WITH HER COOL hand in my warm one, Nalene rested her white-blond head on my shoulder. We sat next to each other high up on a sequoia tree branch, looking down on six darklings: the three dragon lords, Mrs. Salva, Zack, and Alexander Salva. As was the darkling tradition, only the immediate family and the Council were present for the ceremony called Dragon's Last Breath.

We'd both become attached to the darkling, Zack. We felt we should be present when he said goodbye to his father. Leeni's patch of blisters had taken four days to heal. The sheen of her skin remained different in this area, the texture callused. Her breathing sounded normal, but I still didn't want her with me to witness this. She had insisted.

The night Mr. Salva died Nalene had felt something—the cold, the forces, the voices. I hadn't told her about the sword. I just told her Mr. Salva had drowned in the river. Her connection to him that night, and the cold that overtook him, had me spooked beyond anything else in the world.

It was common for mourners to come together for a celebration of life, complete with prayers and stories during the day. At night, the Dragon's Last Breath occurred when the blue and red stars representing Adah, the Mother of Montenai, and Akton, the Father of Montenai, were present for the passage of the darkling's soul to Laith.

I'd read about darkling traditions in books but never witnessed the ceremony. It took constant thought of the Aglatian Sea to keep my fires down. I didn't like being this close to the lords, and looking at the Salvas caused my stomach to churn. Not knowing what to expect, I was prepared to cover Nalene's ears, nose, and eyes if the process became gruesome or scary.

She trembled next to me as we studied the body laid out on a concrete altar. A thin layer of vines, roots, and fragrant flowers served as a decorative cushion or resting place.

"You don't have to watch," I said inside her head.

She looked up at me with her stubborn, hazel eyes. *"I want to."*

I didn't notice much about the lords other than their black suits. Both Nalene and I kept staring at Mr. Salva's lifeless body with the missing hand.

"I wish you wouldn't watch this," I pleaded with her.

She only squeezed my hand tighter.

The Salvas stood facing us at the head of the altar. Lord Akton directed them to back away at least fifteen feet. We could make out their expressions in the dragon lantern light. Zack's eyes stayed glued to the ground as he pressed his lips into a thin line. I couldn't look at him without thinking of the sword—a thought I guarded with all my might from my baby sister. Mrs. Salva waited, her simple navy blue dress wrinkling at the waist where Zack clutched her.

Lord Akton cleared his throat. "Marta?"

Eyes shining under the dragon lantern light, she stepped forward, taking her son with her by grasping his hand. She prayed. "To the Mother and the Father, I relent. To the stars above, I pray thee, take Alexander Salva into your light. Honor him and keep him, until we see him again in Laith. Ever in your mercy, we pray you grant him access to the peace he deserves in your presence."

"Akton's grace," answered all.

I whispered it. We didn't mean *Lord* Akton, but the Father of Montenai, the grand red dragon, Akton, who had burst through a portal from Fallon carrying the Mother, Adah, with him. The story says she carried a mystical dragon egg, now called the Torensphere, which not only played a part in the creation of the dragon lords but today gave them power, energy, and good health.

No one mentioned a sword. My head hurt. Alexander Salva had called the weapon an astrei sword. The only astrei to ever exist on Montenai was Adah, the Mother, but she died, and so did the dragon.

My attention snapped back to Zachary when he finally brought his eyes up to study his father. His face pinched, he struggled not to cry. Despite his best efforts, tears came. He swatted them away quickly. Mrs. Salva swung her arm around his shoulders.

Lord Akton's golden eye glowed as he inhaled. The other two lords joined him. Lord Leasith's eyes lit up blue, and Lord Bulosk's green as they blew fire in a continuous stream at the bit of kindling beneath the body. It ignited, sending orange-blue flame to lick over Mr. Salva's body. The scent of sandalwood, jasmine, and smoke filled our noses as the hot fire consumed him, leaving only the multi-colored flame to crackle from the concrete slab.

Nalene had given in and hidden her face in my shoulder, but I watched as the fierce dragon fire turned everything to ash in just a few minutes. I couldn't breathe fire. The sight mesmerized me. Mrs. Salva's mouth hung open, her brow furrowed. Her husband's body was gone. She held her stomach as if in shock.

It had been too quick.

The blue scales on the side of Lord Bulosk's face shimmered under the yellow moonlight as he stepped forward to present a special blown-glass vessel—the container for Mr. Salva's ashes. No two tombs were alike in the cemetery called Adah's Gateway. The gold handle and plaque at the top were engraved with his name and a symbol of the Wishing Tree. All nonshadowcasters had the Wishing Tree on their placards. Shadowcasters' nameplates contained the royal shield with the dragon Akton looking down on his shadow.

The youngest dragon lord presented the artwork to Mrs. Salva. She seemed so small as he stood towering over her. "Marta. You may stay. In which case, please have a seat and rest. We can give you some water to drink as you wait. Or, you may go and entrust us with Alexander's ashes." He pointed to a tree just ten feet behind him. "His lantern will go there."

"Thank you. It's beautiful," she said, touching the lantern. "We'd like to stay."

Lord Bulosk nodded and stepped aside, allowing the mother and son to find a bench upon which to rest.

Nalene startled me as she wiped tears from my cheeks. Her eyes were wet, too. Neither of us had a father or a mother. It hurt to look at Zack.

"I'm glad he has his mom," she said.

"Me, too."

As the embers died down, Lord Bulosk gave both mother and son some water. Lord Leasith, with the copper scales, stepped forward. Using his bare hands, he scooped the still smoking ash into the top of the lantern. Once it was inside, he pulled the gold handle down, clicking it in place. The lantern glowed so many wondrous colors, and would indefinitely, like the rest of the darkling tombs hanging in the branches of the sequoias. A warm breeze stirred through the cemetery, setting the colored lights to dance in the wind.

When Lord Akton's golden eye traveled up toward our tree, I held my breath.

"Does he know we're here?" Nalene asked.

"I don't know." I concentrated all my will on drawing in the darkness to keep us cloaked. When Lord Akton's gaze finally returned to the Salvas, I breathed again. We should have left then, but we waited.

Once the hanging tomb was in place, Zack and his mother walked slowly away, leaving the dragon lord brothers behind. They blew the altar clean.

It seemed like such a lowly task for the ruling brothers to do, and yet, they seemed to do it with pride.

Lord Akton looked again into the branches. Leeni squeezed my hand.

"What is it, brother?" Leasith asked.

"Drakos haunts us."

The middle lord's eyes widened. "Akton, don't be ridiculous."

"Don't you feel him drawing in the shadows?"

Lord Bulosk's brow wrinkled. He stepped in to touch his brother's arm. "Akton, he's gone. No longer here to torment."

My heart beat right by my eyes. Nalene's nails dug into my skin.

"You don't feel the cloaking?" he asked.

"It's late, Akton. Time to leave," Bulosk answered.

"I'm not convinced he isn't to blame for this," growled Akton.

Leasith got right in his brother's space. He was shorter, more heavily muscled, and the militant one of the three. "How many must die before you acknowledge the danger we harbor?"

Bulosk pulled him back by the arm. "This is neither the time, nor the place."

"Really? Because I think it's the perfect time. Alexander Salva is no more. He left behind a wife and son. We all know *it* has talked to others before," shouted Leasith.

Akton's golden eye glowed, and his hands balled into fists. "Don't go there, Leasith."

"The Torensphere spoke to the little Rehmling child that day in the Rotunda. He didn't hurt her, but he communicated with her. We know he spoke with Alexander. It disturbed him enough that he came unraveled," Leasith said.

"Let's not talk of this tonight," insisted Bulosk. "We really don't know anything for certain."

"Really, Bulosk? What exactly happened to Mr. Salva's hand?"

Akton scanned the tops of the trees once more. "I wish I could *see* like I used to." He took several steps in our direction. "We should leave now."

His brothers looked around at the lights, as well.

When Akton stormed away, the brothers followed.

Even after they had disappeared through the wrought iron gate of the cemetery, I didn't move.

"Natcha?"

"We should go," I said.

She nodded once before disappearing through the water molecules in the air. I spread my wings and flew through the cemetery with darkling tombs twinkling around me.

Drakos was the first dragon lord born of a darkling named Toren.

The dragon egg, or Torensphere, had changed him in the darkling's belly. He had been the first darkling altered by the egg—he came into this world with scales. The moody dragon lord had fathered Akton, Leasith, and Bulosk. Apparently, he also knew how to cloak himself.

So many questions raced through my mind, I wished I had an adult to ask. Instead, I had the sometimes with-it phantom. Like always, Nalene and I would have to make sense of this on our own.

I tried not to think of death, but when it is in front of you, it just fills your head. What would happen to Nalene if I died?

As I cried in my cot that night, I tried to question Serena, the only phantom who could speak. She just sang to me in her haunting way as she always did when I was upset. I felt selfish, but I thought of my own death. I wanted a blown-glass tomb made especially for me, and I wanted to be in the trees with loved ones around me. Instead, I feared I would leave this world how I came into it...alone.

CHAPTER FOUR

THE COOL AIR blew my long skirt off my legs. I watched the trees move with the wind as friends and relatives sang "Happy Birthday" to Zack. They celebrated his birthday on the balcony off the back of the Salva apartment. In another month or so, the air would turn cold, but tonight, the weather was perfect, the leaves just starting to turn different colors.

To his left stood the Rehmling sisters, Bianca and Anka. The Rehmlings were shadowcasters on earth's plane. They cast shadows for their human charge, protecting the human from excess UV radiation and harnessing energy to bring back to Shadowland. They were both so young, but strong. I felt jealous of their ability. I always wondered what it might be like to travel through the portal to earth, to see a human. I also wondered what it must be like to be Zack's friend and make him smile and laugh as they did.

His mother leaned over and placed a chocolate cake in front of him.

Reaching into the deep pocket of my green skirt, I rubbed the smooth surface of my present. Only two months had passed since his father's death, but Zack looked okay. I credited his mother. She talked about his father in the most positive way a darkling could.

Nothing strange had happened to the Salvas since his death. At least not anything I was aware of. I assumed they had hidden the sword somewhere in their house and planned to never touch it again. I knew I wouldn't.

Since his father's passing, Zack had returned to playing with his friends. He no longer had to wander the South Village at night, trying to track down his dad, but instead, could rest.

Ever since Mr. Salva's death, I felt choked with fear for Zack, Mrs. Salva, and for my little sister. I couldn't forget the cold she felt that night when Mr. Salva had been sucked into the river. With everything I had, I would protect her from whatever haunted the Salvas. That's why I'd come alone.

Although Zack's safety was always on my mind, I had considered avoiding Shadowland altogether. Then I'd see Mr. Salva's face and remember my promise.

When the sun began to set, and all the guests had left, I moved toward the balcony. Through the glass doors, I could see Mrs. Salva washing the dishes in the kitchen. Zack's eyes lit up as he talked to her about his presents.

The first glass sculpture I made from the stalactites had been a simple star. The more I had looked at it, the more I realized the color and shape made me think of Adah, the Mother of Montenai. I gave that one to Nalene because she liked everything related to the astrei and spent hours gazing at the sky. Zack would have thought of the astrei sword plunged into his father's chest and possibly hurled the present off the balcony. I was glad I caught myself before giving it to him. Instead, I carved a simple deer with delicate antlers.

Maybe he'll think it's stupid. Before I could change my mind, I placed it on the wrought iron table and flew away.

My emotions caused my heat to engulf me. When I rounded the mountainside with the wind in my face, I dove toward the Aglatian Sea. Plunging into the waves shocked my senses but did the job of cooling my thoughts and calming me. When I looked up on the bank, I saw the whitish strands of Nalene's hair as she stood on a rock. She sat down with her knees drawn to her chest as I continued to soak in the sea.

"Are you o-okay?" she called.

"I think so." I kicked my toes up and floated on my back in the cool water as the yellow moon beamed down upon my face.

"You haven't told me everything," she said in my head.

"I can't right now."

"I'm not a baby, you know."

"There are some things I wish I didn't know or see. I'm not going to upset you with them."

"Don't be sad."

"I'm not." Confused, yes. I was definitely uncertain about so much. Seeing that Zack was adjusting without his dad brought me some relief.

"How was Zack's birthday?"

I brought myself upright in the water before swimming to the rock and resting my arms on the edge. With my chin in my hands, I looked up at her.

"He looks happy. As happy as a fledgling can be after something so awful has happened."

"G-good." She smiled.

"You look much better."

"W-whatever that was. I d-don't ever want to fffeel it again." She shivered.

I nodded my agreement. "We can still go into Shadowland, but I don't want you around the Salvas or the dragon lords for a while."

She reached out to comb her fingers through my wet hair.

"I d-don't wwwant you around Lord Akton. He c-can ffeel you."

"It's a deal."

She disappeared into thin air and reappeared on a rock nearby. Nalene could travel through any source of water. She could even tap into the moisture in Montenai's rock, soil, or air. If there was at least a coin-sized collection of water pooled on a surface, she could use it. The water must be somewhat pure. She can't just pop up in someone's coffee cup.

Her big, taunting smile brought my heat down. I couldn't keep up with her impossible game of hide-and-seek, and she knew it. The one hitch with her skill is she must be familiar with the destination to travel there. She blinked out of my vision and returned to the rock I was using for support. Not a bit of her was wet. It bewildered me. She could travel through water molecules and appear unfazed, her clothes in perfect order.

I pulled myself onto the rock next to her. "Show off."

She giggled. "Who's the show off?"

I looked down to see only strips of my shirt intact. When I ran too hot, I destroyed my clothes, disintegrated them, which really upset me because Cornelius spoiled us with some of the finest clothes in Montenai.

Bringing my arm up to shield my breasts, I stuck my tongue out at her.

Her eyes widened. "Wwwhen d-did you get *those?*"

My face grew warm. Little sisters can be such pests.

CHAPTER FIVE

Nalene's white-blond hair stood up in the wind all around her head, reminding me of a dandelion. The longer strands merged loosely into a braid halfway down her back. She waited for my cue.

"Wwwhat i-is it?" she asked, her hazel eyes wide. The excitement caused her stuttering to be more pronounced.

"Your birthday present." I held the creation I'd carved with my claws in front of her, letting the purple-blue crystal beads sparkle in the sun. I couldn't believe she was ten today. It reminded me of Zack's tenth birthday, and all the horror of his father's death rushed back into my head. With it came my fears about our survival way up in the isolated cliffs.

She bowed her head, allowing me to place the necklace on her.

"I l-love it, Nnnatcha," she said, her voice quiet.

She knew. No matter how hard I tried to hide my thoughts, she often still heard them.

"Don't be sad."

"I'm not." I fixed the strap on her lavender sundress. "Let's go see what our spoils are today, my little pirate."

Excited to spy once more on the pretty nymph mother and the tall satyr who brought us supplies, Nalene twirled around and set off down the mountain. My chest felt tight when I watched her braid swishing back and forth.

The spring sun rose higher in the sky, the birds sang, the bees droned, and I kept overheating. I'd soaked in the cool Aglatian Sea for an hour, but it wouldn't douse my fires.

"W-what's the matter?" Nalene asked. She'd stopped in the middle of the path.

"Nothing, Leeni."

She shrugged before disappearing and reappearing on each small rock all the way down the mountain. Some alarm rang in my head. I'd never seen her do her hide-and-seek so fast.

I practiced turning on and off my cloaking. The slight buzz echoed in my ears, snapped off, then on. Since Nalene was a baby, I'd always hidden her. Her speed was making it difficult for me to cloak her today.

With her ahead of me, I produced fireballs in my hands to let some of the heat out of me. The flames burned bright then smoked.

Her head turned. Hands on hips, she looked up at me. "Why are you ssso hot t-today?"

"Mind your own business."

"Wwwhatever," she said. She continued her *jumping* game, too excited to bother with me and my issues.

At the beginning, Magda and Cornelius had attempted to retrieve us from our home by the sea, but they never got through my cloaking magic. As a tiny hatchling, I was unaware of my defense mechanism that had kept me hidden in the shadows. The phantoms didn't have the sense to allow them through. Serena, in particular, was in tune with my needs and feelings. The more distressed I grew, the more vicious she had become with the two Montenaians who had only been trying to help.

As they had done with me, the two had endured the phantoms to bring milk and supplies for baby Nalene to a phantom-approved drop-off zone, the black rock. I vaguely remembered their fear-filled faces when they approached the spot. At three, I couldn't have done the best job attending to an infant, but somehow, our instincts helped us survive.

When I was five, Cornelius had come by himself and brought two goats: a billy and a nanny goat full of milk. I remember it like it was yesterday. The nanny's name was Cinnamon and the billy, Cosmo, for the fallen leader of the Satyrs. Of course, I didn't know who Cosmo was at the time. Cornelius made me smile. He always wore a derby hat tilted to one side.

As he had walked with the leads around the goats' necks, their bells rang. "Cripes, if my herd could see me now. Goats. I have goats." He had leaned on the rock and called to us. "Are you there, little ones?"

I threw a pebble down the path so he could see I watched him, but I never dropped my cloaking.

He smiled. "So clever. These are your new friends, Cinnamon and Cosmo." He pointed to each goat. "Watch carefully. They will give you milk to drink. You can also use it to make cheese and soap." He scratched Cinnamon's floppy ears. She had tiny buds as horns, a white body, and an orange-brown head. Cosmo was black with a white star pattern on his chest.

Fascinated, I had watched Cornelius express the milk into a metal pail. When he was done milking, he tied the leads to a small tree and left the fresh milk for me in the pail. By seven, I had a herd I cared for up on the cliffs.

Over the years, the goats had provided for us just as Cornelius said they would. In return, we gave them love and a warm barn we had constructed ourselves. It was a funny-looking shed, to be honest, but it sheltered them. We didn't fence them in, but they never left us.

I'd milked Cinnamon this morning. She was the sweetest little thing. We'd done as Cornelius had suggested. By reading the books he'd brought us, I had managed to care for the herd the best I could.

Once the two visitors learned they were *allowed* to come as far as the black rock in the Ballatian Woods, they relaxed a bit. Our return gifts also put them at ease. When we were younger, we left them drawings. As I mastered my soap-making, I left them bars shaped like different sea creatures. It was our sign to them we were surviving.

A bluebird's warble sounded from a tree branch above. Magda turned her head to take notice before continuing on the path. As she walked, all the flowers and plants perked up, waiting to follow any instruction she should give them. With her magic she could conduct plants to grow larger, and in different directions. Her ability to bend light not only helped in casting reflections, but also helped in the fostering of the plants and crops on kirka farmland.

I focused on the soft whisper my cloaking made and the sensation of the cool energy of the shadows drawing toward me. It pooled in the pit of my stomach and buzzed over my skin.

Magda carried a bag of supplies, no doubt more clothes, food, and antiseptic herbs. Her long, blond hair flowed off her shoulders. Cornelius walked next to her, a net of supplies over his broad back. I could see books, shiny trinkets, and fine linens through the mesh. The satyr and nymph made no indication if they noticed our presence.

Nalene usually kept a safe distance. But not today. In an instant, she disappeared and reappeared to the right of the rock.

"*Slow down,*" I cautioned.

She disappeared again and popped up just in front of Magda.

I knew the instant my cloaking had failed. Magda's smile lit up her face.

"Child," she said in a soothing voice.

My heart stopped. I looked from the nymph mother to my Nalene. They looked so alike, my breath caught. Confused, I didn't do anything. I'd always suspected she was related to the nymphs. I'd often wondered if she'd be better in their care.

The nymphs lived in glowing glass domes on the west side of the Montenai River. They had a village of all females who worked their farmlands using magic. All Montenaians knew of their exceptional healing abilities.

They cast reflections in the human world. Like the darklings, they derived something valuable from the exchange. Human interaction had intensified their beauty over the centuries, and, I guessed, helped strengthen them. I've never seen a sick nymph.

Shocked. I waited. *Should I let her go?* Tears burned my eyes. The nymphs might know how to handle her ice and maybe could help her talk without a stutter. She'd have friends.

I don't know how long I stood with these thoughts attacking my mind, my cloaking buzzing around just me. Cornelius hadn't moved.

From the look on Leeni's face, she'd heard a lot of my thoughts. The pink drained from her cheeks, and her hands balled into fists.

"Natcha!"

Two things happened at once. First, Nalene disappeared into thin air. Then the phantoms came, spurred on by her fury and my insecurity.

Gray fog streaked out from around me, the visual introduction of the three screeching phantoms: Serena and Sina have dark hair and eyes, Hana, dirty-blond hair with gray eyes. Their eyes and mouths became hollow black holes as their bodies stretched to twenty-foot tall floating creatures.

"No!" I screamed, stopping them from numbing the only other creatures on Montenai who cared about my survival.

CHAPTER SIX

Eight Years Later

NALENE LAY ON her belly, hanging off a rock by the water. Her head inclined, she listened to the water energy around her. She said each source had a different tone, note, and scale. I suppose that's why she was always singing—to accompany the music she heard all around her. Also, when she sang, she never stuttered. With her fingers, she directed droplets of water to splash against rocks, still others to cause ripples on the surface, and more to mist through the sunbeams, causing a rainbow. The effect was a vibrant musical and visual production that kept me captive.

I stretched my peachy-flesh wings to their six-foot span in order to sunbathe. The back of my halter top dipped low, allowing my wings full movement. Upon the bat-like membrane was a pattern of iridescent white scales, which sparkled like crystals of sand. If I didn't cloak myself, the reflection would no doubt send satyr ships off course as they sailed into port. When I didn't need my wings, I only had to retract them fully into my back. This left two lines of thick shimmery scales running on either side of my spine, descending in size from each shoulder blade to the middle of my back, forming a V. Nalene said it was pretty. Of course, she needed to say that because she was my sister.

I looked over at her. Her skin had turned pink in the summer sun, and her hair was all but white. Our bellies full of fish and crab, we listened to the birds overhead and talked mostly about the satyrs we spied on quite a bit, because what else are two females our age supposed to do during the summer?

Just this morning, Nalene had completed a purple skirt and top, notched just right for my wings, and I had rebuilt the chicken coop and fixed the roof on the barn for the goats. The satyrs produced a myriad of goods in the town called Port by the Sea. In watching them work, she had become an excellent seamstress, learning to knit, sew, and weave. I did more of the manual labor, not because I was that much better at it, but because I wasn't good at the finer stuff like she was.

"I'm so g-glad wwwe did this," she said from her rock. We had rewarded ourselves with a lazy afternoon watching the majestic satyr boats on the aquamarine water.

My mouth opened to answer, but a tremendous *boom* echoed from up the river. I found myself clinging to the rock with my pearly claws. Nalene had shot straight up to stand. We looked across to each other.

"Natcha!" In an instant, she traveled through water to join me on the rock.

"Dear Adah, what was that?" I asked. I grabbed her hand and stood.

The sky north of us moved. Tiny black specks flew in a serpentine fashion, changed course, broke apart, reformed, grew larger and louder. *Birds fleeing danger.* In only a few minutes, we saw gray-black smoke billow above the tops of the enormous sequoia trees.

Nalene quivered next to me.

"Dragon lords," we said to each other.

Fear overwhelmed me. "I need to check on Zack." Something had set off the dragon lords.

She nodded.

"Stay here," I said. I felt a sharp pain in my side. "Ouch!" She had pinched me.

"I hope y-you're k-kidding," she hissed.

I slowed, taking the time to consider her feelings. "Nalene. I want to check on the Salvas. I can't concentrate on them and worry about cloaking you."

"You're afraid something will affect me again."

"Yes. So, please, let me go. I'll communicate with you the

whole time. I promise."

A blast of sea spray rose up and drenched me. I spit out salt water. "Really. Why are you such a little brat!"

"That's a fi-re." She pointed and exaggerated as if I were as addle-brained as a sprite.

I put my arms out. "And?"

"H-hello." Tiny droplets of water swirled just above her palm. "I c-can control water."

"Okay, but don't do anything unless you consult me first."

We locked eyes. There would be no hide-and-seek game while I was trying to cloak her. She'd been so angry on her tenth birthday, the day my cloaking failed, and I exposed her to the nymph and satyr. Nalene had disappeared for over twenty-four hours. It was the longest day and night of my life. I had known she could move through water molecules, but we both discovered that she could infuse the stones of her necklace with water energy and draw from it to travel. I learned later she'd hidden in wild satyr territory and considered never returning to me.

After that experience, we'd come to an understanding. Even though I was older by three years, it didn't mean I made all the decisions and ignored her wishes.

"Travel to the black rock. I'll fly you from there to the Salvas."

"Okay." She disappeared without any argument.

With my cloaking buzzing in my ears, I launched to the sky. To the west, I could see streaks of white foam in the river as satyr speedboats rocketed north to see about the tumult. I headed east over land. Three streaks of fog mirrored my travel below, zooming over the mountainous terrain, until I reached the black rock.

Nalene met me at the supply rock as we had agreed. The bodies of fog halted on her right side and formed into three exquisite maidens—Serena, Sina, and Hana. They didn't appear as scary phantoms but presented a more darkling/nymph visage with us. Semi-transparent, they floated and flickered in the air with a crew of five dark spirits, each kept heeled at their skirts. Barely visible, the shapeless black critters swirled around their lower legs. Only when Serena got pissed did they grow more menacing with high-pitched shrieks that invaded the safe place in your soul and made you want to curl into the fetal position while sucking your thumb.

"It's okay, Serena," I said.

"Natcha?" Her eyes were fully black, usually the first sign she intended to go all phantom.

"We're safe. Thanks for checking. We're going into South Village to check on that little darkling." I had no idea how much she understood. Serena didn't always catch everything. Her mind drifted.

I cringed when I saw her draw her right hand up to consult a cracked mirror she carried with her. Sometimes, when she discovered the mirror was cracked, for the gazillionth time, she'd go into a rage. I had no idea why. The mirror was her trigger, kind of like Nalene was mine.

Her brows creased before she turned from us and disappeared, her crew trailing behind her.

"Oh, th-thank A-Adah," Nalene said. "I fffeared there was going to be a dramafest."

"Let's go," I said, moving toward her. I scooped her up in my arms and launched to the smoky skies, my cloaking buzzing.

Below, we saw the destruction of the bridge that had connected Shadowland to Kirka Village. The darkling streets and South Boardwalk remained vacant. Shutters were clapped closed on various businesses.

In contrast, the kirka side teemed with activity. Nymphs lined the bank. Behind them, their glass domes glowed with reflections of nature. At least seven satyr boats bobbed, anchored in the river because Shadowland's dock had been blown to bits along with the bridge. Most of the fires looked small and containable. Twisted wood and metal littered the bank. Chunks of boats and debris floated down the river. Several satyrs braced themselves against the edge of their boats and concentrated in order to control the winds. With their power, they brought up the waves to douse fires along the bank and on wreckage in the river. Some had abandoned their vessels, rock-hopped to the shore, and were helping a scarce crew of darklings direct hoses on scattered fires spreading along the rooftops of South Village businesses.

"What exploded?" Nalene asked.

"I have a feeling it was the dragon lords' temper."

We landed just off the boardwalk. Under the cover of dogwood trees, the cool shadow washed into me and fed my cloaking. The sun set over the river scene, backlighting the frantic activity in a brilliant orange.

Nalene grabbed my hand. Twenty feet in front of us stood Marta Salva. Her blue-black hair hung in tight corkscrew curls to her shoulders. A red scarf kept it off her face. She held a broom in her right hand, but she wasn't sweeping. She stared glassy-eyed down the boardwalk toward Pia's Park and the cries of outrage at the dragon lords' home. A small group of darklings shouted at two door attendants outside the Wishing Tree.

I ignored the commotion in order to study Good for the Sole. My eyes scanned the white stucco building with its magenta and white striped awning. The sign hung slightly askew, but other than the one shattered front window, it looked intact. A lone boot lay on the sidewalk in the doorway. No other darklings moved about.

"No sign of Zack."

"Yes, but his mom looks okay," Nalene said in my head.

It took everything I had to keep up my cloaking. My conscience told me to step in, grab the broom, and steer her inside to safety. I'd instruct Nalene to make her a cup of tea while I swept the glass from the boardwalk in front of her store and put a temporary board in place. Also, ask her where in the world of Montenai her son was.

I couldn't let her see me. The scales on my back would be alarming. I met Nalene's eyes. She looked like a nymph. Maybe…she could pretend to have come across the river.

When I looked to my sister, her pale eyebrows were raised so high, I thought they'd touch her hairline.

"Sorry," I said. I felt helpless.

"It's okay. I'll go to her if you want me to." Nalene squeezed my hand.

Before I had a chance to decide, I heard more shouting.

"Mom!" A tall muscular male ran down the boardwalk.

Zack had grown at least four inches since I'd last seen him.

He grabbed her by the shoulders. "What are you doing outside?"

She blinked several times and touched his face. "I was just checking to see what was going on."

Sweat drenched Zack's shirt. His wavy dark curls clung to his forehead. "They have Anka Rehmling in the Wishing Tree because they found out she was showing herself to her human charge."

She shut her eyes briefly while she shook her head.

His jaw set, he drew closer to look down at his mother. "I need to do something. The Rehmlings can't get to her. They're frantic."

"Zachary—"

"What good is it to possess something so powerful if you don't have the courage to use it?" he gritted.

"Hush, Zachary!" Eyes frantic, her once fearful expression flared to one of anger.

"Father was not a coward," he hissed.

"Stop this."

The loud bellow of a dragon lord sent darklings running from in front of the immense wooden doors of the Wishing Tree.

Copper scales reflected in the dimming light as Lord Leasith stepped out of the tree, carrying something in his arms.

Lord Bulosk shielded him. "Step away. Go home, now!" growled Bulosk, barreling down the steps. "Ernest, come with me."

The lords got into their official vehicle, a longer version of the typical darkling cart. The Rehmlings' grandfather, Pops or Ernest, moved more quickly than I thought he could.

"What did you do to her?" he asked.

Lord Leasith subdued him with his arm, locking him in the seat as they sped away.

Mrs. Salva stood with her hand over her mouth.

"Zack! Zack!" A tiny darkling ran full speed toward him and straight into his arms.

"Bianca." He held her as she sobbed into his chest.

Mrs. Salva dropped the broom and stroked her back.

"Dear Adah. Please take care of Anka. She's just a little thing," Nalene prayed, snapping me out of my shock.

A rage burned so hot in me, I knew I had to get out of there.

"Natcha, your eyes."

"Go home, Nalene. I can't keep you cloaked.

I didn't have to tell her twice. She disappeared.

"It's okay, sweetie, it's okay," Zack whispered to Bianca.

Her cries were heartbreaking. There was nothing I could do other than potentially catch the whole boardwalk on fire with my outrage. The dragon lords had hurt her sister.

My sister was so sweet and devout. She turned to prayer in times of stress and desperation. My first impulse mirrored Zack's. I wanted to grab a sword and stab someone. With my murderous thoughts making me dizzy, I launched to the sky. *Do not even look at the Wishing Tree.* I knew if I did, I'd be tempted to commit arson.

"Please come home, Natcha."

Nalene's pure voice and heart acted as my homing beacon. She met me on the chalk-white rock ledge leading into our cave. Careful not to touch me, she walked me inside and to the sunken stone tub in the corner. I'd used my claws to carve it. Mountain spring water trickled down the wall in this area and pooled in the tub before continuing down the mountain through a small crevice in the ground. I only needed to plug the hole with a stone to fill the tub to max capacity. Nalene had already done it for me.

"Thanks," I said.

"Y-your eyes are—"

"Scary, I know."

I had no clothes to remove. I'd disintegrated them. When my body made contact with the frigid water, a loud hissing sound filled the cave, and steam rose into the air.

Nalene sat in a wooden rocking chair I'd made. She wept softly as she hugged herself. "D-d-did they k-k-kill her?"

"I don't know, Leeni." I tasted blood as I bit my cheek.

She continued to pray to the Mother and Father of Montenai. I blocked it out because I couldn't come to terms with anything that just happened. The darklings didn't know me, but I knew them. I'd grown up with them.

I leaned my head back on the rock ledge. "I don't think they did. I think they just punished her for interacting with her human charge."

"W-what k-k-kind of b-bar-baric animals are they?"

With my hand over my eyes, I concentrated on taking deep breaths. "Sorry, Nalene, I can't talk about this. I'm afraid I'll spontaneously combust."

"That w-would b-be mmmessy."

I snorted. When I took my hand away, she wore a proud grin. "Did you just make an inappropriate joke?"

She shrugged.

The crystal stalactites of the ceiling settled me a bit, as did our flitting bats leaving their roost in our cave to feed in the night.

"I'm trying not to hate the dragon lords," I admitted.

"Hate is o-only for the evil and the d-d-dark."

"Well, then, you're sister is an evil, dark bitch," I said before submerging completely in the cold water and blowing bubbles out my nose and mouth.

When I surfaced, Nalene was singing in the kitchen.

She had the most ethereal, haunting voice. It mesmerized me. She also knew it helped soften me.

When she plunked a bottle of Port from the satyr vineyards down next to me, along with some darkling chocolate, I managed a grin.

"Have I mentioned you're my favorite sister?"

"I'm y-your only sssister."

"Just take the compliment and get yourself a glass."

THE NEXT MORNING, I visited the Salvas. Zack lived in a duplex in North Village and attended Montenai College. However, I knew he still checked in on his mom. As I'd suspected, I found him in her kitchen, cooking her breakfast. The smell of fresh coffee wafted out from the open sliding doors. Mrs. Salva sat at the wrought iron table on the back deck. Zack came through the door wearing shorts, a t-shirt, flip-flops, and a baseball hat turned backwards. He slipped an omelet onto her plate.

Mrs. Salva had clipped her curls atop her head haphazardly. Even without makeup and wearing night clothes, she was dark and gorgeous. I wondered if she ever considered remarrying. Zack doted on her in such a sweet way, I imagined it made any suitors look less worthy of her attention.

She flashed him a disapproving stare.

His long-lashed eyes met hers. "What? Since when don't you love my omelets?"

"Turn that hat around."

He gave her a sheepish grin. "Sorry. I forgot."

"Better yet, remove it when you come to my table."

"Will do. Do you want a refill on your coffee?"

"Thanks, hon."

He made himself a plate, as well, but only picked at the food. The morning sun filtered through the needles of the trees, casting shadows on his face. When his mother ate her last bite, he cleared his throat.

She gripped the coffee mug with both hands. "What is it, Zachary?"

"She's suffering."

Marta Salva pressed her lips tight and closed her eyes. "What are they going to do?"

"Bianca says none of her own healing energy will even touch the dragon lashes on Anka's back."

My mouth dropped open. *Aglatian Sea. Aglatian Sea.* I thought of the fifty-eight degree water and cooled my dragon down.

His mother's nostrils flared.

"I need you to know something," he said, all the muscles in his body rigid.

Raw fear filled her toffee-colored eyes.

"I've been sword training with the satyrs. I don't want you to worry, but I need you to be aware of reality."

She took a deep, visible breath.

"Something has never been right with Lord Akton. There's always been something dark and twisted about the Wishing Tree."

She shook her head.

"Don't stop me, Mother. Just listen, for once. I need you to hear me." He reached across and clutched her hand. "The Torensphere has given us much vitality and power. The lords have done a decent job of balancing its power but not a great job. It affects us. We can't forget it is a foreign, unknown essence, just as the sword is. It spoke with Anka Rehmling inside the lords' Rotunda. It talked to Father and drove him mad. Lord Akton hasn't been right for a while. And his brothers are terrified of him. They can't control him."

"They have done much for us over the years, Zachary. They helped me with the store. They are your employers at the restaurant."

"I know, and I'm grateful. But I can't ignore what I see...what I saw when I was so young." He wrinkled his face up, and his eyes grew wet. "I saw her back." His lips trembled, and he swallowed. "I just want you to know that if they do anything else to hurt the Rehmlings or come anywhere near Bianca...I don't know what I'll do."

"I understand your anger. I agree; their punishment of Anka was harsh. They overreacted." She played with the fresh cut flowers on the table. "You're all I've got, Zack."

He folded his arms across his chest. "What kind of object must you keep hidden away behind a false wall so that it can't have direct contact with your workers for fear it will drive them insane?"

Her eyebrows shot up.

"They keep it in the Rotunda, behind a false wall."

"Zachary," she scolded.

"Old Gus used to work with Father. Remember? He and I talked recently. He's the one who told me Dad wasn't crazy. The tree wasn't talking to him, but the dragon egg was."

Mrs. Salva pulled the petals off one daisy then started on another. "How's Gus?"

"Did you hear me, Mom?"

She frowned as she looked at the petals. "Yes, loud and clear."

Zack covered her hand with his. "Gus is still making cakes." His face and voice softened. "Sorry. I didn't mean to be harsh. I'm just questioning everything."

"Everyone does at your age." She still wouldn't look at him.

"I wonder how life would be if the Torensphere was in different hands. Gus says it's what gives the lords their magic and healing abilities."

"Gus can be an old fool."

He shrugged before pushing to stand. After he cleared the dishes, he came back and placed a kiss on her forehead. "I want you to know I love and respect you. However, the next time someone I care about is being threatened, I won't stand idly by."

Her mouth dropped open.

"And the next time, I won't *ask* for the sword. I'll just take it."

CHAPTER SEVEN

THE CAVE FELT cold no matter what I did. The Faunlier Mountains stayed burdened with snow as all of Montenai geared up for one of its legendary winters. I sensed in my bones, this one would be brutal. The drastic temperatures in the cave had driven away our colony of bats in search of a more hospitable environment for hibernating. Some of them hadn't made it and returned to die. For days, I had found their leathery corpses littering the twilight area of the cave. I'd discretely removed them so as not to upset Nalene.

She coughed as her usually nimble fingers struggled to fashion my red hair in a fishbone braid. Her wheezing unnerved me, but no matter how close I got to her, no matter how many fires I built, her cold would not relent. And because of her labored breathing, no song came from her lips. The quiet made me mournful.

"That's not getting better," I said.

"I'm fffine, Nnatcha," she rasped.

"The nymphs could help—"

"Ssstop. I don't want to go to them. D-d-don't say it again," she said, tugging at my hair in her frustration.

Why was she so stubborn?

The wind howled at the cave's entrance. She shivered as she completed her handiwork. "G-gonna lie d-d-down fffor a while," she said.

From the kitchen bench, I watched her shuffle to her cot, a satyr

186

throw wrapped around her shoulders. The satyr and nymph no longer needed to bring us wares or food; we were self-sufficient.

Over the last months, Nalene and I had spent more time watching the nymphs and satyrs than observing the darklings. They gave us the skills we needed to survive. The darklings had just taught us about cruelty.

Cornelius still traveled to the rock and left us darkling chocolate, dresses, wine, and books. We owed him so much. Magda, too. In all my observation of the nymphs, I still couldn't understand how they healed. I've never felt so stupid or inadequate in my life. We had always managed to teach ourselves, but nothing I did would help Nalene.

She wasn't fine. I'd raided the nymphs' green houses and forced her to drink teas I'd made from various herbs. Whatever this sickness was, I feared it intended to claim her as the sword had taken Mr. Salva so many years ago. I couldn't help but think of that night, because the markings beside her left eye had returned—blisters, almost resembling scales, bubbled over her bluish-white skin.

Swallowing a lump in my throat, I crossed to the fire circle in the center of our cave. After adding more clumps of klenin moss for kindling, I brought fire to my hands and helped the fire along. Next, I checked on our baby bat, Echo. Echo's mother had abandoned him when the stress in the cave drove the colony away. I'd nursed him with goat's milk. I peeked inside his basket to find him hanging upside down from the handle, rocking himself. He looked peaceful, so I secured the blanket over the basket to keep him warm. I prayed he made it through the winter.

Leeni's horrible wheezing rose above the crackling of the fire. My legs felt like rubber as I crossed through the shadows of the cave to her cot. The whole bed trembled from her shivers.

"Nalene?"

She wouldn't wake, just whimpered. Her eyelids had gone from blue to a purplish color, the veins more pronounced on the paper-thin skin. Studying her up close caused my stomach to twist. *When had she gotten this frail?*

"Leeni?" I cried.

Her bed clothes were soaked through. I gave her a fresh nightgown and blankets, cradled her, sang to her, and applied warm compresses to her forehead. She remained clammy, stiff, and unresponsive.

The necklace. In the last several weeks, we had worked together to infuse her water necklace. She would apply her water magic to each bead, and I would call my heat to lock inside both of our energies. Once she secured the jewelry back in place, she would always smile, a look of blissful relief on her face. Fumbling with the blankets, I reached out to touch the purple-blue beads, anticipating the slight pulse and glow as her magic met my touch.

"No."

I tried another bead, and another. Nothing was left. I put my head down on her chest, hearing the rattling of air through her lungs and the faltering of her weak heart.

When I raised my head, I felt dizzy. My own blood rushed in my ears, drowning out any sounds of our cave. *She's dying.* I stood up and spun around. I wasn't going to let her die. *Damn it, Natcha, do something.*

"Nalene? I'll be back. Hang on," I called in her head.

Placing my hand on the archway of the cave's entrance, I braced myself, because my head felt ready to explode. Taking a deep breath, I stepped onto the icy ledge to meet a horizon pregnant with snow clouds. The red sun punched a thin arm through the wall as it set, causing just a sliver of the Aglatian Sea to dazzle.

"Natcha."

I'd never been so happy to see my phantom. "Serena. No matter what happens, you must stay with Nalene."

Serena flickered in front of me. Her crimson cape matched her lips. Her caramel-colored eyes conveyed fear.

"Please. Don't leave her side. Sing to her. Watch over her until I get back."

She disappeared. When I turned, I saw contrails of her essence blurring the darkness of the cave's tunnel.

With my cloaking buzzing, I launched to the sky and headed to the west side of the Montenai River. I needed Magda, now. No one else could possibly help. I contemplated the best way to approach her. Certainly, I would need to tuck my wings into the wing slits, keep my dragon out of my eyes, explain I was the fledgling from the mountains, and then ask if I could fly her to my cave. That last part sounded threatening, but I knew Nalene was in no shape to travel.

Blinded by thoughts, I pushed through the buffeting winds until something smacked me so hard in the face, I lost altitude. *Birds.*

I dodged several as they swarmed in panic through the layers of clouds. Flying lower allowed me to glimpse the satyr territory below. I couldn't be sure what the moving dark patches were in the delta. Lower still, I soared just above the cypress trees and realized it was a mass of satyrs. The herds ran at breakneck speed toward Kirka Village.

The air grew thick with black smoke. I climbed higher and gained the vantage point I needed to see what had all of Montenai in chaos. Flames shot thirty feet into the air from the enormous dome known as Reflections Celebration Hall. The smaller domes, which comprised Kirka Circle, sounded off as each one exploded in flame. The noise of bending metal and exploding glass was deafening.

Ash mixed with the icy flakes and pelted my face. Choking from the smoke, I darted toward the river and landed on the banks of Shadowland.

I found myself by the remains of the bridge. Straight across, I could see the frenzied nymphs and satyrs as they tried to save Kirka Village from burning to the ground. The morose sky across the river only conveyed doom. My mind went to Magda and her nymphs. Biting my lip helped ground me. I was no help. I couldn't even take care of my own sister.

My cloaking buzzed in my ears as I turned my back to the river. Snow crunched underfoot. I walked just off the path, out of the way of any darklings. Everything felt surreal—shutters closed, gates pulled, darklings gone, except for a strange caste of militant ones I'd never seen before. Armed darkling males ran up and down the boardwalk. They wore a uniform—coats emblazoned with the dragon lords' crest and helmets that had nose guards and hinged cheek plates engraved with a flame symbol. Shadowland never had a guard per se. In fact, darklings were forbidden from carrying weapons of any kind.

What are they doing?

I felt like I was in a dream, a nightmare. Someone had attacked Kirka Village. Was this tiny militia guarding Shadowland? When I glanced across the river once more, I knew which creatures had the temper and fire power to cause that kind of chaos.

Two armed darklings hastened down the path, heading for the Wishing Tree. Not knowing what else to do, I fell into step behind them.

"Lords Bulosk and Leasith are with the nymphs, dousing the fires," said the taller one. "Have you checked in with Lord Akton?"

The shorter guard scanned the area around him. "No one has seen him for hours," he whispered.

I studied the tall darkling He was a nonshadowcaster, reliant on the dragon lords' power for his own wellbeing. When he removed his helmet, I saw a baby face.

"We need to find him. No one is guarding the Wishing Tree," he responded.

Smoke rolled down the boardwalk, and I turned to see the largest sequoia tree in North Village ablaze. Chocolate Syncope, run by the Rehmling grandfather, Pops, had suffered the same fate as the kirka domes. Staring in disbelief, I almost lost focus on my task. But the guards continued their journey, and I followed them, on autopilot.

None of the dragon lords are in the Wishing Tree. I rushed to keep up because they were my way into the dragon lords' mysterious lair.

My chest felt constricted, my breathing erratic. Nalene was dying. Magda was dealing with her own tragedy. The only other power strong enough to heal was that of the dragon lords or...*the Torensphere.*

I refused to second guess what I was about to do. My knees felt like they would give out any minute.

The taller guard walked, his boots thudding on the wooden boardwalk, sword drawn His companion moved next to him, on high alert. A lot of good that would do them. I'm no expert, but I could have jumped both of them from behind, even uncloaked. Darklings were not bred to fight.

Before I realized, we had ascended the steps and stood before the gnarled wooden double doors of the tree. Each creature of Montenai stood in relief upon the doors' surface. Snow had sifted through the great branches of the sequoia and clung to the raised portions of the door, giving white beards to several of the enchanting nymphs. Just above hung the golden shield of the dragon and his shadow.

The tall guard turned the large, brass doorknobs and the doors swung inward. The colorful blown-glass lanterns floating in the grand hallway were the most intricate I'd seen in all of Shadowland, and also the most immense. They floated free through the space and were at least the same height as me. I scooted in just on the tail of the shorter guard, almost smacking into him when he turned to close the doors.

I held my breath until the two guards took a doorway left into a meeting room filled with a marble table large enough to accommodate giants. They slammed the door closed behind them, and I let out my breath.

The inside of the Wishing Tree was more impressive than the outside. The organic material of the tree had been infused with material finery the lords must have collected over a century. I caught myself gaping as I looked around. Antique vases from the time of the fallen nymph leader, Hanleith, rested atop more sleek, modern tables characteristic of the ones found throughout South Village.

Just through the foyer, a cobblestone path descended into the heart of the tree, into the soul of the dragon lords. I understood why Alexander Salva had thought the tree alive. Something in the space was. I sensed it in the air, on my skin…in my head.

"So, you live," it said in my head.

Goosebumps popped out on my skin. *"Who's there?"*

"I think you know."

With my heart galloping in my chest, I forced myself to walk down the path toward the force and the voice. If it was aware of me, then it could alert the dragon lords, so I picked up my pace.

About a half mile underground, the tunnel opened into what appeared to be a lobby or waiting area. Thick tapestries hung on the bark walls, along with oil paintings depicting Shadowland, the dragon lords, and the grand red dragon, Akton, in Montenai's sky. Cello music droned from speakers shaped like antlers set high in the wall.

A wall of glass and French doors occupied my attention. The thickness of the glass rivaled that of the nymphs' great domes. I went inside the Rotunda.

My eyes explored the area—rich chaise lounges, club chairs, carved wooden pedestals with vases, grand bookcases, desks, and a bar. It wasn't my eyes but my ears that honed in on my target. A heartbeat came from the marble wall located across from the club chairs. This alcove appeared rather bare compared to the rest of the space.

My wet boots slapped on the white marble floor as I approached. Heat emanated from the wall in front of me.

I knew with every fiber of my being that behind this wall, I would find the Torensphere. Droplets of water dripped from my drenched hair down the nape of my neck and along my spine. Another sensation crept across my skin, a magic so strong, it stole my breath. When I touched the wall, I felt such an enormous shock, I clenched my teeth and growled.

"I am here requesting your help," I said. "Perhaps, you could hear me out in lieu of frying me to a crisp."

Laughter filled my head. *You're stronger than they are. Fascinating. I didn't anticipate this.*

With my hands in the air, my palms just inches from the wall, I looked like I was surrendering to something. In a way, I was. I needed this creature to save Nalene, because I simply had run out of options.

"How do you feel about travel? Certainly, you must be so tired of staying inside this wall," I posed.

What are you suggesting, dragon princess?

I felt vulnerable and exposed. It could see every facet of me—the light, the dark, each fantastic asset, and evil flaw. "A trip to the mountains. You'll love it. We have the best views in all of Montenai."

My head swung around to study the bookcase behind the club chairs. Didn't every secret passageway or fake wall have a lever in a bookcase?

Really? You're smarter than that, the Torensphere said.

I was running out of time.

"*Red and blue and copper, I see…*"

"What does that mean? Is that a hint?"

"*So many scales returning to me.*"

My breath caught in my throat. Did it mean the lords were returning?

Frantic, I looked through the space. Hundreds of round windows occupied the trunk of the tree, pores in its skin, allowing light to filter down into this room.

What would I use as entry if I were a dragon lord? Something not everyone possessed.

I hurled a fireball at the center of the marble wall. It ricocheted and hit me in the head. The fire didn't harm me but gave me strength as I reabsorbed it. I shook my head from the rush it gave me. Felt like I'd done a quadruple shot of espresso.

"*That all you got? Completely predictable.*"

I considered pleading with the creature, but realized it would not respect any signs of weakness. Pacing in front of the wall, I could feel my heat taking over. Desperation began to impede any rational thought. I almost wished the lords would return so I could deal with them. For some reason, I thought I'd be more successful. I sensed nothing innately sympathetic, warm, or benevolent about the Torensphere. However, it had strength, energy, vitality…components I needed right now.

"*You are nothing like your mother.*"

I halted in my tracks.

"*She was quite beautiful.*"

My claws were out before I knew it. I raked them down the marble wall. It whooshed aside so quickly, I stumbled backward.

"*Brilliant,*" it said.

A black marble table, veined with gold, housed a square tabernacle. I released the latch on the gilded door. When it swung open, I gazed upon the alien egg. It was larger than a softball but smaller than a basketball. Lit from within, it glowed a goldish-fawn color, the shell revealing a mosaic of colors resembling the dragon lord lanterns. I held my breath as I reached out and grabbed it.

With the Torensphere in the crook of my arm and my body overheating, I sprinted up the tunnel. My cloaking buzzed in my ears, but I wasn't sure it hid the egg. No one was in my path so I didn't need to worry.

Outside the huge entrance, I hesitated on the top step, as snow swirled around me. My cloaking flickered on and off. I reached for the shadows, hoping to strengthen my shield, but I didn't feel the familiar surge. Unnerved, I bolted down the stairs and turned left onto the boardwalk. A dragon lord bellowed from the river's edge. My mouth ran dry, and my legs turned to putty.

I am royally screwed.

At the edge of Pia's Park, I saw a hulking figure stalking up the bank. *Lord Akton.*

Everything stopped. White noise filled my ears as he turned his golden eye in my direction and *saw* me.

I don't know how long we gazed at each other. The intensity of the exchange caused my whole body to feel like liquid. When my cloaking suddenly buzzed on, I prepared to launch into the skies, but my wings were as uncoordinated as the rest of me. They wouldn't release, no matter what I did. Desperate, I ran for the Ballatian Woods.

"What are you doing to me?" I asked the Torensphere.

It wouldn't answer. My body felt numb. I barely registered the muscles in my legs as they flexed and contracted. I felt drunk as I plowed blindly through the snowstorm, running into branches and stumbling over tree roots and rocks. The Torensphere's power plunged into my skull, causing a fierce pain to ping inside, ricocheting until it splintered into a thousand lights. The lights converged into a long tunnel, narrowing, narrowing...

My teeth ground together as I thrashed my head from side to side, causing an explosion of stars inside my brain. Pain burned through my veins like lava. Again, I tried my wings. Pressure burst inside my head. Everything went black as my mind and body gave out.

CHAPTER EIGHT

PINPRICKS OF LIGHT floated above me. With my back pressed against a hard surface, I blinked several times as my lungs filled with frigid air. The dots of light reminded me of the windows in the Wishing Tree. *But I knew it couldn't be...*

My eyes registered light and shadow, my ears the howl of the wind. Above me, the gnarled arms of the oaks came into focus. I was in the Ballatian Woods. Again, startled birds filled the night sky, as did the smell of fire.

Wedged deep under my arm, the Torensphere pulsed red hot as I forced my achy body upright.

The essence inside the egg flashed a horrific image inside my head.

"No," I said.

"Yes."

The Wishing Tree had exploded? The fire I smelled was the decimation of Shadowland's center of leadership—the very heart of the darklings' existence.

"You're lying," I said, tears burning my eyes. Disbelief warred with guilt and anguish. Had the Torensphere's absence caused the Wishing Tree to self-destruct? I steadied myself against a boulder and forced my head to stop spinning. *How much time had elapsed since I lost consciousness, and the tree exploded?*

Nothing felt right—not my heart rate, my breathing, my

coordination. I thought of my sister to steady me as the Torensphere's foreign energy pulsed through my muscles and woke me up. Still, my legs refused to move at my desired pace, as if I walked through quicksand. I was almost to the black rock when the Torensphere flashed copper scales in my mind. I tried to ask it questions, but it only rambled and flashed images of Lord Leasith running through the woods, *my* woods. Did Lord Akton tell the other dragon lord about me? Or, had the Torensphere sicced him on my trail?

The storm and elements would hinder most pursuers, but not Lord Leasith. The night filled with the copper lord's bellows of rage, causing my heart to sink. I couldn't trust my cloaking, nor could I trust the egg.

My mind bounced between two gears: get home, drop the egg, get home, drop the egg. Every time I considered leaving the Torensphere, I pictured Nalene. For some reason, the Torensphere responded by giving me a surge of energy, rather than a painful jolt.

The exertion of my escape prompted a sharp pain in my side, which grew worse on each intake of breath. *Push through, Natcha.* This couldn't all be for nothing. I'd committed to my choice. My muscles tensed around the orb. Concentrating, I was able to achieve a tingling, itching sensation inside my wing slits. This bolstered my resolve. Once through the Ballatian Woods, I would be home free. The balance weighed in my favor: the phantoms treated me as their adopted child, and I could fly.

As if on cue, gray rolling fog crept over the snow banks. Black streamers of energy writhed and screeched in the fog's wake. The fog formed into two exquisite maidens just as Lord Leasith came into view down the mountain.

My wings felt full inside my back, ready to release, but my cloaking blinked off. All the blood rushed from my head. *Why is it failing me now?* I relied on my wings and cloaking as another Montenaian might count on their legs, arms, and hands to fight through something.

The phantoms registered my alarm with their black stares before directing their energy to the scary dragon lord stalking me.

My cloaking snapped on once more. But was it too late? Had

Lord Leasith seen me?

I just needed to get home. Back to Nalene. I breathed a bit easier when I saw Hana and Sina hovering just in front of the lord with their black spirits chasing around their skirts like hissing cats and yipping dogs. Then they showed him their inner bitch.

Their mouths became hollow black holes as their bodies morphed into twenty-foot creatures with maws that unhinged like snakes preparing to feed. Now at the peak of their tempest, each phantom wielded her crew of five dark spirits, which they unleashed on the dragon lord.

The faceless, inky black tendrils spread out, preparing to immobilize him. Their din rose above the storm's roar, creating a macabre scene, daunting even to a fearless dragon lord. I turned my back but heard his roars as they numbed him to where he would lose all will. With their diversion, I released my wings in the night air; a tunnel of icy snowflakes lit my runway.

My mind reeled with horrific images of the tree exploding with the lead dragon lord inside. Lord Akton's one golden eye followed me with every beat of my wings, in every breath I took. *It can't be. Dragon lords can withstand fire.*

I couldn't decide if the unhatched creature from Fallon meant to help me or disorient me. It sent a fierce energy up my arm, strengthening me in flight. As I spiraled down toward the cliffs, a dark shape streaked up at me, black eyes flickering in a ghostly face. *Serena.* I had anticipated the egg fighting me, but not my phantom.

"Drop it!" she screeched.

I hovered over the sea. In my twenty-three years, Serena had never used her phantom eyes on me. It left me breathless, confused, and terrified. The stress of my trip weighed heavy on me, and I glanced toward the cliff that housed my cave. Desperate and exhausted, I flinched from her screeching. I felt the cold hit my toes first.

"Stop," I insisted. When I tried to resume flying, she circled me from above, freezing my wings to the point I lost coordination and speed. She continued to pester me, a little bird to a hawk, until I finally had enough. "Serena, you're scaring me!" My anger sparked red hot in my cheeks. I'd never seen her this crazy and out of control. My heart pounded against my ribcage as true fear filled me.

As if finally registering my cries, she stopped. Her billowing phantom shape diminished, and her flickering darkling face returned, lit by her lovely caramel brown eyes. She wrung her hands as she looked to me then the egg.

"Not the baby!" she screeched before flying away, her gown streaking behind her, a crimson gash in the white sky.

Was she worried about the dragon inside? What did she think I meant to do with it? My brain felt ready to explode. The whole while I'd been dealing with Serena, the Torensphere had been yelling at me in my head. It most certainly did not want me dropping it in the sea, which is what it thought Serena wished me to do. The egg made no sense, and neither did Serena.

Before anything else could happen, I alighted on the rock ledge. Blue ice covered it. Cracks ran through it like the ones in Serena's mirror, the glass she carried around like a security blanket. After ducking inside the cave, I proceeded through the outer tunnel into the inner sanctum where the klenin moss glowed dimly. My eyes roved to the stalactites, which usually relaxed me; today, I saw red.

"You swindling little squatters. Get out of here!" I spread my wings and launched toward the ceiling. Ten sprites grinned. White needle-like teeth gleamed against their silver skin. Three males drew their swords. The females hissed at me and began a round of disparaging remarks.

"Oh look, it's the ugly sister." A shapely female hovered in front of my face and hissed.

Another dropped down to view the Torensphere. "Ohhhh, shiny." She looked like she wanted to touch it, but I pulled it away.

"What's up lizard lady?" the first assailant asked.

I snatched her with my clawed hand and landed back on the cave floor. I could feel her biting me, but I didn't release her. Her burning saliva stung my skin. The little bit of pain was nothing compared to the grizzly headache the Torensphere had caused.

The males came to her rescue, stabbing my wings. One wore my favorite ring as a crown. The other had used my scarf to design a black and white polka-dotted suit, complete with a hole for his long, barbed tail.

"Cut it out, you little pests or I will barbecue her."

The males roared at me, but I knew I had them. If need be, I could create a ball of fire in the palm of my hand, and she would be a well-done meaty morsel. I walked back to the entrance of the cave, holding my sprite hostage. As the wind groaned past the mouth of the cave, the legion of sprites bowed their heads and attempted to look pitiful and remorseful.

"But magnanimous lizard lady, it is ever so cold out," they said in their high-pitched voices. One of the males even sidled up to rub his muscular body against my bare neck. Sprites were handsome creatures. Their sparkling eyes came in the colors of gemstones. This one had eyes the color of amethysts.

"Don't rub on me, you pesky, little pirate."

He huffed at me but gave me some space.

I peeked into my hand to see the sprite still biting me. Red pustules had formed on my palm. In no mood, I wound up for the pitch and tossed her out into the night. Her horde followed, issuing horrific strings of curse words and obscene gestures at me before disappearing into the night.

Breathing hard, I tamped down my anger. I couldn't believe the sprites had attempted to infest my cave in the short time I'd been gone. Enterprising pests must have been watching the cave for a while if they knew all the bats had left. *All, except baby Echo.*

Frantic, I looked toward the covered basket by the fire ring. It looked untouched. I wanted to check on him but thought better of it since the powerful essence still rested in the crook of my arm. If the sprites had hurt him, I'd hunt them down and pluck their wings off.

The Torensphere's energy buzzed through my body, reminding me of the dire situation inside my home. Although the kindling still burned in the fire ring, the space felt damp and drafty. Nalene coughed from the cot in the corner. I walked with the now-glowing Torensphere to kneel beside my sister. She turned to me, revealing the devastation of her sweet face. Patches of yellow gave way to black, topped off by persistent blisters. Her white skin and light blond hair waxed dull with her illness. I wiped the cold sweat from her brow and bit my cheek until it bled. With everything I had, I attempted a reassuring look. I could hardly bear to see the pain that contorted her frost-bitten face.

Why was this happening? Leaving my wet garments in a puddle on the cave's floor, I grabbed a dry nightgown from the handcrafted shelf by the wall. With the egg in hand, I approached the cot again. The entire bed writhed from her shivering. Taking care to secure the egg under my left arm, I pulled the blankets up to her chin. She managed a meek smile for me. I climbed onto the twin cot with her and lay on my side to face her, the egg between us.

As hard as I tried to wipe any vestige of the trauma from my mind, she knew instantly something horrible had happened. Her nostrils flared, and an icy tear made a slow journey down her face.

"Don't," I said.

She shook her head. "Wwwhat…d-did you…d-do?"

"The darklings will be fine."

"Nnno, Natcha."

"Yes." I hissed. "You need this."

Although her appearance shocked me, I was encouraged that she was awake and alert.

Her mouth dropped open, and her eyes focused as if listening to the Torensphere. "I-it knows mmme."

Time stopped for a moment. My heartbeat thundered in my ears as I tried to comprehend what she had said.

The covers rustled as she reached out her thin hand.

Overwhelmed by the energy pulsing in front of me and what I'd just done, I tried to speak but couldn't find the words. Inside the dragon lords' Rotunda, the Torensphere had *pretended* to know me, too. What had I brought into my home?

Time sped up. I couldn't stop it. Nalene's hand was already on the orb. I'll never forget the noise she made. It was a scream of agony, so raw, it seemed ripped from her lungs. Her whole body seized with convulsions.

CHAPTER NINE

TEN-FOOT SWELLS rose up and crashed against the chalky rock face. Nalene didn't budge but pushed her face into the spray. She stood wrapped in a wool nymph blanket, looking out on the aquamarine Aglatian Sea. Silver threads glinted from the enchanted woven fabric. The dragon egg had worked wonders. While her skin remained its milky white, her cheeks looked flushed a pale pink. Her huge hazel eyes shone bright with renewed health and contentment.

She wore her familiar rock necklace wrapped in layers around her neck. It wasn't until she became weak in the last two months that she'd had to rely on the jewelry for survival.

I watched the sea roll in and curl its lacy fingers around each nook and cranny of the rocks. It filled my senses, relieved my pain, for a moment. The powerful energy of the water had done nothing for my Nalene when she was so ill. Not even the combined energy of my heat with her water in the beads of the necklace had helped. The thought brought my fire to the surface.

"Temper, Natcha," she said without turning to face me.

I focused on blocking my thoughts from her. I hadn't slept in days. The egg spoke inside my head in a constant rant, blaming me for all the wrong in the world of Montenai. The egg's essence confused me. It had fought me in the Wishing Tree, then strengthened me during my escape, healed Nalene, but now rambled as if it despised me.

Even without the egg's accusations, I wouldn't have been able to sleep. The dragon lords had lived for a century. They were supposed to be strong, perhaps immortal. But they weren't. Lord Akton had perished just four nights ago, the evening I stole the Torensphere.

My plan had veered grossly off course when I'd found Kirka Village on fire. Now the leader of the darklings was gone, and his brothers were vying for my head, or the thief's head. I couldn't be sure if Lord Leasith had a good handle on what I looked like. However, he did know where to look for me—something had set him on the right course up the Faunlier Mountains. The phantoms had been on nonstop guard duty.

I wished none of this had happened. If I hadn't brought Nalene the egg, she would have died. As I watched her in the sunshine, I couldn't help but think of the nymphs. If she had fallen into their care at ten, we wouldn't be in this predicament.

Anger ignited a fireball in the back of my throat. If that temperamental dragon lord hadn't attacked the kirka, I wouldn't have resorted to such drastic measures. Besides, why did only the darklings deserve the power and healing properties of the egg? Half their population leeched off the other half. They had their shadowcasters upon which to rely. Why did they need the Torensphere, too?

Nalene scrunched her nose up at me; she'd heard my thoughts.

"You're b-belittling the nnnonshadowcasting d-darklings? Zack's a nonshadowcaster."

I glared at her. "Fine. I'm blaming those narcissistic nymphs then. They were so busy looking at their own reflections, they became vulnerable to one off-balanced dragon lord."

"You're in a foul mood today."

I rolled my eyes at her while the wind whipped long strands of red hair against my cheeks and eyes. My mind went to dark places easily. I kept replaying events in my head. Every time I thought about that night, I wondered if I should have talked to the dragon lord. Then I remembered he had tried to destroy a quarter of Montenai.

The Torensphere had proved to be a twisted creature. It wouldn't answer any of my questions, particularly when I probed about my mother. In its presence, I struggled to control my fire. Until I adjusted to him, I would continue to take plunges in the Aglatian Sea and dry myself on the cliffs afterward as I did now.

I stretched my wings in order to catch the sun's rays. The rock ledge was clear of ice now, thanks to my heat. With a sigh, I allowed the sun's energy to travel through my back to the middle of my chest and down to the pit of my stomach.

I straightened my long flowing black skirt, one Cornelius had brought. When I thought of the satyr leader and kirka mother, my gut soured. Were they okay?

I broke from my reverie to find Nalene had disappeared from the rock's ledge in front of me. Knowing her, she had traveled to the thin current of sea running through our cave and no doubt sat warming herself by the fire, preparing a fish stew for breakfast.

How she managed to pop into the sea and rise up inside our cave with breakfast still impressed me. The poor fish never saw her coming.

My half-crazy phantom, Serena, could poof out of thin air, too. Her ghostly face suddenly appeared before me as if my thoughts had summoned her. Her dark hair flowed out on its own accord. Her eyes widened in distress. The other two phantoms approached me with this same darkling/nymph visage rather than the scarier one they saved for trespassers.

"Natcha, the lords tried to get through, again."

"Thanks, Serena. I appreciate you keeping guard." I used my most placating tone as I eyed the mirror in her right hand. She consulted it before disappearing again. In all my twenty-three years, I never figured out her means of travel. I don't believe she understood how things worked in her phantom world.

I knew the phantoms continued to drive the lords back, but Serena kept her distance from the Torensphere. My conscience again began a dialogue in my head about the cost of stealing the egg. Turning from the sun, I entered the cave and waited until nightfall to venture back out.

CHAPTER TEN

TRANQUIL SKIES GREETED me, but my mind was anything but still. My head continued to reel with images from the Torensphere, to the point I grew nauseated. Stepping outside the cave and flying away from the entity offered some relief. It also gave me the freedom to lose it, completely. I landed in the Ballatian Woods and sliced my claws across tree trunks, thrashed my way through brambles, and hurled fireball after fireball into the snow banks. Blind rage consumed me, and I wanted to hurt something, anything. When I felt burning tears in my eyes, I got more pissed off; I didn't want to cry anymore. *When had I become this weepy creature?*

I continued my rampage through the woods until the muscles of my chest, stomach, and neck seized up. I didn't know how to fix things. Nalene looked better than she had in her entire life, yet I still couldn't sleep more than two hours at a time.

Even when I shut my eyes, I heard the Torensphere and saw the deceased dragon lord's one golden eye. The thought caused my skin to feel as if it had ignited. I burned through my dress, melting the snow around me. My heat would not ebb, no matter what I did. Soon it rose above, melting the snow, causing the branches to weep. The ground around me muddied, and I searched for a stone on which to sit.

I knew I should go back to the cave, but I wasn't ready. My mind wouldn't slow, my heart wouldn't settle, my soul wouldn't quiet. I felt like I would go completely mad. My emotions changed from one instant to the next. From sobs to laughter to a rage that consumed me with fire and threatened to burn me out like it had the dragon lord.

I felt ill with some disease. The symptoms were despair, anxiety, grief, and guilt.

Soaked with the melting snow, I began to pace, causing steam to rise up from the ground as fresh snow banks gave way to me. The Wishing Tree had been intact and the dragon lord stalking up Shadowland's boardwalk when I launched into the Ballatian Woods. It wasn't my fault he had too much heat. This thought stopped me in my tracks. *Did he have too much heat because I took the egg?*

"No!" I said out loud. Lord Akton hadn't followed me. In hindsight, I knew from the way he held himself and his contorted features that he wasn't well. If he had pursued me, I would be a crispy critter and Nalene dead. It had been a matter of survival. Whose life was more valuable—his or ours? Only Adah could know. I looked up at the stars. I'd have to trust in them. Otherwise, I'd go mad and burn out as Lord Akton had. I wished the Torensphere would stop torturing me with the image of his death. I always blocked it from Nalene. She was having a hard enough time coping with what her survival had cost the darklings and the dragon lords.

Screams echoed through the woods and snapped me out of my thoughts. I wasn't alarmed. Honestly, I'd heard plenty of squalling in my life time. Where there were phantoms, there was bound to be some shrieking. Usually, I could place the sound, whether it be a macho satyr, an enraged dragon lord, or a lost female.

When it came again, I retracted my wings into my back. With my cloaking buzzing in my ears, I sprinted toward the sounds that kept getting louder. Was it a male or a wounded bear? *Something in horrible pain.* In the clearing, under the moonlight, a darkling swung a tree branch at the swarming phantoms. The phantoms contained him but made little effort to numb him. Serena looked more bewildered than ever. The dark spirits clung to her skirt instead of examining the darkling.

I smelled the familiar smoky burnt spice scent of dragon lord nearby so I understood her confusion. "Go," I said to her.

"But Natcha—"

"Go!" I screamed. I'd rather they ward off the massive dragon lord than waste their time on a weak darkling.

When they left, the darkling continued to trudge through the snow in their direction. The muscles in his neck bulged with rage. His one free hand curled into a fist. When he turned, his entire body remained puffed up as if he were ready to fight. The anguish on his face told me he'd really come here to do battle with himself. *Zack.* He wore no jacket, just a long-sleeved, collared shirt, untucked from his jeans.

His eyes fixed on me then widened. "Oh. I get it. Send the naked redheaded phantom to distract the darkling so you can suck his soul."

As the snow melted from my heat, vertical waves of fog released from the ground like freed souls. It shouldn't have given away my location, and my cloaking still buzzed in my ears. *How the heck could he see me?*

He stepped closer and tilted his head, his square jaw locked in anger. Up close, I noticed his five o'clock shadow and ridiculously long eyelashes framing the sad eyes I'd known since he was a little hatchling. His dark hair stood up in different directions from all his thrashing at the phantoms. He smelled like…steak, and something sweet…cupcakes. And he looked…

Dear Adah, he's hot.

The branch came at my head so fast, I didn't have time to react. *Thwack.* I registered a twinge of pain but kept upright, shaking my head a bit to clear the dizziness. Within seconds, I had regained my composure. "Ouch!"

His mouth dropped open, and he scrambled backward with his weapon. "You're…you're not a phantom!"

Uncomfortable. Really wished I hadn't melted my clothes. I crossed my arms over my chest and eased behind a tree branch to obscure other parts. He didn't blink.

"What…*are* you?"

I still registered the warm buzz of my cloaking field. What was going on? "What color are my eyes?" I demanded.

His face flushed, and he looked flustered. "What?"

"You heard me."

Zack stepped closer, his curiosity winning the battle with common sense. "They're brilliant blue." As his eyes lowered to the rest of me, the branch dropped to the snow.

Crap. I wished I could travel like Nalene. I hadn't been around darklings, satyrs, or nymphs. At least, not with them being able to see me. The last two darklings who had seen me were dead. Fear rose as bile in my throat.

I didn't want to sprout wings and launch into the sky in front of him. My wings had caused his father to think I was a demon. I needed to get out of here. "Go home, fledgling. It's not safe in these woods."

I turned my back to him and walked down the path, hoping my casual air would cause him to lose interest. It didn't. I heard footsteps behind me. My long hair stuck to my hot skin so I knew he couldn't see the scales of my back.

"How do you do that?"

I flung my hand up to shush him. He ignored it and continued to follow, slowly gaining on me.

"Aren't you cold?" he asked.

Still ignoring him, I continued to show him my backside and hoped he would stop at some point. He didn't. I whirled around and glared at him. My eyes must have changed, the pupils forming their vertical slits.

"Whoa," he said, drawing his hands up in front of him.

"What part of 'these woods aren't safe for you little fledgling' don't you get?"

His arms dropped to his side, and he clenched his jaw.

Why the heck was he mad at me? "You need to turn around, or I'll call the phantoms back."

"Who are you?"

"I'm your worst nightmare," I growled.

He unbuttoned his shirt, slid it off, and offered it to me. He wore a white undershirt underneath. "Put some clothes on, Nightmare."

My temples pounded with anger. Who was he to tell me what to do? Stupid darkling had the nerve to insinuate I needed to cover myself? I lashed out and knocked the shirt out of his hand.

He looked as shocked as I was.

Hadn't meant to hit him that hard.

"Really? Okay. Give me your best shot," he said as he raised his fists.

So not the sad, little darkling I remember. I had no idea how to deal with this Zack. I didn't want him to see what I truly was. He'd seen my eyes. *I could call fire and hurl a fireball at his head. Then he would definitely think I was a demon.*

"What's the matter? I too much darkling for you?"

I had him pinned on his back in two-point-five seconds. My clawed hands didn't cut but applied enough pressure to each of his wrists so he knew he couldn't get free. I straddled his waist, pinning the rest of him in the process.

Now, I registered fear in those brown eyes, though it dissipated just as quickly as it had arisen.

"You're so warm," he said with a goofy smile.

I head-butted him. *Lights out.* When his eyes rolled back in his head, I felt bad, but I couldn't have him following me farther into the woods, and I didn't want him to know anything else about me.

I flipped his limp body over my shoulder and carried him back to the edge of the woods.

The phantoms appeared in an agitated flurry. "Both lords are relentless, Natcha," Serena said. Tonight, she wore an extravagant, pink ruffled skirt, set off with a high-collared white blouse. I wasn't sure if she picked out clothes every day like any other creature for the image she projected. Did she shuffle through various outfits, wondering if her butt looked big before she decided?

My thoughts went back to Zack as I shifted his weight and struggled to lay him gently on a log. *Father of Montenai. I hope I didn't really hurt him.*

Serena hovered over him. "Well, hasn't he gotten handsome." Sina and Hana took shape beside her and cocked their heads in unison.

I felt a surge of protectiveness. "Hello? Raging dragon lords to attend to."

They snapped to and disappeared into the air. Despite my phantom infantry, the bellows grew closer. I launched into the air, and prayed my cloaking successfully shielded me from the lords.

Never looking back, I flew into the night, welcoming the cloud cover. By the time I arrived at the cave, I couldn't breathe, and I was soaking wet. Hesitating at the entrance, I attempted to collect myself. Why was Zack wandering into the woods alone? How could he see me?

It took a moment for me to realize I was holding his light blue shirt in my hand. Flustered, I hid it under my arm, because I didn't know how to explain to Nalene why I had it.

When I entered, Echo flew to me, emitting his high-pitched squeaks and his low-pitched knocks. Nalene couldn't hear his echolalia, but I could. With the heat streaming off me, Echo settled in my hair. I suppose that was the safest spot. Without stopping, I ran to my cot across from Nalene's and shoved the moist shirt under my pillow. I didn't know where she was, maybe fishing.

I reached up and stroked Echo's fur atop his head. He chirped a bit but didn't hop onto my hand. "Did you get enough to eat tonight?"

With the return of Nalene and my balance, the cave's temperature had regulated. I hoped he had found some recently hatched insects. I also had started a culture of mealworms to supplement his diet over the winter months. He seemed comfortable, so I left him to nest in my hair.

My interaction with the grown-up Zack had done little to cool my fire. I walked to the stone tub in the corner and plugged the hole. Once it was full, I lowered myself into the cold water, causing steam to rise into the air. Echo flew to the cave wall just above my head and hung upside-down from it. When I closed my eyes, I didn't see the golden eye. Instead, I saw Zack's eyelashes. I heard his low voice as he told me I was warm.

He hadn't appreciated me calling him a fledgling. My eyes popped open as I laughed a nervous sound I'd never made before. It really sounded more like a squeak. Self-conscious, I looked around. He'd called me a phantom. What did I look like to him? With my head resting on the tub's edge, I surveyed the stalactites above me. I felt…giddy, jittery, and a bit sick. I slid under, allowing the water to whoosh over my hair and bubble out my ears. My heartbeat preoccupied my thoughts as I closed my eyes to let the water ease the tension from my neck and shoulders.

Remarkable. I had felt devastated and homicidal. And now, I felt…

I shot out of the water and landed in a crouch beside the tub. My pearl-white claws dug into the rock floor. Scanning the cave, I took in our cots, our kitchen, and the fire circle. I heard the gurgle of the sea stream running through our floor. That was it. My cave was quiet for the first time in days. *She took the egg.*

As I threw on some clothes, Echo flew around my head. "Okay. Okay."

I retrieved some food from a wooden box in the corner, our mealworm colony. While Echo lay on his tummy on the kitchen table and ate the squirming mealworms, I paced. I called out to Nalene in her mind. When she didn't want me there, I knew. She sent a message back that registered in my left temple and eye. I'd told her before it was like a tiny sprite stabbing me over and over with a cocktail fork.

That made me think of the last band of sprites who had invaded when I left to get help for Nalene. *Vermin.* Sprites are terrified of bats.

Echo finished his snack and flew to my neck to burrow under my long hair. I stroked his head and ears, so grateful the sprites hadn't hurt him. "You're too smart to take on a gang of sprites. Aren't you, buddy?"

I tried to reach Nalene's mind again but only got the pain of her block. As I cupped my eyeball still tingling from her rebuke, her lithe form popped up in front of me in the sea stream. She stepped out of the water, her wool coat and skirt completely dry. With her huge accusatory eyes, she stared me down, all nymph-goddess-like. Except, they tended to be tall, and she wasn't.

I pinned her with my other eye. "Where's the egg."

"You look like c-c-complete crap. I put it somewhere sssafe to give you a break for a day. See if you can sleep."

I snorted. Smoke streamed out my nose, startling both of us.

"Th-that's new," she said, waving her hand.

"Don't change the subject. We both know that we need to keep the Torensphere within reach."

"Don't talk to me like I'm a hatchling."

"Fine." Honestly, I did need a break. "Where is it?"

"I'm not t-telling."

Echo curled up at the nape of my neck as I counted to ten in my head. If in any way I insinuated that she was childish, she'd shut down. I tried distraction. "Was Max playing football today?"

The satyr, Max, had the torso of a god, a chiseled face, green eyes, brown hair, and we'd seen him get it on with a nymph one night, so we could attest to his *skills*.

It had been a completely innocent spying event. We actually discussed if we should leave. Since we were home-schooled, we decided it may be our only opportunity to learn about such matters.

"Mmmax was p-playing football with the others." She cocked an eyebrow.

At first, I had felt bad when we stayed that night, but then I realized we might never have learned about satyrs and their transformation during *relations*. Apparently, their lower halves turned to those of a regular male when they were intimate. No fur to cover *anything*.

Nalene's eyes looked a bit glazed over.

"You're thinking about his butt again, aren't you?" I asked.

"No," she said, scrunching up her nose.

I knew the moment she detected something was off. She drew closer. I smelled my sister's scent—salt air, water, and honeysuckle, even in winter.

"W-what happened to your head?" she asked.

"I ran into a low branch."

"You're a t-terrible liar."

I tried to keep my mouth closed, my face blank.

She leaned in closer. "I know that g-goofy grin. What have you been up to?"

"Let's stay on track, shall we? Where's the egg?"

"W-why are your cheeks ffflushed like that?"

I sighed the longest sigh I could muster without asphyxiating her with smoke. "Okay. A darkling male was giving the phantoms a hard time, so I helped them get rid of him. I got hit in the head, that's all." I backed away to sit on the bench.

"He hit you in the head! Why are you smiling? How c-c-could he aim so well if you were cloaked?"

Little sisters can really be pains in the butt. "As soon as you tell me where the egg is, I'll tell you about the tall, brooding darkling male with fantastic guns."

All the color drained from her already pale face. "W-w-what guns?" Montenaians didn't use guns. We did have knives, swords, bows and arrows, and the most deadly weapon of all—magic.

"No, no, Nalene. It's a term the satyrs use to describe muscular biceps."

She darted to the bench across from me and plopped down. "Ssspill."

"Tight shirt, ripped muscles and all," I giggled before getting a grip. My smile fell. "It was Zack."

Nalene leaned over our driftwood table to stare into my eyes. "Natcha?" She looked like she'd seen a ghost, I mean a dragon lord. "I think the egg mmmay have scrambled your—"

"I head-butted him unconscious."

She snorted a laugh that echoed up into the high ceiling before she leaned back in place and covered her mouth.

"It's not that funny."

"I-it is, actually. I was ssstarting to worry about you." She laced her long, elegant fingers together on the table.

She could be so prim and proper.

"The egg is buried in the c-cave we loved to play in as kids."

Since she made a concession, I made a confession. "I got naked with a guy and I liked it."

With her jaw unhinged, she didn't look like a nymph goddess anymore. "But you said—"

"Yes, but I had disintegrated my clothes and scared off the phantoms. Then he bashed me with the tree branch, so I tackled him and knocked him unconscious."

"How very romantic," she said.

I tilted my head as I considered her meaning.

"Oh, Mmmother of Montenai. In your world, that truly was romantic. It was like your fffirst d-date."

I shrugged. "He's really cute, and he smells like food."

Nalene slapped her hand to her forehead.

CHAPTER ELEVEN

FIRE FLOWED THROUGH *my veins, dark lava fueling my rage. I tasted ash in my mouth, but my mind drew a blank. Thoughts and memories thrashed inside my head, trapped birds. They hit a wall over and over, never breaking through to a blue sky of clarity.*

The simplest things brought me back. As river water dripped from my pants to the snowy bank, I recognized the lanterns hanging along the boardwalk. Yes, the boardwalk I'd created with my brothers. I knew just beyond was the Wishing Tree, its enormous presence always my touch stone.

I raised my eye and...froze. My brutal childhood flashed through my head. But my pain and struggles as a young dragon lord were merely a warm-up for this instant in time. This fractal moment when my gaze met hers...she held the Torensphere. Who knew a thief could cause my dreams and reality to merge? In mere seconds, I questioned the truth of everything in my lifetime—agony, fortune, loss, and now...regret.

"Natcha? Please, Natcha." A familiar voice called me. I was myself again. What just happened? The voice beckoned once more, and I took off running, desperate to reach the source. With my arms and legs pumping fast, I ran through the arched, iron entrance of Adah's Gateway. Countless lantern lights twinkled amidst the branches of the trees, but I could only focus on a bright gold one that drew me deeper into the cemetery.

"Natcha."

Before I knew it, I was perched on the tree branch, claws digging in as I studied the hanging urn. The nameplate read, "Lord Akton."

Dizzy, I reached across to touch it but slipped.

I plummeted…down..down…my wings wouldn't release. I flailed out to catch a branch, dig my claws into anything around me.

My eyes popped open, and I gained awareness of my surroundings. My bed. *Just a dream.* Nalene's face came into focus. Brow furrowed, she grasped her necklace with one hand. The other stayed locked in my clutches. My claws dug into the skin around her elbow. Rivulets of red streamed and found each pore, creating a road map on her delicate forearm.

I let go of her arm as I tried to quiet the heat that whispered inside me like an evil accomplice. My thicker skin shined with sweat. "Are you okay?" I croaked.

She continued to grasp her necklace. Blood coagulated and the punctures in her skin slowly closed. Tiny, round, purple bruises stayed behind.

"Wwe need to t-talk," she said.

Her nightgown glowed lavender under the lights of our ceiling. She sat at the foot of my bed as I retracted my claws and attempted to smooth my hair out of my eyes. The clammy feeling continued as if I had a fever. It didn't matter how far away the Torensphere was. It still got into my head while I slept.

"T-tell me about Akton," she demanded.

His name caused me to flinch. I retreated to the stone wall that acted as a headboard to my cot and pulled my knees to my chest. The cool rock eased me. However, I assumed it would take some time for me to recover from the dream.

"You wwwere screaming his name." Nalene's rich timber wavered.

When her hip brushed my shin, her cool essence crept over me, sedating me a bit more. She would continue to encroach on my personal space until I caved.

"Not much to tell really," I said in my cavalier way. "All the dragon lords were gone. I crept inside the Wishing Tree. You should see the riches and treasures those lords have amassed over the years. Anyway, I made it outside. As I was leaving, he was returning. We locked eyes with each other."

Her hazel eyes stayed fixed on mine. They seemed to dazzle with her water magic. My body began to rebel against me. I felt my muscles twitch and mouth run dry just as they had done the day I took the Torensphere.

Her cool hand covered mine and squeezed. "Nnnatcha. What else? You c-c-can't keep this inside."

Panic seized me. My respiration, heartbeat, everything veered off course, lost rhythm. My mouth opened and closed, but no words came out. I couldn't breathe. *Too hot.*

"Yes, dragon princess, that is the pain he felt," the Torensphere said inside my head. A pain lanced through my skull, a tunnel narrowed, and everything went black.

TIME WENT BY. I couldn't be certain how much. The first thing I registered was the cool dampness on my forehead. My eyes took in the dark shadows as they shifted over the stalactites of the ceiling. Was nightfall upon us already? It had just been morning.

I expected to see Nalene but found Serena flickering next to my bed.

"Shut up! Stop it!" When distressed, her voice became otherworldly shrill. She cupped her hands over her ears.

I pushed to sit up. "What did I say?" A damp washcloth fell to the sheets.

Serena's hair stood out more than usual. Her eyes were all pupil, like those of a startled animal. It wasn't often that I saw Serena weep. She floated back and forth in front of my cot, creating a frothy dessert in the air with her movement. Before I could comfort her, she disappeared.

Exasperated, I forced myself to get up. I stood with my shoulders hunched in the soft glow of the cave, wondering if I'd driven Serena away for good and if Nalene was furious with me. I didn't try to touch Leeni's mind. She most likely needed space. The memory of the diseased, half-crazed dragon lord had made me physically ill. Would I go mad like him?

Every joint ached as I snatched the hem of my nightgown and flung it up over my head. The sound of a billowing sheet echoed into the darkest crevices of the ceiling, announcing the stretch of my wings. Finally, like the popping of knuckles, the cartilage in my wings crackled with the release of pressure.

After dressing in boots, a skirt, and an open-backed green sweater, I filled a basin with the spring water that trickled down the wall of the cave. At the washstand, I splashed water on my face then brushed my hair in front of the mirror. In the last week, my life had changed in a way I could never have imagined.

Grief, guilt, and resolve kneaded my insides until I became dizzy and had to grab the sides of the washstand to steady myself. I told myself that Akton would have died anyway. My appearance before him and theft of the Torensphere were not the cause of his demise. I was gone before the explosion. It was the Rehmling sister—the little one with the big hair. The rumors swirled that she had been in his presence when it all happened.

If I didn't accept this story, at least for the time being, I knew I would snap. I owed it to Nalene to keep it together, at least until we saw how things would shake out. I forced myself to heat some fish broth to calm my stomach.

Afterward, I stepped out to the ledge overlooking the water. A million phosphorescent creatures created a waving tapestry in the Aglatian Sea. Banners of snow unfurled in the wind from the mountain's peak above me. My mind wandered to the satyrs. It was always amusing to cloak myself and watch them. Their music and singing were wonderful, and I needed soothing tonight. However, another force pulled me. Not the Torensphere, but Zack.

I flew toward the stars, allowing the cool mist of the clouds to envelope me, before plunging down toward the sea's spray. When I alighted at the farthest stretches of the woods, I heard voices. The phantoms rarely came this far. If I were smart, I would never come this close to Shadowland.

The Montenai River gurgled in the late hour. My eyes found the twisted, atrophied skeleton of the darklings' Wishing Tree. *It was still there?* At first, I thought my eyes deceived me as I looked into Shadowland's South Village. Dragon lights lit the structure from within.

Voices carried through the still woods, drawing my attention away from the disaster zone. After scaling a nearby old oak with a U-bend perfect for swinging or hanging out, I cloaked myself in its branches and listened. I smelled him first.

"Zack. I don't expect you to understand," huffed Bianca Rehmling. She strolled next to him, her ringlets bouncing as she shook her head for emphasis. From my usual eavesdropping on the satyr camp, I'd learned Bianca spent less time as a shadowcaster now and more time as a healer in Toren Hospital. You catch a lot being an invisible lurker.

I'd overheard the satyrs talk about her healing abilities almost paralleling those of the nymphs. I also learned she had a thing for Lord Bulosk. This could explain Zack's bad mood the other night.

Something inside me didn't like the way Zack looked at her. Or the way he doted over her, making sure to grab her by the arm to steady her over the rough terrain of the forest.

"Bianca, I understand that Lord Bulosk rescued you from the burning tree. I get it. But he's brothers with Lord Akton who lashed your sister close to death, and then tried to burn you alive inside his lair. Did you forget all that? Besides, he's old."

"Really? That's all you got. He's old." Her hands found her hips.

"Merely weeks ago, you were referring to him as a reptile." Zack paced in front of her. "I'm sorry to be cruel, but I believe you're not thinking clearly due to the strain."

"My mental function is just fine. Things are very clear."

"This has nothing to do with my feelings for you. This is me talking as your *friend*."

"I don't believe you," she said.

"They have the ability to mess with your mind. You know this."

"He's not brainwashing me." She put her hand to her forehead. "I can't talk to you about this. I just can't." She turned back toward the lights of the village and walked away, wisps of her breath visible in the air.

He didn't follow but stood still with his jaw clenched, his hands shoved deep into the pockets of a black leather jacket. After several tense minutes, he spun around and looked up in the trees. "How was the show? Did you enjoy that?"

His eyes scanned from treetop to snow bank. My cloaking hummed softly in my ears. And yet, I knew the instant he found me.

"Hello, Nightmare. Stuck up in the tree like a little cat, are you?" With his arms folded across his chest, he walked toward the tree. "Well? Do you enjoy spying on darklings?"

It took a few moments for me to realize he expected an answer. I'd grown so accustomed to watching the Montenaians, not talking to them. I couldn't quite figure out what to say. I leapt down from the branches, startling him.

He squinted as he scrutinized me. "Are you a nymph?"

I shook my head.

"Skin so fair. Not a phantom or nymph…" he continued. "You smell of the sea. You must be a siren or naun—" He froze.

Had my eyes changed because of my nervousness or excitement?

Zack took one giant step back. He uncrossed his arms. "The heat." He never broke his gaze with me. "The strength."

I stayed glued to the spot. Wet snow dripped from the branches above. Some fell across the shoulder of my sweater, mixed with my body heat, and caused a hiss. It would be better if he were scared of me and stayed out of the Ballatian Woods. But I hoped he'd stay and talk a bit more before he freaked out. I saw the whites of his eyes, and I knew he considered me dangerous.

"You have eyes like *them*," he spat. His head turned toward the village, then back to me. "Who are you?"

This was not going well. I culled the air with my senses. The dragon lords were nearby. I knew they were patrolling, constantly on the lookout for the thief. And yet, here I stood, not 300 yards from their beloved Wishing Tree, their lair. Perhaps the bump on my head had affected me.

"Lord Leasith said the thief was female. That she ran into these woods." Zack shook his head. "I could yell and have the dragon lords here in two seconds flat."

When he strode toward me, I turned to run. His gasp triggered every alarm in my body. He must have seen my back, my scales. While they were light in color, they did have a tendency to reflect in the moonlight.

"Leave me alone," I said. After sprinting up the path, I rounded a sharp corner and launched into the air, flying low for cover in the tangle of trees. With my heart pounding double-time, I looked back. Hurt and confused, I focused on my cloaking. How could he see me when others couldn't? What would he tell the others? Serena's scream filled the night. She'd followed me and come to my rescue.

CHAPTER TWELVE

NALENE HELD ME close and stroked reassuring circles on my scaly back where my sensitive wing slits were. Her icy hands attempted to soothe my hurt feelings. She had felt and heard my every thought through our connection. She knew the absolute rejection and shame I'd felt from Zack's reaction to my scales. Fear. Disgust. He must think I was like the dragon lords, but worse, I was a thief.

"Nnnatcha, stop," she insisted. But no matter how hard I tried, the loop continued to run through my head of him steadying Bianca with a gentle hand, and then his face scrunching up when he saw my scales.

The tears stopped when I got a grip and realized he could lead them straight to us. *Straight to Nalene.* I lifted my head from Nalene's shoulder and grabbed her face. "I need you to leave."

"Wwhere d-do you p-propose I go?"

"Leave now. Go to the nymphs."

Her bottom lip jutted out. "Sometimes I hate you. It wwwould be easier without me. I haven't mmeant to burden you, Natcha."

"You didn't do this. I did. Go to the kirka. They'll take you in. You look just like them."

She pressed her lips together.

Lately, I'd been calling the nymphs conceited. Well, all except for Magda. Now I'd told her she was like them. "They're smart, Leeni. I think they can help you with your body temperature."

Nalene stood up from the bench, smoothing the black sweater she

221

wore. It contrasted with her pale skin, making the sharp lines of her face and enormous eyes appear more severe. "I d-don't need to be healed. I c-can travel through water. I know how to mmmanipulate the molecules. Will they *cure* me of that, too?"

My eyes burned from crying. Why was I so stupid? In addition to insulting her, I had managed to endanger her with my naïve crush I'd had since childhood. Would Zack tell the dragon lords about me? *Of course he will.*

A chill breath tickled my cheek before Serena appeared and whizzed past me to address Nalene. "They're coming. They're coming," she lamented while wringing her hands.

I stood up so fast, my head swam. "The dragon lords?"

"No, the sad darkling and…that nymph." Serena continued to avert her eyes from me. The fur trim on the hood of her crimson cape cast her face in shadow. "They are almost to the rock."

I wished I hadn't upset her with whatever I'd said in my nightmares. I was already unsettled, and now, she deferred to Leeni. That never happened.

Serena turned her menacing phantom eyes on me, prompting me to stumble back. "We may have to attack. They will come and kill the baby." She raised her hand to consult the eternally cracked mirror. Her shriek of anguish sounded like a wounded animal. It vibrated through the space and sent stalactites crashing to the floor.

After she disappeared, Nalene looked at me in horror. "The b-b-baby?" she whispered.

"Pfff. She's so melodramatic," I reassured her. "And she's obviously confused."

Nalene met my gaze with one of maturity and absolute disbelief. My sarcasm and jests were no longer effective in defusing things for her. She grabbed a nymph light from the driftwood end table. It glowed a deep scarlet with her mood. Darn mystical nymph lights. Sometimes it's better if you don't know everyone's feelings.

She arched an eyebrow. "Well, dragon sister. Let us greet our nosy guests. I have a fffew words for Zzack."

"Zack," I repeated.

I found myself running my hands through my hair and checking my face in the mirror above the washstand. Although my skin was pale, it didn't pink easily because of its thickness, so it looked in relatively good shape. However, my pupils assumed their vertical shape; my irises glowed aquamarine with a pattern of lines bursting from the pupil like cracks in dry land. I focused on my breathing and thought of the cool Aglatian waters to bring my fire down, which, in turn, diminished the dragon in my eyes.

I couldn't contain the jolt of energy that surged from my toes to the ends of my hair. Danger usually was the impetus for this feeling. Today, it was the blend of fear and excitement. I looked at Nalene. My thoughts must have flooded her mind.

Her hazel eyes lit with her water power, and she pursed her lips in amusement. "G-getting ready for a b-b-big date, are you?"

"Stuff it!"

She snickered before growing serious.

"I don't know if confronting them is such a good idea," I said.

"You're right. Let's wwwait until they reach this side of the mountain, fffind our home, and lead the d-dragon lords straight to us." Her nostrils flared.

"Leave the light. It makes it harder for me to cloak you."

With a huff, she returned the nymph light to hover just above the table's surface. Eyebrows raised, she watched me. "If they can sssee you, then I d-don't want to hide."

Folding my arms across my chest, I sighed the long exasperated sister sound she'd grown to hate. "We need to stay hidden. We have no idea what they want or what they'll do."

She nodded.

Fists clenched, I stood and crossed the small stream of water to the mouth of the cave. The churning fog of the phantoms greeted us as soon as we emerged. The only way off the cliff face was for me to fly and Nalene to travel through water.

"Let's cut them off by the black rock," I said. Something was happening with the phantoms if they were allowing a strange darkling to reach halfway up the mountain.

Leeni pressed her face into the moist breeze and disappeared. I spread my wings and launched off the cliff's face. Usually, I dove toward the water and skimmed low to admire the colors of the water world below. Today, I flew as fast as I could before my foolish ways gave away our location.

When I landed, I saw Magda wrapped in a silver cloak, standing by the rock. Her power caused the flora around her to bow and acknowledge. The movement of twigs, branches, and leaves caused a mini-avalanche of snow. Zack stood to the side of her, at a respectful distance.

Nalene stalked a few steps behind me. *"Careful, Natcha."* She communicated in my head.

The nymph's hair lifted in no breeze as her eyes scanned the area. "Come out, Nightmare," she said in a husky voice. Zack darted his eyes to her, looking displeased with her mocking tone.

Confusion filled me. It spread across my chest like the worst heartburn I'd ever experienced. This was the female who fed me, clothed me, and monitored my life from afar. Why had she led him here? She had known of my existence but had respected my privacy for over twenty years. Why would she betray me now?

"The Torensphere," Nalene and I both said to each other.

Zack looked to me, then the nymph. "You can't see her?"

Allowing my dragon eyes to glow, I stared him down. He swallowed and narrowed his eyes.

"I've never seen her, except from afar when she was a wee hatchling," Magda said. Her eyes moistened, and a smile spread across her face.

A yearning inside me swelled to a peak. Her show of emotion knocked the wind out of me.

"Her hair is red like the glow of our fires, her eyes the color of the sea. And when she was a toddler, I saw her magnificent wings spread in the sunlight to reflect like a prism across the bluffs."

She had been close if she had viewed the bluffs around our home. Magda had to have stood in the southernmost reaches of the satyr fishing town of Port by the Sea to have glimpsed me. When I was young, I couldn't always control the cloaking.

I monitored this lovely creature, knowing she could siphon Montenai's essence and channel it to level her enemies. Magda had exercised extreme control in not retaliating when the dragon lord had burned her village. "*Whose side is she on?*"

"*Not ours,*" Nalene communicated in my head.

"Why is he here?" I asked, furious Magda had betrayed our location to the darkling.

She fixed her eyes in my direction, although I kept my cloaking on.

Zack stepped forward, his jaw set. How quickly curiosity had mutated to disdain. I should have insisted the phantoms mess with him the other night. I regretted ever speaking to him.

My mood must have spurred on Serena. I watched with relief as three bodies of fog writhed over the terrain and threaded through the trees behind our visitors.

"You have caused the worst kind of strife in Shadowland. *Thief.* Our leader is dead, his brothers struggle to reign, and a violent faction of darkling militia has formed."

His words sank into my thick hide like hooks. It only made sense he'd figured out I was the thief. I was the only creature the phantoms let pass into the Ballatian Woods. Hurt and defensive, I struggled with my words. "That militia was there before the Torensphere disappeared. Lord Akton, no doubt, created it. Do you blame all of his destruction on me?"

Magda stood rigid.

"I came to seek your advice that night, kirka mother, but your village was on fire because of the dragon lord. I needed—"

"My mother is sick," Zack started toward me, but Madga grasped his arm.

This news about his mother disturbed me, but I tried not to show any emotion.

A piercing shriek ripped through my head. "*Don't listen to a traitorous nymph. They are the ones who weakened the darklings,*" the Torensphere said in my head. "*Do you know what Akton's last thought was, dragon princess?*"

Dizzy, I shook my head, trying to block out yet another one of his rants. I knew he'd be showing me darklings with rashes covering their faces, sick from Shadow Fever. Or, Lord Bulosk's sad eyes as he looked at the burned Wishing Tree. My fire surfaced as my anger built. I directed my intensity at Zack.

"Your leader was gravely disturbed and abusive. You're completely delusional if you think one creature caused all the strife in your world. Nonshadowcasters are sick because they have always been more susceptible to things." I dropped my cloaking so Magda could see me.

"Natcha?" Nalene called in a trembling voice.

I brought fire to my palms.

The nymph mother stepped in front of Zack. "We're sorry, but we desperately need your help. Surely we can come to some agreement regarding the Torensphere."

Zack stepped past her. "I'm not sorry. Whatever kind of beautiful creature you are on the outside, inside you have a black heart."

"Natcha!" Nalene warned, again.

"I could have the phantoms suck your soul," I said in my most menacing voice. It wasn't low like Magda's, but it had enough gravel to convey my inner monster.

Zack's jaw dropped. Magda tilted her head. I doubt many had ever spoken to the nymph mother in that manner. I didn't care. Their presence had brought the return of the egg's essence. It hissed and howled words to me, sending a blinding pain to ignite behind my eyes. I saw it glowing in my favorite "treasure cave" from childhood. It flashed my most distressing childhood memories to me in a fast, nauseous display. I thought it had been quiescent in the cave, but it had only been mining my memories.

I stepped back and clutched my stomach. Something wet dripped from my nose. Looking to the snow, I saw droplets of blood. Time sped up. Suddenly, I found myself on my knees with Nalene in front of me, shielding.

"Where did she come from?" Zack asked.

"Hello, child," Magda said in the same soothing voice she had used on Nalene's birthday.

"Y-y-you need to leave," she gritted.

I peered around her leg, attempting to draw in the shadows to restore our cloaking, but the essence made me so dizzy, I couldn't focus.

Large icicles dislodged from above and pierced the snow just in front of their feet. If they had moved an inch, it would have injured them.

"Impressive," I said inside Nalene's head.

Magda stood her ground, looking undisturbed and fascinated.

Nalene placed an elegant hand on her hip. "I mmmean no disrespect, but you are t-t-trespassing and endangering my Natcha...sister. I don't advise you return any time soon."

A layer of snow powder rose up and suspended in a wall in front of them.

When it dispersed, Zack had turned to face the three phantoms. Instead of attacking him, they flowed through him and stood around me, sheltering. Knowing Nalene would disappear into water, I took to the air. *"The cave,"* I said in her head.

When I landed in front of the cave of my childhood, the one we fondly named Satyr's Treasure Trove, I felt the surge of the Torensphere as it clutched at every fiber of my being. Disoriented, I turned to find Nalene at my back. Cold rarely disturbed me. The water usually calmed me, but I couldn't move my feet. The only way in was underwater. The thought of it suddenly repulsed me.

"Wwwhat is it?" Nalene asked. "You're scaring me."

"Don't you hear him?"

"Sure. He sssings to me."

"Sings? I get rants and nosebleeds. You get vitality and ballads?" I never expected the creature to be happy with me for stealing him from Shadowland, but I couldn't comprehend why it...*he*... was wooing Nalene.

Nalene patted my back. "I'll go talk to him."

"You do that. All I get is insults, violent images, and displays of power!"

That brought on more raving. *"Miss...taken. Miss...taken,"* he hissed.

"I am not mistaken, you jerk!"

I turned to see the color seep from Nalene's cheeks. "W-was that him?"

"Yes."

She shook her head. "I-it can't be. He doesn't sssound like that a-at all when he t-t-talks to me."

"Well, maybe he has a split personality disorder," I spat. I'd had enough. After a big gulp of air, I dove into the water.

Once inside the cave, I coughed from the essence that enveloped me. My once cool, comfortable refuge felt stifling. The egg lay in the middle of a pile of seaweed. Nalene appeared beside me. Her cheeks flushed a peach color. Her eyes shone with a healthy glow as she gazed lovingly at the Torensphere.

All the fluid in my body seemed to dry up. My eyes felt gritty, and I couldn't create enough spit to swallow. "I am not mistaken."

Stupid, stupid, Natcha. Why did I think I could manage an entity it had taken three dragon lords to control? I had been so desperate when I thought Nalene was dying, I'd lost all reason. I was in over my head. This creature was complex, dynamic, dark—and charming with my sweet sister.

"You need to stop," I said to him.

A prickling sensation ran up my jawline to my right temple. It felt like he meant to broil me alive.

"Leeni. We need to get out of here."

Nothing was right. I'd stolen the egg. The dragon lord died. My nymph foster mother, as well as half of Montenai, was after me for being a thief. Zack hated me. I struggled as thoughts that brewed in the background fought to become evident in the foreground of my mind. This place felt ready to explode. The Torensphere had changed the atmosphere in the cave. *Why?* The longer I stood there, the more I couldn't catch my breath.

"Now, Nalene. Come now." I clawed at her wrist.

She pulled back. "O-okay. I'll mmmeet you at home."

Feeling like my skin would melt off, I dove into the cavern's pool now warmed by the Torensphere. Once I pushed through the tunnel to the great sea beyond, frigid water soothed my body and cleared my brain. I surfaced, gulping for air.

After catching my breath, I took to the air. The icy rock ledge leading into my home had never been such a welcome sight. When I landed, I stood for a moment just breathing the fresh air.

By moving the Torensphere, I had sparked a change. It was thriving in its new location, with its new freedom. The warm, dry air had reminded me of...*an incubator.*

What had I done by bringing the egg here? Darklings were sick. Too many Montenaians were suffering. *Why had I ever trusted it with my baby sister?*

CHAPTER THIRTEEN

MY BEST MILKING goat, Juniper, nuzzled my hand as I carried her grain bowl to the stanchion. Without hesitation, she jumped up onto the milking stand, ducking her head through the slot that held it in place. I'd included alfalfa, her favorite, and she allowed me to clean her udder and begin expressing her bag into the bucket. The rhythmic stream of milk hitting the metal lulled me, and I leaned my head against her side as she chewed her grains. She was my favorite doe. Her disposition was quiet and steady, the opposite of mine.

Early morning was my favorite time of day, and I needed this breather after the tumult of yesterday. In her fur-trimmed cape, Serena sat next to me on a stool, or pretended to sit the best a phantom can.

I had given her the silent treatment after her failure to guard us yesterday from Zack and his threats. Nalene and I had fought over the Torensphere, and I could not forgive her for siding with the entity. The two of them had me so out of sorts, I had slept in the barn with the goats. Well, not really slept. The Torensphere would not shut up.

After a few quarts, Juniper was done. I moved the milk aside and let her down so she could graze along the mountaintop with her herd.

The chickens were next on my list of tasks. I collected the eggs from the nesting boxes and cleaned out under the roost. Once they had fresh water, feed with crushed oyster shell, and new straw, I took my basket of eggs and focused on Serena. She'd been gazing into her mirror for the last fifteen minutes, which tempted me to break the quiet because I couldn't stand this obsession of hers.

She mumbled under her breath something about "home." When I retreated to the cliffs, she followed. The other phantoms had worked double-time through the night. Lord Leasith was determined to get through, but my phantoms were ferocious when it came to the dragon lord. After I got mad at her about Zack, Serena had shadowed me nonstop.

It's hard to ignore an agitated phantom. The black spirits rotated around her skirt as she stood overlooking the Aglatian Sea. Their muffled screeches wore on my last nerve. I plopped down several yards away by a rock I'd dragged up earlier to start my latest project. Wings stretched wide to capture the sun's warmth, I protracted my claws and focused on the crystal in front of me. I carved it with a fierce intensity that brought my heat to the surface of my skin.

I'd never let anyone see me before, and now, when I should have sequestered myself in a faraway cave, I had exposed myself to the leader of the nymphs and a darkling. Worse, I'd caught myself crying. Pissed, I wiped the tears away. I'd never been a weepy creature. The tears thing had me more unnerved than all the impending danger.

All of Montenai was out of sync. The phantoms were behaving erratically. My sister and I disagreed gravely over the plans for the Torensphere, and I knew the dragon lords were relentless.

Try as I might, I couldn't get Zack's troubled voice out of my head as he talked about his sick mother. I hadn't even wanted the egg in the first place. I just didn't want my sister to die. I hadn't tried to return it yet, because I was terrified Nalene would become ill again.

No matter how hard I argued, I couldn't get her to agree on a consult with the nymphs about her troubled breathing or what we called her "ice." If I knew there was an answer, some hope she'd never get that ill again, I'd turn the Torensphere over in a second.

Why is Nalene so stubborn?

When finished with my creation, I retracted my claws and studied the result of my work with the stalactite. I pushed the tiny sculpture into the deep pocket of my skirt. Nalene had at least a hundred such sculptures lining the shelf by her cot. She'd always loved shiny things.

Leaving the Torensphere around her unattended was like placing a big fat diamond in front of a sprite and not expecting it to take it. Sprites were notorious for stealing Montenaians' treasures. How could I have been so stupid?

With the hum of my cloaking in my ears, I launched into the sky, which was a solid wall of gray. The snow took the form of tiny ice pellets and needled my skin. My senses were certainly heightened. Usually, such things didn't bother me.

Cloaked, I made a pass over satyr territory. They played and worked along the water's edge. Their songs reached my ears and buoyed me. Whether tending their vineyards or fishing from their boats, they always had music as their companion.

I didn't sing, but Nalene did. In fact, she had been humming a haunting tune lately, which I surmised originated with *him*. Serena followed behind me, the tail to my kite.

"Natcha. Turn back," she said.

My head reeled with different thoughts, which I knew were not my own. Just before I landed, Serena dove in front of me. She flashed her phantom eyes at me, and wrapped my body with her numbing cold. It was a good try, but she'd never been able to subdue me completely like she could the dragon lords.

The claws of my feet dug into the silt at the mouth of Satyr's Treasure Trove. Warmth infused the soles of my feet. The Torensphere knew of my visit. I resented the creature within for violating my thoughts and feelings.

Hesitating at the entrance, I suddenly wished we had cleared the cave of our riches before the Torensphere had taken up residence. These were our prizes, our sacred things collected over the years.

A plethora of treasures had washed up along our shore from the satyr's across the way. We had handsome knit scarves, variegated colored bottles from their winery, wooden flutes, and even guitarellos in our little museum.

"Am I not another one of your treasures you've pilfered?"

With my palms facing each other, I formed a fireball.

"Not necessary, little thief."

"Really? You made my nose bleed last time we conversed."

"If you are worried, sit along the rocks and chat from there."

I huffed but did as the Torensphere suggested. Serena dangled over the water ten yards out, creating a frothy snowball in the air about eight feet in diameter. The closer she was to the Torensphere, the more frenetic she became.

"Do you know of the astrei?" he asked.

"Yes, the Mother of Montenai, Adah, was an astrei."

"She brought me here from Fallon."

I knew the story. Even as a hermit living in a sea cliff cave, I learned of our history, mainly from the books Cornelius had brought us. Before the Blessed Incursion, darklings lived on the west side of the river with the nymphs and satyrs but were much weaker creatures. The families relied even more heavily on their connection to humans for strength. Those who were nonshadowcasters were seen as burdens and often neglected. They didn't live long lives. Many satyrs existed as nomads to escape the domineering personality of the kirka ruler at the time, Hanleith. The aggressive nymph would never have tolerated a dragon lord burning her village. Of course, there were no dragon lords to contend with at that point.

"Adah stole me from my mother."

I'd never heard anyone speak of the Mother of Montenai with anything other than praise. Now that he wasn't screeching at me, I was able to listen to the deeper tones of his male voice. My interest piqued, I engaged. *"Why did she take you?"*

"I don't know. I was only newly laid. I do remember we were at war."

"She was said to be twice as beautiful to behold as the nymphs. Astrei were the creatures that tended dragons in your world."

"Yes."

I'd seen paintings of Adah in the dragon lords' Wishing Tree. She had three sets of gossamer wings. While petite in stature, barely five feet, she was said to be more powerful than the seven-foot satyrs in my world.

"It was a violent, harrowing ride when we came crashing through the portal from Fallon, the land of the stars."

Adah rode the red dragon, Akton, through the portal. Akton's immense figure had eclipsed Montenai's sun. The Montenaians thought the world was coming to an end. Akton blasted the sky with toxic flames, causing a torrential heat that damaged the ozone layer. He managed to close the portal before landing in the Shadowland woods, exhausted and bloodied from battle.

Adah lay in the snow, a wracked, broken creature when the first brave shadowcasters approached to see the otherworldly visitors. They didn't fare well. In fact, they were Akton's lunch.

"She was mortally wounded. Akton's fury was felt by every creature in Montenai. She had freed him from enslavement. In their world, the powerful sorcerers ruled, and the dragons served them. The astrei cared for the dragons. At least that was the term used. In truth, the astrei used their magic to suppress the dragon's fire, which weakened them and kept them under the sorcerer's control.

"Quite often, the astrei grew fond of their dragons and formed a life-long bond. Akton was a rebellious spirit. He had been sentenced to death by the sorcerers…at Adah's hand. The astrei had begun to question the practices exercised by her rulers.

"Adah, saw an opportunity. She grabbed one dragon egg and climbed upon Akton. They rode into Fallon's brightest star."

I knew the story. An army of dragons, astrei, and sorcerers pursued them. Adah fought bravely, but two of her wings were severed. In their world, the wings carried the essence of the creature.

The sorcerer's magic seeped into her open wounds and overtook her like a slow-acting poison. She stayed conscious through it all.

The dragon, in his rage over her pain, took out one-third of the forest before a pregnant darkling, Toren, stepped forward and provided an herb from the nymphs to ease the astrei's suffering.

The torment abated, but still the blood in Adah's veins turned cold within three days. In the morning, as Montenaians dug their way out from one of Montenai's record snows, they saw a blue-white burst in the sky. Adah had crossed to Laith, where we go after this life.

"Akton was overcome with grief when she died." The Torensphere had been communicating in a lulling tone but interrupted my thoughts with his familiar menacing one. *"He took to the sky and suffered the fire death just*

like his halfling legacy did just a few weeks ago.

"*Lord Akton,*" I replied in his head.

The power I felt the previous night crawled over me, and my mouth went dry. "*Now he glows red from above and she a blue-white. The satyrs, darklings, and nymphs refer to them as the Mother and Father of Montenai due to their impact on the land at the time. Montenai kindred are said to see Adah or Akton when they cross over to Laith,*" I finished.

"*Yes, little thief.*" He flashed an image of a golden eye in my mind. My head spun. I was sick and tired of this creature's mind games.

"Stop it!" I yelled into the watery cave. "*How could I know?*" I pleaded with the creature.

"*You stole me from my brothers,*" it shrieked.

A needling pain pulsed in my head. In an instant, I was airborne. I'd accomplished enough for the day. The being had actually conversed with me. I'd win him over, perhaps. I needed to be quick about it.

I didn't trust this alien creature from Fallon. I'd seen the power it wielded while encapsulated. What would happen if it hatched?

CHAPTER FOURTEEN

A RED FOX crossed my path, yellow eyes glowing in the night, reminding me of two moons. The fox carried a squirming mole in its mouth and disappeared down a game trail. I took to the air, traveling north over satyr territory, the marshlands, and uninhabited Cypress Forest. It felt great to stretch my wings and attempt to clear my head. I hoped that increased physical distance from the Torensphere would ease my mental state.

I had left Leeni brooding in the cave, but I had my bodyguard, Serena. In twenty-three years, Serena had never traveled with me beyond the woods or the mountains. I couldn't say she never went there herself since I didn't know where she went when she disappeared. Tonight, I traveled with my cloaking buzzing in my ears and my fierce phantom riding shotgun.

The air felt almost balmy in this area. I rarely came this far north on either side of the river. My route would lead me straight into Kirka Village. I stopped just shy of where the land opened to wide fields and farmland. Perched in a cypress tree, I looked in awe at the spectacle before me. Fire. Wind. Magic.

Under nymph floodlights, a diverse crew of Montenaians was creating a large, glass dome in Kirka Circle to replace the one destroyed by Lord Akton's attack.

Nymphs chanted and gestured toward the land, procuring minerals from the soil that suspended in mid-air as a fine powder. Lord

Bulosk breathed his flame on the elements while the satyr, Cornelius, inclined his head, directing the winds to swirl around the perimeter of the materials to create a thick, curved glass.

The other domes looked to be complete. While the field remained bare, I knew it wouldn't be for long. Once the nymphs had their main circle intact, they would work fast to restore their surroundings to a lush, fertile state.

It dawned on me why the dragon lords hadn't hunted me down, at least not yet. Their truce with the nymphs must have entailed first restoring their village. If Lord Bulosk was preoccupied on this side of the river, Leasith must be guarding the Wishing Tree. I realized the dragon lords had become quite vulnerable without the power of the Torensphere and strength of their oldest brother.

I looked across to the east side of the river. The blown-glass lanterns of the dragon lords illuminated the skeleton of the tree. There still was no bridge across the river. I wondered if that was part of the agreement as well. The nymphs didn't want rebellious darklings to have easy access to their village.

I felt Serena's coolness as she rested at my back. I couldn't cloak her, but when she wasn't in full phantom state, she didn't cast any light. Mesmerized, my eyes stayed on the scene below me, but my nose detected a familiar scent coming from the west, the Hinterlands. *Fire.* As a dragon creature, I can detect smoke from miles away. I searched across the vast distance. Torchlight blinked and darted through the thick, wild terrain. Smoke rose from various sources, clustered together in a narrow swatch of land. Why was there so much torchlight and fire in an area that remained uninhabited except for the random cabin?

When I left my perch, I drew Serena with me. As I skimmed the treetops, I felt and heard the change in my phantom when her black spirits awoke and began swirling her aura. I had never wandered this far west of my home, but my senses told me trouble brewed here with the nymphs and dragon lords preoccupied elsewhere.

Cypress trees gave way to a more variegated forest. The slender skeletons of bare hickory trees stood starkly against the snow-covered fringe of red and white pines. The sprawling arms of river oak marked a thin leg of the river that cut through the land. In the heart of this mysterious wild, campfire flickered, and voices rose in the night.

My heart jumped to the level of my throat when an encampment of at least fifty tents came into view. Cloaked, I drew closer. I eyed Serena, hoping she'd bring her dark spirits to heel. Their usual din would give us away.

Once we landed in an ancient cedar tree, I could discern the makeshift camp situated by a wide bend in the stream. My eyes roved over canvas tents, fires with stews brewing, and a weapons area with darklings busy cleaning and repairing swords. I recognized the embossed metal helmets of the militant darklings I'd first seen the night I'd stolen the Torensphere. The swoosh of flame on the cheek plate did something to my insides.

The darkling rebel militia? *Of all the crappy luck.*

The canopy of the dense forest effectively obscured much of the camp, but my heightened senses zeroed in on a clearing at the edge of the compound.

The sharp lash of a whip rent the air, followed by a guttural animal cry. The sound, full of anguish yet suppressed fury, came again, twisting something inside of me. I lost feeling in my toes. Shouts and moans created a gruesome chorus, raising all the hair on my body. I counted ten darklings being detained and *questioned.* Long chains and rope bound their wrists and ankles and tethered them to each other. Blood stained the ground around the males heaped together, some lying, some sitting in the snow. Those that remained upright yelled their protests at their captors.

One of the darklings lay shirtless in the snow—his arm bent at an impossible angle, and his leg twisted inward. Against a tree trunk glinted a nasty device known as the crippler. Shaped like a scythe, the arc of metal was blunt for breaking, not cutting. This weapon hadn't been used since the reign of the nymph queen, Hanleith.

Heat surged in my gut, as fury pounded in my chest, making me dizzy. I leaned into the fern-like needles of the cedar and inhaled the spicy scent.

My intent had been to see what was here. I wanted to erase the images in front of me. A trail of blood in the snow led to a monstrous, sprawling oak tree. One soldier held a whip at his side, another stood by the tree, shouting in the face of a darkling tied to its trunk. *Zack.* Blood wept from wounds across his back. The tree trunk was so wide, the binding stretched his arms straight out to form a T. He had no shirt or shoes in the winter night.

"You know exactly what's going on," the captor spat. "You're in tight with the nymphs and Bianca Rehmling."

I thought my rage and sorrow might blind me or set the trees on fire. My chest ached as I looked at his condition. Tears welled up in my eyes as I clenched my fists so tight, my claws dug into my skin. When I turned to conspire with Serena, she was gone. *Really? Now? When I need you?*

The dark spirits started their muffled chorus. I located the sound about twenty feet in front of me. When Serena began her shrieking, I decided that if I was going to have a sidekick, a phantom is the way to go. *Holy Mother of Montenai,* she lit the night in all her horrifying glory. Grown males screamed. Few darklings had experienced a phantom up close. Serena's reputation, however, preceded her. The phantoms had become part of darkling lore in the last two decades.

First, she moved to dispose of the evil rebels in charge of the *interviews.* Cloaked, I flew behind her, straight to Zack. *Focus on his face, Natcha.* I couldn't look at his bloodied back and keep my cool. He hadn't moved, despite the cries from the soldiers, but shook all over from the cold and pain. Eyes shut, he pressed his left ear to the bark of the tree, as if listening for some answers.

"Zack."

A crease formed along his forehead. When I slashed the ropes that pinned him to the tree, his stiff arms sprang back, ripping a cry from deep inside him. His eyes popped open. I didn't dare touch his back, so I bent low, supporting his legs from behind. This way he wouldn't collapse backward. He huffed air, a raspy, thready rattle, as he swayed in front of the tree.

With the commotion of the rebels at my back, I needed to trust my phantom to guard me. I held Zack steady and gave him time. He looked down as I poked my ahead around his leg to look up. My cloaking buzzed, but I knew he could see me.

"Nightmare," he croaked through cracked lips. Then, he laughed. As he shook, I just squatted at the back of his thighs, still steadying him.

"Thank you, Natcha."

He used my real name. Nalene had let it slip to both him and Magda. I liked that he knew it. Drawing back, I tested his strength. He placed a hand on the tree trunk and managed to hold himself up.

"I'm okay," he said in a hoarse voice. "If you can, please help the others."

When I turned, I found a much different scene. The prisoners still huddled together in the snow, but there were no soldiers guarding them. The torturers lay on their sides, eyes wide and unblinking, victims of Serena's power.

Cloaked, I slashed through the prisoners' bindings.

"Hey…what the…" came from the terrified males.

"Be very still," Zack insisted so they wouldn't flail or fight the invisible force whooshing behind and over them.

He kneeled next to the guards, rifling through their pockets to find the keys to the metal cuffs. "Go, Natcha. I've got this."

I hesitated for a moment as I looked at his bloody and swollen face.

"Go."

I do not condone violence, but I gave the frozen torturers a good kick. The one, who wielded the whip, got a single claw to the face. It was a small wound that I hoped would leave a scar on his cheek.

When I joined Serena, she faced a motley crew of rebels wielding swords, spears, cripplers, and bows and arrows. I fought with the element of surprise, ducking sword strikes, whips, and darkling knives. The majority of the militia members were nonshadowcasters. I knew this because I detected no shadow energy to pull for my cloaking. They wore the Shadowland crest, a gold shield with a red dragon looking down at its shadow. From their bits of communication, I gathered they were loyal to Lord Akton, serving on his behalf.

About ten percent were shadowcasters. They were able to throw a dark shadow, which usually would cause their target to experience dizziness and nausea. The few who were able to hit me with their casting were gravely disappointed because it only fed my cloaking and helped me disappear. Their faces of triumph when they thought they had vanquished me quickly changed to terror when I popped back into view. Through it all, I took extra care to memorize faces, for many weren't wearing their fancy helms.

Did I cheat? No. I let them see my face, my glowing dragon eyes, popping out of my cloaking long enough to give them a fighting chance before I kicked the weapons out of their arms, or delivered blows to their heads to stun them. I rarely used my claws unless nothing else would disarm or subdue them.

I crouched down to check a few of Serena's victims. I'm pretty sure she left them breathing. All the color had drained from their faces, and they lay curled in the fetal position.

At some point, I took in a deep breath, turned, and found no foe, just Serena. She flickered in her darkling visage, her pretty hood up around her face as if just out for a stroll in the winter night to look at the stars. I knew she could return to her phantom state in an instant if anyone stirred.

"I need to destroy their supplies," I said.

She blinked but didn't answer. I knew she would wait for me. Adrenaline coursing through my veins, I flew up and down the rows of tents, collecting all whips, ropes, swords, and bows and arrows and dumping them on the bonfire to incinerate them. My clear third eyelid closed diagonally to protect my eyes from the heat and smoke as I repeatedly threw fireballs on the heap, creating an alchemic stench that caused my head to swim, but I persisted in my methodical way.

In the last tent, I found scrolls of parchment with detailed plans scribbled in messy penmanship. After rolling them tight, I shoved them in my large pocket. My dragon eyes glowed in the dark of the tent, finding one last weapon, which glinted brighter than any star in the sky. This time, I wouldn't hesitate with the astrei sword. My fingers curled around the hilt. When I recognized the texture, my mouth went dry.

Scales. *Real* golden dragon scales, not just the mutated version the lords sported. The pommel at the end of the sword's hilt looked like an ornamental dragon's eye. A full-dress golden saber knot hung down.

When I pulled the sword up, the knot swayed and found my skin. A sharp prick caused me to cry out. The saber knot had morphed into a miniature dragon's tail, wound around my wrist, and hooked into my flesh with the barb on the end of its tail. I understood how Mr. Salva lost his hand ten years ago.

A powerful magic crawled over me while voices whispered foreign words inside my head. Screams of triumph, torment, and tragedy fired through my synapses. My stomach felt like I'd dropped from the sky in a downdraft. Every hair on my body stood up. I couldn't drop the sword if I'd wanted to—the tail had my wrist locked into place. With the barb latched on to me, I didn't dare let go of the hilt for fear I'd be maimed.

Mouth agape, I stood with my red hair straight out from my head, examining the intricate etchings of stars that covered the sword's steel blade. Engraved on the branched handguard were three sets of wings.

"Drop it! Drop it, Thief!" The Torensphere warned in my head.

"Natcha?" Nalene called.

"Little busy right now," I communicated back.

She tried to sneak into my thoughts, but I blocked her out. I gathered she was with the egg. If *he* wanted me to drop the sword, then I planned to hold on. Besides, I didn't want to lose my hand.

I recognized the black scabbard worn by Mr. Salva and his tiny son so many summers ago. It lay nestled in the dirty blankets comprising a soldier's pallet on the ground. Using two hands, I steered the tip of the longsword into the scabbard. As I sheathed it in the hide, I felt the dragon tail quiver. When the blade had sunk completely inside, the tail released and returned to being a decorative cord. Squatting, I reached out to feel the material. My fingers caught on half-inch hooks over the surface of the piece. That wasn't what disturbed me. The skin rippled under my touch as if alive.

"Natcha!" Serena yelled to me.

I grabbed the sword and scabbard and exited the tent. My hair still stood on end, and I had an epic case of the heebie-jeebies, which didn't get any better when I saw my phantom sidekick floating toward me, looking frightened. I'd never seen her scared. Scary, yes, but never scared.

"Careful with that," she said.

I hesitated. Serena didn't always remember things. Had she seen the sword the night Zack's father died? I couldn't be sure. She turned from me to look at the immense bonfire. I bent down to strip one of the immobile male's belts from his waist and then threaded it through the loop of the scabbard. With the scabbard secured around my waist, I yanked the remaining tent and its contents toward the bonfire to finish my purging of this blight on Montenai.

Now completely exhausted, I caught myself swaying on my feet. Serena floated behind me, my quiet sentry. Through the distorted fumes of the fire, my eyes met Zack's. He had a blanket draped over his shoulders. The released prisoners had found a few supplies, administered first aid, and were almost ready to leave the area in carts and satyr all-terrain vehicles. Zack stood to the side of an ATV, its trailer loaded with injured darklings. Even with the vehicles, they had at least a two-hour trip through the Hinterlands to Kirka Village.

I couldn't read Zack's expression. If he noticed the sword, he made no indication. After a slight nod, he climbed into the vehicle, switched the high beams on, and set course through the woods.

When I turned to Serena, her stare was distant. I wished her thoughts and communication were more coherent. Did she have any ties to these creatures in her past life? I gave her a tight-lipped smile I hoped was reassuring. She overwhelmed me. I'd seen her freeze a lone male, but I hadn't been sure about her taking on a whole camp. I would never doubt her again. No wonder she had been able to keep our mountains and woods clear of trespassers for all those years.

My head swam from the fumes, the adrenaline, and the noise. The Torensphere ranted in my head. *"You have no idea what you've wrought."*

"Really tired of your gloom and doom." I prepared to launch into my own tirade about unhatched dragons with negative attitudes, but the bellow of dragon lords stole my moment.

Serena's eyes flickered black. I'm not sure what I had expected. Serena had screeched to wake all of Montenai, and I had created a bonfire that no doubt was visible from another plane. Cloaked, I took to the air, while she followed at a decent distance so as not draw attention to me. She didn't engage with the dragon lords. I wondered if it had anything to do with her being out of her familiar territory, or did she feel as completely drained as I did? Did she ever get tired?

Homebound, I tried not to think about the entity at my waist, the look on Zack's face, the screams of the Torensphere, or the fact I was neck deep in this crap and would either need to fight my way to the surface or drown in it.

Serena stayed silent as she floated alongside me.

"Nice work, Serena. Thanks for your help."

She turned to me with her startled prey look. "Akton?" she asked, her chin trembling.

Her expression broke my heart. When the cliffs came into view, she disappeared.

I circled my home, debating about what to do with the sword. For the first time in my life, I didn't trust my sister. I'd seen her reaction to the Torensphere. Passing the familiar cave entrance, I headed for the barn. My herd greeted me with their bleats. Juniper nuzzled my hand. Despite it being dark, she thought it was time for milking and feeding. I gave them some treats before kneeling in the southeast corner of the barn. Using my pearly claw, I worked the board loose. Once I'd laid the sword and belt against the cold ground, I replaced the board and moved the hay back over it.

When I turned, Nalene stood in the doorway.

CHAPTER FIFTEEN

NALENE AND I fought like never before. She wanted to know about the sword. I wanted her to promise to stay away from the Torensphere. We went to bed, neither of us satisfied with the other. I slept with the sword, refusing to show it to her. My sleep had been horrible for weeks; what difference did a sword in my bed make?

A light snow fell in the early morning. I tended to the goats and brought Nalene fresh milk as a peace-offering. She only looked at it in silence, her eyes red and puffy.

"What is going on with you?" I asked.

She pressed her lips tight and shook her head. Echo perched on her shoulder so just his cute little pointy ears and his thumbs jutted out from beneath her hair. It said something about her health that my bat felt comfortable sleeping the day away nestled against her skin.

"Why, Nalene?"

"Y-you've b-b-been blocking mmme out." She looked down at the table, drawing imaginary circles with the pad of her index finger on the faded driftwood surface.

"I'm too old to have someone reading my private thoughts," I countered.

She looked up. "I d-d-don't invade your mind. I j-j-just check-in when you are fffar away from mmme. And most of the t-t-time, it's more you leaking your thoughts to me."

I was so tired of arguing and worrying. It didn't seem like any decision I'd made up to this point had been the right one. No words I chose at this moment would be the right ones, either. She had become just impossible to live with or trust.

The muscles in her jaw twitched, and her nostrils flared as tears filled her eyes.

I sighed. "I'm sorry. I'm very frustrated."

When she stood up, she startled Echo. He chirped and found a more peaceful resting place—a stalactite hanging over the tub.

"You must know everything. You're always right. What is it going to take for you to trust me? Maybe, I know a lot more than you ever could," she yelled in my head before disappearing.

"Nalene? Nalene?"

I felt her block as the usual sensation of a cocktail fork to my eyeball.

Feeling physically sick, I sat on the bench and took deep breaths. I could go after her, chase her all over Montenai trying to make amends. But I needed to check in with Serena and Zack. Besides, if Nalene didn't want me to find her, there was no way I'd be able to with her hide-and-seek skills.

Convinced I had to act, to do something, I pushed my sister and my problems to the back of my mind. I rolled the rebel's plans in some soft leather to protect it and shoved it in the deep pocket of my purple dress. In the other pocket, I placed the crystal sculpture I'd made at the barn with Serena fretting over me in the aftermath of my meeting with Magda and Zack.

The layered Montenai sky was as clear blue as could be when I stepped out on the ledge. The warm sun found my face and made things better if only for an instant.

After a quick flight over water, I landed and hiked the ridgeline to the east of our cave. This allowed me some time to gather my thoughts and cool down. The terrain was rugged and untouched for the most part, except for game trails. After I reached the summit, I looked out at the sea to watch the birds dive to the surface and come away with breakfast. Mama otters lay on their backs, wrapped in the kelp, nursing their young. Others used rocks to break open the shells of mollusks and clams.

I continued hiking through the mountains for an hour, lighting fireballs and dispelling some heat. Serena came to mind several times. I wished I had an effective way of communicating with her. She didn't always focus or process direct questions about her past. What did she know about the Torensphere and the dragon lords?

Cloaked, I flew back to the other side of the mountain and landed just past our goats. I called for Serena as I trudged through melting snow. I was halfway to the black rock when she appeared in front of me, wearing a long, white dress. I'd never seen this dress. Blood covered the skirt.

She held her mirror and did not meet my eyes.

"What a lovely dress," I said, hoping to capture her attention.

Her smile touched the corners of her eyes. "Thank you. It's a surprise," she gushed. She looked so young and hopeful, it stole my breath. What trauma had she suffered that she never passed over to Laith?

"What kind of surprise?"

Eyes cast down, she appeared bashful. Then I saw her usual tempest spark. Her face went from joyful to a mask of anguish. Eyebrows arched, mouth slightly open, she wailed at the crimson stain on her dress.

Dumb Natcha. Why did I call attention to the dress? "It's okay. It's okay," I pleaded with her, my hands up to try to stop the impending storm. She disappeared.

"Come back. We'll fix it," I said. Frustrated, I formed two fireballs in my hands. I'd love to hurl them at something, but I didn't want to catch the forest on fire.

The sword hung from my belt, the weight a constant reminder of its presence. I considered drawing it from the scabbard and taking my frustrations out on the air with my awesome swordplay, but the voices had scared the crap out of me last night, as had the stabbing dragon tail.

"That's a wicked trick, Demon," a male voice said.

All the blood drained from my head. Zack *had* seen me the night his father died. *Did he think I was responsible for his father's death?* I turned to face him.

"Peace, Natcha." His voice was still hoarse. Bruises and cuts swept down the left side of his face. I wondered if it was from being hit with a fist or bumping against the tree trunk when being whipped. He lifted a dark, woven basket in the air, and the ethereal scent of meat filled my nose. He put up a brave front, but he kept a comfortable distance. "Can you turn those off?"

I couldn't be sure if he meant the fireballs or my eyes, which likely changed when I had smelled the food. I doused my fire and my dragon eyes with thoughts of the sea.

He found a downed tree and settled on it with the basket. "Hungry?" His thick, dark eyebrows shot up in question.

Unnerved, I placed my hands on my hips. "Why are you here?" I didn't like that the phantoms were just letting him roam anywhere in our territory.

"To say thank you and offer a truce." When he lifted the lid of the basket, the smell of roasted chicken and herbs wafted my way.

I didn't move.

"I promise, I don't bite." He chuckled. "Now, can you say the same?"

Stepping closer, I culled the air, using all my senses to track any threats in the surrounding area. Before I knew it, I sat on the log at the farthest end from him. He opened the other flap of the basket and withdrew a linen cloth that he spread on our makeshift table. On this, he placed a plate filled with chicken, diced potatoes, and okan, a green vegetable quite tasty when fried. My mouth watered. He handed me the utensils wrapped in a napkin matching the blue color of the cloth. The Lords' crest was embroidered on it. This gave me pause.

His face fell when he realized the affront. "I'm sorry. It's on everything in Shadowland."

I nodded as I unrolled the cutlery. Here I was sitting next to handsome Zack while considering if he was trying to work up the nerve to kill me, the demon he had seen ten years ago. "You first," I said.

Our eyes met. I kept a cool façade, even though I trembled inside. He raised his own fork and cut a piece of chicken. I watched as it crossed his lips. He chewed and swallowed. I raised my eyebrow.

"Interesting. I don't *think* you would poison yourself. Then again, you have displayed a death wish by coming into phantom territory and challenging my sister and me."

He wore the leather jacket with a white thermal shirt underneath. I could see his light brown skin and black chest hair. His masculine scent distracted me from the food.

"Speaking of your sister, she around?"

"Always. So don't try anything funny."

"Natcha. I'm a chef. Seriously, what could I do?"

I smoothed the skirt of my purple dress over my legs. My index finger traced the intricate embroidery on the material. "You came at me like a satyr warrior or a darkling militia member."

He pressed his lips together. "I'm sorry I hit you that night. I thought you were going to hurt me."

A little growl escaped my lips.

His eyes widened.

"I still can." While my heart felt warm, and my whole body tingled in his presence, I couldn't forget his anger toward me about the Torensphere. To him, I was a dangerous, perhaps murderous, alien creature.

Since I had him on guard, I reached over and tasted the chicken. It was like something straight from Laith. I tried to play it cool, but before I knew it, I'd eaten all the chicken and started on the potatoes. "This is amazing."

I watched his pride swell. It was evident in the color that seeped into his cheeks. He looked down and fussed with the contents of the basket, obviously uncomfortable with the praise.

The dragon lords' scent wafted from the basket.

When he lifted his chin, I met him with my dragon eyes. "Where are they?"

Brow furrowed, he looked to the dessert in his hand then at me. "What's the matter?"

I looked at the chocolate cake in the plastic wrap.

"Natcha, I work at Drakos, the five-star restaurant in town."

My claws extended as I scooted a distance from him on the log.

"I prepared everything myself. It's okay." He held the chocolate cake out to me. "It's their restaurant. Of course, their scent lingers on things."

"You first," I said.

He pulled his chin back as if I'd offended him. But he grabbed a fork and took a taste of the food. Once he swallowed, he licked his lips and smiled. "Yum." Chocolate frosting clung to the corner of his split lip.

I scooted forward to my previous position and took the fork from him, claws retracted. *Yum* was right. After several bites, I decided he didn't intend to poison me but rather lull me into a food coma.

Afterward, he reached in for two more items. "Now to test your grit." He handed a bottle to me and kept one for himself. *The Fire Bomb.* Lord Akton stared at me from the label.

I swallowed a lump in my throat the size of a dragon egg. My breathing sped up. I wondered if Zack was trying to mess with my head, or if he'd just not thought when he grabbed the bottles with the dead lord's image on them.

"Are you okay?" he asked innocently. His eyes shone with genuine concern.

"Sure," I said, brushing it off.

The clear glass bottles revealed an amber liquid with floating gold specks. Each bottle had a thick rubber base.

"Do you know how this works?" he asked.

I shook my head. I knew they served these in III Brothers' Pub, but I never went near there, especially after Mr. Salva died.

He grinned. "Allow me." He slammed the base of my bottle down so hard on the tree trunk, I was sure it would shatter, but it didn't. I heard a "pop" like a cork releasing. A darker liquid infused the drink from the base, swirling and bubbling. When it was finished, the liquid coalesced and flickered the orange and red of dragon fire.

"You ready for this?"

"Pff. Please," I said. "You go first."

He laughed. "No, no. Females first. I insist." He handed me the now warm bottle then slammed his bottle to make the fire appear.

The glass warmed my hands, indicating the liquid's temperature had changed. I studied the fancy closure. It had a swing-top bail and stopper. Zack leaned over and used his two thumbs to pop it open.

"You've done that before," I said with a giggle. *Why am I giggling?*

"It's my favorite drink."

"Do we chug it?"

"You might want to take a sip first. See if you can handle it." He winked.

"We'll chug it. On three."

"Whatever you say, but I warned you," he teased.

When I hit three, we both tossed back our heads and chugged. I loved it. Cinnamon is one of my favorite flavors. I finished first. The kick came after as a pleasant tingling in my nasal passages.

Eyes wide, he surveyed me.

I cocked my head like "what?"

His mouth hung open, and the smallest beads of perspiration formed along his hairline. I caught him sniffle a bit, and his eyes watered.

"That was delicious." I flashed him a megawatt smile.

"Glad you liked it." As he packed up the basket, I caught him wiping his nose on a napkin.

Afterward, he stayed by my side, studying his hands clasped in his lap. I wanted to ask about the rope burns around his wrists, the fate of the rebels, and the status of the dragon lords. Most of all, I wanted to know how his mother was doing but was too afraid to ask. She was all he had. He cherished her. I'd seen him cook for her since he was a small hatchling. Food was his way of showing he cared. Except with me, in which case, I believed it was more like bringing a meaty steak to distract an attack dog.

A deluge of thoughts streamed through my head; I felt nauseated. Did he really think I was a demon? Did he want the sword back? How sick was his mother? Did he still kiss Bianca Rehmling? How bad did his back hurt from the abuse he suffered at the rebels' hands? I studied him once more—torn jeans, black boots, no hat or gloves. He had to be hurting, but he'd hiked here to find me.

"So," he said, looking up the trail to the top of Mount Faunlier. "I'm a chef. What do you do?"

"I lure darkling males into the woods then eat them." As I snorted at my own joke, I suddenly thought of his father and wondered if Zack thought I'd harmed him. My laughter died.

"That story doesn't ring true."

I bit my lip.

"If you were truly a bad demon, you would have killed me first, and then raided the contents of my picnic basket. And you wouldn't have tried to help my father."

Shocked, I met his eyes. "Do you want to talk about him?" I looked back down at my skirt and fidgeted.

He swallowed loudly. "It *was* you," he rasped.

Blinking several times, I forced back tears. Fear, anger, and regret filled me, leaving a metallic taste in my mouth. As I surveyed the pristine snow and blue sky beyond, I realized I had nothing to lose. He deserved to know it all.

"When you were nine, I watched your family."

"Your sister, too?"

"Yes." I shrugged. "We were lonely little hatchlings. The only way we learned about the world was through observation. I shadowed your father often."

Hands shoved in his jacket pockets, he gave me a slight nod.

My throat felt like it was closing up. I'd never told anyone the full story. Something cooled my hand. I looked down to find his dark hand covering mine. It gave me strength to continue. Whether I should or not, I trusted him with the details.

The cool breeze lifted the dark curls off his forehead.

"Your father spoke with Lord Akton at the Wishing Tree before he went to the pub, drank, and then stumbled to the Montenai River. It was the Torensphere that must have driven your father to the edge. Instead of explaining about the entity, Lord Akton let him think he was mentally unstable, hearing things from the tree."

He squeezed my hand. It reassured me just like Nalene's touch could.

"My little sister wasn't with me. I had left her at home because I didn't like her to see your dad in that state."

Zack grimaced. "I wished I hadn't seen him that way, either."

I bit my bottom lip. "He came out of III Brothers' Pub with a satchel I believe held the sword. When I saw him making his way to the river's edge, I came back to find you."

"You led me to him," he said.

"I was trying to help, but he'd already swum into the current with the sword."

The color drained from Zack's face. "I heard him yelling."

In an instant, I could hear Mr. Salva again, and see his frost-covered black beard and desperate eyes. Nerves fluttered in my stomach. I shivered although I wasn't cold. "He thought I was a demon from the sword."

Zack caught my eye.

"I'm not. I was just a clueless fledgling in the wrong place at the wrong time." I hiccupped, wishing I hadn't eaten so much. "He meant to throw the sword away, into the river."

Zack's brow furrowed. "The light."

"Yes, and voices."

He swallowed as he glanced at the scabbard on my hip. "It has been my family's secret for generations."

I nodded. "Adah's sword." My fingers found the cold belt buckle as I moved to return the piece to its rightful owner.

He placed his hand on my arm. "I think you may need it more than I do right now."

"No. If anything, the other night at the rebel camp proves you are in grave need of it."

Zack flinched.

"Sorry to bring that up." The last thing I wanted to do was bring him pain, but that's all I'd done by talking about his father and the sword.

He shrugged. "It has only brought my family trouble. If it has accepted you, then I trust you with it."

Dumbfounded, I fixed the buckle back in place. "How did you even get it in the first place?"

"The astrei sword has been in my family since my great grandfather retrieved it from the river's edge a century ago. He was just fishing from the banks one day. For some reason, he felt compelled to keep it rather than turn it over to the lords. It never lit up or did anything for him. The scabbard hide always squirmed when you stroked it. But no barbed tail, light, or demon voices surfaced like with my dad." Zack rubbed his hands on his jeans.

"We didn't touch the sword after my dad died. The night you stole the Torensphere was the first time the sword actually released for me when I stroked the scabbard. The strange voices overwhelmed me. A horrible force crawled through me and knocked me unconscious."

"What did you do?"

"When I came to, I returned it to the scabbard and put it back on the shelf in the closet." His bruised face contorted. He leaned forward and rested his elbows on his knees. "I can be brave, but I'm not crazy. That was just too wild, dark."

I nodded.

"When I saw you and no one else did, I knew it was because of the sword."

Perhaps his father had seen me because he possessed the sword, too. Zack must have been mulling the same idea around in his head. I knew the instant he remembered it protruding from his father's chest. His whole body became rigid. I grabbed his hand and squeezed.

"I tried," I whispered. My throat felt tight, and I struggled with my emotions. "I tried to get him away from the river." As tears slid down my cheeks, the whole tragic night replayed in my head. I felt what I'd felt as a little twelve-year-old—confused, scared, and so helpless to stop anything that was happening in front of me.

Zack stared at me, scrutinizing me so intensely, it cowed me. I had to look away.

"I'm sorry for many things: the night I didn't save your father, the fact I took the Torensphere—"

"Why'd you take it?"

My stomach rumbled. So much rested on how I answered this question. I wanted his trust, his understanding, but I also didn't want to reveal my sister's vulnerabilities.

My right hand found the sculpture in my pocket. My fingers rubbed over its smooth surface. "To survive."

He blinked several times. "Your sister's sick."

Well, now it was out in the open. "I tried to go to the nymphs for help, but their village was on fire. I acted out of desperation."

With his lips pressed tight, he stared off into the forest. He was angry.

I felt the tension between us. "I'm sorry your mother is sick."

He wouldn't look at me. "In my life, I've always been so certain. My next step is always evident." Shaking his head, he exhaled a long breath. "I don't know what to think of you."

I looked down at my hands.

"I owe you my life," he said.

Uncomfortable, all I could manage to do was shrug.

"How did you know we were there in the Hinterlands?" he asked.

"It makes sense in the current situation if I monitor the dragon lords' movements."

He blinked several times, as if still processing everything.

"I was watching Lord Bulosk and the others constructing the new kirka dome, when I smelled the fires. Serena sensed things, as well." When he looked down, I studied his long lashes. "You don't really think they meant to kill you?"

"Yes, that's exactly what they planned to do."

I tucked a strand of hair behind my ear and watched an eagle soar, wings fanned out, so majestic. With my wings more like that of a bat, I couldn't soar. There was a lot I couldn't do. Like save Zack's father, heal my sister, or control the Torensphere. However, I did save Zack. If I hadn't been spying, he wouldn't be sitting next to me now.

Even after observing them for years, I still didn't understand the darklings. "What are those darklings rebelling against? Aren't they loyal to the dragon lords?"

He shook his head. "They rallied behind Lord Akton when he wasn't quite balanced. Akton told them the Rehmlings were traitors, and then Bianca Rehmling was the last one to see him alive. They blame some of the shadowcasters for his death. They particularly hold a grudge against Lord Bulosk since he's..." His chin jutted out. "...*friends* with Bianca Rehmling."

"Was she your steady?" I almost smacked myself in the head. So many important matters to address, yet the first thing that came out of my mouth was this?

"What's it to you?" He grinned.

I looked away. "Nothing, I just wondered."

"I dated her at one time, but no, we're just friends."

Nervous, my hand went to the scabbard. As I stroked it, the hide quivered. I don't know what I thought I'd accomplish, but the sword did not make me feel any braver.

"So, are you here on the behest of the all-powerful dragon lords to negotiate terms of the return of the Torensphere?"

"Behest?" His eyebrows shot up. "Who says behest?"

"Who carries food around in fancy linens?" I scrunched up my nose.

"I am not working with the dragon lords, nor am I working against them. I have my own agenda."

His mother. A knot formed in my stomach. "You think the return of the Torensphere will make her better."

"I hope it does."

Without thinking about it, I sparked a flame in my hand to dispel some heat. He raised an eyebrow, so I extinguished it.

Zack reached up and grabbed my wrist. My first reflex was to snatch it back, but I caught myself.

He held my fingers so he could study my palms. "Where does it come from?"

I leaned away from him while he grasped my hand. "I don't know how I bring fire. I just have always had it."

His thumb rubbed over my palm; he stayed transfixed by my skin.

"It's so soft. I thought it would be rough."

I snatched my hand away.

"Sorry. I was just curious."

My heart raced, and my face flushed so hot, I was sure I'd char through my dress. *Icy Aglatian Sea. Icy Aglatian Sea. That felt so nice the way he stroked my hand.* I looked at my palm as if it was no longer my own.

"Why can't they see you?"

"My cloaking. It has worked my entire life, except with your father and now you."

He frowned. "Where did you come from?"

"You ask too many questions." I stood up. Leaning forward, I placed the rebel scroll in his hand. Then, I gave him the crystal sculpture I'd made for him. "Don't worry about your mother. I will take care of things in the next twenty-four hours. I'll return the Torensphere."

He stood and grabbed my arm. "Natcha. Things are dangerous. The lords are out of their minds about their brother's death and that half the village is sick."

"I snuck it out of the tree, I can sneak it back in."

Zack shook his head. "The dragon lords are most on edge about what happened last night."

"What does everyone in Shadowland *think* happened last night?" I looked up at him.

"They know about the phantom. The others you freed thought you were another phantom and told the lords just that; I guess due to your cloaking. The lords were shocked to hear any phantoms had traveled out of the woods."

"Why didn't you tell them about me?"

He looked away as color filled his cheeks. "I don't know. After you freed us, I thought maybe you weren't all bad. Maybe you had a really good reason for doing what you did."

He lifted the crystal dragon in the sun, seeming to admire the light that shined off each facet. "Magda enchanted the forest to drive them off your scent, and I told them I'd seen the phantom coming out of satyr territory." He brandished a proud grin.

My stomach fell. "You lied to the dragon lords?"

"No. You said yourself you came through the Cypress Forest."

Heat flushed my cheeks. "Thank you."

"I just bought you some time." He lifted his hand and touched a strand of my hair.

My heartbeat sped up. I stepped away to run up the path. An orange flash of color drew my eyes to a juniper bush. I just caught the white-tipped tail of a fox as it disappeared from sight.

Without a backward glance, I took to Montenai's sky, striated with rich shades of blue. I cloaked myself, although I knew he could see me. What was the point of having the ability to cloak if it didn't always work?

CHAPTER SIXTEEN

A COLD PRESENCE infused the air behind me as I landed on the cave's ledge. Nalene's hand rested on my shoulder. A sliver of fear sliced into me. I'd never been afraid of Nalene.

"Hey," I said, turning to meet her.

"I caught lunch," she said, looking radiant.

I forced myself to eat the salmon so she wouldn't suspect anything.

Afterward, stomach bursting, I rested in my cot and read one of the history books from Cornelius. Music played softly on the compact satyr player. I continued to focus on blocking my thoughts from Nalene and the Torensphere. For the most part, I believe I was successful with her. The Torensphere was another story. *He* had been quiet, which made things more difficult to assess.

Nalene came to snuggle next to me like she used to do when we were little fledglings. I smiled.

"Wwwhat has you so thoughtful t-today?" she asked.

"Just trying to understand the point of everything."

She tsked. "Nnnatcha, it will all work out. D-don't worry so much."

She certainly had changed her tune since I'd first presented the Torensphere to her. I opened the book and looked up the Father and Mother of Montenai, paying particular attention to the part about the egg, the dragon lords, and Adah with her three sets of wings. The pictures of her wings confirmed for me that they had inspired the design on the sword's handguard. It was the same passage I'd read over a million times.

When Akton, the grand dragon, met the fire death, he left behind a glorious egg. The brave darkling, Toren, collected the egg and tended to it night and day. The egg sang to her but never hatched.

One hot summer night, Toren delivered a male baby. He was like no other in Montenai. She named him Drakos, for he had golden scales and purplish-brown eyes. The Montenaians feared him for his differences.

The Torensphere had manipulated her embryo, giving him the dragon's traits. Drakos had a mercurial temper. His temper grew, and soon the dragon-darkling was a volatile adult male. He married a darkling, Pia, and they had three sons, the dragon lords. The oldest they named Akton for the Father of Montenai. They named the middle son Leasith, in honor of Pia's father. The youngest they named Bulosk, in honor of Drakos's father, who had been loyal and faithful to Toren and did the best he could with Drakos.

The fierce dragon lord killed Hanleith, releasing nymphs, satyrs, and darklings from her reign of terror. Many thought he meant to take her place as leader, but he had no interest. He was restless in Montenai. He died attempting to use the portal in the Sequoia Forest to cross to the human world.

The Torensphere passed into the hands of his sons. They took refuge in the Wishing Tree and worked to restore order and balance to the creatures of Montenai, particularly the darklings. The darklings, who had once been weak, sickly creatures, thrived in the essence of the sphere and the power of the lords. They had always cast shadows for humans, but they never thrived from the radiation they gleaned from the earth. Some did better than others.

"T-t-together, they c-c-created Shadowland as it exists today with the Nnnorth and South Village," Nalene whispered.

"Not how it exists today," I said. "But how it was before I stole the egg from them."

"Ch-change is inevitable. Wwwe need to move forward," she said.

"I liked you better as the little fledgling who liked to piss me off with hide-and-seek."

She giggled.

I tread lightly. My gut told me Nalene would not agree with my plan. "This isn't a history book; it's a fairy tale." Anger festered inside me.

"It's p-p-pretty accurate, Natcha," she said. She played with the ruffles of her taffeta skirt. She liked taffeta. I didn't. It made too much noise. Hard to be stealthy with your skirts rustling.

"They underplay the fact that the dragon killed so many darklings. Also, they don't tell that Drakos was a raging, abusive, lunatic who beat his wife and oldest son, Akton, causing him to lose an eye."

She didn't respond. As I closed the book, I felt guilty for taking my frustration out on her. *Nothing in there at all about a sword.* When Nalene looked up, I tried distraction. "What have you been up to lately?" Usually, when she disappeared, I knew she was gazing at the stars or spying on the satyr, Max. She had a wicked crush on him.

"The sssatyrs have a big fffeast tomorrow night. They'll be conducting a wine-tasting and playing music."

Her hand trembled a bit as it rested on mine. I felt her water energy surge. It was more powerful than ever. "I wwwant him t-t-to see me. C-c-could you rrrelease the cloaking?"

"Leeni. Don't go anywhere near the satyr camp for a while."

Her jaw dropped. "Why?"

How did I protect her from the Torensphere? I swallowed a lump in my throat. How did I protect her from herself? "I've been monitoring the dragon lords. They plan to raid the satyr camp because they think the satyrs are hiding the thief."

She stood up from the cot. "Who would t-tell them such a thing?"

"I think the nymph is trying to protect us."

"Even mmmore reason for me to be p-present. I'm not going to let anything happen to the satyrs because of sssomething we did."

"*I* did."

"Nnno, Natcha. We're in this together. Remember?" Her hazel eyes locked on me.

I stood up and turned on my dragon eyes then stepped closer so she could feel my heat. "I did it. Don't forget I did it to save your life."

"Wwwhy would you th-throw that in my face?"

"Because I don't want anyone else to suffer. We need to be careful. You're spending too much time with the Torensphere."

She hugged herself. "He's lonely."

"I know. I took him from the only creatures he's ever known. I'm working on a resolution."

She squeezed my left arm. "D-don't do anything reckless."

"I won't."

Releasing my arm, she walked to the stream and soaked her hand in the waters. I must have used too much heat.

"I'll unlock your cloaking tomorrow night. I think it will be good for you to interact with some normal Montenaians."

She stood up. "Really?"

"Yes. Better to be friends with the satyrs when the dragon lords come. They'll protect you."

"Wwwhat about you?"

"I plan to negotiate."

She scrunched her nose. "Rrright. The female who head-butted a mmmale she liked in the w-w-woods."

"Give me a break. I can do diplomacy." I arched an eyebrow.

She laughed the little hatchling sound I'd grown to love, but the grown female before me seemed like a stranger.

CHAPTER SEVENTEEN

ZACK STOOD, HANDS in pockets, looking out at the Aglatian Sea. I had taken my view for granted. This particular vista placed us at the level of the clouds. Despite the winter sky, the water remained a clear aquamarine and teemed with active sea life.

I shouldn't have brought him here.

"This is more beautiful than I ever imagined," he said.

I'd flown him here. I don't know why I trusted him. He kept bringing me food, which seemed to be weakening my senses. We stood on the rock cliffs immediately across from the satyr beach area.

"I'll do it tonight," I said. I stomped my black boots in the snow, causing the buckles to jingle. "My sister will be preoccupied. She can't know." I made sure not to give away her name. Even now, while I schemed about this betrayal, I still tried to protect.

He frowned. "I'm coming with you."

"You don't understand its power. It could hurt you."

"I've already been hurt," he said, pointing to his bruised and cut face.

I sucked in my breath. That ordeal was terrifying for me. I couldn't imagine how he was coping with things. "You okay?"

"I'm alive." He held out his arms and looked toward the sky.

Wisps of clouds drifted around us.

"How did it happen?"

Zack's forehead wrinkled. "They came for me in the night. My mom tried to barter by offering the sword. They took the sword *and* me."

"Your family has been through so much," I said.

He shoved his hands in the back pockets of his jeans. "The first rebel who tried to remove it from the scabbard lost his hand. After that, they made me carry it to the leader's tent."

I waited.

"My hands were bound. They had my friends over by the tree and threatened to use the crippler on them. I couldn't risk trying to fight with the sword. You know the rest of the story."

I fidgeted with my black sweater, attempting to pull it up more along the sides of my back to cover my scales.

His hand reached out to trace the V of my wing slits. "So pretty."

Blood rushed in my ears, and my mouth hung open.

In an instant, he removed his hand and cleared his throat. "So, about this Torensphere business…"

"That was a smooth transition," I teased.

He smirked. Then his face became serious. "I've lived with the Wishing Tree, the dragon lords, and the shadowcaster magic all my life. These are things I've thrived on since a young hatchling. It won't harm me."

"The fewer individuals involved in this, the better."

"Whether we like it or not, it seems everyone is involved when it comes to this. Its presence has affected all Montenaians."

I tilted my head.

"Magda's daughter, Korena, has lost her sight."

"How does the Torensphere figure into that?"

He shrugged. The blue of his thick sweater contrasted with his skin, and made his brown eyes seem that much deeper in color. "They can't heal her."

"She's blind?" I squeaked. "I've never known of a sick or injured nymph."

"Exactly," he said.

I blew out a long breath. "Well, it will be over tonight." I shoved my hands into the pockets of my layered black skirt. "The dragon lords' power and the nymphs' healing abilities, all of it, will fall back into balance." Unease flip-flopped in my stomach. The fact my actions had made everyone sick had my head pounding. If I had the chance to undo it, would I? I knew I couldn't bear to watch my sister suffer. Even now, I felt conflicted because I didn't know what would happen to Nalene without the Torensphere.

"I don't want them to hurt you, Natcha." He looked at my face, not with disgust but something else.

I remembered the day in the woods when he made me cry. "Why are you being nice to me?"

He drew his chin back and blinked. "I like you."

"I'm a Nightmare that needs to be monitored."

Zack crossed his arms over his chest. "I'll admit you intimidated me, at first. Just remember, that nickname is self-imposed."

"You think I'm a monster. You hit me with a tree branch," I argued.

He clenched his jaw. "Can you read my mind? You have no idea about my feelings. You have very limited knowledge of the world." Color flushed his cheeks.

I kind of liked making him mad, but I didn't enjoy insults. "I know you like Bianca Rehmling, and she's in love with one of the lords." Once it left my mouth, I regretted it.

"Keep trying, Natcha. I'm not leaving you alone with the Torensphere and the dragon lords.

"I can knock you unconscious, again."

"That won't be necessary," Serena said.

When I turned, Serena rose to her full phantom height, over twenty feet tall. With her eyes dark holes and her mouth able to swallow a darkling whole, *she* was every creature's nightmare.

"Uh, Serena. What are you doing?" I asked.

"He shouldn't be here," she screeched.

"Somebody's in a bad mood." I grabbed Zack and launched into the sky. She shrieked after us until I dropped him off on the other side of the mountain in the Ballatian Woods.

Zack yelled over Serena's shrieks. "I'll meet you at the black stone tonight. Eleven o'clock!" Then he ran. My phantom followed him, trailing her rolling fog and sending her cold essence at him. She weakened and slowed his progress until he cleared the woods and stepped onto the path leading to the South Village.

She returned to me in her darkling female form. Hard to believe this was the same creature.

"Thanks for that, Serena. I hope you can hold him off tonight, as well. He doesn't need to be any part of this. They'll banish him from Shadowland like they did Anka Rehmling when she fell in love with her human charge."

Serena wrung her hands as she floated in front of me. I decided I could use the walk over the mountain to steady my nerves. With the satyrs distracting Nalene and Serena holding off Zack, I would be free to bring the Torensphere back to the Wishing Tree.

CHAPTER EIGHTEEN

I LEANED AGAINST a cypress tree as I looked across the delta at the satyrs' lights and festivities. Nalene had arrived hand in hand with Max to the celebration. Interesting little tidbit she'd kept from me. I had no idea my cloaking had failed or that she had befriended the handsome satyr. From their body language, they looked rather familiar with each other. No one looked alarmed by her presence. She could pass for a nymph, no problem.

Max fawned over her, bringing her wine and meat from the barbecue. Funny, you'd think goat creatures would be vegetarians. I snorted smoke out my nostrils as I giggled. This new talent didn't excite but alarmed me. Honestly, I was scared to blow my nose or sneeze. Would flames come next? I had always wanted to breathe fire but never thought about the repercussions.

The yellow moon rose higher in the sky. I could make out Akton's red star but not Adah's—too much cloud cover tonight. My cloaking buzzed over the surface of my skin as I headed south toward the Satyr Treasure Trove. My friend, the Torensphere, had been quiet. When I landed on the silt of the bank and peered into the waters, I felt the familiar warmth of *his* essence.

"Little Thief."

"Good evening." Without hesitation, I dove into the watery cave. When I surfaced, I found the Torensphere in its spot, glowing its kaleidoscope of colors. Reds, blues, golds, and greens mottled the

fawn-colored egg. Again, I thought of the blown-glass pieces created by the dragon lords.

"I inspired them."

"I'm sure you did," I said, approaching slowly. Despite my third eyelid, my eyes felt dry, as did my throat.

"How is it you come without your sister?"

"You go home tonight." A heat spread through my chest and up into my head. His power was impressive. "No need to battle me, Torensphere. I will return you to your brothers, unharmed."

"No."

The claws of my feet dug into the cave's rock floor. "Yes. It's time. I appreciate that you nursed Nalene to health, but now the darklings and your brothers require your help."

"They are not my brothers."

When I squatted closer, I swear an eye blinked inside the sphere. I drew back, realizing the Torensphere planned to give me a hard time.

"I stay. Miss...taken."

When I reached toward my belt, he interjected, *"Do you know at all about dark magic?"*

Perhaps, *he* was right. The sword held some kind of wicked-powerful mojo, and I already had one magical object creating strife in my life.

I leaned in and extended my hand to touch the egg. "Ah!" The shock wave made my teeth chatter. "What kind of gratitude is that?" Seething, I launched a fireball at it. It ricocheted off the surface. I caught it and absorbed it back. I lunged once more, and the Torensphere shocked me again.

"Screw this." I rubbed the scabbard's hide, causing it to shiver and release the sword. Once my right hand closed around the hilt, the dragon's tail appeared, found my wrist, and locked it to the hilt. This time, when I drew the sword, I felt empowered not scared. The voices returned, but they were subdued, just white noise.

The Torensphere's murderous rants filled my head. *"You will die a long and horrific death."*

"Such a pessimist." Brandishing the sword, I approached the egg once more. No shocks reached me.

"Not an inch closer."

"You have a choice to make: I will use the sword or my hand to retrieve you."

Nothing. Not a peep.

I swooped in and collected the sphere, cradling it with my left arm. Once it was secure, only then did I return the sword to its scabbard. With one deep breath, I plunged into the cavern's waters and swam out toward the sea. The sword weighed me down, and the Torensphere disoriented me with his rants. When I surfaced, I couldn't figure out which direction I was facing. I didn't see the satyr camp or Akton's star.

"Great," I spat.

He began Nalene's song. I knew it was his way of signaling to her something was amiss.

"Natcha!" she called in my head.

I blocked her out.

My body heavy, I launched from the water to skies so thick with clouds, I couldn't see but a few feet in front of me, even with my dragon vision. The cloud cover obscured the moon, the stars, and any of the sky's map. Panic settled in a tight band around my chest, but I continued to fly, blind. A familiar shrieking brought me back on course. *Serena!* Relieved, I choked back a sob. I loved that scary phantom with all my heart. All I needed to do was follow her shrieks.

When I dropped down through the trees, my eyes found Zack with Lord Leasith standing next to him. *So much for sneaking into the tree.* Why couldn't it have been Lord Bulosk? He had the reputation of being the more reasonable one.

As I flew closer, Zack's eyes darted to the side. *Was something behind him?* I hovered in the air as I scanned farther down the path and found Serena. Lord Bulosk stood just in front of her, blocking access. A large mirror leaned against *my* black rock. Magda stood next to the mirror, creating a reflection of Lord Akton in the glass. It had Serena in agony. The pain on her face broke something inside me. I blinked back angry tears.

"What are you doing to her?" I shouted.

Lord Leasith stepped forward and scanned the skies, attempting to locate me by following my voice.

My head pounded as adrenaline rushed through me. I had planned to drop the Torensphere and leave, never to be seen. Nothing made sense. Serena's shrieks caused my fire to surface. Perhaps, I could still reason with everyone, but I needed to free her first. If I had to hear her misery one more second, I would lose my mind.

Cloaked, I flew in a circle until I hovered immediately above Serena. In her blood-stained, white dress, she wailed and repeatedly launched herself at the glass. She had no corporeal form to make any impact, and her freezing power didn't work on the inanimate object. The reflection remained constant no matter what she did. In her darkling visage, she looked so young and so real in all her devastation.

"Akton. Akton!" she shouted.

When I lobbed a fireball into the mirror, it shattered, eliminating the torture device. Serena's head snapped back. As she looked up at me, I saw those lovely eyes bleed to black. The dark spirits woke and swirled her skirts.

Yes. I have my lethal sidekick back.

Two ribbons of fog streamed over the undulating forest floor to join her. Sina's and Hana's presence created a wall, blocking the path that lead back to Shadowland. Magda and Lord Bulosk tried to move away.

"Serena, wait," I commanded, but it was too late. She'd already targeted Magda.

Magda's eyes rolled back in her head before she dropped to her knees and collapsed into the snow. Lord Bulosk knelt in broken glass by the rock, checking the nymph's still form.

"Stop, Serena. Please stop!" I said.

Lord Leasith located me by my voice and breathed a stream of toxic fire straight at me. It covered my face and neck, making me cry out. It didn't burn, but it did sting. Stunned, I shook my head, trying to alleviate the pain.

"I'm returning the Torensphere to you."

Things were completely out of control. In an attempt to defuse the situation, I landed five feet in front of him and released my cloaking.

"You have a lot of nerve, thief," Leasith said. "Careful. I've got your rebel within claws' reach."

"Rebel?" I looked at Zack. Magda's strong nymph vines bound his ankles.

"He thinks the written plans implicate me as a rebel," Zack said.

My heart sank. I'd given the plans to Zack so he could help the darklings prevent any more violence from within their own community.

How had things gotten so messed up? Before Lord Leasith could shoot more fire at me, I cloaked myself and flew high into the branches. I couldn't think. Zack was in danger. The phantoms were ticked off, and I still had the Torensphere lodged under my arm. It continued to send little unpleasant surges into my body.

The cloudy night brought to mind the satyrs and what they could do with the winds. My stomach soured. Were they all teaming up to take me down?

Serena and her phantoms broke through my confusion. With all her shrieking prowess, she rose up behind Lord Leasith and delivered her icy trap. The spirits nipped at him, repeatedly freezing then refreezing parts of him each time he pulled lose from their power. He bellowed with frustration.

With Lord Leasith contained, Zack looked up to me in the trees. *"Go,"* he mouthed.

Instead, I dove for him, my cloaking whispering in my ears. With a swipe of my claws, I freed his legs. He didn't move. "Run!" I hissed.

Serena and her spirits swarmed the copper dragon lord, but Zack just stayed put. I yanked him by his shirt front. "What's the matter with you?" I asked.

"Ambush," he whispered.

I turned to find Korena, Magda's daughter, standing just on the other side of the path. A red fox with glowing, amber eyes crouched at her feet.

A thorny vine wrapped around my right ankle. I called my fire to disintegrate it. Another vine shot out of the ground and wrapped around my left arm, immobilizing it and the Torensphere. Shocked, I formed a fireball in my right palm and called my heat to my skin's surface.

With her golden hair flowing off her shoulders and her blue eyes glowing bright, Korena captivated and perplexed me. *Could she see me?* Quickly, I drew in the shadows to strengthen my cloaking.

As I burned again through the vines, I watched the fox. No sooner had I broken free, when another vine caught my left arm. *He can see me.* The nymph had some connection with the animal. *Clever.* When doubt leads to hesitation in battle, you may as well fall on your own blade.

My mind raced, but my body stalled. I wanted to drop the Torensphere, but now that Zack was in danger, I couldn't release it until this whole mess was straightened out. I needed it as my bargaining chip.

This time I didn't hesitate. I stroked the scabbard and released the sword. Serena zoomed past me and froze the fox and nymph. "Well, better late than never, Serena," I muttered.

I turned with my bright astrei sword to find Lord Leasith's large reptilian eyes on me. When I darted to the side, he followed. *Note to self: glowing blue sword eliminates cloaking.* "Aw sprite's balls!"

A force struck me from the side. I flew through the air a good five feet, landing face first in a snow bank. A tremendous pressure pinned me there. Sharp knives raked down my right arm and shoulder. As I rolled, blue scales blurred in my vision. *Lord Bulosk.* Dizzy from the impact, I grasped the sword with my last bit of strength. With his other hand, he yanked my wings back at a painful angle. The Torensphere popped out of the crook of my arm.

So much shouting ensued. Snow flew up around us. Dragon lords bellowed, Serena shrieked, and then the ground dropped out from beneath me.

CHAPTER NINETEEN

I NEVER HAD a chance to catch my breath before I crashed to a hard surface with strong arms around me. The floor shook as another presence appeared to my right. Lord Leasith held the Torensphere; Lord Bulosk held me, his razor sharp claws digging into my skin.

We were inside the Wishing Tree. I recognized the swanky décor and expansive marble floors. From what I could see, they had completed some restoration work. But I couldn't see much since Bulosk's enormous claws pinned my head to the marble. I brought my heat to the surface, hoping to scorch him and earn my release.

He laughed. "Hatchling, do you think I can be burned?"

Yes, Akton could. I hoped they couldn't hear my thoughts.

I took some satisfaction watching Lord Leasith's face as he struggled with the Torensphere.

"You okay, Leasith?" Bulosk asked. He strained as I bit his wrist as hard as I could.

My pearly claws extended, I dug one into his right side. "That's for Serena," I growled. He didn't even flinch.

"There's something wrong," Leasith grunted. His blue eyes glowed with intensity as a tremendous heat filled the room.

"Let go of me," I demanded.

"Be still," Bulosk growled. The primal sound made my own growl seem like a whimper. It reverberated deep inside me, flooding my body with waves of panic.

Lord Leasith managed to walk to the wall where the marble alcove used to be. Now, it looked like a plain bark wall that was part of the sequoia tree. He breathed fire at it, causing the wall to slide to the side. There was no fancy table and tabernacle like before. Instead, a simple square space had been notched into the plaster wall behind the bark façade. He placed the egg on a black cushion before whispering some magic that locked the Torensphere within. I could hear the creature's rants.

Bulosk squeezed my wings together to the point I saw stars. I struggled with him until something tore free. I screamed in pain.

"Don't move," he demanded.

"Easy, Bulosk. Don't kill her, yet."

Bulosk released my wings as Leasith grabbed my wrists, pulling me to my feet.

"Well, it bleeds," Leasith said coldly.

I saw a trail of blood, *my blood*, streaking the white marble floor.

"Do you have her?" Bulosk asked.

I knew the Torensphere had exerted its power on Leasith because he was puffing air like he'd just been wrestling a dragon...*technically, he had been.*

"*It* will not escape," Leasith answered.

His huge hands immobilized me. I could feel the scabbard still attached to my belt, but the weight of the sword was gone. *Disappointed.* Here I'd brandished some epic weapon from an alien world, and all it had done is give me away.

"I was returning your precious egg," I insisted as I dug the heel of my boot into Leasith's shin. He just grunted. "It's going to hatch, you know."

Leasith narrowed his light blue eyes at me.

"Not that my opinion means anything, but *it* hatching would really suck." What also sucked was that my cloaking failed to snap on no matter how much I concentrated on drawing in the shadows to power it.

Bulosk retrieved a set of iron cuffs with two-foot chain from a desk in the corner.

Who keeps handcuffs in their desk drawer?

While Leasith held my arms, Lord Bulosk locked the cuffs around my wrists. I felt like a dog on a leash as he led me to a five-story wall of books. The library wall contained an open spiral staircase that took a reader to each landing. On each level, a rolling ladder attached to the lighted mahogany shelves. As I gazed up at the display, the brothers worked together to unlock one cuff, wrap the chain around the railing of the staircase, and replace the cuff to secure me.

The lords studied me with their intense dragon eyes while I looked up at the sublime library I coveted as much as I did darkling chocolate.

"Is that *Cosmo's Comedies*?" I asked. The collection of stories apparently was the fallen satyr leader's account of his life, full disclosure.

Leasith scrunched up his nose, and Bulosk cocked an eyebrow.

"I could get out of these bindings very easily," I said. "I won't because my unfettered presence seems to incite violence in you two." I tried not to wince, but I kept burping up bile and my head spun from my throbbing wing. My cloaking flickered on for a moment, and then died out.

Lord Bulosk studied me like a specimen under a microscope. "Not what I expected."

"Where did she come from?" Leasith asked.

I could hear shouts outside. *Zack? I'm probably just hallucinating.*

Bulosk straightened the silk sleeves of his collared shirt. "Leasith, would you please go contend with the interlopers."

Leasith squinted and frowned. He obviously didn't want to take orders from Bulosk.

"Siblings," I huffed.

Leasith breathed flame at my face. It came just short of my skin but singed my hair.

"That was completely uncalled for," I spat. "Besides, you almost hit the books!"

Bulosk shot his brother a dirty look.

"Fine. Just know, Leasith plans to handle the traitor *his* way. No diplomacy with murderers."

I snorted at the older dragon lord. "Did you just refer to yourself in the third person? I read that's what psychopaths do."

Leasith ignored me. Bulosk waved a hand at him like *whatever*.

The militant dragon lord turned from me and strutted from the room.

Lord Bulosk's scrutiny overwhelmed me. His green eyes glowed against his dark skin and hair. I admired his blue scales. My scales were so plain. He paced from side to side, checking every angle, before stooping down to bring us face to face. There's something even scarier than looking into the eyes of a dragon lord—it's having him look back with *fear*.

"Where did you come from?"

"I just am," I growled.

Thick arms of magic wrapped around me. I focused on breathing while trying to bear the pain in my torn wing. I usually healed quickly, but I've never suffered such an injury. Panic fluttered inside me as I felt Lord Bulosk's power squeeze tighter. A warm essence filled me, replacing my terror.

"Is that better?" he whispered.

The stabbing pain dulled to a distant ache. He'd eased my discomfort with his power.

"Oh, Mother of Montenai. You're still tying creatures up in here?" With her arms crossed, Bianca Rehmling stood just inside the vestibule of the dragon lord's lair. Her brown, doe-like eyes scanned my entire body and took in my torn, blood-soaked clothes. Her nostrils flared. "Please, tell me you didn't do this to her," she seethed.

Bulosk whipped around so fast, Bianca took a step back. "Get out, now!"

Her mouth dropped open. I don't think anyone had ever spoken to her that way, especially not her new mate.

"You have no idea what this is. Go, Bianca. Please." He strode toward her. Her face scrunched up like she might cry. Then she turned and ran from the room. He began to follow her but caught himself.

When he returned, he reached over and grabbed my chin a lot more gingerly than I expected. Turning my face from side to side, his eyes grew wider. "It can't be. How old are you?"

I waited him out. He drew even closer. *Perfect.* I head-butted him with the last vestige of energy I possessed. He stumbled, that I noted. I couldn't tell much else because I blacked out from the pain.

When I came to, Bulosk stood just outside the doorway, conferring with his brother.

"She's what?" Leasith asked.

My brain felt bruised. I made a mature decision—my head-butting days were over. I threw up on the floor. *Good work, Natcha.* I'd given myself a concussion. The cuffs and chain were stretched tight from the top of the railing, raising my arms above my head and to the side. I had collapsed so I now sat with the pressure on the right side of my butt, knees bent, and ankles to one side. *Uncomfortable.*

Leasith crossed the room in minimal strides. He squatted down, placing his face mere inches from mine. He whipped his head away. I could have sworn I saw tears in his eyes. "This isn't happening."

Bulosk paced in front of me. He rubbed his head where we'd made contact. That gave me a sense of satisfaction.

"Did you tell her?" Leasith asked.

Bulosk shook his head.

With one swipe of magic, Leasith released my metal cuffs. I shifted to my hands and knees. Closing my eyes didn't help relieve my dizziness.

Leasith approached me, again. His scales blurred before me as I tried to focus my eyes. "You killed him, you know."

"Shut up, Leasith," Bulosk said.

"She did."

"He was sick." Bulosk yanked his brother away from me.

"You took the Torensphere, and he tried to compensate," Leasith said. He paced the floor and scrubbed his buzzed hair with his hand.

I pushed back to sit on my feet, and looked up at them. The rants of the Torensphere were growing louder. He made it hard to hear the next sentence.

"You killed your father!"

CHAPTER TWENTY

MY CHEEK PRESSED against the marble. A rushing sound filled my ears, which reminded me of the river. Tears burned my skin before spilling to the floor. The stone didn't cool my face but heated with me. Refusing to look up, I focused on my breathing and dug my claws into the hard surface to root myself.

"You shouldn't have said that to her," Bulosk spat.

Leasith paced in front of me. His highly-polished combat boots were a welcome distraction. The Torensphere screamed inside the false wall. *Miss...taken. Miss...taken.*

Leasith halted for a moment. I looked up to see the bronze scales on his arm as he put his hands on his hips and turned. "What did she do to the Torensphere? It's not right," he said in a choked voice.

Bulosk crouched by me, concern suddenly in his eyes. He touched my shoulder, claws retracted. "She doesn't look well."

Glass exploded from above. The Rotunda rained tiny, colored diamonds. Bulosk threw his body over me, not pinning, but in a protective gesture. Leasith charged toward the threat. Remnants of a construction tarp floated down. When Bulosk raised his head, I peered out and saw Serena dominating the space at full phantom height.

"Don't touch the baby!"

"Mother of Montenai! How did she get in here?" shouted Leasith. He breathed fire at her. She shrieked, fluttered, and reformed in front of him. I glanced at the small puddle of tears in front of me. With the last of my strength, I pushed away from the dragon lord. It didn't take much effort, he was already moving off me to go to his brother's side.

When I drew to my knees, Serena floated to me in her darkling form. Her strapless organza gown looked impeccable. "Natcha."

Behind her, both lords stood, mouths agape, eyes wide in disbelief. My phantom had obliterated the glass basilica they had blown to fit over the top of the tree.

"Serena," Leasith gasped.

He began to walk toward her, but she turned and flashed her menacing eyes. She placed her cold hand on my shoulder, which I registered as a faint pressure.

"Are you hurt?"

As she questioned me, the dragon lords remained still, observing. They didn't notice Hana and Sina drop through the new *skylight*. The phantoms hovered just behind the lords, waiting for Serena's cue.

With Bulosk at a distance, the throbbing returned to my wing, but I didn't focus on it too much. Instead, I watched, fascinated by the way my phantom disarmed these supposed omnipotent creatures. The space filled with their heady magic, creating a thick soup in the air. I felt it brush up against me, but my fire shielded me.

"You meant to hurt her. To kill her. That's why I ran away. I will always keep her safe," Serena shrieked.

I saw her essence clash with the heat of Bulosk's arm. It gave the illusion that his arm was distorted—like an artist blurring the lines of a painting. His lips took on a bluish cast.

Leasith put his large hands up in a placating gesture. "Serena, we want to help. We didn't know."

"Where is he?"

"Who?" Bulosk asked. He shook his arm as if it were asleep.

"Akton," she whispered.

All the hairs on my body stood on end.

"He doesn't visit anymore." She began to wring her hands and pace in her floating way, stirring the already thick air.

Leasith stepped forward. "He's gone."

Her dark tresses shook as tears filled her eyes. With the tears came the phantom blackness. Having lived with her my whole life, I covered my ears. Still, her shrieking stirred the dark spirits and the other phantoms into a frenzy. I feared they'd drain the life out of all of us.

The lords growled, trapped in their own home while the phantoms froze their muscles, their will. Serena had completely lost her mind. Leasith fell to the ground. Digging his claws into the marble, he attempted to pull himself away from them.

"Natcha." He panted, and his eyes glowed full dragon blue, *like mine* but lighter.

Realization crushed me—I knew who I was. The fierce creature I'd always thought of as my scary bodyguard was my mother, a deceased darkling. My father had been a dragon lord. Akton's brothers had hurt me. They had upset Serena. Did I have compassion, or was my heart as cold as a reptile's?

"Bulosk! Bulosk!" Bianca Rehmling tripped over me as she ran *toward* the phantoms.

How stupid can you be?

When Sina focused on her, she stopped in her tracks.

I stood up to appear more formidable. *Really wish I had the shiny sword.*

Bianca's fierce eyes locked on me. "You need to make the phantoms stop. They'll kill them."

"I'm fine," I said, gesturing toward my bloody dress and wing. "Thanks so much for asking, Shortcake."

Her lips formed a tight line, and her hands found her hips. She looked to be winding up for a full onslaught of angst but caught herself. She blew out a breath and relaxed her arms at her sides. "Please."

I raised my eyebrows. *Better.* "Serena, please stop." It took several more shouts before she hesitated in the air. Nothing about her resembled the lovely darkling in the woods who had raised me.

Weakened, both dragon lords writhed and trembled in the aftermath.

When Serena returned to her more darkling form, tears streaked her face.

"I'm sorry, but Akton became very ill," I said, my voice frail and quavering. I had seen her stay confused for days on end, to the point she was unreachable. But the eyes that fixed on mine were clear.

"I need to go," she said before disappearing, taking two phantoms and fifteen shrieking dark spirits with her.

My heart sank. I couldn't believe she'd left me with the lords. Shocked, I took in the scene. The dragon lords still hadn't found their feet. Seemed like a good time to get the heck out of the tree.

As I headed for the door, my cloaking continued to buzz on and off. My wing hurt too much to try flight. If I could disappear, I would. Anything to get away from the rage that threatened to consume me the longer I stayed in this place. What had the lords done to Serena that she ran away to her death? They'd failed their brother, Akton. They'd failed their own kind. Things were not settled.

The Torensphere chanted something inside the false wall.

Zack stumbled over the threshold, pale and out of breath. He held the sword. "Natcha."

Trust is so slippery. I wanted to trust him, to believe he may be the only creature on my side...except maybe for Nalene.

The scent of the sea hit me so hard, I felt dizzy. *Is she on my side?* I turned in time to watch Nalene rise from the puddle of my tears. Her hazel eyes flashed with anger. Leasith blew flame at her. She raised her hand and sent ice to cover his face. I'd never seen her do that. I didn't think he could breathe through the mask.

"Leeni?"

Leasith breathed fire, and the mask splintered and melted away. She ignored him. The false bark wall shook in front of her. Nalene merely touched her palm to its surface, and it slid to the side. When she grabbed the Torensphere, both dragon lords attempted to move toward her, but they were still drained from the phantoms.

"Please, Nalene. No!" I screamed in her head.

She didn't acknowledge me but disappeared, and so did the rants of the Torensphere. I had been ready to spring into action, but she had been so quick.

A cool hand slipped into mine.

Zack.

"Let's leave here," he whispered.

I let him lead me up the tunnel and out into the night.

Magda stood on the boardwalk. "Natcha," she called.

Zack dropped my hand to grip the sword with both hands. I didn't hear the foreign voices but wondered if he did. He showed no sign of distress from the weapon.

Madga took one step back. "Mother of Montenai," she said as she stared at the blade.

"Don't do anything," he hissed. "Don't move your hands, your eyes, your mouth. In fact, don't even dare to breathe."

"Natcha?" she turned watery eyes to me. "Zack, please. You don't understand."

But I did. I understood her desperation over her daughter's condition. I'd acted out myself because of my sister. And look at the mess it had caused.

"I can't talk right now, Magda." Numb, I leaned on Zack for support as my cloaking buzzed on.

His eyes widened with surprise. I'd cloaked him, too. I didn't pay attention to anything around me until we entered the woods, my once safe haven. Magda didn't pursue us. No doubt she was checking with the dragon lords to see about the Torensphere. She was in for a shock.

Just past the first copse of trees, I saw something shiny in the dark.

"Our ride," Zack said. "At least no one found it."

I raised an eyebrow.

"I drove it here earlier, thinking we may need it after you turned the Torensphere over to the lords. I never thought they would draw the wrong conclusions when I presented the rebel plans to them, or that Magda would tell them everything about you…and me, creating more confusion.

"They let me walk away from the Wishing Tree, but they followed me into the woods." He shook his head, his nostrils flared. "It's my fault they hurt you. I'm not sure why I thought I could outsmart a dragon lord. I didn't even hear Leasith sneak up behind me when I reached the rock."

Fumbling at my waist, I found his hand and squeezed. "It's not your fault. You did everything you could to help me. I should have given you the sword."

"I didn't think I would need it." The muscle in his jaw jumped. "Magda," he said, shaking his head. "I went to her originally because she has always been so kind and wise. I shouldn't have trusted her."

I shrugged, which caused my wing to ache.

"Because I was talking to the phantoms at the rebel camp and had the sword, the darklings and lords became suspicious of me. The dragon lords have been incredibly paranoid since their brother's death. When I showed up with full plans to take down Shadowland, I just hurt my cause."

"The unknown is terrifying. They didn't know what I was, so they attacked."

Exhausted, I removed my cloaking. I was just unable to sustain it any longer. Zack held the sword out in front of him while keeping his left arm wrapped around my waist. We made slow progress to the satyr ATV. I gave him the scabbard to slide on to his belt. He finally slid the sword into its sheath before helping me climb onto the back of the vehicle. Carefully, he positioned himself in front and started it. I hugged his waist and rested my head against his back. It was rough going, but I tried to breathe through the pain from each jolt along the way.

Halfway up the mountain, by the black rock, he slowed and maneuvered carefully around the battle zone. Broken glass shimmered in the moonlight. No matter how hard I squeezed Zack, I couldn't prevent my heat from surfacing as I thought of Serena. He stopped just past the rock and turned off the engine.

"Hot!"

I let go.

He turned to look at me.

"The engine overheat?" I asked, dazed.

"No," he chuckled. "You did."

I looked at the scorch marks on the back of his shirt. "Did I burn you?"

"I'm fine," he said. "Maybe just hang on to my shirttail." He winked before turning around and starting the engine.

Following my instructions, Zack found the barn. With my injured wing, I knew we'd never make it to the cave. I've never been so happy to see my herd, but they were not alone.

CHAPTER TWENTY-ONE

CORNELIUS'S EYES TOOK in Zack's tattered clothes, bruised face, and cut lip. Zack had drawn the sword. This is where the satyr's eyes focused. Cornelius wrinkled his brow as if trying to process the meaning behind this *harmless* darkling carrying the alien weapon. For anyone could see that it was alien. Something about a blade glowing white-blue in the night is anything but subtle.

I wasn't prepared for the look the buck gave me. Compassion, anger, confusion—all played across his face.

"I came as quickly as I could. Without the phantoms to stop me, I made it through the woods and tracked the scent of the goats."

Zack took a protective step in front of me. "What do you want?"

The satyr nodded once. "I don't mean any harm to you or her."

"Natcha," Zack said. "Her name is Natcha. Maybe in all these years that would have been something you could have investigated a bit. You know, learning a child's name."

The pain in my wing returned with a vengeance, so I leaned my head against Zack's back. A burning flame sparked at the apex and flared to the base. However, the emotional pain was what crippled me. I'd lost Serena, Nalene, and my homeland. For years, I'd been safe, hidden. My guards were gone, and anyone could get into my world. I'd never felt so vulnerable.

"I didn't know anything until it was too late. One of my head bucks investigated when the winds began to shift. Max told me the story of his friend disappearing into thin air."

I couldn't believe Nalene had just used her water magic in front of the crew of satyrs.

"Are you losing control of your herd?" Zack challenged.

Cornelius towered over Zack. In an instant, he could grow his full head of horns and hurt him, but he didn't. Instead, he fidgeted, folding his thick arms across his chest and staring at us. His horizontal pupils were dilated, his nostrils flared. "My son is responsible for the winds, and he will be punished."

My stomach dropped. I didn't appreciate his son aiding the nymph and dragon lords' ambush of me, but I also didn't want to consider how the herd punished one of its own.

Cornelius looked down, his face showing a terrible sadness. "And Magd—"

"Manipulated me, allowed the dragon lords to rough me up, and used me as bait," Zack said.

"She needed the Torensphere—"

"I was returning it." I shook my head. "None of this aggression was necessary."

"She had to make sure she got the Torensphere. It was essential for her kin," Cornelius said.

"I needed it for my family, too, but now it's gone," Zack shouted.

The satyr's face dropped. "Is this true?"

"Yes. The *disappearing nymph* took it. Good luck finding her." I would not tell him my sister's name.

"At the very least, allow me to bring you some medicine for healing," he said.

He was the only father figure I'd ever known. I believed he was hurting as much as I was, just in a different way. I'd never seen weakness in him. With this one act of defiance, his son had exposed Cornelius's vulnerabilities. His strong, trusting nature had been used against him tonight by two of his loved ones.

"Thank you," Zack said firmly. "But we can manage. And I mean no disrespect, but this is Natcha's land. Even though the phantoms didn't stop you, the satyrs and nymphs can't just waltz in here when they like."

Cornelius caught my eye. "Understood. You know where to find me if you need anything, Natcha?"

"Yes."

He looked so defeated, I wrestled with wanting him off my land and wanting his help. At this moment, he looked like he really needed to feel necessary.

"I'll make sure my herd and the nymphs respect the boundaries."

We didn't move as the satyr turned and headed through the meadow. I took note of where he descended the cliff. He traveled farther north before disappearing off the edge. I breathed a sigh of relief because my cave was in the opposite direction.

Zack sheathed the sword before taking my hand and leading me inside the barn. We fed the goats treats and worked to make a pallet for sleeping. Under nymph lights, we laid out satyr blankets. These reminders made the betrayal sting that much more. I shook it off and followed Zack back outside.

He made a fire. I could have done it in an instant, but I realized Zack needed to work off his angst. He never stopped moving— building and feeding the fire. I cooked eggs over the fire using an old metal milk pail. Juniper provided us fresh milk to drink. We didn't talk except for in the preparation of the food.

Afterward, we sat under the stars. I couldn't help but think how I had always dreamed about spending time with Zack under this sky, and here I was doing just that. Yet, I was miserable.

"That was delicious," Zack said, milk clinging to his upper lip.

At first, I laughed because he looked like such a young hatchling, but then my eyes watered. "Cornelius brought me my first goats." I watched his smile deflate.

"I understand why you're conflicted. I am too. But we need to send a clear message to everyone. With the phantoms gone, they don't suddenly have free rein over your land, free access to you. There are too many strong feelings right now about the thief. I'm worried you'll have unwanted visitors coming to retaliate." His brown eyes intense, he touched my chin. "You did what had to be done."

I raised my eyebrows. "Well I sure made a mess of it."

"In the end, you tried to fix a wrong."

"I don't think they will see it that way. To them, I'm a thief, a murderer." I shifted my position on the log. The pain in my wing would not diminish.

"They know better. The dragon lords have no one to blame but themselves for their disturbed brother's death."

It didn't matter what anyone said. Inside, I knew my actions had contributed to the demise of Akton. My ignorance about these creatures and their politics with the nymphs had also fueled what transpired tonight. They didn't know me. In their world, I really was a thief, a murderer. Why did I expect them to meet me with anything other than aggression? I thought I could just appear out of thin air and hand them the egg? I laughed at myself. How naïve could I be?

"Natcha?" Zack's brown eyes studied me.

"Why did I think that would work?"

His mouth formed a grim line. "Because, you hoped they'd had enough. That they realized there was room for diplomacy after all the violence of the last month. A good leader doesn't act on his own agenda of vengeance or retribution; he looks at his followers and considers what actions will ensure their safety and prosperity."

The burning at my back had me regretting the refusal of Cornelius's offer of treatment or medicine. Dragon claws had caused the tear, and my usual rapid healing was not happening. My thoughts kept diverting to dark places, which I knew didn't help my overall physical condition. Every time I heard Lord Leasith announcing I'd killed my *father*, I had to dig my claws into the log I sat on and breathe through a panic that deprived me of all my senses.

"Natcha. Natcha. Come back."

I wiped my face. "Did you hear?"

He narrowed his eyes.

"Of course you didn't. You weren't there yet." I let go of his hand because I felt my heat threatening to overwhelm me, and I didn't want to burn him. *Maybe they had lied about Akton.* I knew they hadn't. When I looked at my claws, thought about my scales, my hair…I knew I was

Akton's daughter. I didn't know what to do with the range of emotions that ebbed and flowed through me, shaking loose my beliefs, my truths, and washing away my foundation. What was left of me?

"Hey." He brushed my hair out of my eyes. "You're scaring me."

"He must have hated the very thought of me. Why else would he leave me with the phantoms to die in the woods?"

"Who?"

"Lord Akton."

Zack's mouth formed an O.

"I'm more messed up than I ever thought possible."

He reached out to stroke my arm. "Natcha."

"I'll have to live with the fact that I contributed to my father's death. I deserve the irreparable damage to my wing."

Zack shook his head. "I'm sorry you lost your father, but it wasn't your fault. And, there is no good reason in this world for him to have abandoned you." He touched my good wing, his fingers caressing the membrane as if it were the finest silk. "I wish I knew how to heal."

"Me, too."

He pursed his lips in thought. "This wing doesn't look so good."

Everything around me faded at that moment—the sound of the owls, the fire, the pain in my wing. His lips pressed delicately against mine so quickly, I almost didn't register it.

"It's terrible."

His eyes widened in alarm. I suppose he thought I meant the kiss.

I grabbed his shirt front. "The wing is terrible. You'll need to do that again."

He did. A warm rush surged through my whole body.

I heard a twig snap. Growling, I pulled away from Zack and looked toward the fencepost. Green dragon eyes glowed in the night.

"Hello, *Uncle* Bulosk. You have terrible timing."

Zack's fingers dug into my arm.

Lord Bulosk looked so uncomfortable, I almost felt bad for him. He held his hands out, signaling he meant no harm "I'm alone, and I'm not here to hurt anyone."

I didn't move. Zack jostled me a bit as he untangled himself from me and stood up to face the lord. The ring of the sword unsheathing brought me to alert. Heaving a tremendous sigh, I managed to stand. I feared if I didn't intercede, things would just grow more intense.

Bulosk eyed the weapon but kept his arms extended. "There has been an unfortunate sequence of misunderstandings and mistakes. I take full responsibility for the hardship we caused Serena, Zachary, and you, *Natcha*."

"I'm not a rebel or a traitor. Neither was my father." Zack's split lip trembled.

"I know that," Bulosk said. "And I have always been so sorry about your father, Zack."

Zack sheathed the sword. Dizzy, I reached out to steady myself on him and give him some reassurance.

"I came here to mend your wing."

"Well, it's about flippin' time," I snarled.

Zack snorted next to me. "That's my Nightmare. Mistress of diplomacy."

CHAPTER TWENTY-TWO

BIANCA REHMLING STOOD in the grand foyer of the Wishing Tree, arranging flowers in a crystal vase.

"Are you gonna be my aunt?" I asked.

The gaze she cast my way would have paralyzed a lesser creature.

I smiled. "So weird. I mean. You know. Because we're about the same age, you and me."

Her blue-black ringlets cascaded down her back. She wore a fuchsia sheath dress, which hugged every curve. She continued to arrange the roses while monitoring me as I paced in a circle around her.

"No offense, Shortcake. But my Uncle Bulosk's old. I mean, older-than-dirt old."

She didn't look at me or say a thing.

"That feels awesome. Thank you," I gushed.

She huffed before looking up at me.

"The dark shadows you keep casting. What a rush. Like ten espresso shots."

We held each other's gaze for several seconds. I tried flashing my dragon eyes, but she laughed at me, so I breathed smoke out my nose instead. She fanned it away.

"Raawrrr," I said, spreading my wings, flashing my dragon eyes, and extending my claws.

Bianca stepped closer. I think she reached my chin. She snatched my right claw to study it. "I know a good manicurist in North Village."

I retracted my wings and claws. "Why are you so…likeable?"

After flashing a disarming smile, she grabbed her purse off the mahogany table. "You miss her, don't you?"

My goofy grin fell from my face. "Yes."

"I miss my sister, too."

I knew she meant her baby sister, Anka, who chose to stay in the Hinterlands with her human mate-turned-half-nymph, Ben. Patrick Benjamin Solomon had a strong aversion to the dragon lords. He was trying to cope with his new powers the nymphs had given him while accepting that he may never be able to return to earth's plane.

"I'm going to be late for my lunch date with the *old* guy." Bianca stopped in the doorway as she flung a gray cape around her shoulders. "He's right. You are trouble."

"Who's right."

She turned. "Zack. And Adah knows, he likes trouble."

For a few seconds after she left, I stood there, speechless.

"Nightmare, you're gaping again." Zack walked in from the Council Room. He'd been discussing things with Lord Leasith. I was still trying to get used to having to talk to everyone and let them see me. Also, I was working on accepting that the dragon lords were not my enemy and I should not plot ways to attack them.

"Why does Bianca do that?" I tapped my new brown suede boots from Good for the Sole on the marble.

"Do what?"

"Wear dresses like that?"

"I dunno. Because she looks pretty—"

I raised my eyebrows.

"Short. She looks pretty short in them."

I hooked my arm in his. "Did I tell you about the time I saw a satyr get it on with a nymph."

Zack closed his eyes while shaking his head. He allowed me to cloak him while we flew to the Faunlier Mountains.

I still lived by the sea and continued to care for my goats, chickens, and bat. Unfortunately, I did it alone. With daily trips to Shadowland, I was making amends with the dragon lords and visiting with Zack. In a few days, I planned to meet with Magda and Cornelius to resolve things with them.

All my life, I had focused on survival. In the next months, I would try my claws at forgiveness. But I would never forget.

Zack and I found our favorite spot in the highest sea cliffs of Montenai. Literally perched in the clouds, we looked out at the aquamarine water, admiring the patchwork of colors created by the creatures and reefs. He leaned in to capture my warmth. The snow had started to melt, giving us some hope spring was around the corner. Pelicans dove and scooped up sea bass in their beaks. Triumphant, they flew into the sun.

I couldn't fix things, but I would try my hardest to help, somehow. My mind and heart, however, would not mend. There was too much for me to sort out. My motley family had disappeared. Nalene gone. The phantoms no longer haunted the Ballatian Woods.

At least twenty times a day, my thoughts veered toward my sister, and I worried what might become of her. I couldn't touch her mind. She never returned to the cave or barn.

Serena, *my mother*, did not appear when I pleaded with the air for her return. When I thought of both of them, I felt so much regret, particularly Serena. Would I have tried harder to connect with her if I had known who she was? Despite keeping busy, nothing filled the void they'd left in my soul.

My wing tingled. I turned to face Zack. He stroked my wing, my shoulder, and then my face. When he leaned in, I met him halfway. His kiss cooled me, grounded me, held me. He was the only peace in my world. So much uncertainty whirled around me. The nymphs, the dragon lords, the satyrs, the darklings—what would become of us all?

I pulled Zack to me by the front of his shirt and kissed him harder. "You're not allowed to leave me." I tried to sound matter-of-fact, but my voice broke.

He smiled. "I wouldn't. You're too *dreamy*, Nightmare."

I laughed, snorting fire out my nose for the first time.

Zack was fine. Eyebrows are overrated.

GLOSSARY OF MONTENAI TERMS & CHARACTERS

Adah – Mother of Montenai. Considered a deity in the world of Montenai based on her importance during the turning event called "The Blessed Incursion" in which she rode through a portal on the red dragon, Akton. She brought the power of the Torensphere to the darkling population. Adah is an astrei—a creature with three sets of wings. Little is known about the astrei from the world of Fallon other than they tended/controlled dragons in that world. Adah is now a blue star in the sky. Dying Montenaians are said to see her when crossing over to Laith (the place after death).

Adah's Gateway – darkling cemetery where urns that resemble dragon lord lanterns hang from sequoia branches. These tombs eternally twinkle like stars in the sky.

Aglatian Sea – the Montenai River feeds into this body of salt water. The Aglatian Sea is located in the southern border of Montenai. South of the Faunlier Mountains, its aquamarine waters provide a thriving fishing community for the satyrs in their village of Port by the Sea.

Akton – red dragon who crashed through a portal into Montenai while fleeing a war in the world of Fallon. Considered the Father of Montenai due to his importance in bringing the Torensphere to the darkling population. Now just a red star in the sky.

Alexander Salva – father to Zachary, husband to Marta. Nonshadowcaster who worked as a chef to the three dragon lords in the Wishing Tree.

Anka Rehmling – darkling and shadowcaster. Casts shadows for human, Patrick Benjamin Solomon (Ben).

Astrei – creature of Fallon with three sets of wings. Adah, the Mother of Montenai, was an astrei.

Ballatian Woods – the forest between the Shadowland South Village and the Faunlier Mountains. Known to be haunted by phantoms. It is comprised of variegated flora: oak trees, pine trees, and mountain laurel.

Bianca Rehmling – darkling and shadowcaster. Casts shadows in the evenings for human Ben Solomon. Older sister to Anka.

Blessed Incursion – Montenaians' term for the event when the red dragon, Akton, came through the portal to Montenai. He carried with him the astrei (Adah) and the Torensphere (mystical egg possessing magic). This incident changed the lives and beliefs of all Montenaians.

Chocolate Syncope – Pops's chocolate shop housed in a sequoia tree. It's located along the Boardwalk in North Village.

Cornelius Jeremiah – head buck of the Fardoragh herd of satyrs.

Darklings – live in Shadowland. They love the shade of the sequoias on their side of the Montenai River. There are three types of darklings: shadowcasters, nonshadowcasters, and dragon lords.

Dragon's Last Breath – ceremony performed by the dragon lords as funeral rites for deceased darklings. It requires them to breathe fire and transform everything to ash in preparation for the soul to crossover to Laith.

Drakos – first dragon lord born to Toren, the darkling who attended to Adah's wounds and oversaw the care of the mystical orb/egg. He had golden scales and a mercurial temper. Married to darkling, Pia. Together they had three sons: Lord Akton, Lord Leasith, and Lord Bulosk.

Drakos Dregs – Shadowland soda that has a kick. Fledglings like it because all flavors (black licorice, butterscotch, and cinnamon) are a bit spicy. The cinnamon flavor, aka The Fire Bomb, is known to cause the nasal passages to burn.

Drakos Restaurant – gourmet restaurant operated by the dragon lords. Located in South Village.

Echo – baby bat that Natcha and Nalene raised.

Fallon – the land from which Akton and Adah came. Known to have astrei, dragons, and sorcerers.

Faunlier Mountains – mountain range on the east side of the Montenai River. It is south of the Ballatian Woods. The Mountains give way to sea cliffs and the Aglatian Sea.

Fledgling/hatchling – the darkling term for child.

Good for the Sole – shoe store in South Village owned by the cordwainer, Mrs. Salva (Zack's mother).

Hanleith – nymph ruler of Montenai prior to the Blessed Incursion. After her fall came the rise of the three dragon lords and development of the separate communities: Shadowland, Kirka Village, and Port by the Sea.

Kirka/Nymphs – creatures of Kirka Village. They are usually fair of skin and hair. They control plants and light. They cast reflections in the human world and gain vitality and sustained youth this way. After the Blessed Incursion, they formed their own matriarchal village separate from the satyrs and darklings. The male equivalent to the female nymph is the satyr.

Kirka Circle – main circle of domes in the Kirka grasslands. Reflections Celebration Hall stands at the center of ten smaller domes consisting of boutiques, eateries, and homes.

Kirka Village – a town of only nymphs (females) on the west side of the Montenai River. The town consists of glass dome homes, a main circle, and farms.

Korena – beautiful, young nymph assigned to cast reflections for human, Ben Solomon. Daughter of Magda.

Laith – where Montenaians go after death.

Liza Rehmling – nonshadowcaster and darkling. Bianca Rehmling's roommate and cousin. She is studying to be a teacher.

Lord Akton – oldest dragon lord named for the dragon, Akton. He is mostly darkling with some dragon characteristics and the ability to manipulate magic. He has one golden eye and red scaling with strawberry-blond hair. Has the ability to make darklings "see." Head of the Shadowland Council.

Lord Bulosk – youngest dragon lord with blue scales, green eyes, and dark hair. Part of the Shadowland Council. He is mostly darkling with some dragon characteristics and the ability to manipulate magic. Looks more like darklings than his brothers.

Lord Leasith – middle dragon lord with copper scales, light blue eyes, and brown hair. Part of the Shadowland Council. He is mostly darkling with some dragon characteristics and the ability to manipulate magic.

Magdalena (Magda) – leader of the nymphs. Mother of Korena. Magda is the main healer of Kirka Village.

Marta Salva – Zachary's mother. Nonshadowcaster who owns and operates Good for the Sole store in the South Village.

Montenai – the world on a parallel plane to earth. The main creatures include: darklings (dragon lords, shadowcasters, and nonshadowcasters), nymphs, satyrs, sprites, and phantoms.

Nalene (Leeni) – sister to Natcha. Lives in the sea cliffs of the Aglatian Sea. Her abilities allow her to travel through water. Although she most closely resembles the nymphs with her golden hair, she was orphaned from birth.

Nana/Violet Rehmling – the grandmother and caregiver to the Rehmling sisters. Married to Pops. She is the daughter of a nymph and a darkling.

Natcha – orphan sister to Nalene. Lives in the sea cliffs of the Aglatian Sea. Her fiery red hair matches her temperament and her ability to control fire. She can draw in the shadows to cloak or hide herself from view.

Nonshadowcaster – darkling who lives in Shadowland but doesn't have the ability to cast shadows. Often lives in the South Village close to the Wishing Tree, the home of the dragon lords and power hub of Shadowland.

Out of Shadow – the shadowcasting movement in support of fledglings taking turns shadowcasting. Adults and fledglings belong to a pool of shadowcasters and share the responsibilities evenly. Shadowcasters learn in a school environment rather than just from their parents. The model allows shadowcasters more freedom to participate in Shadowland life and not be chained to the human world.

Patrick Benjamin Solomon (Ben) – young human charge of Anka and Bianca Rehmling.

Phantoms – creatures who haunt the Ballatian Woods. The three phantoms are Serena, Sina, and Hana. Serena is the only phantom who can speak. Serena and Sina resemble darklings, but Hana is fairer like a nymph. They are able to immobilize a creature with their cold essence and use of five dark spirits, which each of them wields.

Pia – mother of Lords Akton, Leasith, and Bulosk.

Pia's Pop – Shadowland soda that fledglings love. It comes in strawberry, blueberry, raspberry, peach, and pomegranate.

Pops/Ernest Rehmling – grandfather to Anka and Bianca Rehmling. Owner of the candy shop, Chocolate Syncope.

Port by the Sea – fishing town of satyrs (some nymphs stay here as well). It is a large area, which encompasses marshlands, cypress forests, hinterlands, wine country, and the harbor where the Montenai River gives way to the Aglatian Sea. As the name indicates, the village holds an open invitation for Montenaians to come sip satyr Port wine by the Aglatian Sea.

Reflections Celebration Hall – large dome structure located in Kirka Circle. This is the nymph gathering place for meetings, ceremonies, and celebrations.

Satyr – creature of Montenai with the upper body of a regular male but lower body of a goat. Control wind. Fantastic artisans, anglers, and vintners (makers of wine). While they cherish the nymphs, they prefer to live independent of them in their fishing village of Port by the Sea.

Serena – phantom who haunts the Ballatian Woods. Has the ability to deplete Montenaians' essence.

Shadowcaster – a darkling with the ability to travel via portal to the human world. He or she is assigned a human charge at a very young age (age four to eight) for whom to cast shadows. The shadowcasters work in families. They don't attend school but spend time in the human world protecting humans from excess UV radiation and harnessing the sun's energy on that plane to bring back for the vitality of all darklings. Some can cast dark shadows on other creatures in defense—stings, causes nausea and migraines.

Shadowland – home to the dragon lords and darklings. It's nestled under sequoia trees and skirts the east side of the Montenai River. Most shadowcasters live in North Village to be closest to the portal to earth. South Village is home of the Wishing Tree, nonshadowcasters, and the dragon lords.

Shadow Fever – nonshadowcasters may become ill and potentially die from this disease. It is characterized by a web-like rash on the face called the Silton rash.

Silton rash – rash associated with Shadow Fever. Web-like rash that appears on the face.

Sprites – considered pests in Montenai. These tiny, winged creatures have needle-like teeth, jewel-like eyes, and silver skin. The males have barbed tails. They are known to steal shiny items and slew insults at any creature around them. They are terrified of bats.

III Brothers' Pub – bar named for the dragon lords. Located on the South Boardwalk.

Toren – darkling. Mother of Drakos, grandmother of Akton, Leasith and Bulosk.

Toren Hospital – Shadowland's hospital named for Toren, grandmother of the dragon lords. The architecture is similar to a French Chalet. It is situated in the middle of Shadowland, between North and South Village.

Torensphere – the mystical orb/unhatched egg brought through the portal by Adah, the mother of Montenai. The dragon lords watch over it and harness its power to keep Shadowland strong.

Uncle Vincent/Vincent Rehmling – helps run Chocolate Syncope with Pops. Anka and Bianca Rehmling's uncle. Father of Liza.

Wishing Tree – enormous sequoia tree in which live the three dragon lords, Akton, Leasith, and Bulosk.

Zachary Salva (Zack) – Bianca's roommate. Darkling who is a nonshadowcaster. He studies the culinary arts. Son of Alexander and Marta Salva.

Continue Reading…

THE DARKLING CHRONICLES

Shadows 2

The last two books in *The Darkling Chronicles*

Sacrifice

So much pain to bear for something new to come.

Despite a rocky start in life, Nalene has survived twenty years in the sea cliffs of the Aglatian Sea. She struggles daily to master her water energy rather than succumb to it. An icy constitution has forced her to rely on her sister for care, protection, and guidance.

But the tides are turning and powers shifting in Montenai. Once a sickly creature with no purpose, Nalene emerges a strong, willful guardian. This reclusive orphan has everyone's attention, including a new seer who predicts "only one can survive" the battle to come.

Challenged by dragon lords, championed by outcasts, Nalene meets strife at every turn. As a crisis of faith wages within her, she forges ahead because she won't give up on hope. What is she willing to sacrifice to fulfill her destiny?

Home

A family tragedy at the age of twelve thrusts Serena into the world of shadowcasting. She relishes the dragon lords' protection and training but loves her new job and human charge even more.

Because of her great-great-grandfather's alliance with a vicious nymph queen, Serena finds other Montenaians refuse to trust or accept her. It doesn't help that she has the same birthmark and orange spark in her eyes as the relative who brought shame to the Brisson name.

Stepping through the portal to Paris allows Serena to escape her family's reputation as well as her mother's harsh traditions. Every day Serena pushes to be "worthy of the dragon," regardless of her brother warning her the path leads to horrible loss.

For years, the lore of dragon and astrei has molded the practices and beliefs of Montenaians. No one has felt this more than the phantom, Serena. This Drifter's history is the key to Shadowland's fate. Can she protect them from a dangerous future and still find her way home?

ACKNOWLEDGMENTS

A heartfelt thank you to these amazing people: editor, Nancy S. Thompson; cover artist, Robin Harper of Wicked by Design; cartographer, Jared Blando of TheRedEpic.com; and formatter, Angela McLaurin with Fictional Formats. Thank you for your patience and dedication.

My deepest gratitude to my superheroes (beta readers): Martina, Annalee, Crystal, Karen, Cheryl, and Stacy.

Thanks for the support and inspiration: Michele May, Barbara LaRochelle Cutrera, and Alison G. Bailey.

Finally, to the readers—thanks for taking a chance and stepping through the portal!